BEYOND MEASURE

PAULINE HOLDSTOCK

BEYOND MEASURE

PAULINE HOLDSTOCK

Cormorant Books

Canada Council Conseil des Arts
for the Arts du Canada

 ONTARIO ARTS COUNCIL
CONSEIL DES ARTS DE L'ONTARIO

The publisher gratefully acknowledges the support of the
Canada Council for the Arts and the Ontario Arts Council
for its publishing program. We acknowledge the financial support
of the Government of Canada through the Book Publishing
Industry Development Program (BPIDP) for our publishing activities.

Printed and bound in Canada

National Library of Canada Cataloguing in Publication

Holdstock, Pauline, 1948–
Beyone measure: a novel/Pauline Holdstock.

ISBN 1-896951-49-X

I. Title.

PS8565.O622B49 2003   C813'.54   C2002-905083-9
PR9199.3.H548B49 2003

Editor: Marc Côté
Cover and text design: Tannice Goddard
Cover image: Portrait of Beatrice Cenci, Elisabetta Cirani, 1638–1665.
Printer: Transcontinental Printing

CORMORANT BOOKS INC.
215 SPADINA AVENUE, STUDIO 230, TORONTO, ONTARIO, CANADA M5T 2C7
www.cormorantbooks.com

PROLOGUE

1552

THE SCAFFOLD HAS BEEN MOVED from the courtyard of the Palazzo del Podestà to the square outside, and there is not one rope but two. It is windy, and the rain is driving across the waiting crowd. There is no protection in the square from the buffets of this April day. Men and women cover their heads and stand like cattle with their backs to the weather. The pale stone of San Fiorenzo is streaked with dark ochre. A sudden gust lifts a long piece of canvas and slaps it back against the scaffold. The thin man who sells almond cakes at holy days and hangings is cursing his luck. There are fewer customers in the rain, everyone too intent on keeping covered, keeping dry. A door in the palazzo opens and an officer comes out accompanied by two orderlies bearing trays of little cakes, some stamped with the *palle*, some stamped with a lily.

The orderlies proceed to distribute these tokens of a liberal, loving justice among the crowd. At this, a dark, dishevelled man who has been watching from a doorway steps forward. The smugness of the official gesture, the patronizing intent and the assumption that those who eat will not question, provoke in him a rage that informs each nerve. He strides over to one of the orderlies. The thin man swings his own basket of now unsellable cakes to the ground to watch. The dark man clasps his hands together and, before anyone can stop him, brings them up sharply under the tray. The cakes fly up, flipping like coins before they land on the wet ground. In the distraction, the man has managed to upset the second tray, too, and is busy stamping as if he is trying to put out a fire, while all around men, women and children scramble to pick up the fancies before they are spoiled. The thin man picks up his basket of merchandise, his restored prospects, pleased at the way fortune, too, can flip and flip again. He will sell all his cakes.

Meanwhile the dark man, Matteo Tassi, has eluded everyone, and the officer is busy arresting an alarmed and protesting bystander. The confusion is so great the crowd almost misses the moment it has been waiting for: the bell in the *campanile* has begun to toll, the gates to the courtyard of the palazzo are opening, and the drummers are coming out, keeping their slow rhythm in time with the bell. As they come out onto the square, the shouting begins. Behind them comes the crier and six of the guard and then the hangman and then the priest. Six more guards come out; they are wearing black cloaks and black hoods that cover their faces. They walk in formation, in a block with the condemned in the centre, the two of them, in long white shifts, like ghosts of themselves. The shouting stops, leaving only a buzz and a murmur against the drums, like a fly against glass. The second condemned is a woman, just as Matteo Tassi had feared. It is the wife of the man who will hang. Such uncertainty in the air now. Is this something to cheer?

There is an eerie quiet. The ground under Tassi's feet has turned to water, and he is being carried closer on the back of a swiftly moving current. The woman, with her hands bound behind her back, trips on the long shift that tangles round her legs. She falls in two heavy movements, first to her knees and then forward, hitting her face on the ground as the crowd breaks into laughter. A matron shrieks at her, "Murderess! Poisoner! Murderess!" though no one recalls hearing that she was tried and found guilty or even that she was accused, and poison has never been mentioned in connection with the attempted murder of a profligate and well-connected cleric. The woman's husband stares down at her but cannot help. She rolls awkwardly and pushes herself back onto her feet. There is a small private moment between husband and wife, as each inclines the head to the other, looks in the other's eyes, while their constricted universe expands within the block of guards. The woman catches the perfume of something forgotten, and the faces and the jeering crowd recede until they are faint tremors at the edge of knowing. For the husband there is only the sudden pity, a cloudburst in the desert of his heart, and then he turns and is aware again of the press of people.

It is a small, merciful gift, this fall, for the woman in this her most terrible hour, for she is left now with only the pain, a vertical shaft of fire extending from her upper lip through the right side of her nose and her right eye. She cannot see the faces or hear the laughter. Nor does she see how her husband is having difficulty on the first step of the scaffold. He cannot make that step without dirtying himself.

Matteo Tassi does not see much more. The man and woman are placed very close together, almost touching, and the crowd is silent now in its unholy communion of expectation. Tassi is sick with it. He has difficulty turning in their direction. It is as if the light that passed between the pair has scorched his eyes. He has lain with this woman, has walked with her in a furnace of desire. From the line of half-remembered lovers, she has stepped forward and assumed a sacred vitality, more potent than any he has known. He will not stay to see her end.

The woman, in her cocoon of pain, does not hear the prayers of the priest, does not register the untying of her hands, the retying, this time in front of her so that she can climb the ladder. She does not see the guard or feel his breath on her face, but as he turns her in the direction of the priest, she sees for a moment her husband's face, her husband looking so startled, as if he is puzzled to see her here at all. The blood from her nose runs a little to one side and into her mouth, tracing the memory of a smile.

A guard takes her to the foot of the ladder. It is a complicated matter to get her onto it, lifting her shift, placing her foot, her hands, and then she is on the first rung. The hangman from his ladder, set at an angle to hers, is coaxing and she, with determination, begins to climb, lifting her hands together and grasping the next rung with a snatching motion before her weight can topple her backwards. She lifts and snatches, pulling herself up, her feet wide apart, kicking the shift away as she goes, first one side, then the other in an ungainly ascent, her whole body applying itself to this new task, this new achievement. The small clouds above her invite. Below, the crowd roars as she gains each new rung. The hangman climbs with her, staying abreast.

The woman and the crowd achieve a kind of rhythm, each awkward, violent movement on the ladder performed in silence and greeted on completion by a massed roar from the square. As she nears the top, she can feel every slight vibration of her body amplified by the ladder returned to her through the soles of her feet.

The hangman tells her to stop, and in less than a thought the noose is round her neck. The shouts of the crowd fly up like a flock of starlings at the sound of a gunshot. The hangman pulls the knot tight. Every movement is difficult. He unties her hands and ties them again behind her back. He says, "Lean with your knees or you'll fall." Below, her husband has started to climb and the crowd begins again, a chant this time, ragged.

She can feel a slight breeze in her hair. It seems all there is between her and her desire for this to be over.

Her husband climbs, leaning into his ladder, moving one foot up and placing the other on the same rung before he moves again. The top of the ladder creaks against the timber of the scaffold. The crowd is jeering, led by those at the front who can see and smell his shame as he climbs. The hangman has moved his own ladder, has already ascended and is waiting at the top.

The husband considers leaning back, out, falling to break his neck. It is a possible dream; it lasts no longer than a breath. Someone is telling him to stop climbing, as if he could, or would want to. Nothing is real now, not the roughness of the rope around his neck, nor the hands fumbling with his own. The crowd calls from another place. His body now could be sliced open, cut apart for them to gawk at and finger, and it would be no more than meat displayed. He is not there. He is at the puddle where his wife fell. He is at the place where their eyes met, where he last tasted life — which is only love — after the long drought.

He is still at that place when the ladders are pulled away. As his tongue comes out, the crowd screams its satisfaction.

Matteo Tassi is not among them. Matteo Tassi, the dark man, is already halfway to his house. In his mind he is halfway to Siena, where he will try to forget. In his heart he, too, is at the place the hanged man found, a place he has never known. He thinks he can hear the swifts circling the *campanile*, piping back at the bell that is still tolling.

OUT IN THE GULF of Genoa, a ship rears and plunges toward the shore. In her hold she carries one hundred and ninety-eight pieces of lead, fifty-one carpets, seventeen bales of pilgrims' robes and five barrels of gall-nuts, along with three men, nine women and eleven children purchased in Alexandria and another, listed in the bill of lading as a piebald child. The word "child" has been scored through and overwritten with the word "female."

The girl cannot remember how she came to be on board the boat. She has no memory of her family, nor of how she came to lose them. She does not even remember her own skin, which had saved her — just as it had so many times almost cost her her life. Perhaps the gods who turned away in her people's hour of need feel some compunction to atone, for she is spared the memory of the marauding soldiers who came upon her family. Perhaps that is her small, merciful gift. This is where her life begins, here on the boat that lurched out of nowhere to carry her toward the coast of Italy. This is her first memory: she is waking on a bed of scratchy straw. She tries to move her leg because of the thistles in the straw, but her feet are shackled. There are more than a dozen others with her in this narrow room where daylight enters from a square hole in the ceiling. There is a lantern. It seems to swing as if in a wind, sending long loops of light forward to one side, backward to the other. There is the noise of movement everywhere but no one is walking. And then, too, there is the sensation of movement although she is still. Her ankle is raw and her neck hurts; she has no idea where she is. She looks through the gloom and finds the space disproportionately long and narrow, the walls inexplicably curved, hugging great stacks and bales of stuff secured with planks and cords. It is a long time before she thinks "boat." At first, hearing the grating of chains, she thinks "prison" and cannot understand the tilt and fall of the floor, the hiss and roar of what she thinks is wind. Stiff from sleeping and awkward, she tries to get up. When she gets to her feet, still bent, arms spread for balance, blood flows from her, runs warm down her leg under her skirt. She wipes it away with her hand. There is more coming down. The man nearest to her spits in her direction, passes his hand over his mouth. She squats to see the blood still flowing. There is no one to tell her that her woman's sorrows have begun. Instead it seems a sign of something she knows but has forgotten. Something that would cause her own body to be weeping blood. It comes to her from a great distance, this knowledge of blood and its impatience to be out. It is about to burst like a dam behind her eyes. And then like a dream it vanishes. The man is cursing her. There is nowhere to go. She stands up again, balancing this time with the roll of the ship: the sharp tilt as the floor on one side lifts, and the precipitous sliding fall as it returns. Tilt and fall, tilt and fall. She becomes aware of the smell of vomit, as pervasive as the shadows. She steps on someone lying nearby and the dream almost returns, but the body under her foot yelps and people begin to shout. Like a sky full of rocks aimed at her head — but still she does not remember her skin. A woman, her ankles shackled, shuffles over and presses a rag into her hands. It is already damp and sticky.

After that she remembers nothing more until a man's face against a blinding blue sky, loud as a shout up against her own. The man's eyes are blazing anger, his breath is hot on her face and he is spitting something at her, words she doesn't understand. The dark hold has become bright broad day. She is standing on a raised platform. A crowd of people look up at her. Between two buildings she can see shining water that reaches to the edge of the world. The man's hand is on her arm, shaking her, jolting her. She does not understand what he wants. He shoves her toward the faces and at the same time holds her back. What does he want her to do? She says in her own language that she doesn't understand and the man looks pleased. He is smiling now, satisfied and nodding to the crowd, gesturing with one hand up to his mouth and the other behind him waving in the direction of her own. He looks back at her and barks an order again. She repeats, "I don't understand," and he smiles again, nods, "*Può parlare. Eccola che parla*," tapping his mouth with both hands, flicking his fingers outward, toward the crowd. And now the people are calling, gesturing in her direction. The man

7

beside her finally takes her arm and extends it. For the first time, she is conscious of her skin and the fact that she is naked. He holds her arm out to the side and runs his free hand up and down it as if he is trying to calm or soothe her, or as if he is gently wiping away the markings that cover her. He does the same on the other side. Then he opens both his hands to the crowd, who fall silent, waiting for whatever calamity must surely overtake him for this rash act. He passes his palms over his face and down his neck as if he is washing. The silence hangs a moment in the air before it is fractured; a lock has been turned, a door opened. People begin to talk again and call out. The man shouts back and finally a man with no hair at all to cover his brown scalp comes forward. He climbs up onto the platform and puts his hands on the girl's shoulders to turn her around. She closes her eyes. He runs his hands along the length of her body. The girl begins to shake. Someone in the crowd is baying the words of a song and people begin to laugh. The girl opens her eyes and a shift is pushed into her hands. She has barely time to put it on before she is taken by the arm and led away from the platform to a table where another man sits with ink and paper. The bald man is waiting.

The tiny noise of the broker's quill on the page of the ledger makes her skin crawl. She begins to shake again.

The men are engrossed. They all speak the same language as the barking man. Finally money passes between them and they shake hands. The bald man takes her by the wrist and leads her away.

He walks her to a wagon loaded with bulging sacks, a mule with a moth-eaten look about the face waiting between the shafts. A carter comes and she is made to climb up into the wagon. The carter follows, carrying a large fruit that she does not recognize. It is as big as a human head. He wedges it between two sacks, pulls others toward the front and arranges them so that he can half sit, half stand and drive in comfort. He makes a sharp clicking noise with his tongue and she has to grab the edge of the cart as the mule moves on. He looks at her and asks her a question. She says at once, "I don't understand," and the man seems pleased. He uses a switch on the mule, and they go creaking and swaying up the hill away from the wharf and on through the shade of narrow, crowded streets. The man glances in her direction once or twice and inhales as if he would speak, but she is careful to keep her eyes fixed on the road. In a little while they pass through a monumental stone arch out onto the open road. Two storks fly overhead, their slow wing beats like breath blown hard against the fist in winter. The man turns and says, "*Cicogne. Primavera.*" She says at once, "I don't understand." He looks her way from time to time. Sometimes he speaks. Each time, she answers the same thing: "I don't understand."

IN A LOW STONE BUILDING that once was a byre, now a workshop, on a hillside overlooking the city of Firenze far below, an old man with grey hair to his shoulders and a full grey beard is making a sketch in a small notebook. It is nighttime and he has to peer closely. Ceccio, his boy, is preparing the room, making sure they have everything they will need for their work. The old man, Paolo Pallavicino, bends over his drawing. In the centre of the page, a child dances, balanced for an instant on the ball of one foot, in his raised hand a lily, beneath his foot an egg.

A heavy block stands in the middle of the byre. Ceccio has hung the sharpened knives on hooks at its end, laid out the saws, placed the barrow nearby, and the two buckets, one containing a sponge, underneath. He has six lamps on the table and he is lighting them with a taper, careful not to burn himself or spill the oil. The lamps flare, casting their brilliance on the turn of his cheek, his long lashes. He stands on a stool to hang them from the hooks in the low roof beams and their light spills gold on his hair. In his concentration, his tongue protrudes slightly between his teeth, giving him a stupid look. Paolo Pallavicino does not see. He bends over his notebook. Under the foot of the dancing boy, the egg is upright and unbroken. On the page the boy's mouth smiles with secret intelligence. It is Ceccio's mouth but it smiles with a beauty all its own.

Paolo has drawn the boy many times before, rendering his head in pen, in silverpoint and in paint. He never tires of it, perhaps because the heads, though they are very beautiful, are not Ceccio. They have, to be sure, the same broad brow with eyebrows that lift to an angle and wing outward from the midpoint, and beneath them the same large and wide-set eyes. They have the same fine nose with its straight bridge and perfectly formed nostrils set a little wide. There are the same cheekbones and the same jawbone, the small cleft in the rounded chin, the lovely lips with the small bow above, the pout below. Lips to kiss. And yet none of it is Ceccio. On Paolo's page there is no greed or malice or cunning, only generous goodwill. The eyes are limpid. One gazes into the middle distance, the other wanders farther, lost in a dream. Every time Paolo takes up the challenge of Ceccio's face, his hand is bewitched by the beauty of the line, the set of the sturdy column of neck in its collar of bone, the shell of ear . . . Paolo can reproduce a line with great accuracy, can render the finest degree of shading, but his hand, charmed into dawdling in the abundance of soft blond curls, betrays his eye and blinds it to the duplicity that clouds Ceccio's gaze, the stupidity that swells his lips.

⌇

IN AN UPPER ROOM of a house on Via del Cocomero a man, old before his time, lies on his side while his daughter rubs warm oil into his sore hip. She, Sofonisba, has put on a face of patience and fortitude. Her father, Orazio, is complaining loudly. The weather, he says, is the worst it has ever been. It will kill him. "My hips," he says, "my hips." Sofonisba says, "There, there, there," over and over. "My father," she says, "my poor father." If he had been working on the wall today it would have been, "My hands, my hands," but the rain has kept him inside and he has been sitting all day working on the panel for the Sisters of Sant' Anna. Sofonisba's stomach is in a knot with the effort it requires to maintain calm. Sofonisba Fabroni is not a patient person, except when she herself is painting. Then there is no Sofonisba to be patient or impatient; when she is painting, her body is simply a tool for the application of paint to wood or to plaster, and her mind is one with it. Time does not exist then; the question of patience is irrelevant.

Sofonisba's arms ache, and she stops rubbing her father's hip for a moment, closing her eyes against him when he protests. "You've stopped? I need you to rub until it has gone." He turns over heavily on the bed, so that she can rub the other side. The wind outside is gusting still, sending the rain in bursts of noise against the shutters and filling the dark streets with sudden, unearthly voices.

For I understood, without any doubt, that life is twofold:
the material existence common to the beasts and the plants, and that
existence which is peculiar to a man eager for glory and high endeavour.
— GIROLAMO CARDANO

PART I

ONE

1554

Paolo Pallavicino has been invited today to view Giuliano's latest acquisition. Paolo is an artist, an inventor, a student of Nature, a fabricator of curiosities. He lives in a new house built especially for him by Giuliano, his patron, on the grounds of his country estate, *La Castagna*. The stuccoed house sits lower than Giuliano's villa on the hill, just beyond an old fieldstone byre. A former granary stands beside it. Giuliano has given both outbuildings over to Paolo's use. Paolo's house itself is new, built with good stone, finished with the same smooth stucco as the villa. The terra cotta tiles of its roof will long outlast both men. Although he is reluctant to part with coin that can be clutched in a fist, Giuliano has spared no expense to see that Paolo is comfortably established. Paolo is as much a chattel of his patron as the shrill peacock that perches on the roof.

Giuliano's own house sits comfortably where the incline of the hill eases away to a broad shelf before rising again to the summit. The estate is on good, productive land, cultivated by Dominicans for one hundred and seventy-six years before Giuliano arrived with his money. *La Castagna* is a fine house with a stark beauty all its own. The lines are severe, the yellow stucco of its walls unadorned; high windows are set in two even rows across the front, a tall door in their centre. A third storey projects above, its covered balcony running on all four sides under the exposed timbers of the eaves. Protected by the rise of the hill at its back from the north wind that sweeps down from the Mugello, it is open on the southwest to a view of the city spanning the river below. In summer, in a certain light, the dull gold of the Arno winds through the valley floor like a river of wheat.

Giuliano likes to use the Medici name after his own, although his connection with it through a series of marriages is tenuous. It is his only public pretension, a fancy easily accommodated by the rest of the family since he is wealthy, he is polished, and he has neither political aspirations nor heirs. The doors of *La Castagna* are open winter and summer in welcome to his many guests, for Giuliano lives all year up here on the hill with his wife Lucia, when she is not at her sister's washing down nostrums for a fruitful confinement. Giuliano enjoys his farm. He keeps an extensive vineyard and a productive olive grove, but his interests are more esoteric.

Paolo Pallavicino is doubly important to him. Not only does he have the discriminating eye necessary to discern the wonderful, and the skilled fingers to fabricate it, he is also something of a wonder himself. There is no artist quite like him and Giuliano gladly provides his living while he works.

A whole suite of rooms houses Giuliano's collection of antique curios, plate, and works of art. The table for viewing stands in the centre of the largest room. Eight chests contain the works in glass and gold and silver, medallions, antique bronzes and mirrors that Giuliano has amassed. Here too are precious gems and corals as well as an ossified tumour from a calf's skull and the third station of the cross carved on a peach stone. It is Giuliano's pleasure to visit this room, his *guardaroba*, in the evenings, either alone or with Paolo, and have the Master of these apartments, his valet Gaetano — of the white beard and the endless patience — present perhaps his latest acquisition, or perhaps some well-loved piece that he had almost forgotten he owned. One day it will be a set of firing pieces with silver handles, the next the horn of a sea creature mounted in silver and supported by dolphins of bronze. There is no end, he likes to say, to the ingenuity of the mind of man, nor to the delight that it can afford the cultivated man.

In a long stone barn a little way off from the house he keeps a menagerie of uncommon beasts, which he calls his ark. It makes no difference to Giuliano whether a thing be an artefact or a freak of Nature. What matters is only that no other man possess it.

Giuliano can hardly wait to present his latest acquisition. He knows she is extraordinary — a little slave girl, no longer a child, nor yet a woman, not exactly a Moor, nor yet a fair-skinned Christian. She will be perfect for Lucia, who shares his love of the rare and the curious.

The markings on the little girl remind him of the drawings of the giraffe kept by one of his great-uncles. As a boy, he longed to see the creature in the flesh, to run his hand over the neck.

Today Lucia returns from a visit to her sister. He will give her the girl. She has asked for one constantly.

~

GIULIANO'S INVITATION — or summons, Paolo is not sure — is a source of anxiety. He has at this moment a new subject in the byre in readiness for an anatomical demonstration tonight.

Paolo's mind is a mercurial thing, fluid and swift. His interest has long since moved from the feathers that litter his *studio* like the sweepings from some celestial courtyard. He has, in the course of only two years, investigated lenses, seeds, flotation, mortars and glues, armour and fire, in the course of which he accidentally ignited Giuliano's grain shed and burned his own collection of notes on lenses. Of late his interest has alighted on the nature of the animal and the essence of life itself. He searches intently for the vital spark, the seat of life, hoping always to discover its exact location.

Giuliano condones, even encourages, these anatomical investigations. Sometimes, when there are guests to entertain, he himself will attend, but not tonight. Paolo can only think that he has had some sudden objection of conscience.

Although Paolo's guests are due to arrive at any moment, he cannot risk refusing Giuliano. He leaves his house and walks up past the byre to the villa.

It is a relief when Giuliano greets him at the door with open arms and a welcoming smile. He lets Paolo pause for breath after the climb and then he takes him straight to the stairs.

Paolo's value, for Giuliano, lies in his judgement. He is his most trusted adviser, able to assess the worth of things, at a glance, allowing him to sleep soundly in the knowledge that he has not been duped or led astray in the quicksands of artistic merit.

He has, he says, a marvel of Nature to show him. More pleasing by far than a dwarf, more mysterious than a hunchback, this child-woman is neither devil nor angel. Her skin is as pied as the spotted cow that stands in the meadow. The girl, he says, is called Caterina. Dressed in a grey shift, she is waiting by the long window in the *guardaroba* (she can steal nothing for she is wearing no pockets or sleeves). He has thrown open the shutters.

SOFONISBA FABRONI TURNED seventeen on the day her father, Orazio, announced that it was time to take her to Paolo Pallavicino's house to view an anatomical demonstration. Three weeks later, as soon as he received word that Paolo had a subject, Orazio closed up his shop and set out with his daughter early in the afternoon. At once he began to have misgivings. All the way through the narrow streets of the city, Orazio fretted about the security of his shop and whether he had remembered to tell the boy to put both bars across the shutters and whether he had remembered to lock the gold leaf in the strongbox as he had intended. Father and daughter left by the Porta San Gallo and turned westward on the steep road to San Domenico. They had not gone far before Orazio insisted on stopping and changing mounts. The mare was too skittish for his bones. He gave it to Sofonisba and rode instead on the mule. For the rest of the journey Sofonisba enjoyed her elevated view from the mare's back and tried not to listen to her father's curses about the intractable nature of mules.

La Castagna is a fair climb from the town. When Sofonisba and Orazio arrive at Paolo's own house, there is no one about. Orazio calls out but Paolo does not appear. Instead, his boy Ceccio comes to take the mounts. He says Paolo is up at the villa and they are to make the house their own. Orazio takes him at his word and goes, grumbling and banging the dust out of the skirts of his mantle, up the stairs to find Paolo's bed. Sofonisba watches to make sure the boy stops with the mounts at the water butt before he takes them away. The boy is beautiful with the golden curls of an angel, but that does not mean he has any sense.

Upstairs Orazio pulls the shutters closed against the low sun and lies full length upon the bed, his nose to the ceiling, his arms out at his sides, like a corpse before it has had its boots removed and its hands folded on its breast. It is his favourite position. Sofonisba listens, holding her breath. She wonders how long it will be before her father calls out to her to come and rub his hands. Or his feet. Or his knees. She walks quietly away from the stairs.

Orazio sighs. His bones ache. He wishes they were instead over at the farm where his cousin Iacopo keeps Giuliano's vines. At least Iacopo has a wife who would look after them. The trouble he brings upon himself for the sake of his daughter. All this — this arduous journey, this tedious and revolting demonstration they are to attend — all for the advancement of her skill. And to silence his fellow painters once and for all. It has become tiresome for it to be known everywhere that his daughter executes parts of his work. The question is always being raised at the meetings of his Guild, the *Arte de' Medici e Speziali.* He hopes he has found a way to silence them.

At the last meeting of the *Arte,* Sofonisba's name came up two or three times in connection with Guild affairs. Once, when the question of eligibility was being discussed, Antonello Morelli had asked Orazio pointedly how his daughter was. Orazio had had a schoolboy impulse to strike him. Sofonisba's name came up again when they discussed the fulfilment of contracts and the regulations for subcontracting. Again there was only cowardly innuendo.

By the time the wine went round, Orazio was ready for a challenge. He banged his fist on the table. "It's time you listened to me." Which took everyone by surprise since the last item for discussion had been cleared amicably.

"I understand you well enough. Slanderers. Cowards," he said. "My Sofonisba is not good enough" — though no one had said it — "for you. Well, let me tell you, she is as good as any of you."

There were faces round the table that were sheepish, but more for the fact that they felt themselves accused than that they had actually harboured such thoughts; it simply seemed appropriate to look that way. Orazio, after all, was mad enough. But there were others at the table who jolted awake, who could recognize from any distance — even through a haze of wine — the tones that made up the prelude to a fight. It was almost a duty on their part to cry "Never!"

"As skillful, as sure, as gifted, as expert as any of you," Orazio looked around accusingly. "And I know how to prove it. There!" He flung down the letter he had brought to the meeting. The seal was familiar. Some of the others had received the same letter. "The Arcivescovo Andrea is asking for proposals. For a wall in fresco at his country house and for a panel in oil. Well, never mind tenders. Let us propose an open contest. What do you say? I'll approach the Arcivescovo and he'll set the terms. Sofonisba shall enter."

Now here was something more interesting than the endless bickering among themselves.

"If she wins, you can stop up your baggy mouths and quit your slander once and for all."

"And how shall we know if it is Sofonisba's work?" asked Landucci, who loved to work in details and was already taking up ink and pen.

"Because if she wins," Orazio had said, "then she will have to paint equally well. You will see for yourself. And if she loses," he took the quill from Landucci's hand and put it back down on the table, "well then, you shall not have to worry." He raised his cup. There was a general raising of cups, which he took to mean assent.

"Good, then. I shall speak to the Arcivescovo on Thursday, right after Mass."

Antonello belched and held out his glass.

That Sofonisba should be an artist was not surprising. From her earliest years she had lived in the company of painters, and was raised by Orazio's model, who was also his mistress. Orazio's work was much admired and his reputation kept him busy with commissions. In his younger days his circle of painter friends was wide. They came and went in his house at will. The day after his wife died in a fearsome miscarriage, Orazio moved his mistress into the household as nursemaid. When Orazio was working, Sofonisba played at her father's feet. She made thick, red chalk marks on the plaster wall Orazio used for mapping out the images in his head. The nursemaid slept. When Orazio was not working he rolled with the nursemaid on the wide bed. When Orazio was neither working nor rolling, he was carousing with his friends. There was always something to celebrate: a new commission, a feast day, the birth of a child, the death of an enemy, a successful vintage, the execution of a murderer, sun, rain.

Sofonisba grew to be bold and relaxed. She knew that if the guard came hammering at the door, and if the boy finally let them in, and if they thundered past her and bellowed at Orazio, and threw over the tables and chairs in their search for the felon he was supposed to be harbouring, she would not be harmed. She would sit placidly in the corner, playing with a piece of wax, laughing when one of them stumbled or tripped.

Later, she came to know that the leering men and their pawing hands were harmless if the smell of wine were only heavy enough. Then they could be rebuffed, if not with a remark that took them out at the ankles, then with a physical blow from her elbow jabbed into the diaphragm. She had used the trick enough times to know how to make the air come out of them in a squared off cough, and almost their breakfast, too. She knew, besides, that her father, whatever his shortcomings, was her protector; however vile and out of hand his companions might become after a meal, Orazio could be counted on to throw them out, with his own hands if he had to, if they made to harm so much as an eyelash of his daughter's eye.

But there are fewer companions now for her father, who has fallen into old age like a drunk falling into a gorse bush. His bad temper and his petulant fretting have become customary, and coin is almost all he desires — that and renown. Those who still associate with him do so out of respect for his work, which does not mean that Sofonisba goes unnoticed. For men like Matteo Tassi, who career through life like boys in an orchard, she is one more fruit to snatch at. They are drawn to her for the movement of her breasts and hips, the sweet turning of her figure, and the softness of her skin, never giving a moment's thought to how unlike she is to the fair-haired loveliness they paint on their panels: the delicate opalescent skin, the painted lips that offer half a smile and never open to show teeth.

There is nothing delicate about Sofonisba. She is a strong young woman, tall enough, somewhat broad, and very dark with the burnished colouring of Naples or of Sicily. She does not fit the Florentine mould for beauty, nor does she care, for at fifteen she had had a revelation. She had been standing in front of one of her father's paintings eating a peach. The painted Saint Francis was beckoning to a courtly youth who was standing with his back to a table laid for a small but rich feast. The two figures were almost complete but the viands on the table were still suggestions. There was a pheasant with a twisted neck, there were grapes and there was bread, two round loaves, and there, roughed in on the very edge of the table as if about to fall out of the picture was the peach the young man had replaced, his hand still outstretched behind him, in the act of turning toward the saint. Sofonisba's mouth had come suddenly alive with the shock of sweetness. She glanced down at the peach in her hand, caught off guard by the sharpness of the contrast between the velvet of its skin and the slickness of its saturated flesh. Cupped in her palm it made its shape and its mass known to her so that in response she knew suddenly, intimately the cave of her palm and in knowing that she knew also her mouth's hollow and its own moist lining of flesh, contained behind the silky walls, her teeth smooth and strong against them. Everything inside of her and outside was known to her, was contained in that single moment, so that she was aware of the difference, the strangeness, the otherness of every part of creation and how every part had each its own hundred thousand qualities of roughness or darkness or breadth or tensility or moisture or fragility or luminescence or colour or . . . She put her own peach on a corner of the table and then, risking her father's wrath, she reached for his mixing board.

Later that day Orazio had worked on for a while, trying to ignore the convincing peach — with a bite out of it! — that somehow had rolled onto the table in his painting. He knew of course that it was Sofonisba's work but it had unnerved him in the way he had been unnerved by the visions of the necromancer that his friend, the goldsmith, had taken him to see: the chimeras that he knew to be deceptions appearing and disappearing in the smoke and he, knowing it to be fakery, but at a loss to say how it was done. The peach was eerily lifelike, as if when he looked back again he would find it drier, discoloured at the bitten edge. Well, good then. He already had more work than he could handle. She would be very useful.

That same afternoon, Orazio looked out of the window to the courtyard and saw Sofonisba sewing caps for the *gettatelli* with the woman who did the cooking. He called her inside. He said the time had come for her to help him in his work. Sofonisba waited, expecting to be told to mix colours or to prepare a size.

"You can finish this fruit," said Orazio. "Start here with the pomegranate." Sofonisba took up the brush.

Sofonisba walks quietly through Paolo Pallavicino's study, his *studio*. It takes up almost all of the ground floor of the house. Only a small room with a hearth and a chimney is left for cooking and eating. An outside staircase leads to a covered balcony and the chambers above. Sofonisba assesses the size of the *studio* and the space at Paolo's disposal and compares it to the cramped conditions of her father's shop.

She looks in at a recess in the back wall. It forms a smaller room with its own window. It is lined with shelves like an apothecary's shop, its space almost entirely taken up by a small desk where Paolo prepares his colours. She tries the drawer but it is locked and she guesses this is where he keeps his paper and parchments and his silverpoints. The shelves are packed with jars of oil, tablets of wax, incising knives, ink pots, bowls. There are two pestles, two thick glass grinding plates, a plaster mould, a slab of marble, small copper pots of different sizes, an oil burner, knives and scrapers, rags, pens, sticks of chalk, chunks of pigment. There is enough material here to open a shop to commissions. But Paolo has no need.

The *studio* itself is high-ceilinged and wide. There are two tables, one almost lost under a drift of feathers. Last year, at the *festa* of San Giovanni, Paolo Pallavicino's reputation as a master of spectacle was secured by the giant mechanical dove of his devising that opened its wings above the Piazza Santa Croce and let loose a thick flurry of white eider feathers to float about the heads of the spectators. The white down stayed aloft. It swirled and eddied against the blue sky. Snow in June. No one can forget it. Some said it was a taste of Paradise. In the town there are high expectations of a reprise in June of last year's *festa*.

The second table is empty and stands by the window, Paolo's own drawing desk with its easel top and its stool beside it. The drawing surface of the desk is raised and a piece of thick rag paper is tacked up ready, its surface primed the colour of plaster, cloudy white, like a blind eye.

A narrow shelf supported by iron brackets runs the length of one wall at shoulder height, opposite the door. It carries only a few books. The legend Paolo studies belongs to Nature. Her secrets, he likes to say, are everywhere transcribed, her notations inscribed on every leaf, on every bone, on every feather. A man has no need of school. A man has only to use the eyes God gave him. Besides the books, the shelf carries a row of stoppered jars, a stack of plaster tablets bearing the imprint of leaves, some drawing tools, several wax models, both human and animal figures, and a small bronze cast of the head of a cat. Paolo's notebooks flop untidily on the end.

Sofonisba would like to look but does not dare. No one has said when Paolo might return.

She runs her hand through the pile of wings and feathers on the table. They make a husky sound like wheat in summer. Here is every kind of feather, a confusion of lost flight, tools for sculpting air, inscribing sky. Curled swansdown lifts when the pile is stirred, daggers from the magpie's tail, notched flight feathers from the buzzard's wing slide to the floor.

Sofonisba picks up a gull's wing that Paolo has stretched on a reed and fixed with rabbit glue in a flightless arc. It has a faint smell of rotting fish at the base where it has not been cleaned, but its line is beautiful and invites the fingertip to trace. Gulls fly far inland on the blustery days of early spring, when they tumble and scream in the air above the ploughs outside the city. But here too are the wings of birds that have never taken flight, pairings of cuckoo with rooster, crane with goose, wings of Paolo's own creation, no sooner conceived than discarded. She sees the feathers now for what they are, the workings of Paolo's untidy mind, the underside of genius.

Sofonisba is hungry. She hopes Giuliano's fabled hospitality will extend down the hill and manifest itself in some form of sustenance before the night's work begins. Meanwhile, she is at a loss. Paolo is not the most attentive of hosts. Ceccio has said the subject is in the byre. It will require some courage. But she has come here to learn, after all.

⌐⌐

PAOLO SENSES HIS PATRON'S EYES searching his face when he pauses at the door of the *guardaroba*.

A small figure dressed in a loose gown of grey wool stands by the window. Giuliano's brief and enigmatic description did not prepare Paolo for what he sees. Under her dark curls the girl's black brow is splashed with a curious white mark in the centre. On the left side the blackness flows round her eye to extend across her cheekbone and down in an irregular shape, tapering to the outside edge of her mouth. Here it picks up and begins to widen again, as it flows past her chin and winds down around her neck. The right side of her face is white and bears only a tracery of black, the shadowing of leaves on a limed wall. She keeps her eyes turned toward the window, her pied arms hanging loose at her sides, her darkly mottled feet planted squarely.

"She speaks?"

"Yes, she speaks. Vittorio had his wife teach her before he brought her here. The man knows how to wring the best price."

"What's your name, girl?"

"Caterina, sir."

"And who is your master?"

"*Signor* Giuliano."

"Are you a good girl?"

"I am."

"Where do you come from?"

"I come from the boat."

Paolo laughs. "But before that?"

The girl's gaze slides back to the window.

"You'll get no answer. *I don't know. I don't remember. I don't understand.* You can ask whatever you like. Have you a mother or a father? A brother? A sister? *I don't remember. I don't understand.* She's as stubborn as any of them."

"And where is she from?"

"Alexandria. Taken from there to Genoa. But before Alexandria who can say? She's not an Ethiope, not a Tartar, yet she has something of the look of both. Sometimes it's best not to delve.

"Do you want to draw her?"

Paolo hesitates.

"Ah, but you have work of your own to do. I had forgotten."

But Paolo would like to draw this girl. Would like more than anything to see the whole of this strange skin that is so like the hide of a beast, yet smooth, hairless. He has seen this skin on pups that he removed from the belly of a bitch.

"I have no tools with me."

"I have drawing tools, and a piece of velvet on the table here if you require it. I had them move the table close to the window for you. I've inspected every inch of her. She's a marvel. The instruction you derive is yours but the drawing you make will be mine."

"Of course. It will be an honour."

"Take off the gown, Caterina."

The girl's eyelids open and she looks from one man to the other.

"Take off the gown. You will not come to any harm."

The girl undoes a lace at the neck of the gown and pulls it from her shoulders. She wriggles out of it and snatches it up at once to cover herself. Paolo takes it gently and gives her the piece of velvet. She is shivering; it is a movement that begins not on the skin but in the belly.

Paolo pushes a chair into position and motions to her.

"Get up. Get up on the table."

"Up on the table. Now, Caterina."

Paolo sees how the shivering increases, sees how the girl's attention turns in on herself, leaving her eyes blank.

"With respect, *Vossignoria*, I think we shall succeed with patience."

Giuliano laughs. He puts his arm round Paolo and claps his shoulder amicably.

"I shall stay away," he says. "I've seen all this. Just do whatever has to be done to make me a fine drawing."

He turns to go.

"And don't rush. Your subject has all the time in the world."

⌒

PAOLO'S SUBJECT FOR TONIGHT is a pauper who died at the gates of the Stinche as if he were taking himself to the prison in the last hope of charity. It is not clear why he died. He is not an old man, is not perhaps yet forty, nor is his body entirely famished. Paolo's agents brought it up to the house this morning, wrapped in sacking and hidden under bales of straw in the cart. They took it to the stone byre and laid it out on a heavy table in the centre and when Paolo had seen that all was in order he left it there with the doors locked. When Sofonisba's knock comes, there is no one to answer it.

"The dead bastard's in there."

It is Ceccio, standing a little way off, the low sun making a halo of his unkempt curls.

"I know."

"The maestro won't let you in. Not till we've got him ready."

Sofonisba thinks what a good subject this boy would make. He has a lightness about his figure, his neck and his wrists not yet thickened. She would show how the soft, blond curls seem to dance.

"But you can see him. Want me to show you?"

"If you will," says Sofonisba. Almost before she has finished speaking, Ceccio is forcing a loose board in the door, prying it up and sideways so that it gapes at waist height. He holds it while Sofonisba bends down to look. She straightens up, shocked, then takes a breath and kneels down to peer once again into the crack in the boards. Ceccio giggles.

Light falls into the byre from the gaps in the stone under the eaves. The man's body is lying on a heavy table. She is looking straight past the soles of its bare feet away down its length, past the male member curved in its nest of hair, past the cave of the standing ribs to its barrel chest with the minute nipples just breaking the line of sight and beyond them the scrawny neck and then the dark stubble of the chin. The man's hands lie at his sides, the palms upturned. Her heart panics. The head is raised slightly on a block as if on a pillow and she can see the lovely lines of the mouth at rest, the closed eyes. There is no border between sleep and death.

She gets up and looks at Ceccio. He makes a lewd gesture with his hand at his groin. Sofonisba brings the back of her hand smartly to his head and he stops smiling.

She is filled with confusion. What is it about the corpse? It lies on the table with its eyes closed — and she is at its feet. Why does she think of Christ? Why does she? She knows the Christ figure. It is vertical. Its arms are outstretched. Its mouth drawn down in pain. This man could be asleep after a long and difficult journey. Or in Heaven.

"Want to see something else?"

"No. I want to eat. My father will too when he gets up."

"I can get you something."

"But first I will look again."

~

THE GIRL IS NOT BEAUTIFUL. And she must know this, wherever she came from. She is an aberration. Against Nature. She is not beautiful and yet her face has a pleasing form and her eyes are lively. Her hair is abundant and tightly curled. Her cheek bones are too broad and too high perhaps, but not out of keeping. She is pleasingly proportioned. But her skin — the mark of Cain could be no worse. To live inside such skin is to be clothed in disgrace, to go about the world as a herald — the blasphemy will not be suppressed — of God's cruel indifference. Paolo wonders how she came to be purchased at all. How she survived her birth. He pictures her on the dock at Genoa where the newly arrived captives are displayed on barrels. He wonders why she is not at the bottom of the harbour.

He pushes the chair closer to the table. The girl stares at her feet but cannot seem to move them. Paolo puts his arm behind her to help her, but still her shaking continues and her feet remain planted. Paolo sighs quietly, and bends toward her as if he will lift her up, drapery and all, and deposit her like a bundle of bed linen on the table. But he is not quick enough. She turns and steps back, leaving him stooped, his arms extended, like a farm boy trying to force a pig into a pen. Twice, three times he tries to get behind her and each time she turns, rotating her hips away from his reach in a strange dance of seduction and flight. Paolo laughs out loud, seeing their dance suddenly through Giuliano's eyes. He straightens up and turns away with a shrug, folds his arms.

The girl senses this is a signal. She steps up carefully and climbs onto the table to kneel in the centre, facing the window, her back to him, her head bowed.

Paolo turns round. He tilts his head and wonders what she imagines will happen next. The shivering has stopped. Her attitude is one of abandonment. She has left her body, as the condemned do. He goes up behind her and lifts the velvet away. She does not resist. Paolo catches his breath. He wants only to look and to look.

Her mottled back is in shadow. The soles of her feet, upturned beneath her, are dusty and show white. He walks round and stands facing her with his back to the window. A second time he catches his breath, though he is careful not to let her see. What he had expected were dark blotches, disfigurations of uneven hue and texture, blemishes, perhaps some of them raised. What he sees draws his eye and fixes it. She is holding her arms in close, crossing them in front so that only the upper half of her breasts is exposed. The skin there is smooth. She is in the full light of the window and, though there is no tree outside to cast shadows, her body is dappled. The markings are irregular in shape, larger than oak leaves in places, and the colour of the blackest loam. They are dispersed over her pale skin. So smooth he wants to touch. Her thighs, too, are covered with the markings. He comes closer. The light striking her side obliquely shows the surface of her skin to be entirely without flaw. It is as sleek, he thinks, as the flank of a horse. A piebald colt. No wart or scab or boil upon it. He touches her waist, would have liked to stroke but instead reaches across to unclasp her fingers from her arms.

As he does so he catches the look in her eyes and he knows his own eyes are too greedy, too curious. He cannot see enough. He examines her closely, lifting her limbs to see the underside, peering under her hair at the nape of her neck, parting her legs. When he has seen every inch of her, he sits down and closes his eyes. The girl waits a while, a while longer and then she makes a move toward the edge of the table.

Paolo opens his eyes. "No, don't get down," he says. "We shall begin." He takes up Giuliano's drawing board and a red chalk and begins with quick strokes to lay her figure on the page. His eyes travel her skin inch by inch, flick away to the page, return, inch by inch, measuring, noting every marking, noting more than the girl knows herself.

The girl keeps her eyes fixed on something outside, far away through the open shutters.

⁓

SOFONISBA AND HER FATHER sit on the benches in front of Paolo's house and watch the day seep into the west. The sky there is flooded with rose and lavender, marigold and violet. The distant hills darken and mass. In the valley the river turns first to gold, then copper; eastward it is already a deep Lenten purple. The guests have seen their host only briefly when he came down from the villa. Ceccio brought them onions and broth and pieces of salted fish. Orazio said that if he did not find them some wine he would have his master pull his ears off. He cannot wait for this night to be done, wonders why he ever suggested it. He grumbles to himself, cross that he expends his time and strength preparing Sofonisba for his trade when he would do better simply to marry her off. It is a thought Orazio entertains often, despite his fear of losing his most valuable assistant.

Sofonisba too would like the night to be over. She cannot stop thinking of the uncommon beauty of the bones of the man's face even in death, the humble patience of the cadaver, waiting in state to serve them. She gets up and goes into the house to light a lamp. It gives a feeble glow but will look brighter in a little while. In daylight the undertaking was nothing but education, an apprenticeship in anatomy, but the approaching darkness gives the night's enter-prise a flavour of sin that she did not taste before. They have torches by them, ready to light when Ceccio comes to tell them it is time.

Paolo Pallavicino insists on performing his demonstrations at night. The idle and the foolish, who might otherwise have a mind to peer in on what he does in the stone byre, will be deterred by the dark and by their own ungodly imaginations; for while it might be for-ward thinking and plumped with prestige to conduct an anatomical dissection in a public lecture hall in Padua, it is quite another thing — it is in fact tainted with criminality — to perform the same by the light of lamps in a disused cowshed at the dead of night. In this way, by throwing a cape of terror about his activities, Paolo seeks to preserve their sanctity.

The terror at first was almost too much for Ceccio. Once, when it was time to get up and assist Paolo, he tried pretending to be unable to rouse, lying there with his long-lashed eyes closed against the dark, moaning as if in sleep. But that only moved Maestro Paolo to anger. He had taken hold of him and shoved him to the corpse's side, made him kneel and there, by the dead man's face, make his apologies for his tardiness. "Poor shred of a lost soul," Paolo had said. "You're lucky I don't lock you in here to spend the whole night with him." But the moment that Ceccio fears most, the moment that gives him nightmares of the worst unwaking kind, is when Maestro Paolo asks him to carry the unwanted parts away. Because Ceccio has little wit and Paolo Pallavicino too much, neither of them would think to use the barrow. Maestro Paolo would be scrib-bling notes still with his hair singeing in the flame of his candle, while Ceccio would clasp to his chest some unnamed, unnameable mass wrapped in a damp and stained sheet and already smelling putrid. Tonight Ceccio stumbles once, the thing is so heavy, for Paolo Pallavicino has isolated the upper torso on the block, leaving the arms attached for ease of handling. The rest is almost more weight than Ceccio can manage in one trip.

Yet it would never occur to him to leave Paolo's employ. There are, he knows, terrors greater than this at large in the world. His Uncle Federigo is one of them. Federigo calls himself a necromancer. He does the work that Paolo can ask no other man to do. Ceccio thought once to return to this man who gave him away to Paolo for a price. He went with him up to the ruins above the villa. He cannot remember now what made him go. Promises? Threats? A memory of his mother's voice? There was not just Federigo but four, five more men with the smell of wine heavy on their breath. Ceccio remembers following the staggering path to the ruins, shivering with cold. So cold he was that when they finally stopped climbing he drank what was offered. His shaking hands made the neck of the wineskin jab at his lips. They wrapped a blanket over him, over his head. One man lit a fire, placed him near. The fire began to crackle and leap. When he felt its warmth he thought he could stay there and sleep with the voices all around. In a little while he did indeed begin to dream; yes, it was a dream, later he was sure. He dreamt of hands and legs about him, bare flesh on his, hot breath, his back parts exposed. Something unspeakable at his face, at his mouth, his eyes crying hot tears, fear and darkness welling from the centre of his being and leaking from every part of him. He remembers pain beyond words. He woke next day in the hay cart calling for Paolo, calling.

Ceccio does not think to go away again. Paolo has told him he will stay forever. He both fears and needs Paolo. He will stay with Paolo until he dies. He has the wits to direct his own way among the many artisans who could use a willing boy, but why should he? Paolo puts food in his mouth, gives him a warm bed and never beats him hard. And if Paolo himself is overtaken by sudden urges in the night, well, they are soon over. And this other thing he does, this meddling with the dead, it does not happen often.

Tonight Ceccio will keep the working table clean. He will keep the wick on the lamps trimmed and hold a candle near for Paolo if there is a difficulty. He will bring the laver whenever Maestro Paolo needs to rinse his hands.

Paolo has set the torso upright on the table. He sharpens the knife he will use for flaying. It is no good asking Ceccio to do it. It would not be done to Paolo's liking. Apart from fetching and carrying, Ceccio has only one real use. There was a time when Paolo thought of finding a more suitable lad to assist him in this demanding work but he kept Ceccio by him nevertheless, hoping perhaps that the beauty of the boy might serve as a charm against the defilement of the knife, as if the mere presence of beauty, like terror, could bestow sanctity. And Paolo now thanks God he did, for Ceccio has a prodigious memory, a talent so great, an ability so extraordinary it might be supernatural. He parrots back, without understanding but in perfect order, every word Paolo speaks during a dissection. The old man wonders sometimes to himself if this is diabolic possession, but the marvellous faculty is too useful to ignore. It is, when afterwards he is making notes, like being given the gift of reliving the night.

Tonight the work will be easy. He is going no deeper than the bed of muscle that lies like a smoothly undulating landscape beneath the skin.

UP AT THE VILLA, Giuliano is pacing the terrace in his stockinged feet. His wife, Lucia, is combing her hair in her bedroom and thinking of the sweet, cool linen of her bed. Caterina, the girl, lies like a dog in the passage, but with her eyes open against the night. Giuliano crosses his arms over his skinny ribs while he considers what to do. His long fingers clutch the embroidered silk of his vest and twist it. The fingers of his other hand run restlessly over his wispy beard, opening and closing like the ribs of a fan. How he wishes he had Paolo's attention tonight. He needs his advice. He hooks his fingers and plays them on his mouth as if to tap out words that would be of use. Lucia was not happy. He chose the wrong time, he knows it now. She was tired after her journey. The two grooms he had sent with her for protection had ridden too hard. The cook's wife, who was supposed to provide company was about as entertaining as a piece of dough. It was a mistake presenting the girl to Lucia as soon as she returned. How could she show delight when she was tired and dusty?

He had had his wife wait in the reception room, had seated her square to the door so that he could see her face when he came in with the girl. She was astonished. She was certainly astonished. But he knew it was more than that. A small frown had gathered between her eyebrows and then her lower lip had pulled sharply down as her neck tensed. She drew back against her chair as if being tugged by an invisible attendant. Two, three times she opened her mouth to draw a breath and speak, each time looking to him and back at once to the girl.

"I cannot think what to say," she said at last. "Let her wait outside." Then, "Will she run away?"

"Of course not," said Giuliano. He closed the door. "Where would she go?"

Lucia stood up. She took the huge breaths of one released from great danger.

"I don't know what to say," she said again. "What is wrong with her? Is she clean? What is this affliction that covers her? What were you thinking?"

Giuliano did his best to calm her fears but Lucia simply closed her eyes and moved her head with a tiny motion from side to side, as if stopping his words from finding the passage to her ears.

When he had said all he could possibly think of to reassure her, she opened her eyes.

"We will decide what to do with her in the morning. If there is no disease, let her sleep in the passage. And now I am very, *very* tired. God keep us, protect us from harm, and bring us safe to morning."

THE BYRE IS WELL LIT. It might be a chapel, the table an altar. The torches the guests brought with them burn in sconces on the walls. Four lamps hang from the rafters above the table. The table is rugged, constructed especially for this work. The knives and saws hang from hooks on the sides. Two buckets stand underneath and a short-handled axe lies beside them. Sofonisba's heart is pounding. Her gaze returns to the mound on the table, discretely covered with a sheet. She clutches her drawing board and her box of tools. She has two pages prepared for silverpoint. For the rest she will make sketches in chalk. Paolo has set two stools by. He invites Sofonisba and her father to make a drawing of the subject before he begins. Sofonisba sits down. While she is opening her box and taking out her silverpoint, she hears Paolo removing the sheet. It will require a conscious effort of will to bring her eyes back again to the table.

"There is no need," he is saying — for her benefit, she knows it — "to be afraid of the flesh. The flesh itself —" She looks up and there it is, the sad, comic stump of the man, his arms too long now for his truncated body, what is left of his neck angled slightly, suggesting the absent head to the struggling mind. "— gives no cause for fear. Only the spirit that informs the flesh in life has power to do us harm."

Ceccio is lighting candles at a small table to the side, where cloths are folded and a basin of water stands ready for washing. Sofonisba's eye is still denying what it sees on the table. Orazio reaches out and taps her arm.

"Begin."

Paolo continues to talk quietly about the nature of flesh, its affinity with earth, with clay, with stone, the importance of water.

His voice is soft, as if he is trying to soothe a skittish horse. Sofonisba lays down lines upon the page. It is a fair enough resemblance to the form in front of her but she cannot give herself to the work. No amount of words from Paolo can remove the sense of shame that afflicts her for the pauper's present disgrace. There is an obscenity here infecting them all. It is a relief when the real work begins. Ceccio is ready with a small lamp. They leave their books on the stools and stand up to view.

With a small triangular blade, Paolo makes a long incision starting between the two collar-bones and running down to the navel. He makes two others from each side of the severed neck out to the end of the clavicle where it meets the scapula. He talks softly, describing each action. He draws his blade down from the top of the shoulder, beside the mound of the humerus and continues the incision round underneath the arm. From there he makes a long incision to the waist and repeats the procedure on the other side. He uses the blade to work a corner of the skin free so that he can grasp it and begin shearing away skin and tissue from the muscle underneath. He pauses only to take up a broader knife with a slight curve to the blade. He works deftly, keeping the blade at an angle. The skin and tissue come away steadily with a dry papery sound, exposing the muscle and its smoothly sheathed contours, a virgin landscape under the eye.

When Paolo has finished, he has removed the skin of the chest and abdomen in two perfectly symmetrical pieces. He tosses them in the bucket and has Ceccio help him turn the torso over.

"The back will be easier, not having the interruption of the nipples."

But Ceccio looks beyond cheering.

"We will take it off in one piece. Ceccio will have to maintain tension on that side."

Paolo undercuts, creating a flap for the boy to grasp.

"Now . . ." He works as before, pushing rather than cutting with the angled blade. ". . . the skin you see is a most wondrous membrane. It keeps the moisture within our bodies, while protecting us from dissolution and putrefaction from the moisture without. It is the veil that stops us from dissolving in ether, the veil that shades us from the scorching of the sun." Paolo pauses. "There are those who say that skin flayed from the corpse of a hanged man has magical properties, the power to ward off evil. Moreover, if you wear the skin for a week, they say, what you most desire shall come to pass. Nonsense. The skin of a hanged man is as the skin of any other. It is its own miracle, a paragon of suppleness and strength and exquisite sensitivity and, when hairless and smooth as in youth and in the female form, a thing of beauty beyond compare."

Ceccio thinks differently, and the guests too, who at this moment are eyeing the skin of the dead man, wrinkled and folded back on itself, the colour of tallow in the thickest places, almost grey elsewhere.

Nor does Paolo pause long to admire but pushes it to one side as soon as the last corner tears free. He takes a sponge and cleans the muscles of the back, pleased that their smooth surfaces are intact with no place where the knife has inadvertently bitten. He washes his hands and dries them to preserve his grip and takes up his knife again to remove the skin from one arm. He makes one long incision down the back edge of the arm from the shoulder to the smallest digit, then pulls and peels the skin back and down, working with the knife as he goes. Ceccio holds underneath each arm to keep the torso from slipping. When they have finished, the hand appears to cling to a long and terrible scarf it does not want to surrender. Paolo plunges his hands into the basin again and bathes them up to the wrists.

"Good then," he says. "Ceccio will clean up while we take some air. Afterwards I shall explain all to you."

Outside it seems everyone needs great gulps of night air. The scent of lilies arrives on the gently moving breeze. Paolo is wrong.

The thing is not entirely inert, not yet wholly clay. It is still in process, the way the human body is always in process. It breathes off still the last of its life so that its presence invades the room and finally pervades it in a way no statue could. Sofonisba walks a little way off in the darkness, breathing the lilies, breathing the wild marjoram crushed underfoot, breathing the clean wet grass, the sun's warmth trapped in the grey stone, the coldness of stars.

In the byre, Ceccio drops the pieces of skin into one of the buckets. A dog appears in the doorway, making a soft yearning cry to itself. Ceccio throws a hammer at it. A thought has just occurred to him.

Paolo Pallavicino's drawing will be executed in silverpoint on the prepared right hand page of his notebook. The subject will nestle in fronds of delicate fern. The beauty is there within the terror, Paolo knows it. What is apparent on the block is not, is never, all of it. An observer witnessing the viscous remnants on the knife, the ragged cuts and the smeared aprons of the man and his assistant would not guess, must be shown the unnamed landscape. That is why, when he comes to the end of a dissection of many hours, he rests only a short while before he takes up his silverpoint and his paper, "to make fair the foul."

Orazio has already gone down to the house. He said, though it is not true, that he had done all this many times and had no need to do it again. Sofonisba made a number of drawings. There was nothing left to fear. The pauper she glimpsed through the slats of the door had been reduced to the partial carcass of a cadaver. Sofonisba saw only an arrangement of muscle and the way each part was laid down in the manner most apt for its purpose. Her drawings were stark and accurate. They showed the strips of white fascia and the satin sheen of the silver blue sheath, the muddle of skin still attached under the palm of the hand of the flayed arm, the coarse grain of the wood block beneath it. She made six drawings from different angles, setting them in regular formation on the page like pieces of choice meat on a cook's table. She listened well to all that Paolo explained. She recorded each layer of muscle, from the broad transverse fan on the surface, through the thick diagonal straps, to the beautiful smoothness that runs the length of the spine. She felt as if she should offer thanks to the lump of flesh on the block for the simple truths it had revealed.

When she had finished, Ceccio walked with her back to the house, lighting her way.

It is the most still hour of the night. Paolo has finished his drawing of the flayed torso and is working on embellishing it with fern leaves. The only sound is the tiny scratching of his silverpoint. There is no one to hear. The torso is positioned vertically. The fronds of fern imitate the lines of the subtly plaited muscle, and their grace and airiness set off its solidity and mass the way the softness of drapery enhances the marble of a bust. Springing from its base, they rise and arch like ferns around a tree stump in a wood or on a hillside, and indeed there beyond it, in the top left hand corner of the page, is a suggestion of a distant valley. The valley recalls to the spirit the consoling contours of hill upon hill receding, bluer and bluer in the misty air, but the springing of the ferns leads the eye back and back to their centre, concentrates the mind on the skinless torso there, rendered without arms and attaining now a perfect humility, which is beauty itself. For just as any root or trunk or bud exists to serve the tree, so each part of the body exists to house the soul and serve it in perfect compliance with God's will. Paolo Pallavicino is exhausted but he will finish the last crenellation on the last frond; he will not blur the fine-toothed edge: he is offering its beauty as restitution for the indignity, is burying the flesh in loveliness.

TWO

In the morning, Lucia sees things a little differently. The girl is not so bad. She is not beautiful. None of them are. Even the pleasing ones are spoiled, scarred from the cuts they receive to mark them against running away. No need to mark this one. She is brindled like her sister's bitch. She would scare the liver out of the Devil if he came upon her without warning. Yet her face is neither scarred nor pocked. She takes a sidelong look at the girl. It is a pleasant face under its strange mask.

"Think of it," Giuliano says. "She cannot have any disease or Vittorio Cibò's bald head would be pied by now."

He does not tell her what she knew already from one of the servants, that Gaetano had cried, "*God save us all!*" when he first caught sight of the girl.

"Imagine," he says, "how you might dress her when we have guests from the town. Imagine," he says, "what Cosimo will think, who thinks he has seen everything."

Lucia gives him a thin smile while she makes up her mind to devise a set of rules about where the girl might roam and when.

"Take her for a walk about house and the gardens," says Giuliano. "Let her see the extent of her good fortune. And give her sweetmeats. You will secure her allegiance at once."

Lucia says, "We'll see." But she likes the idea of taking the girl outside. It seems more salutary.

Out on the terrace, the sun is already warming the stones. The air is fragrant with the white flowers of a vine that has cast its lot with a dark cypress, and tangles in its branches. Lucia takes a deep breath. The girl does the same. Lucia is amused but does not show it.

"Come," she says. "I'll teach you some more words." Though there is no need to go anywhere. All the world lies before the terrace where they stand, the low clipped hedges, the sandy, raked paths, the glossy lemon trees, the small birds descending like rain on the white billows of the pear blossom. It is all there for the naming, the fat bee grumbling in the nodding foxglove, the leaves of the distant olives turning in unison to flash silver, the ants in file along the foot of the wall.

"Bee," Lucia says, and waves a hand vaguely in its direction. One day she will teach all these words to the child she is carrying. She will present each word to him as a gift and her child will own it all. The words are of no use to the strange creature beside her.

"Flower." She waves again.

Beyond all this, down in the valley, the intricate puzzle of the city spanning the river with its complicated dance of roof against roof, spire, tower, wall, window, and the great brick dome of Santa Maria dwarfing all. Where to start? At the blue-green, the green-blue hills rising one behind the other in the distance, merging with the mist of sky? How to name the world? Bird, flower, tree, bridge, church, sky. She will let Gaetano or someone else sort it out. It does not occur to her that the girl may know a considerable amount already.

Vittorio Cibò, when he brought the slave back from Genoa, made it abundantly plain to his wife, Elisabetta, that the sooner the girl learned their language the sooner he could present her to Giuliano. Elisabetta, gripped by fear of the girl's outlandish appearance, had at first resisted in the way she knew best. "Father in Heaven!" she had cried. "Devils are devouring my eyeballs! Tear them off me! Tear them off me! The devils! The devils!" and on and on in this vein, rolling the back of her head against the wall, back and forth, back and forth, making the linen she wore round her neck wind tighter and tighter, until her face grew purple and her eyes bulged, lending support to her claims. Vittorio had seen the spectacle many times. A good slap was all that was needed to curb the fit. It worked every time and indeed, as soon as it was administered, Elisabetta set to work.

She trained the girl in simple duties, teaching her the language as she went along. The girl repeated the names and the actions, her new language building quickly, at first single words, like beads on a wire, then whole phrases. It was like singing, echoing the rhythms, the rise and fall, mirroring the shapes of the mouth's cave, the movement of the tongue within it, pitching her voice on the air as if mimicking a bird call: *here is bread; here is water.*

But there are phrases inside the girl's head that Elisabetta did not teach her and that Lucia will never hear. The girl hooked the words together herself, whole phrases that hung like disembodied voices in the blind place behind her eyes. *Where is my father? Where are my sisters?* She has no memory to feed the words, but holds them trapped in her head — together with the answers that she does not know she has — like birds starving in the dark that might on release become dragons, ravenous. *Where is my brother? Where is my mother?*

"Come," Lucia says, abandoning the thought of naming the world. It makes her tired. "I'll show you some things you've never seen before." They follow a path that leads to the right, past the kitchens and the stables, and then turns down the hill a little way, toward the barn.

"Look," says the girl, and points. Lucia ignores for now the fact that the girl has used this imperative with her and looks. Past the barn, down toward Paolo's house, a figure is crawling on the roof of the byre.

"That? That's Ceccio, Maestro Paolo's boy. Who knows what he's doing up there. He's as much devil as angel and if you meet him, never trust a word he says."

Lucia is feeling slightly sick. Perhaps she has stared too long at the girl's dizzying face, or perhaps it is the smell emanating from the door of the barn, a foul mix. She loses interest altogether in this naming of the beasts. Even her initial impulse, her desire to see the strange confronted with the strange, is snatched away by nausea.

"Go on," she says. "Go inside and look."

The girl hesitates and then steps in out of the sunlight. The barn has been furnished with trestles to support the cages, some piled one on top of another until they stand three or four high. To the girl, all the creatures are equally familiar, equally strange. And all are equally nameless. Those that cannot hide watch her warily. The birds are dry leaves caught up by a gust of wind in the corner of a courtyard. They lift and whirl crazily in their cages, settle for a moment then lift and whirl again.

The girl moves forward slowly, glancing behind in case *la signora* should suddenly disappear, in case a guard might on the instant replace her and the door creak shut. And then she is face to face with a creature she has never seen before. It has neither feathers nor fur but the skin of a snake, only rougher, and it stirs a memory she cannot place. Something about snatching at small, cold bodies, something about the rough, dry underside of a rock and the heat of her palm, and then there is only chaos, memory fallen away, leaving only a residue of dread. The creature has a crest of skin that stands up around its face like a high stiff collar. It turns its head awkwardly to stare at her, its eye a gold bead under a wrinkled lid. In the next cage there is a bundle of sprung quills, like the shafts of flightless feathers, and it is moving. Her mouth turns down with distaste. While she watches, a ripple runs through the quills like wind through standing corn, though the air is still. She frowns and then she is distracted by a movement at the far end of the room where something is leaping for her attention, *her* attention! The chittering she has been hearing is coming from a little man-thing, a creature bouncing back and forth in its cage, bobbing and weaving. It has hands and a tail. She smiles. It shows its yellow teeth back at her. A little, hairy old man. It stops chattering when she reaches its cage. She bends down and it is for all the world as if a man really is living there inside its skin. The eyes are looking right into hers, are speaking to her. They are telling her something she can understand, something she knows, though it is in a language she does not recognize, or has forgotten, the way she has forgotten the names of the other animals. It is a story of loss and sorrow soaked in shame. It makes her want to leave the barn at once, makes her draw great breaths of air as she follows her mistress back along the path to the villa.

        ✑

DOWN AT PAOLO'S house the Fabronis are preparing to leave. Sofonisba is disappointed to have experienced none of Giuliano's famed hospitality. Orazio is disgruntled. Their host is still asleep after his night's labours, and the mare is skittish again. Orazio and Ceccio buzz round it like flies, while Sofonisba rides it in tight circles and does her best to keep her temper.

It is at this moment that a certain Alessandro, generally regarded as a slack-brained, but useful fool, son of the apothecary Emilio da

Prato, rides down from the gates.

"*Salve! Salve! Cari amici miei!*" He sings it almost and is at once dismayed to hear the sound of his own voice, ridiculous in the air. He is doing his best to look like a successful man of business as he rides into the yard, mercifully unaware of the faintly chicken-like appearance of his yellow hose and cape of red silk. He has come, on the only worn-out nag his father entrusts him with, sweating and panting up the hill to Paolo Pallavicino's house, losing a stirrup and getting stung by a hornet on the way, to take an order from Maestro Paolo. At least that is what he told his father. He did not mention what he had heard: that Orazio Fabroni was going to be there with his daughter. So besotted is he with Sofonisba that his body is not his own in her presence. His feet grow huge and trip him up, his hands lose their ability to grasp, and his neck and chin crane out of his clothes and wave about like a starving turtle's. It does not deter him. This morning when he set out he was pleased with his plan. All sorts of things took place at the house of Paolo Pallavicino, a man even less bound by convention than Orazio. A chance meeting up at Paolo's might lead anywhere at all.

"*Che fortuna!* What a pleasant surprise to find you both here."

But Alessandro, always one step behind the rest, belongs to life's latecomers. The fussing with the mare continues unabated and even as he dismounts, Orazio is hauling himself up onto the mule.

"Give her more rein and she won't jump so much. Ceccio, help her for God's sake."

"I have important business with Messer Paolo." Alessandro is like an archer shooting far wide of his mark.

Orazio decides at last to notice him. "Alessandro, lad. We are just leaving," he says. "Maestro Paolo is still sleeping and this brat is as good as useless. Don't expect any refreshment."

It is not promising. How to proceed from here?

"Get hold of that mare's bridle will you? Ceccio is as much use as a monkey." Alessandro strides over, aware now of the opportunity he has overlooked. But the successful man of commerce and the commanding horse-handler vanish together as the mare turns her head and breaks the skin of his hand with her long grey teeth.

The fidgeting and fussing of all the horses and riders in the world could not muffle his yelp. He is not sure in the circumstances quite where, or even whether, he should bleed. But now suddenly he has the attention of Sofonisba herself.

"Let me see."

She reaches down and takes his hand in hers. It is enough to unman the most worldly: a woman behaving as his familiar, intimate almost. He is more afraid of her than he is of the horse.

She shakes her head. "You need to spit on it," she says and does just that herself.

Alessandro whips his hand away as if he has been burned. He looks from Sofonisba to his hand and back again. As ever, this confusion. Has she made a fool of him? In front of the others? Is he to be indignant? But is it an honour perhaps? Or an intimacy? What must a suitor do, spat upon? She looks down at him with her eyebrows raised. Without a word she is plainly saying: "*Well?*" What does she expect? He has to do, say something.

He settles on, "Thank you, *Madonna*," and to his horror she throws back her head and laughs. Alessandro abandons all hope and retreats at once to the safety of business. There might a scrap of dignity be salvaged.

"If you will excuse me now, *Madonna*, I have an order to take."

"Yes. Come every day and make me laugh."

Wit. That is the thing. If only it weren't so difficult.

"It will be my pleasure," he says. "My small gift to you in return for the great gift you bestow on the world." God, but this is hard work. And now she is asking him what he means. She is not supposed to ask. He wishes for a lightning strike, a small earthquake but the world is horribly complacent. Not only that, his feet have somehow grown roots and he seems unable to move from the spot.

He uproots one foot and take what he hopes is a chivalrous step backwards. Garblings about gracious ladies and their mere presence come tumbling from his lips, and she is laughing again. At him.

"Well, enough," says Orazio. "Let me know, sir, how your hand heals. We shall meet again soon, no doubt, in town."

"You are kindness itself . . ." Alessandro chirrups a few more banalities at Orazio's receding figure. The tasty Sofonisba, as wilful as any four-legged beast, is already on her way up toward the gates. He had been so close! Anyone could see her father was ready for his company, yet the old man had no choice but to follow. If he valued his mare.

It is an old story and Alessandro is used to it: life is nothing more than a maggoty carrot on a stick. Always disappointing even if you grab it. He is more than ready for coarse little Ceccio and a few lurid tales to distract him from his sorrows.

The two of them sit side by side with their backs against the wall of the byre, while Ceccio delivers an account of the last night's proceedings. Though he is thirsty from his journey, Alessandro finds his mouth filling with saliva.

It is as if he is in the very room. Ceccio repeats all that was said, word for word.

"'I shall expose the anterior musculature first. The first incision takes us . . . from between the collar-bones . . . right . . . down . . . to the navel, like so. And one quick cut . . . turn it . . . more . . . on each side out to the mound . . . here . . . of the humerus.'"

Although Alessandro is not a man of imagination, when Ceccio speaks it is as if pictures form on the air.

"'The back will be easier without the interruption of the nipples . . .

"'. . . the skin you see is a most wondrous membrane . . .

"'There are those who say that skin flayed from the corpse of a hanged man has magical properties . . .'"

When he has finished, Alessandro makes him repeat the part about luck and how it may be changed. Ceccio knows an opportunity when he sees one.

"I can get one for you. A skin. But it'll cost you."

Like a bird, harmless and welcome on a window sill, the thought comes.

"I can. Want to see?"

Alessandro hesitates.

"No. You don't want to see it now." Ceccio laughs. "Come again when it's ready and I'll show you."

Clothed in luck. It is appealing.

"How do you know it is empowered?"

"My Uncle Federigo tells me."

The mention of Ceccio's uncle suggests a raft of additional reasons to acquire a skin. Ceccio's Uncle Federigo tells him many things — which Ceccio regularly passes on to Alessandro — and all of them point to the misfortune and evil that lie in wait in the world: men who would rob you and leave you for dead, wolves who will eat your throat if you stay in the hills too long, werewolves that come at night, never mind that Maestro Paolo says they don't. There is lightning, and thunder, and there are wicked sows to bite your leg, bitter herbs to make you spit blood and go blind for the rest of your life, rivers that can climb their banks in a moment and drag you to darkness. And then there is the Devil; Ceccio himself knows all about him. Ceccio has told him many times how the Devil flung him on the hay cart beside the shed, and he woke to hear Paolo Pallavicino calling for him. In such a world a man can make good use of a mantle of good fortune.

He considers for only a moment longer before he asks how much Ceccio wants.

⌒

ORAZIO HAS BEEN THINKING. All the way down from Paolo's he was thinking. When he got back to his shop and the house on Via del Cocomero, he was compelled to lie down and think some more. All that trouble. The bone-breaking journey up there, the long night, the journey back. What was it all for? To ensure that Sofonisba's skill would outstrip all the others'? To stop their mouths? Wouldn't it just be easier to marry her off? He could wind down the business with only one mouth to feed. And no son. And no son. What, really, was the point of a daughter?

In the afternoon he is up and off to see the notary Tomasso. He hates going to see Tomasso. It is like being shaved with a blunt steel, or going to be bled, or shriven. Or leeched. Yet Tomasso is his friend as well as his notary and his advice is always good. For Orazio — and for Tomasso too — friendship is a two-handed saw. It is push and pull and never at rest. Orazio loathes to hear what Tomasso has to say. Tomasso loves to expound. Yet when the two are finished, Orazio will walk away entirely satisfied while Tomasso will have to soothe his nerves with a concoction of balm and honey. He will remain angry for days — which only serves to prime him for Orazio's next visit, making his rhetoric all the more robust . . . And so the cycle begins again.

Tomasso has to be honest. People have begun to talk, he tells his friend. They are saying that he, Orazio, is not a fit father because he puts his daughter to work for him like a common apprentice boy. They can vouch for it. They have seen when they come to the shop: Sofonisba wearing an old *lucca* to protect her gown, a cord around it to draw it closed like a string around a beggar's sackcloth; Sofonisba with her hair coming down, her face smeared with paint; Sofonisba hardly with the time of day to look up from her task and offer the common courtesy of a salutation. It is not good enough. People are saying it is a pity, a crime, to see a young girl so used. If Sofonisba's mother had been alive it would not be so; Sofonisba would be sitting like the richest merchant's daughter with the leisure to dream under the shade of a cherry tree. It is not proper.

She should have been married long ago, yet Orazio has not made overtures to any man, has not even begun to suggest a dowry. There must be young men who would have an eye for such a broad-hipped companion but unless Orazio starts putting about some ideas, no one can even guess at the terms that might be offered. And what use is that? It leaves everyone in the dark. It is not the way things are done. By eighteen a girl's prospects, if not settled, should at least be clear.

Tomasso lets the neglected daughter slink away to lick her wounds and turns his fire directly on the father, wanting to know why he has to be always conducting his affairs in that dim place somewhere between the irregular and the disreputable. If it had not been for the excellence of his work, Tomasso tells him, he would have been shunned long ago. His work is good, there is no denying it; it secures him the respect of men greater than the grumblers: bankers, cardinals, even, once, the Duke; but the company he has kept has not always been savoury. Now it seems he is applying his own shaky code of behaviour to his daughter.

Tomasso reaches across his table to grasp Orazio's arm.

"Orazio," he says, "sometimes it seems to others that you think only of yourself."

Orazio looks away abruptly. "Sometimes I think of your flapping mouth," he says.

It is always a mistake to try to talk to Orazio without a cup of wine.

"Listen," says Tomasso. "What I am telling you is for your daughter's good and for the honour of your name. You are already an old man, like me. We shall not be many more years serving our Lord on Earth. Think of Sofonisba. You do her a great wrong to keep her at work for you."

He pauses and braces himself for Orazio's response, but Orazio is quiet.

"Those who say you are thinking only of yourself say that you keep her by for your old age. I don't intend to say anything about the propriety or otherwise of subjecting a maid here, there, and everywhere to the public gaze, nor about the propriety of her presence in the company of some of your more ribald, not to say criminal, friends —" There is a harsh, exasperated sigh from Orazio's direction and Tomasso hurries to finish. "— but only this: when you are gone, there will be no work coming in, and then what shall she do? She will be old herself and unmarriageable. And who shall look after her? The sisters of Sant' Anna themselves may not have her after the life she has led."

"But they'll have her now, while they want their walls painted."

"But that is precisely it. A woman who leads the life of an apprentice can hardly enter as a postulant."

"They should have you in the *Signoria*," says Orazio, getting up. "You are a contentious old bastard."

As much as Tomasso seethes at this and sucks his teeth and sticks out his lower lip, it is all lost on his friend, who does not turn round from the door.

"I'll see you tomorrow," he says.

"If we live that long," says Orazio.

All afternoon, Tomasso fumes. He likes people to listen to him. Nothing makes him angrier than being ignored. It would help his digestive system immeasurably to know that on his way home Orazio stopped at the shop of Emilio da Prato and invited him to dine.

⌒

ALESSANDRO IS USED to navigating life with no discernible compass or star. He is used to squalls and rips, to believing disaster to be always ahead. But he wakes on this particular morning to the prospect of a smooth and sunlit passage. He cannot believe how his luck, after only a few days, is already mending. It seems that just talking with Ceccio about the hanged man's skin has been enough to turn his fortune.

Even the air feels changed. The wind in the night wrenched itself round to blow from a new direction, bringing down trees and tearing off shutters in the process. Alessandro slept through it all, waking only to a sense of movement ceased — and this inkling of fortune turned. When his father told him what had transpired, he was sure of it. Even his father had noticed.

"You're a lucky fellow, Alessandro. You don't deserve it but there you are. The deserving get their reward in Paradise. You're getting yours now. Think about that. I'd take it as a warning if I were you." His father could strip the sheen off any piece of intelligence, expose its underside. But Alessandro didn't mind. Orazio Fabroni, it seemed, had indicated to his father that he — Alessandro, son of Emilio — might be welcome to pay his respects to his daughter. To his daughter! He was joining the company of those who win all of life's prizes, deserved or not, and he relished the thought.

"Only make sure you do honour to our name," his father had said. "Remember to take with you some small gift, nothing ostentatious, and try not to say anything stupid to her. Or to her father."

Buoyed by groundless hope and for once in his life blissfully unaware of the shoals of misfortune, Alessandro set out later that day for *La Castagna* to deliver the order he had wrung from Paolo Pallavicino.

The same wind that had rocked Alessandro to sleep kept Paolo awake, waiting restlessly for morning. Who knew what curiosities such a wind might uncover? It blew all night on the hill, rattling doors and shutters and making loose tiles click. The boughs of the trees squawked against one another like chickens and the smoke from the chimney blew back into the room for warmth. In Giuliano's menagerie the monkey screamed all night and the dogs in their kennels wept with pity for it in their strange sympathetic voices. All of which seemed to Paolo to be hopeful. In the morning he set out for the vine fields. He visits the farm often. Iacopo, who keeps the vines for Giuliano, supplements his income by trading in curios that he claims to have unearthed in the fields, but that for the most part he purchases from an army of small boys who come up from San Domenico to scavenge for him. He pays them a handful of *soldi* to excavate the pink-orange soil of the notoriously fruitful hill and they reward him with their finds: a bronze horse, small tiles still glowing with their peacock glaze, the hilt of a sword. What the vine keeper cannot sell to Giuliano he keeps for Paolo. Paolo has taught him to keep everything, even the oak galls and the empty wasps' nests. Who could say what this morning might hold?

Paolo walked out into the high wild day and smelled the resin from the torn sprays of cypress above the house. The land outside his house had the dishevelled, unravelled look of autumn more than spring. Leaves, bits of bough, and twigs littered the ground. Twining flowers that had only just begun their meticulous ascent waved their plight. Yet everywhere Paolo's sight was ravished by the survivors of the storm's violence: the hop-like clusters of wisteria buds, the sleek magpie perfecting the gloss of its back, the saxifrage untouched at the base of the wall. But this was commonplace beauty, and Paolo was after the rare.

At the farm a chestnut tree was down. It had fallen on a pigsty and killed one of the animals. Two of Iacopo's sons were working to saw limbs from the tree. Iacopo had hung the sow to drain. Its head was crushed. Iacopo made a joke about stew. It was not the sort of joke Paolo found funny. He would get more sense out of Margherita. He could hear shouting coming from the direction of the house.

"Where is Monna Margherita? Inside?"

"No," Iacopo said. "Monna Margherita is outside." *Fuori di sé.* Outside herself. Paolo smiled. Puns are more to his taste. He is working on a book of them.

"Don't disturb yourself," he said. "I'll find her."

The shouts from the house were increasing. A small figure ducked out of the doorway as he approached. Paolo knew at once who it was. She was shielding her head with her crooked elbow, expecting a blow. She dodged around the side of the house. Monna Margherita appeared in the doorway.

"Filthy little dung-cake!"

Paolo Pallavicino shook his head.

"You!" said Monna Margherita, and turned on her heel. Paolo Pallavicino, undaunted, followed her inside and sat down.

"It's not your affair and you don't have to put up with it. You don't have to put up with anything. You just wait for the magnificent Giuliano to pour food down your throat. Food we've grown with our hands." She was bending down to him so that he would have no trouble identifying these same hands, pushing now dangerously close his face.

"You're angry."

"Oh! Oh, I am? And you had the kindness to come all this way just to tell me? How can I thank you?"

"Where did she go?"

"I should know where she went? I should care?"

"Giuliano sent her to you?"

"Oh no. It was the Pope. He came here especially to deliver her. You saw them passing through, didn't you? They stopped for supper."

Paolo Pallavicino folded his arms patiently.

"She's bad luck, that's what she is." Monna Margherita picked up a piece of wood from the hearth. There was a movement outside and at once she spun round and dashed to the window.

"Get away!" she yelled. "Get away from this house!" She waited until the unfortunate had gotten far enough away to come within her sights — and threw the stick.

Paolo Pallavicino felt a deep discouragement. We are all children, he thought. All of us children with ungovernable impulses and no one to correct us. Who shall throw a stick at us?

"Monna Margherita," he said, "you are a fine strong woman you, and your house can withstand a little storm, the loss of a pigsty . . . Let the girl be." Though such a speech was an invitation to attack, was baring the naked chest, saying, *Strike here.*

He sat still for her torrent of abuse: how he could keep his ugly nose out of her affairs; how no one knew the aggravation and the suffering this creature might cause; how Giuliano held Iacopo in such low esteem that he passed him this slave — like the pox — knowing that his wife, Lucia, had already fallen sick from her. How Iacopo could ever be such a weasel as to accept her was past understanding. Anyone could see she been touched by the evil eye.

"What are you going to do with her?"

"Me? I'm going to do nothing. If she comes within twenty feet of me or my house I shall set the dogs on her. But Iacopo . . . Iacopo wants to sell her for two ewes."

Hopeless, hopeless children. Fighting in the street.

"So Iacopo wants to sell her?"

"Yes. Ugly, disfigured thing. It will make us a laughing stock. She looks as if she's been splashed with dung. There will be neighbours spreading rumours and now the pigsty's falling down."

And suddenly she was weeping, crying like a baby. "I'm frightened. I'm so frightened. I don't want her near the house. I don't even want her in the barn. She'll let the Devil in while we sleep."

Paolo Pallavicino made soft clucking noises with his tongue. But he did not touch the woman. Very quietly he backed out of the room, cursing mildly when he was outside because he had forgotten to mention what he had come for. But it no longer mattered.

He walked round the outbuildings, listening for where the girl might be. She was sitting in the shade behind a low byre, with her back to the wall and her knees drawn up to her chest. When she saw him she drew her fists and elbows together quickly and covered her face with her forearms.

Paolo bent down on his haunches. "Caterina?"

She let her arms drop. Her eyes were rimmed with red. One of them was bruised underneath, suffused with a purple tone that he saw now was repeated in places on her arms.

He got up and went back to the house.

Monna Margherita was smacking at the fire as if it was an animal and she would like to kill it. She did not turn round.

"You want?" she said.

"I'll get you your two ewes."

"And the pig."

"You've got the pig. It was old. You lost nothing. I'll get the two ewes for you if you'll let me take the girl off your hands today. But you'll have to trust me."

"Trust you?" said Iacopo when Paolo told him. "Give me your cloak and I'll trust you."

Paolo sighed. He lived on the same estate as this man. He had the same discouraged feeling he had had earlier. He took off his cloak and laid it on the rubble of the sty.

"Come on," he said to the girl. "Don't stand there."

~~

PAOLO HAS ARRANGED his desk facing into the room, a table in front of it a little to the side, a stool close by for the girl to step up on. Ceccio has been watching, looking in on them through the window. He is not at all sure about this slave. He had heard all about her from one of Giuliano's boys, but the girl in the flesh baffles him. He does not know whether to laugh or run. Instinctively he knows she is out of reach of his banal cruelties.

"Remember?" Paolo says, and shows her the drawing he is working on for Giuliano. He reaches for the strings at the neck of her gown but the girl turns away and undoes them herself. She stands between the table and the desk, keeping her back to the window and Ceccio's searching eyes. Her own eyes flick repeatedly to the drawing on the table. Paolo steps round and gestures for her to climb up, but as before she refuses. This time she shakes her head resolutely and is more determined than before. Nothing Paolo can do or say can induce her to so much as touch the table. Paolo resigns himself to working from a new angle.

"All right," he says. "Kneel down." And he points to the floor.

Ceccio stares at her exposed back.

Paolo walks around the girl, considering. She is kneeling as she did the first day, sitting back on her heels, and her hands are in her lap. He would like to render her long, patterned back. The markings begin by splashing her shoulders with heavy dark rain, deep brown-black on skin the colour of ewe's milk. There is hardly a space between the splashes. The white might be torn threads of lace over her shoulders. From her shoulder blades, the heavy rain thins to an even stippling and then reverses at her hips to become a dark ground overlaid with large, irregular flakes of white.

"Look," says Paolo. "You lift up." He has one hand on her arm, the other on her buttock, pushing her up, the way you push a horse into a stall. "You extend this leg, behind."

Ceccio covers his mouth, laughing now an imminent option.

She is shaking, and Paolo is finding it all too difficult.

"Look," he says and gets down awkwardly on one knee beside her. "Like this." He shows her exactly what he wants: an upright kneeling pose, one leg extended behind, the body forward at an angle making one long line from knee to nape, the hands held out in front as if in offering. And she, like a dark shadow, repeats the pose.

Ceccio, aware — as they are all three — of the triangle of forbidden space between her legs, wishes he had a friend here to see this: the two of them, she without a stitch to cover her, and the old man, all unconcerned as if it were the most natural thing in all the world, kneeling — but not to pray — with a girl beside him newborn naked. He watches while Paolo gets up, tilts his desk top and locks it in place, pulls up a stool and sits down to work, bending over his book with great concentration. The girl kneels rigidly, as if there is something on the table and she is staring straight at it.

And in the girl's mind there is indeed something on the table, though she does not see it for what it is. There is a young man on the table. It is a young man of great beauty yet there is no way that she can know this. He is lying on his back, and blood runs from the places where his nose and ears should be. It is a visitation from Hell and it is Heaven's only kindness that she does not recognize it.

There is not much more for Ceccio to see. When he goes by again later, they are still there. He stares in at the door. The girl glances at him just once. She hasn't moved. Her nose is running, perhaps with tears, and every few breaths she sniffs, swallows. Paolo is talking to her. His face bears the same look of concentration he has in the byre. It is the look of someone listening intently. There but not there. He is talking to the girl, telling her about her skin, telling her things she already knows: it is a strange condition; there is no one else in the world with such a skin; it is her cross and her affliction and she is lucky to be alive; there are those who fear her, believe she is the carrier of God's displeasure; there are those who would rather she not mar the face of Creation. He, Paolo, however, is not disturbed. His eye delights in the rhythms of the markings. Nevertheless, they have no place on the body of man; they offend the eye that searches constantly for perfection, as the soul searches for its Creator.

He tells her, too, some things she could not know: that he, Paolo Pallavicino, with the knowledge and the practical experience that he has acquired over many years, would be equipped to lift the markings from her; that he might divine a way to remove her unsightliness and make all one on the surface of her skin so that it might no longer offend the eye of the beholder and strike discord in the harmony of God's Creation. He talks about lye and about lime. He talks about healing fumitory and blue flag and thyme. He talks about peeling an orange, and he talks about the renewal of the flesh.

He takes Ceccio by surprise when suddenly he says, "Enough," and flings his notebook on the table as if it means no more to him than a rag for wiping his face. "We will do more tomorrow. You make me tired. There's Ceccio at the door. Go with him and talk to the beasts. Get her out of here, Ceccio."

The girl picks up the shift and the gown that Paolo tosses to her and slowly puts them on. She can see Paolo's beautiful, pout-lipped boy with the yellow hair waiting outside the door.

Paolo believes it is no accident that this girl has come to his attention. She has been provided for his own purpose. It is his God-given duty to enlarge the boundaries of his knowledge, to measure and plot each part of Creation, even the most lowly. Paolo Pallavicino believes that to extend oneself beyond one's limits is to honour the almighty God whose creature one is. In his imagination he continues to address the girl. You are in good hands, he says, and, You are in the hands of a master. He says, I shall make you, God willing, as pleasing a female creature as can be found. No? Why would you tell me no? Are you afraid? Then walk away. Walk out now in the streets down in the city where no one knows you. Walk with your pied face uncovered and see how long it shall be before you come to harm.

The girl follows Ceccio along the path that leads up the hill to the menagerie, keeping her distance. He says he is going to get the salamander for Maestro Paolo. He says the maestro will cut it up. He turns his head often to speak to her.

"What happened to you anyway? Did you fall in the mire? Did the Devil shit on you?"

At each question the girl fixes Ceccio with a hard stare until he turns round again, and then she says, "No." She says, "I don't remember."

In the barn, Ceccio shouts, "Wake up, wake up and see the monster!" He drags a stick along the doors of the cages, rattles their occupants. He screams back at the birds and mocks the monkey, dust motes flying from his hair as he cavorts before it. The salamander watches with its golden eye and the girl watches it. She can see no sign of movement, not even a rise and fall of breath.

Ceccio finds a straw and pokes it through the meshes of the wicker, the skin around the straw contracts. The salamander doesn't move. Ceccio picks up the cage.

"He wants to cut you up, too, you know that?"

"No," says the girl.

"He does. You heard what he said about peeling an orange?"

The girl does not know what he is talking about until they get back to the house with the salamander. And there is Paolo sitting outside and he is indeed, as if to demonstrate, peeling an orange with a little curved scalpel of steel, and the rind is falling away in flakes of brilliant fire.

Paolo has a lot to think about. He does not want to be disturbed. He sets Ceccio to gathering wood for his fire and he sets the girl to washing his two shirts that stink like cat's piss. He wears an old brown robe that gives him a decidedly monkish air. When Gaetano sends a boy down with a message, he listens, but it is a distraction he does not want to attend to. He is busy all day. At nightfall he makes Ceccio set down a mattress of straw for the girl outside his door. Ceccio sleeps in his bed.

The next morning there is uproar. The girl watches wide-eyed as Giuliano himself comes striding into Paolo's house with Gaetano, a white-bearded sheep attempting imperiousness, behind. Giuliano is all arms and legs, a tree in a storm, a walking tree. A walking, weeping tree.

He shakes his head. "Paolo, Paolo, Paolo," he says. "You cannot.

Lucia saw her yesterday and now she is delivered of an ill-formed thing. As still as a stone."

He wipes his hand across his nose and mouth, draws his sleeve across his eyes. It is the gesture of a young child. Gaetano coughs.

"I don't know what to do," Giuliano says. "The women say she still bleeds."

Gaetano intervenes just in time to save his master from an undignified display of self-recrimination. "What *Signor* Giuliano is saying," he says, as if Giuliano is speaking another language, "is that you must remove this slave from the property at once. It was understood that she was over at the farm where she was to be sold . . ."

"As she has been."

". . . and taken away. *Sua Signoria* does not want her within sight."

Paolo sighs. There are certain drawbacks to the enjoyment of a Giuliano's patronage. Sometimes he would like to live as a pauper in the town.

"Of course," he says. "Of course."

Giuliano puts his arms out in gratitude. Paolo embraces him as a father might embrace a son, promising him that the world will do no further harm.

In the afternoon, Alessandro comes with his order of pigments and white lead from his father's shop. He has suffered no misfortune on his ride up the hill, and Paolo's welcoming smile and his generous attention only accord with his new sense of well-being.

Paolo does not have to feign gladness. He has made up his mind that when he gives Alessandro the payment he will have him take the girl away too. Alessandro can take her down to his father. They will like a girl in the shop. Think how useful. If they don't, well then, they can sell her. It has been a day of capricious squalls and showers. A day to be impetuous.

"Spend an hour with Ceccio," says Paolo. "Take your rest before you begin the journey down."

When it is time for Alessandro to leave, Paolo puts his hand on his arm, says, "Listen. Today I will give you something special. Wait there."

Alessandro's slow-moving thought senses something amiss. A man gives away only a broken cart. When Paolo comes out of the house, he has with him the very girl Ceccio has been describing with such perverse relish. She is a monster. His head buzzes so loudly he hears nothing of what Paolo is saying.

A little later, with rain beating from the west, Paolo stands at the gates of *La Castagna* and watches the bony nag and its two riders begin its descent to the city. He stands a long time. His shoulders darken with rain and dry again before he turns back.

THREE

ALESSANDRO IS NOT HAPPY. This girl, sitting up behind him, makes his skin creep. Her bad luck is written all over her body. She will infect him. All around his waist his skin feels uncomfortable where she is holding on. When Paolo Pallavicino helped her up as they were leaving, Alessandro felt his face flame scarlet.

As soon as they are safely away from the gates and out of earshot, Alessandro stops the horse. It is not just the girl. His mind was already occupied and his nerves unsettled by what Ceccio showed him. He can smell it still. They went up, the two of them, from Paolo's house to the byre. The skins were supposed to be on the roof where Ceccio had laid them to cure. One of the pieces, secured by a single stone, was hanging from the eaves like a bat. Another had blown down and lay folded over on itself in the shining grass. They could smell it from where they stood, and it was obvious that Ceccio had cleaned it less than perfectly. Green stains like old bruises had begun to spread on both sides. When Ceccio bent and lifted a corner, a mass of tiny maggots squirmed away from the light: the powers of evil at work on his fortune.

He pulls his body away from the girl and tells her to get down. He repeats it twice, but she only frowns. He pushes her hard, steadily in the stomach until she slides awkwardly off the back of the animal.

"You walk now," he says. He can hardly believe he is put in this position. He wants nothing to do with her. She will destroy every good fortune that might come his way, and he will remain as far as ever from Sofonisba.

The girl trots now and then to keep up. Alessandro glowers down at her. The nearer they draw to the town, the more concerned he grows. He does not know what to do. She is more conspicuous than a leper. He has a light cloak and he gives it to her to cover herself. She puts it over her head, and the grey wool of her slave's gown shows clearly at the bottom edge. Her mottled feet stick out below. They mock him, these feet. They mock all his hopes. Just as Sofonisba will mock him when she hears about her. She is Misfortune itself walking up to join him. His short-lived, decomposing fortune.

Instead of crossing the city, Alessandro goes all the way round to come in at the Porta Carraia and cross the bridge there, slipping along by the warehouses and trying not to attract attention. By the time they reach the shop, a towering, narrow building, with rooms piled one on top of the other, the shadows outside are already long and workmen are lighting the torches on the walls of the new palace. The only people who had seemed to notice him and his travelling companion were the few schoolboys who jeered and laughed and pulled their noses at her.

Once inside, Alessandro is under no illusions about her reception. His father's reaction falls just short of rage, and it seems to Alessandro that he has known what to expect all along.

"You are a witless lump. You were born a witless lump and you show every sign of remaining one." He cuffs Alessandro a few times to punctuate this short speech, though he has to reach up to do it. He goes to strike the girl, but recoils. He asks Alessandro how he expects their patrons to enter an establishment that houses a leper. A filthy leper.

Alessandro knows better than to answer.

"And your own interests. What will this do to your own interests? Do you think Orazio will entertain our suit for Sofonisba when we have lost our fingers and noses?"

Alessandro manages to say, "She isn't — " before his father cuts him off.

"Don't speak when I'm speaking," he says and promptly falls completely, stonily silent.

Alessandro wants to tell him that Paolo has suggested they might sell the girl. He has the papers. *Young female. Obedient. Of most exotic appearance.* But he knows from experience that whatever exact moment he chooses to open his mouth will be the precise moment his father chooses to speak again.

"You'll sell her that's what you'll do," his father says at last. "And may God be pleased to recognize my charity which keeps her beneath my roof tonight. If she's not gone by Saturday when I get back, I shall turn her out myself and you will follow."

Alessandro takes such a deep breath that it sears his nostrils and gives him a twinge between the shoulder blades. He nods so earnestly, so energetically, with his lower lip thrust out in what he hopes is a shrewd and worldly way, that his father feels compelled to hit him again as he goes by.

SOFONISBA'S PAINTING FOR the Arcivescovo's contest will display all she knows about perspective and anatomy. It is a Christ figure, Christ in his tomb, and it will represent the greatest mystery of all, life in death. It is, of course, the pauper on his altar in Paolo's byre. For days she has struggled to reconcile what she knows about the dissolution of the flesh with what she believes about the resurrection. She thinks she has found the answer in the face which is both dead and undead, asleep but waiting. It is flesh that has surrendered. But all of this, she knows, is secondary to the main purpose of the painting which is to display, through the acutely and accurately foreshortened figure, her consummate skill with the art of perspective.

Today, however, Sofonisba is pleasing herself, glad to be released from the pauper's perfect humility, the memory of what he was reduced to for her instruction.

She has a new subject. She works quickly and there is a rhythm in her movements. She turns aside to load her brush, turns back and the brush has made its mark almost before the turn is complete. She turns aside again, loads the brush again. Her arms open and close in rhythm, a shadow of a dance. She is painting darkness in the triangle of canvas immediately above her subject — which is herself. She has put on her best gown of heavy dark green satin. She is painting darkness over and over, the shadows deeper and deeper. She has a mirror set up on a chair on top of a table next to her easel. She has fixed it by a wire to a hook above the window. It is angled down at her so that her point of view is that of light entering a high window, falling on her eyelids, her cheekbones, her breast. Her painting is a second mirror, its image the same as the first except for the eyes, which on the painted plane look straight ahead toward a second painted figure. Sofonisba has no idea how long she has been painting.

"It will be very good."

She swings round at the voice, unable for a second to remember where, or even who, she is. Matteo Tassi is standing in the doorway, his legs planted squarely, his chest thrust out. There is an unkempt look about him as if he has just risen from his bed.

Never mind that he has only come from Siena, when Matteo

Tassi comes into the room it is like a hot wind blowing up from Africa. He stirs everything. Men begin to sweat and women, to feel faint. He is a small one-man bluster blowing in from the dirty street, fingering the bed curtains and pinching the women, upsetting the servants and spilling the wine, kicking the cat, kissing the dog, and pissing on the statue in the courtyard. He is a travelling entertainment. He comes in grinning, showing off his crooked teeth. He slaps you on the shoulders, whispers in your ear, and takes you off at once to hear his latest filthy tale. A small man, yet he fills the room, the house. There is no ignoring Tassi and Tassi ignores nothing. Look how he turns from his scummy story leaking into your ear, catches your wife's eye, your sister's, goes to her all suavity and polish. *Madonna bellissima! Madonna magnificentissima!* The flourish, the curlicues. And yet all women smile for him. Because they do not smell his rankness, or because they do? When Tassi is in the house, life is suddenly an amusement, a holiday, and you wonder that you have been blind to it. Trouble and care melt like ice in spring. Life, the bolting horse galloping into the future, stops suddenly in its tracks and looks around. On every side is a fair field drenched in sunlight and decked in the sweetest herbs and flowers.

Sofonisba is always ready for a fair field. When Tassi comes she throws down her brush and opens her arms. She is ready to be entertained, would never say no to a wild gallop into a flowery meadow, lush grass to lie in. But then Sofonisba is strong. No one owns Sofonisba, not even her father upstairs who thinks he does, her father who crackles and fumes about her carryings-on like a smoky fireplace in a gale. Sofonisba leaves her glaze to dry and calls the boy to bring them wine. She missed Matteo's company while he was in Siena.

They raise their glasses, hail the woman on the canvas who paints on unconcerned.

"It will be very good. Only remove the gown and it will be excellent."

And there it is again: the sense of disappointment, of failed expectation that always shadows Tassi's spectacular entrances. He is a good sculptor, an unparalleled bronze caster, an amusing and generous friend, irreverent and entertaining, but always there is his lechery to contend with.

He comes over to her, and at once his hands are on her. It is as if he carries with him a pair of gloves that have a life of their own. There is no conversation to be had ever until you have taken them off him and put them down somewhere out of sight.

"It is an allegory, Ser Matteo. You would understand that. It is an allegory of painting."

"But that is it exactly. A muse clothed is against Nature. The muse must be naked. She is naked truth. The naked flame of inspiration." He stands by her shoulder. He is shorter than she, and Sofonisba can feel his breath on her neck, and smell the wine. She tries to carry on but it is impossible. His hand is on her waist. She moves quickly out of reach and goes to the table to clean her brushes.

"Well, Ser Matteo?" She tries to sound brusque, purposeful. "You did not come here to give me a lesson."

"Not in painting." Tassi says and leers.

Sofonisba sighs like someone hearing an old, old riddle for the fourteenth time. "So there must be another reason."

"Two," he says, "First we have to see Maestro Paolo up at *La Castagna*. He has work enough to feed us all until the feast of San Giovanni."

"Second?"

Tassi's face breaks into a broad grin. "I have something for you."

"For me?" She loves him again.

"A gift."

Sofonisba smiles. "You always bring me gifts. You are too kind." Though he has offered nothing yet.

He grins again. "You will have to come to my house to receive it."

"I can't come to your house."

"Why not? You have before." It is a risk to remind her; the formal feast he had promised that night had been a drunken debauch, and she had had to break the curfew and leave with her hood covering her face and her father drunk beside her.

He grins again. "You'll like it." He has not in fact yet thought what he might be able to produce as a gift, but he is not a man to be hamstrung by petty details.

"I shall come with my father."

"Of course. He will enjoy it too. Where is he?"

Sofonisba shakes her head and laughs, says, "Get out of here, sir. Go and see him. He's at Santa Maria Nuova. *All'Ospedale*." For, yes, she does remember the drunken night and the way constraints and inhibitions fell away. Despite everything, she likes Tassi. She likes his grin. She likes the deep grooves, incisions almost, that appear beside his hooked nose and run down in a long curve to disappear around the edges of his mouth. His teeth are crammed crookedly against each other. She could swear he has too many. There is something about Matteo Tassi. He is not a handsome man. He is too short, too broad. Sometimes he seems to have no neck at all. But still there is something. And always she is angry with herself after he has gone — because always she feels as if he has taken something of her away with him. She feels as if he has put his hand on her bare neck. She feels as if he has whispered lecheries in her ear and she has allowed it.

Tassi finds Orazio working at the back of the loggia of the *Ospedale*. He is painting *fresco* without any assistant, working on a section of wet plaster near the bottom of the wall, his bowls of prepared colours standing by. Tassi can see his difficulty and knows how to make himself useful, knows just when to hand a new colour or wash out a brush, when to take over.

It is more than a year since Orazio has seen him, but the old man begins to grumble straight away, complaining that he has no assistant for this job, a painting of Christ casting out demons. He had hired Ilario but the man has a growing reputation and left yesterday on business of his own.

"Strange how when money whistles a man becomes a dog." Orazio grumbles that he does not have the patience to work with a younger man again. They are too much trouble. Employing Sofonisba, he says, is out of the question. She has taken many commissions at private institutions — two in the Via San Gallo alone — but he will not have her painting in a public thoroughfare, like a house painter.

"So here I am, instead, like a priest on my knees." Glad to accept Tassi's help, Orazio doesn't ask him about his latest absence. Tassi is always coming and going. Orazio has heard all the rumours. That the woman who was hanged two years ago was his mistress. That he had a part in having the husband arrested. That things did not turn out as he had expected and he ended by running for his life and has never settled since. There is a grain of truth in everything, though it was not for his life that he ran, but for his heart, carrying it away from ruin. But Orazio would care neither one way nor the other. Orazio is simply relieved to be able to sit on the step and watch him finish the work.

When it is done, Tassi helps him take the bowls and the buckets through to the courtyard. Orazio tells him a little, but not too much, about the Arcivescovo's contest. He has no need to be so miserly with the details, so jealous of his province. Tassi has no interest in commonplace commissions to decorate the walls of money-laden patrons with no taste. He is more interested to learn from Orazio that Paolo Pallavicino has set his sights on the post of *Direttore dello Spettacolo* for the *festa* of San Giovanni on the twenty-fourth of June. Giuliano will no doubt see that he wins the twinkling ears of their Lordships and gets it. The man who is appointed will oversee the procession.

Orazio says, "You should go up and see Paolo. He could find you work." Tassi knows this. The entertainments are grand and complex with a host of responsibilities, from the design of the cars for the procession, to the creation and construction of the central *edifizio* and the provision of fireworks and music. There will be plain labour, too, with good wages. With fees paid by the *Signoria* he would at last have some funds at his disposal, a rare luxury. But it would be more than that. San Giovanni is a marriage of amazement and splendour, an indulgence, for him, of the most extravagant kind. Who would not want to attend?

FOUR

The loss of the girl did not occupy Paolo for long. He immersed himself at once in other matters and began to fill pages in his notebook with ideas and sketches for the celebrations. Wings, feathers, shining scales coursed across the pages, reflecting the fluidity of his thought, his mind like a river running on from one turn to the next, never delayed for long. Today, however, it must flow around Iacopo, the vine keeper. Something of a boulder, this man. It was an irritation to have Iacopo's coarse-mouthed son here again this morning, thumping on the door with the side of his fist, demanding payment for the little slave girl, a detail Paolo would prefer not to be bothered with. He surely owes no debt. With the girl went the opportunity to investigate the nature of her skin. Iacopo's loss is as nothing compared with the loss to the advancement of science.

Two ewes! He sent Iacopo's son back with a message for his father, saying he had already given his own cloak and an agreement was an agreement. He did not think for a moment that the vine keeper would assent, but getting hard coin out of Giuliano was like getting a *Te Deum* out of a statue. Paolo as usual has no funds at his disposal and he has no finished work on hand to sell. He did ask Tassi some time ago to cast a small bronze for him and gild it, a monkey's forepaw that could hold down the pages of one of Giuliano's great books. But then Tassi had disappeared again. In any case it was planned as a gift, the monkey in question being one of a pair much loved by Giuliano. To present it for payment would be the mark of an inferior man, churlish. That particular bronze must remain as the gift he first intended. It will make Giuliano all the more earnest when he presents Paolo's name for the *direttorio*.

There is little else that he has done of late that could conceivably be assessed by the master of the *guardaroba* as valuable. He has his drawings of the girl of course, but Giuliano already has one. They would hold no more value than his studies of clouds, of water.

The problem creates a muddy undercurrent to the morning's work, but it does not win Paolo's complete attention until Ceccio announces that Matteo Tassi himself is riding up the hill toward the villa. Paolo knows at once that Matteo will have the bronze cast with him and will be expecting payment for his work. Paolo wishes he had paid him his fee in advance. Matteo will have to wait now.

Paolo has another idea. He closes his notebook and goes to the shelves in the alcove of his *studio*.

He lifts down a plaster mould from the top shelf and lays it on his desk. It has been prepared in two pieces, set in a small cask cut through its length. Paolo opens the two halves. The impression is almost perfect. It was the most demanding anatomical work he had undertaken and his heart is gripped again by the emotions of that night. He had in the past carried out more intricate investigations, made incisions and sections that required greater dexterity, more intense concentration. This particular dissection had in contrast been straightforward — and yet it had exhausted him. He can remember how he felt when the men came to take the subject away. He was sending the woman to her grave emptied, scooped out like a melon, the child, her child, still curled as it was in her womb, lying now in a pail under a tumult of blooms. He had torn them from the stems in guilt and something close to rage.

"Maestro, Maestro!" Tassi comes into the *studio* with his arms extended. Tassi lives life with arms extended. "*Salve! Buon giorno!* May Christ save your soul but may his Lordship give you a good living first!" He laughs. He has ridden up from town on his thick-necked mare that loves to run if he kicks her hard enough. He has a wind-blown look about him. He would look at home behind a plough.

"I should like that very much," says Paolo. "I'm still waiting."

"Well, this should help." Tassi puts his satchel on the table, but already Paolo is starting on a sorry tale of financial woe that revolves around an unwanted slave, a debt, and the miserly bent of certain prominent citizens and leads, just as Tassi expected, to the reason Paolo would like to postpone his payment for the work.

"You have already been paid for the materials, if you remember. I ask you to wait only for your fee."

Tassi's heart sinks. The work was easy. He cast the paw itself. There was no model to make and there was only one firing, and luck was with him. But still. Paolo is not the only man here short of funds. He unwraps the paw and sets it down on the table. It is an admirable thing, perfectly balanced. It rests on three points: the heel of the palm, the thumb and the shortest digit. And how human the fingers, the hard, narrow nails, both less and more than claws. A ferrule of finely wrought gold caps the wrist. From the long narrow back, two digits reach up and curl forward into air. It is both heavy and delicate at the same time. For the moment, Tassi's feeling of being cheated evaporates before the purity of the work, just as the paw itself had vaporized in the furnace.

"This could bring you *twenty* ewes."

"No. It is a gift for Giuliano."

Tassi shakes his head in disbelief. "Or twenty-*five*!"

Paolo smiles, asks what would he do with twenty-five ewes? He is not a farmer.

Tassi imagines he would dissect them one by one, but does not say so. He can think too of a ribald response, but since this is Paolo he refrains from voicing it.

"There is something else I have in mind," says Paolo.

He has, he says, a very special undertaking, a life-size figure which in the final stages will require the assistance of an expert bronze caster. The word "life-size" puts Tassi on his guard.

"I don't know," he says, "if I could build a furnace large enough for such a casting." He makes a show of frowning and concerned head-shaking. "I don't know." He is thinking of Paolo's endless sketches and calculations for the bronze horse which has exercised Paolo's imagination as long as he has known him. He prays that this is not the undertaking. He knows instinctively that involvement in such a project would require the devotion of a monk.

"My shop," Tassi says, "is far too small. The courtyard, you know, is not much bigger than this table."

"'Life-size,' Matteo, not 'large.' I didn't say 'large.'"

"A child?"

"Almost. It has never been done before. And when it is done not all who see it will understand its beauty."

"Where is it?"

"The subject?" Paolo's voice is sharp. This is trespassing. "It is laid to rest and its soul in limbo. I have a mould from which you can work." He gets up stiffly, rubbing his knees. "Come with me."

The two halves of the mould, the two profiles of the unborn child, lie side by side. Facing each other, they might be twins.

The impressions are complete, every detail is present, from the fine edges of the minute fingernails to the tiny crescent-shaped swells at the sides of the nostrils. Each hair on the head is there, each eyelash on each closed eye. Tassi looks closely. He can see every line, like the finest filaments of a spider web, etched on the soles of the child's feet. He looks around for a figure in clay or wax, begins to ask where it is and stops himself as he realizes there has been no secondary model.

"It was not difficult," says Paolo. "The body was as firm as wax. I oiled it well, especially the hair, so it would not stick." He looks at Tassi. "It should render a perfect bronze."

There is no doubt. But Tassi feels the weight of responsibility and resists.

"You would not want to finish the thing yourself? To be sure?"

Paolo says no. His prospects for San Giovanni are good and he will not have time. The mould is perfect and Tassi is the finest craftsman he knows.

"Who has ordered it?" asks Tassi, wondering about Paolo's commission and his own cut.

"No one has ordered it. But Giuliano will buy it. I'm sure of that. It is an investment. You put in your time. Interest accumulates. You withdraw your fee."

Tassi laughs. "In the future."

"Of course in the future. Do I look like a rich man?"

"You look like a dear father and I'll do anything for you, Maestro. You know that. Now, my dear father, it was a long way up from Firenze and your dear son has a mighty thirst on him."

"And shameless manners." It is difficult to tell whether the old man is amused or offended, but he takes Tassi to his table and pours him some wine, pouring some for himself too.

"And this slave? What was wrong with her?"

"I'll show you." Paolo creaks away and comes back with his notebook and shows Tassi the page.

Tassi sees only a young girl naked under the dappled shade of a tree.

"You would have to see her."

"Where is she now?"

"Alessandro took her."

Tassi snorts with laughter. "You cruel old man."

"He'll manage."

"I meant the girl."

Tassi would have liked to sit and talk with Paolo all morning but Paolo cannot rest unless he is at work.

"To business," he says and gets up again to fetch the monkey's paw.

"It has come out perfectly."

Tassi nods. He is pleased; he likes to please Paolo, who always has work and has promised an introduction to Giuliano. And Paolo is pleased; he likes to please his patron who has promised him an introduction to the Duke. Paolo's thought is for the remaining monkey to present the paw to Giuliano. Then Giuliano will be pleased; Giuliano loves theatre.

"Walk up to the menagerie with me and we can talk on the way."

The birds call in alarm to one another when the men approach. In its cage at the other end of the barn, the surviving monkey is hurling itself from wall to roof to floor, rebounding like an object thrown. Paolo mutters softly to it, perhaps to soothe it, perhaps to curse.

"First I have something to show you," he says to Tassi. He lifts a cover on a wicker cage and Tassi bends down to look in. The crested salamander he has seen before has been transformed by some magic of Paolo's. Its dull earth-coloured ruff is hung with tiny medallions of silver almost as fine as leaf. They shiver at the faintest movement and catch the light, turning to gold with the reflection of the reptile's skin.

Tassi bends closer. The animal twitches, creating a shimmer of light. He sees that the medallions have been drilled through at the circumference and attached with the finest silver wire threaded through the creature's hide. Beads of yellowish matter have formed at the points of entry and begun to trickle down over the scales.

He looks at Paolo.

"It will heal. I have blue flag and matricaria. I do a little at a time. Perhaps when it is finished I shall have created beauty," says Paolo. "With Nature's assistance."

He puts the cover back and moves on to the rowdy monkey. He suffers scratches and a bite on the thumb when he opens the cage but slips a leash on the animal at last and they leave to walk for a while in the grounds to calm it.

Tassi, too, needs air to breathe. Judged by goldsmiths' standards, the silver salamander was coarse work, but marvellous nevertheless. He wishes he had thought of such a thing.

They take the path that leads from the menagerie, past the kitchens at the side of the villa and through to the formal gardens in the front.

They walk between low hedges of rosemary the colour of the Virgin's robe. The monkey tears at the blooms and the smell of pine surrounds them.

There is San Giovanni to discuss. Every year the pageant is more elaborate than the last. Paolo says he has been thinking of clouds. He is thinking, he says, of a representation of Heaven and of the passage of the soul to Heaven from Earth and how clouds might be employed to represent the movement. An Assumption perhaps; but not the Blessed Virgin, for the people had witnessed it many times and were thirsty for something new. Giuliano, he says, wants spectacle, is anxious to impress his uncle who, after all, is the one who really holds the purse in that family.

"Give him a dragon," says Tassi.

Paolo raises his eyebrows, "Wings."

"Fire," says Tassi.

"Golden scales."

"Enormous size."

"Great terror."

"A martyr."

"A saviour."

"An assumption."

"Clouds," says Paolo, and smiles. "I shall need some good painters," he says. "You'll be willing?"

"Of course. And Orazio. You should get Orazio if you can." Though he means Sofonisba.

"And some competent assistants."

"Alessandro?" But even as Tassi turns to Paolo to say the name, Paolo is saying it too, with the same inflection.

"Or *in*competent," says Tassi.

━━

TO ALESSANDRO, miserable and in a bind, the sight of the rumpled Tassi caught in the late sun, rakish in the doorway, is as welcome as a delivering angel. Alessandro has spent today and yesterday in a state of impotent anxiety, shut in the shop with the girl cowering at the back.

For two nights he has hardly slept at all, listening for movement from the girl lying outside on the balcony. His father had refused to put her out in the street where she could draw attention to them, refused to let her sleep anywhere but up on the top floor with him, where he was supposed to keep an eye on her. Alessandro had been afraid to close his eyes. Every scandalous crime ever committed by slave against master came back to him: the girl who had stolen the rings off her sleeping mistress's fingers, the lad who had cut the throat of the master's son. No end of them. Hideous night blooms, they flourished in his head in place of dreams. Last night the need for sleep dulled his anxiety, but still he had lain awake. Every time he was about to succumb, the whimpering of the girl outside resumed. It grew only worse when he summoned his courage and threatened to throw her off the balcony.

It was not until dawn that she was quiet, locked in a nightmare of her own.

In the morning, Alessandro's foggy brain was blessed with an idea that arrived like a shaft of sun. It came to him in the middle of another tirade from his father.

"I can't think of any other man," his father was saying as he prepared to leave, "any other man in the city who would be so foolish, or so heedless of his own and others' well-being . . ."

It was at the word "heedless" that Alessandro thought of Tassi. Tassi. Why not? He could get him drunk. Matteo would do anything when he was drunk. He retired to his room to think about it. The scheme he devised had thin promise but if it should succeed it would be worth the effort: the girl would be off his hands by the time his father came back tomorrow, and Tassi — who could do no wrong in a certain lady's eyes, however badly he behaved — Tassi would find himself tainted and besmirched.

When he was sure his father was well on his way he went to the door of the shop and summoned a lad to take an invitation to the workshop of Matteo Tassi.

When Tassi appears, Alessandro could almost genuflect, he is so relieved. He takes him up to his room two floors above the shop and Tassi follows him in with slaps and punches, his eyes all over the room, looking for the slave, looking for pleasure. He roars with laughter at the little cakes and the hopeful cards, dumps his heavy satchel down on top of the cards, says. "You've nothing to wager. Your father keeps a tight purse."

"Come here," says Alessandro.

The girl is sleeping, curled, in a corner of the balcony. He wakes her with his foot, not kicking, prodding merely, as if testing for life.

"Ah," says Tassi. "I have heard about this girl."

She twitches awake and scrambles up, knocking her head on an iron bracket that sticks out above.

Tassi raises his eyebrows. He has seen Paolo's drawings, but he has not imagined.

"There is nothing wrong with this girl. A most excellent serving girl. She works hard. She can cook, she can sew, she —"

"Bollocks!" says Tassi and steps in front of Alessandro. "You sound like a peddler. What's her name?"

"Caterina."

"Here!" Tassi holds out his hands to her. "Here, Caterina, here!" beckoning in invitation with a movement of his head.

She steps forward but keeps her hands by her sides. Tassi reaches down and takes her by the wrists. He edges her to the low wall that encloses the balcony.

"Go! Go on!" with his head again signalling for her to step up. She plants her weight firmly where she stands and does not move. Tassi pushes her forward, backing her against the wall, forcing one leg between hers, lifting her leg at the knee with his until she has to put her foot on the wall for balance.

"There, go, go! Stand up, girl. Stand on the wall." All the time pushing forward and up with his arms until he has her there, standing with both feet, swaying, bent forward and terrified upon the wall.

"Stand up! Stand up!" roars Tassi, as if it would be good for her. "Stand up!" Still grasping her wrists, he raises his arms, locked at the elbow, stiff, above his head and out, forcing her to stand upright.

"There!" he says, triumphant, and lets go. "Now I can see you." Over her shoulder, her eyes wide open, the girl catches sight of a cat walking on the tiled roof below.

Tassi cannot afford a serving girl. He has a boy already who is too useful to let go. He helps him with his work, knows how to pack the moulds for casting, can keep the furnace going. But the boy's appetite is prodigious, he eats half the profits and is still hungry. Tassi has himself seen him steal half a chicken right after his breakfast at noon. Another mouth to feed is out of the question. Nevertheless he is tempted. This girl is more wonderful than he had imagined. And if he can't keep her, why, just like crazy old Paolo he could give her away. What a gift to bestow! *Monna Sofonisba, accept with my humble compliments this rare and curious gift!* And meanwhile, to see if the strange markings meandered farther than the neck . . .

Alessandro is watching his eyes.

"She's yours. If you win, you can have her. If I win, perhaps you can have her still but you have to pay for her."

If Alessandro were alert he would notice the way Tassi seems to hesitate and calculate. He would deduce from the length of the pause that the otherwise impetuous and hasty Tassi is playing a part, that he has indeed some real interest here. But Alessandro is never alert.

"Wine!" says Tassi and whisks the girl from the parapet. "No transaction is possible without the spirit of friendship to warm it. You know me. I did not come empty-handed." He stalks back into the room and opens the satchel on the table, draws out a large flask.

"Cups," he says. "Bring cups. One for you, one for me and one for her. We'll drink hers first." He roars again with laughter, but when Alessandro returns with two cups he sends him back for another and fills it. He takes a mouthful, fills it to the top again and hands it to the doubtful girl.

Alessandro takes the bag off the table, settles down on a stool and begins to deal.

"Another drink before we begin," says Tassi.

By the time they have finished their card game, the girl is asleep in the corner. Tassi and Alessandro are singing, although Alessandro himself is feeling like a nap, indeed has only just slipped into one when Tassi kicks him awake again.

"So what's your price?" Tassi is sorry to have lost the game, but then he could not fix everything and it will all turn out. That is all that matters.

"Six florins," Alessandro has addled his brains in Tassi's wine and is quoting, in his confusion, the price he himself would be prepared to pay to have her taken off his hands. Tassi misses the slip. He knows only that he is hearing a ridiculously low price.

"I don't have it on me but —" he goes over to where his cape lies on the floor, "— my cape alone as you can see is worth seven right here." He sweeps it out to the side to show the lining.

It taxes Alessandro's brain to catch up with this new development. Tassi it seems is actually offering him something.

"No?" says Tassi, flinging the cape round his own shoulders. "Then we shan't waste any more time."

"No. No, *yes*. Yes," says Alessandro, knocking his stool over and gripping the edge of the table as if it were the reins of a horse about to bolt. If the room would only stop rocking. "But not the cape alone. What else do you have?"

Tassi sighs but does not mind. Every drawback he encounters is one more challenge in the entertaining match of Tassi versus life. There are chances to win points at every turn. He raises his eyebrows and pauses before he says, "Nothing that would interest you."

"But something. What do you have?"

"Nothing. You will have to keep the girl." Tassi slides the satchel out of reach with his foot, and it has the precise effect he intends.

Alessandro drags himself upright and lurches for the bag. "Let me see. Come on. A debt is a debt. You don't walk away so easily."

He rummages in the bag, says, "Ah!" though he has no idea what his hands have found. He pulls out a small urn. It is very light, made of some curious material he cannot fathom. Having no judgement of his own and no clues to help him, he doesn't know what to say and covers with, "Aha!"

"Out of the question."

Well, he could play that game too. "Is that so? Then perhaps the whole deal is off."

"Good then," Tassi is half-smiling as if his teeth are closed on a secret. He holds his hand out for the urn.

Alessandro, unsure now, holds it closer. "Tell me where you got it. What's it made of?"

Tassi shakes his head. "You wouldn't believe me. And you'd have no use for it."

Alessandro sits down heavily and locks his hands firmly round the urn.

Tassi leans over him and whispers hotly in his ear.

Alessandro is very quiet, concentrating. He looks up. "True," says Tassi, nodding, eyebrows raised in earnest. "Especially," thrusting with his hips, "in matters of the heart."

Alessandro turns the urn round and round in his hands, looks up and says, "The cape as well."

"Done!" says Tassi.

"Done!" says Alessandro. His hands are rummaging in the satchel again. He pulls out a small jug of wine. He would have preferred it to the urn.

"*Bugiardo ingannevole*!" he says, "You kept this back."

"Too late," says Tassi, putting it back in his satchel. "*Vernaccia*. You don't need it. Not until you have the woman — whomever she may be — on hand." He makes a lewd gesture with his fingers and laughs. "*A portata di mano*."

Taking the long way home, helping the girl keep to the shadows to avoid the watchmen, Tassi considers Alessandro's disappointment when he put the jug of *vernaccia* back in the satchel. He might have walked away with her for as little as a jug of wine and kept his cape. But Tassi never regrets anything.

When they reach his house on Via del Rosaio, the shop boy lets them in. Tassi rents the ground floor of this dilapidated building squeezed tight between two others. To the right of the door, the interior space opens to the street by day; this is where he keeps his shop, letting down the shutters at night. At the back is a chimney place where he builds fires for his work and sometimes cooks. Tassi sleeps in the only bed, letting down a heavy curtain that divides the area front to back. On the other side of the entry is a narrow room with a table and two benches, at the back an alcove where he stores what little food he might have. The shop boy sleeps where he can, sometimes in the bed with Tassi, or, if Tassi has company, on the floor.

The boy lifts the taper to the girl's face and breathes a sigh of relief.

"I thought it was blood," he says. "I thought she was covered in blood."

"This," says Tassi "is my little parti-coloured friend, Caterina."

But the boy is already distracted, looking hopefully at Tassi's satchel to see if he has something to eat. Tassi tells him to get back to sleep — on the floor.

The bed is warm from the boy's body, and the girl, still a little drunk, is asleep again as soon as she is in it.

Tassi goes to look for oil for the lamp. He wants to see, to really see, this strange creature's body. The boy has used up the last. Tassi fills a lamp with his best cooking oil and carries it to the bed. He sets it where it will throw light on her skin — wishing he had four lamps like Paolo when he works — and there, with no one to watch him watching, he sits for a long time. His sculptor's eye sees the surface of water beaten and dented with light and tracks the moving shapes that travel like flat shining clouds over its surface.

When the girl wakes in the morning, she finds herself on the floor. She is in a strange room, and the man Tassi is lying beside her with his hand on her belly. She is cold. Carefully, she slides sideways and gets up.

Tassi reaches out and grabs hold of her ankle, unbalances her so that she comes down again onto the floor. He pushes an empty wineskin out of the way.

"Lie down," he says. "Be still."

He gathers her in beside him, reaches behind on the floor and drags a bed cover over her. She leans in against his warmth.

They are lying in the dark of the closed shutters. After a while, Tassi rolls over and hooks one half open with his foot. He settles beside her again, resting on one elbow, pushing the cover down with his other hand. The light plays over her shoulders, her hips.

"I'll tell you something, Caterina," he says. "I like your ugly skin."

She makes no reply. What could she possibly say? What he says makes no sense at all.

"*Chiaroscuro*," he says. "It should be your name." He reaches for the wineskin and upends it over the white dove on her forehead. She laughs and flinches under the thin trickle.

"I baptize you, Chiaroscuro, *in nomine patris et filii et spiritus sancti*. Come on." He gets up and makes her stand. "*Chiara*," he says, baptizing her again with his eyes. "That's your name. Hungry, Chiara?"

She nods.

"Come on, then." He gives her a blanket and takes her to the kitchen, where he surveys the shelf. Sometimes he has chestnuts, or ripe olives, a piece of salted fish when he can afford it. Today there are only a few almonds that have been gnawed by mice. Tassi sits down beside her. He puts an arm round her shoulders.

"Tomorrow," he says, "you will eat cheese and fish."

ORAZIO FABRONI'S HOUSE on Via del Cocomero extends in one wing behind his shop and looks onto the courtyard at the back. A staircase leads from the courtyard to a covered balcony and the family's living quarters. Outbuildings and a kitchen make up the third side of the yard, with a neighbour's house, where the cook lives, closing in the fourth.

It is comfortable house, a house, Orazio has always thought, to pass on to a son. He is in his upstairs chamber, which opens onto the long balcony. The room is light and airy. The shutters are wide open and a breeze blows across him from the long window on one side straight through the open door on the other. Orazio can hear Alessandro and Sofonisba talking below. He would like to know what they are saying but he catches only fragments. He cannot concentrate when his hands are hurting. He lies on his back on a divan with his arms stretched out to the sides. Two basins of fermented goat's milk, each raised on a stool on either side of him, receive his sore hands. His gnarled fingers curl under the milk and he sighs. As much as his hands hurt, he would not be in the youth's shoes at this particular moment. So unyielding, his daughter. A fellow like Alessandro could not stand up beside her. A mistake perhaps to encourage him to pay his respects in person. Better to arrange it all without them. Though he could not say with confidence today that Alessandro is the son-in-law he would choose were it not for the attraction of his father's apothecary on Via Bardi.

Messer Emilio's business is thriving like a lusty unstoppable lad. It could provide an artist with all the minerals and pigments he could wish for. The perfect union. Pigments are the leeches in an artist's pocket. Drawn from the earth at great expense, they eat gold coins. Grinding them and mixing them is a chore. They suck away the hours in a day. Or: a man can pay a boy to do it for him and lose more money still. Or: he can put his daughter to the task but where is the sense in that when she could be painting, completing commissions as fast as they come in, the output from the shop the same as if a paid assistant was at work? So: why not marry the daughter to the apothecary's son and reap the respect due to a father-in-law when the bill is drawn up? And Ser Emilio's health is even worse than his own. It could be a match with a number of advantages.

Down in the courtyard, seated on the stone bench beside the woman who turns his insides to fire, Alessandro is as awkward as ever, despite the fact that his moment has come, and this time he has a gift. He has the urn — and Sofonisba has seen it. But it does not help. With the money his father gave him he could have purchased a pearl for her brow. But the money is squirreled away along with other unearned gains in a locked box in his room. Instead he has this ungainly pot. He wishes he did not.

"Is that for me?"

Like a dog trembling for attention but fearing it, Alessandro can barely meet Sofonisba's eye. He holds it out and mumbles platitudes about humble gifts and no gifts fine enough.

Sofonisba laughs with her lips closed and it does not signify delight. But what is he to do? He has practised these words and cannot improvise. She takes the little urn from him.

It is narrow-necked, wide-shouldered and short, tapering in again to a narrow base. It has been wrought with a curious design of dancers that have been raised from its surface.

"What is this?" Sofonisba turns it over in her hands and taps the bottom. Alessandro smiles. At last he has managed to interest her.

She turns it round and round. She taps again with her finger nail. It makes a dry hollow sound.

"What is it?" she says. "It is not wood. Not clay." Alessandro does not know. He knows only what Tassi told him, that it was bought in one of the *botteghe* that trade in works of art excavated from Roma. It is charmed. The charm is powerful and not of the kind that he could discuss with Sofonisba — or any of her sex. It is the very reason he wants her to have it.

"What do you think?" says Sofonisba and throws it suddenly upward so that he has to catch it. "Not bone," she says, "and yet it's light. Tell me."

Alessandro tries to look enigmatic and to his horror Sofonisba is overcome with snorting derision.

"It is very ugly," she says, recovering. "I do not want a dun-coloured thing like that."

Alessandro's confusion is turning to anger when she says suddenly, "I shall paint it," and takes it back. Shreds of hope to salvage. Her words send him scrabbling. She is turning the urn over in her hands again. Instinctively he knows he must drop this dead weight of anger, cling to lightness if he is to succeed.

"Make it beautiful," he says "and then, *Madonna*, I shall tell you what it is." And he feels himself suddenly elegant, light as air and able to play this complicated game.

Orazio's suffering extends from his hands. He aches all over. He closes his eyes, grateful that Matteo Tassi returned today as he had promised to release him from his pains. He had been at Santa Maria Nuova again, working alone all morning to finish the last section of the wall. Because the work was *fresco* and proceeded from the top down, he spent most of the day on his knees and his haunches, sometimes lying down on his side to paint the lowest extremities next to the flagstones. Even his shoulder hurts. His hands, however, are the worst. The lime in the plaster has set the skin between his fingers on fire, and the pain is competing with old ailments brought on by years of painting. The knuckles of each hand are swollen to a great size and two of the fingers on each hand draw in and under, toward the palm, leaving two to hook the air, useless, like claws. He has devised a way to hold the brushes still but while he paints he counts the minutes to his release.

Tassi had said, "In God's name," and made him get up. "You need Ilario for this," he said. "Here." He took the brush himself and lay down. Orazio smiles to remember. So different from Alessandro. Chalk and cheese. Tassi is uncouth, undesirable even, but there is no false note about him. An open-hearted man. A spendthrift, yes: never a penny to his name. Money runs like water through his fingers and yet somehow a person is always in his debt, always beholden for some generous act. He'd even carried the buckets into the courtyard and washed off his brushes for him.

"My most dear old friend and father listen," Tassi had said, sluicing lime from the path. Father! The familiarity! Yet somehow he had license.

"I have a gift for your daughter, sir, and with your leave I should like to present it to her tomorrow. I know, knowing you and your household intimately, as I do, that she has no maid of her own to serve her and it just so happens that I have this very day at my house a young girl '*of most exotic appearance and lively nature.*'" He laughed. "But I beg your permission. It's a gift that requires feeding and housing." Orazio did not answer at once. "But one that makes a dowry more attractive."

It was an arrangement Orazio found hard to fault. It was a brash, inflated gesture but who was there to offend? Sofonisba, for one, would be grateful for a girl to help her.

Tassi leaned over and breathed heavily in Orazio's ear. "You can see if you find her 'lively.'" He grinned. "If you come with your daughter to dine we can make a night of it."

Orazio agreed.

"And when she has served her mistress," Tassi said, stacking the buckets and straightening up, "perhaps the master may serve her." Slapping him on the back, paying him the compliment of treating him like a vigorous youth. Flattery, yes. But did he care? He looked forward to the evening. And then, too, he had a special affection for Tassi, who could be a foul-mouthed lout and a broad-hearted friend all at once. Better by far than an idiot. And Orazio has a taste for the foul himself.

Sofonisba returns to the workshop as soon as Alessandro has gone. She puts the urn on a shelf and resumes her work on the Arcivescovo's panel, the Christ in his tomb. Difficult as it was to begin, the painting is progressing well now that she has unlocked the conundrum at the heart of the subject. The work is not hard. She has decided to apply the conventions of perspective that she has absorbed from her father's workshop as readily as Ceccio absorbs words. She works from the detailed anatomical drawings she made of the torso, and from her vivid memory of the pauper's corpse glimpsed, entire. She paints for a while, colouring the flesh and lending it substance with delicate applications of azurite and cinnabar. But she does not find the familiar rhythm. Her mind is distracted by the squat brown urn. It offends her eye. Unable to ignore it, Sofonisba decides to give it her full attention. She will meet Alessandro's challenge. She interrupts her work to mix a small portion of gesso with a little glue size. She tries it on the urn. It adheres. It dries quickly. By the end of the afternoon, black figures in cinnamon-coloured tunics turn on a blue ground in an endless dance around the urn. Tomorrow she will lay a little gold leaf in bands at the neck and the shoulder. She wonders about the artist who created the little pot. Was his soul as ugly? Or may a beautiful soul create an unlovely thing? The thought has a dangerous correlative.

⌒

BY THE TIME MATTEO TASSI jumps onto the table and calls for silence, Sofonisba has almost forgotten that he had promised a surprise. He has invited six friends in all. His favourite, Bianca, is not attending, in deference to Sofonisba and her father. Bianca is Tassi's whore, whom he loves with a passion but cannnot afford to keep. Instead there is the young Lavinia, as rotund and accommodating as a barrel. She is not quite respectable either, but at least she does not ask for money. She is the younger sister of Giovanni, a copyist, who is also present. Giovanni is invited everywhere for his voice as well as his sister. He loves to sing, can improvise on any theme, and knows how in every sense to strike the right note. Tassi has high expectations for his performance tonight. In addition, he has invited Niccolò Ricoldi, who designs floors in mosaic, and Umberto, his friend and mentor. Niccolò was almost unable to attend, having been fined on the spot for breaking the canopy outside the house of the Podestà when he tried to climb up on it the night before. Penniless, he was on the point of being carried away when Umberto arrived with his long mule's face and his money. Umberto always has money — and always declares it to be his last.

Orazio is glad to sit with Umberto at the table. They talk about matters the younger men wouldn't understand: the way doubts assail them in the small hours when sleep deserts them, their fear of being left no time for repentance when their hour comes. They pour more wine and begin to remember instead the sins of their youth, basking in old glories like two old *condottieri* in the sun. Tassi has to call again for silence before they notice him.

"My ladies, my lords, my dear friends," he says, "we humbly beg your leave," — nor does he mind the catcalls and the cries of "*Su! Sbrigati!*" — "to lay before you a marvel of Nature that will astonish your faculties and delight your senses. But first," he says. "But first, we ask for silence.

"Behind the curtain at the far end of the room sits one of Nature's creations, not of our land but from a distant kingdom, and it may be easily put to fright by our strange and sophisticated tongues." All of which is cheerfully understood to be untrue. Nearly everyone in the room has taken the liberty of peering behind the blue curtain strung across the alcove; there was nothing there but a low platform with four small lamps on it and a coiled rope attached. Nature's creation sits in the cupboard at the back of the recess and has been there for two hours, undetected. Far from being alarmed, she is on the point of falling asleep for lack of air and for the wine that Tassi gave her to ensure her compliance. The girl's — Chiara's — forty-eight hour acquaintance with Tassi has taken her through mistrust and alarm, sudden fright, reassurance, warmth, relief, comfort, amusement, pleasure, ecstasy, release and trust. The man can do as he pleases; this much she takes for granted. A man might use her or abuse her and what is plain is that she has no choice in the matter. But that Messer Matteo will hurt her? It does not seem a possibility.

"And now," says Tassi, "I beg your indulgence. A few moments of darkness." At this, his boy takes a candle and slips behind the curtain. Tassi jumps down and snuffs out all the candles and extinguishes the lamps. The audience is primed. If he were to bring in a chicken they would gasp, a pig they would be astonished.

Behind the curtain there is creaking and movement and above it the guests can see the light from the candle flickering. And now the boy must be lighting the lamps on the platform, for they can see the glow. He ducks out backwards, leading with his behind, and the audience applauds in the darkness. Lavinia yells with laughter. The boy has the free end of the rope, which he pays out, bringing it to a spike that Tassi has driven clean into the floor just by the table. He passes it round and back across the floor, taking it once more under the curtain. "Perhaps he's going to hang himself. Horizontally," says Niccolò. Umberto says for his part he would hang himself any way he could if he had to live with Tassi. Lavinia says she will hang herself if she has to wait any longer.

The boy is a while more, doing as Tassi has instructed, feeding the rope under the low platform — which is on castors and where

Chiara is now seated, cross-legged — and out to the back of the alcove. He coughs twice.

Tassi, beaming, strides to the curtain.

"My friends, my honoured guests, you who have seen every wonder of God's world, you who create with His grace new worlds of your own, behold now in the house of Tassi, the bronze crafter, Light and Dark at play in perfect balance." He draws the curtain aside and loops it over a hook.

There, illuminated by lamps placed at the four corners of the platform, sits Chiara. Sofonisba, like the others, leans forward. She thinks at first she is seeing a Moor, the girl is so dark, her hair so curly. Then she sees that the darkness is not uniform but dappled like the shadows of leaves cast on a wall. The girl is naked to the waist except for a gilded wire from Tassi's workshop round her forehead and bracelets of the same, high on each arm. Sofonisba judges her to be thirteen, fourteen. A cord of thick gold silk girdles her hips and a narrow, fringed apron hangs from it in front for modesty. As Sofonisba watches, the platform jolts and begins to move forward. The room is very quiet except for the sawing and creaking of the rope. If Tassi had hoped for magic he is thwarted by the eagerness of the boy, who hauls more energetically than smoothly on the line, so that the platform creaks and jolts forward erratically. Its seated figure looks her spectators in the eye. No one laughs.

Niccolò is the first to respond. He breaks off bits of bread and throws them to the seated figure as if they are flowers. The other guests applaud and begin to do the same.

Tassi, still the showman and still sober enough to see where all this will lead, steps away from the curtain and walks behind the guests to where Sofonisba is sitting. Smiling, he takes her hand and holds out the other toward Chiara.

"Come," he says to Sofonisba. "Come and receive your gift. My gift to you." He helps her over the bench and leads her away from the table and round to Chiara. Chiara's eyes dart from one to the other, waiting for her cue.

Sofonisba, close now, marvels at the smoothness of the girl's skin.

Chiara begins to speak: "Monna —"

"Not yet," says Tassi. He gives the girl a cup of wine and she holds it with both hands and drinks greedily, noisily.

"Where did you get her?"

"From Genoa. From a prince selling Barbary yearlings."

"Yes, and I was carried into the world by a wild stork." Sofonisba laughs with delight. "But I like her."

Tassi grins. "You like her?" He jerks his head at Chiara. "Say it," he says. "Say it now."

Chiara looks at Sofonisba and says, "*Monna Sofonisba. Sto a Sua disposizione assoluta. Sono Chiara, la Sua schiava lealissima.*"

Sofonisba spins round to Tassi.

He shrugs and smiles.

"Chiaroscuro," he says and puts his hand on Chiara's breast, Sofonisba's hand on her neck. His guests slap the table in approval.

"Stand up," says Tassi, and Sofonisba takes her hand away and helps her to her feet. Tassi turns her round and his guests applaud.

"She's cold," says Sofonisba and she makes the boy help her take down the curtain so that she can wrap it round the girl's shoulders.

Tassi says, "Wait," and leads the girl around the table to show her off.

"Come along. Enough." Sofonisba says. "She shall sit by me."

"Enough, then," says Tassi. "You have eaten all the food, my greedy friends. We shall have to drink instead."

Chiara, sitting next to Sofonisba, sways a little. Sofonisba moves her to sit in the corner of the room. Chiara is grateful for the support of the wall. She lets her eyes close on the room of strangers, listens to their voices and then hears nothing more.

For one of Tassi's suppers it is a sober affair. Giovanni and Umberto are both asleep. Only Lavinia is still eating and drinking — and smiling between belches. Orazio says it is time to go. With difficulty Chiara is woken and dressed in her grey woollen gown and bundled down the stairs and out the door. Orazio with his arms round Tassi says, "All suitors should know how to engage an old man's fancy." Orazio and Tassi embrace and bid each other goodnight.

Tassi says, "This is just the beginning."

Sofonisba sees his inviting smile. Only a fraction wider and it would have been a leer. She thinks of the lilies outside at Paolo's house. Great white lilies with tawny pink depths and stamens the colour of oxblood. The air was fragrant with them but when she had bent her head and inhaled, their perfume caught her at the temple. It was a sensation only just this side of pleasure, a grain of pollen more and it would have crossed the line to pain.

⌒

TASSI IS IN GOOD SPIRITS. Who would not be? He sings in a ragged voice with a smile on his face while he makes up the fire. The morning is fair, spring masquerading as summer. The air is balmy and sweet and all along the road the traveller is assaulted by new fragrances the warm breeze has stirred. At least those are the words of his song, though here in Via del Rosaio the fragrance is an underlying blend of boiled cabbage and shit beneath the stink of the tanneries that wafts up from the river. Still, what the song offers is all a man needs when he is happy, and Tassi knows it. He never wants for more than the pleasures of the senses but today, anyway, he has more. He is in favour with the smiling Sofonisba and her store of laughter that can melt a man; he enjoys the good opinion of her father; adding one and one he arrives at the prospect of unlimited pleasure: license within the house, the freedom to come and go without scraping his nose on the ground for Orazio, the possibility of savouring that throaty laughter — with or without marriage — in private.

Tassi's boy, waking to the cheerful rumpus of his master making up the fire, salivates at the thought of food, but is sent out instead with sleep in his eyes to buy wax from the convent for Paolo's bronze cast. Bronze is the medium that Tassi loves best, the most sensuous in every one of its complex stages, the most mysterious and the most like life in its finished form. When he has a large commission, he transports his moulds to the great foundry on Via Buffalini. For smaller pieces he risks the wrath of his landlord and builds a furnace in the yard.

While the boy is gone, Tassi lays out the two halves of the plaster mould, the blind twins in love with their mirror images. Using only his eye to measure, he fashions a small embryonic figure — the *anima* — from clay. It is the core that will hang inside the wax model and, later, will remain, a false heart inside the finished bronze. Rudimentary, smaller and less sharply defined but with the same contours as the foetus, the *anima* is a shadow of it in the way that the snow lions in February are shadows of those that were carved in January.

The boy returns from the convent with enough wax to cast an entire nun. Tassi uses only a part. The dimensions of the finished sculpture will scarcely equal those of a small cat curled. Its core will be taken up with the clay. He breaks the wax he needs into a tall copper pitcher. While it melts on the fire he prepares the mould, carving a channel out of the plaster in each of the two halves. When they are joined, there will be a funnel to receive the wax. Carefully he sticks iron pins into the *anima* and, in a process of trial and error, positions it securely in the mould, closing the two halves round it. The protruding pins keep it away from the inner walls; it hangs inside, clear of the shell of the mould, trapped and at the same time free, the way, Maestro Paolo once remarked, the rough unfinished soul hangs inside the body, a disparate element, longing for fire. So the artist's work, said Maestro Paolo, was the mirror of God's creation, Man.

Tassi closes the mould and seals the seam lightly with a thin smear of plaster, then binds it with cloth so that it looks now like a small, rough cask. He sets it upside down on the bench, the hole in its base ready to receive the molten wax. When the wax is clear and almost smoking, Tassi calls the boy to pour. He takes the mould in both hands and swirls it once, twice in a figure eight, as if he is engaged in a new game of skill, about to throw dice from a great tumbler perhaps. The boy is well trained. He pours again. They work quickly, alternately pouring and swirling, Tassi using that same expert motion. When the mould refuses to accept any more, he sets it in the shade to cool.

He leaves the boy to clear up and walks off into the town, looking into the shops of friends, the back corners of taverns, allowing time for the mould to cool, making his way, though he does not admit it to his feet, to Sofonisba.

When he gets back he will break out the wax figure and, when he is certain it is hard enough, he will clean up the surface, bringing the details of the features into sharp relief. Still he will have only the preliminary stage completed. When the wax figure is to his liking, he will encase it in a new jacket of clay. He will circle it with iron bands for strength and then he will fire it on the bricks in the centre of his furnace. The furnace will burn all day and all night, melting out the wax and firing the clay mould and its *anima*. In the morning, all that will remain of his exquisite wax model will be the shape of its absence. Then, with the mould removed but still hot, he will stoke up his furnace to Hell's heat and turn solid metal to liquid, molten fire. At this moment he will become smith, alchemist, priest, and midwife all.

"So you like my gift, do you?" Tassi has his hand on Chiara's neck as if she is a young colt in the market.

Sofonisba and Chiara, working in Orazio's cluttered shop are as unadorned as penitents, Chiara in her grey woollen gown, Sofonisba in a dusty black *lucca* splashed with lime. When Tassi sees her like this he feels she belongs to him. He can imagine her by his side as he works in his shop, content after a night of pleasure.

"I love her. She is my little mottled sister. She's going to follow me wherever I go." Sofonisba puts her arm around the girl's waist and draws her away.

Three days ago she had woken to a rush of delight as she remembered her gift. She had lifted her head and, yes, there was the girl's form, curled under the covers on the chest at the end of the bed. She had reached out with her foot and pushed at the girl's shoulder. She sensed that the girl had woken though she was still lying perfectly motionless, staring, Sofonisba surmised, into the room and wondering for that moment of waking where in Heaven she was, and who or what was poking her. It would be a fine amusement to see her face. Sofonisba jabbed again at her shoulder and this time the girl carefully turned her head. Sofonisba laughed at the terrified face with its dark staring eyes.

"Well?" she said. "*Non puoi parlare?*" The girl swallowed and sat up and said hoarsely, " *Monna Sofonisba. Sto a Sua disposizione assoluta.*"

Sofonisba laughed again at the thought of her days enlivened by company.

"Stay there," she said and got up and put on her gown. "Stay there." She left the room, returning after a while with a small calf-bound notebook and piece of red chalk.

"So take off that cover, my little ugliness, and show me this body the Lord sees fit to give you." She saw by the girl's eyes that she understood what was required, though she stayed quite still.

"You're mine now, remember? *A mia disposizione assoluta.*"

Here was power of a kind Sofonisba had not tasted before. Even the boys who ran errands were not in her sway like this girl. It was the power of man over beast, husband over wife and daughter.

She walked round her until she found an angle that pleased her and then she settled to draw with the chalks. Two, three, four more times she made a drawing and all the time Chiara remained naked as the night and with a bladder full to bursting.

"Don't move," Sofonisba said, though the girl was watching so intently that she had hardly blinked. "Don't move." And Sofonisba, too, is intent, absorbed, the expression on her face like one who is starving and receives food. At last she had had enough and she let Chiara dress and use the chamber.

"Do you want to see?" She turned her book and showed the girl the page where she had drawn her head, in three-quarter profile, with the neck and shoulders. She watched the tears that began to well and slip down the strange, smooth skin.

Nothing in Sofonisba's experience had taught her how to respond.

"Come," she had said. "You can't be a miserable little wretch around me or we'll never get on."

Since then, she has drawn her many times though Orazio has insisted on receiving an account each day of the duties Chiara has performed. He says if he is to feed another mouth then it must be worth his while, though already he has pronounced the girl something of an asset. She asks nothing, expects nothing in return for the labours she performs, is grateful, and does not resent the blows he has to administer. Her presence is as unassuming as an animal's. Only once has she shown resistance. Sofonisba had thought to use her to make notations on the way the light strikes a horizontal figure, but no amount of scolding or cajoling could induce the girl to get up on the table.

"I love her, too," says Tassi. "I'll miss her."

"She was with you for only two days."

"And three nights."

"Well, a good thing. She is safer here with me than with you."

"What makes you say that?"

"You have a hand in every pot."

Which reminds Tassi. He begins to prowl, looking for something.

The blue and gold urn enmeshed in a silver net is hanging in the window. Tassi walks past it and then stops and doubles back. He looks from it to Sofonisba and back again. A smile slides across his mouth, a snake parting the grass.

"*Madonna!* " he says. "Where did you get this?"

"Why?"

"I think I recognize it."

"What do you mean?"

"Something I sold to young Alessandro."

"And?"

"He didn't give it to you, surely?"

"He did. He always brings me gifts."

"But are they always as wonderful as mine?" Tassi sits down abruptly just as Chiara passes him and he pulls her onto his lap.

Sofonisba laughs. "Not nearly. I had to paint this one." She twirls the pot and it flashes in the sunlight, making the linnet sing. A sudden thought occurs to her and she turns round suddenly. "You know what it is made of."

Tassi grins.

"You know."

He nods.

Sofonisba senses a trap. "Tell me."

"I couldn't, *Madonna*."

"Tell me, Messer Matteo."

They are both laughing but only Tassi is amused.

"I'll tell my young friend here."

He gets up, pushing Chiara to her feet and shepherding her toward the door. He has one hand on the latch and one hand to the nape of her neck. He leans and whispers something.

"What?" she says.

He repeats it, bows to Sofonisba, says, "Honoured lady," grins again, kisses his fingertips at her and is gone.

Tassi guesses the wax to be firm enough to withstand removal from the mould. He is almost running by the time he reaches his house.

He lifts the mould onto the bench. The moment of discovery is pleasure. The moment preceding it is bliss. He unwraps the swaddling and runs his knife down through the plaster on the seams. With the mould lying on its back, he carefully prises the two halves apart, knocking on the top section to free the figure, excitement a soft kick in his belly. The wax infant is whole and perfect in the last detail.

His boy chuckles, says, "*Buon giorno, ometto.*"

Tassi lifts the bottom half of the mould and taps it sharply down. He tilts it to let the infant tip onto his spread fingers, says to the boy, "We're giving birth."

Without warning he is overtaken by a shudder. His stomach contracts. The thing in wax is too like life, the same dimensions, the same colour surely as the foetus that Paolo must have extracted from the mother. Tassi's legs feel as if he has been attacked from behind. He puts it down and throws a rag over it, growls, "*Lascialo stare!* Leave it alone!" as the boy reaches to have another look. He shoves the boy out of the way and tells him to bring the *luto* for the jacket. He has a sensation of reeling though he is standing perfectly still. He leans heavily on the edge of the bench and the moment has passed by the time the boy returns with the clay.

He draws a breath and uncovers the figure. He can look now. It has ceased to be a visitation from elsewhere, a manifestation of mystery, and has become again the product of his own hands. He lifts the damp sacking off the bucket and scoops out a portion for the boy to knead. It is the same mixture of clay that he used for the core, an unlikely mixture of straw and dung and clay and wool shearings, a child's mess. Tassi shares his recipe generously when his friends ask, but still he has the most success, perhaps because the boy's fingers never tire of working it.

Tassi takes the finest of tools to the model to draw out each fold, each crease and hair. In a little while he is lost in the flawless perfection of its form.

He softens new pieces of wax on a copper sheet and fashions four slim candles, about the thickness of a lily's stem, and a long funnel-shaped piece. He attaches the pieces to the head, the shoulders, a knee, a heel. Now comes the hardest part, for he must coat the figure, complex now with its pouring tube and its vents, in clay. It is delicate work, laying the fine clay over the surface of the wax without spoiling the cleanness of the form, without harming the junctures where the vents attach. Tassi's fingers are thicker than the infant's wrist but his intuition is sure, unfailing, his patience with the slender willow tools limitless. Once he has achieved a certain thickness in the clay, the work goes more quickly.

At last the wax foetus is entirely encased. The ends of the vents, small circles of wax breaking the surface of the clay jacket, are the only sign of what might be hidden inside.

Tassi lodges it out of the sun in a warm dry corner of the courtyard, where the stones, giving up the day's heat, will help to cure it for firing.

FIVE

When alessandro set out for Orazio's house in the afternoon, he could not have been more pleased with himself, more confident. Sofonisba had painted the urn. He had heard it from Tassi. Good, then. She had entered the game with him. She was waiting for his next move. How easy after all to leave the blunderings of one's boyhood behind and become a man in the world. Stepping out along Via Bardi, he had believed the gift to be working, just as Tassi had promised. Women, Tassi had said, once they had felt the urn between their palms, had been known to lie down and lift their skirts. Well, he knew exaggeration when he heard it, and he knew Tassi, but all the same, all the same . . . The next move in the game, he had to confess, was delicate. Sofonisba was going to ask him what it was made of. It was not going to be easy to think up an answer for her. The composition of the urn. Tassi had warned him to keep it a close secret. He would think of something plausible by the time he got to Via del Cocomero. There was no need to worry, he was a changed man. Something elegant would trip off his tongue when the time came, something to surprise even himself.

Alessandro still does not understand what happened. He looks like an old man as he returns home, his neck sunk into his shoulders. The time that elapsed from the moment he went through the shop, crossed the courtyard and tossed his cape — with panache, he thought — over one shoulder to climb the stairs to the reception room, to the moment the flower pot crashed down and hit his heel, narrowly missing his head as he left, was shorter than the time it takes to get from the *Introit* to the *Kyrie*. He still can't fathom what happened. First there was the shock of seeing that revolting little gargoyle crossing the courtyard in the other direction. He was so stupid. He was always so stupid. "Oh, is Tassi here?" he had said. For everyone upstairs to hear. Simpleton. "Is Tassi here?" He could kick himself. But it wasn't so stupid. He saw the girl. How was he to know she had changed hands? "Tassi?" Sofonisba had looked around as if he might have just come in. "Tassi? No. . . . Oh, I *see*. You think . . . No, no, no. Chiara is *mine*. Tassi *gave* her to me. Sweet man." She hadn't changed hands in a regular transaction. She was Tassi's gift. Tassi's *extravagant* gift beside which no stupid lit- tle turd pot could hold a candle. "*Tassi? No. . .*" He went through life missing opportunities, missing advantage. How could he not have seen that the slave girl was an asset? Why should it be given to Tassi to see? At that moment, standing in Orazio's house with Sofonisba staring at him, he hated Tassi more than anything in the world. If Tassi went into a tavern without a penny, drinks were poured down his throat. If Tassi was hungry, he'd get invited to Careggi. If Tassi was out of work, the poxy King of Napoli would suddenly call for a poxy bronze-caster. "*Tassi gave her to me.*" *That* was how it happened. It was her voice like that. *Tassi gave her to me. Sweet man.* That was the moment when his whole future collapsed. He lost his head. "Oh, he did, did he? Well, Tassi's good at giving gifts, isn't he? But you watch out, you just watch out for Tassi's gifts. You never know what you could be in for — a case of leprosy or the tip of an elephant's prick." That was exactly what he said. The thought makes him colour. Her disbelief. "What was that I heard you say?" That was when he — idiot — had repeated every word. He tried to explain, to put the blame on Tassi, but he only made matters worse and anyway she wasn't really listening but had started looking for things to throw. And then he was backing down the stairs. The flower pot *would* have brained him if he hadn't quickened his step to avoid that dirty little girl who was just then coming back. It is all connected. He knows it is. Only the most powerful talisman can help him now.

Chiara has a cut on her shin from one of the shards of the flower pot. The shop boy had grinned and warned her to look out for herself.

Upstairs things are breaking, too. She goes along the balcony and stops at the door to the reception room, pushing it open just a little and waiting until she hears a heavy object hit the wall before she judges it safe to slip quickly in.

Orazio is standing on the far side by the window like a man under a tree waiting for the storm to pass. But he is smiling.

"Ah, Chiara." Sofonisba opens her arms and flings them round her.

"At least Chiara will understand. Come with me."

In the shop, she snatches the urn from the silver net and dashes it to the floor. It rolls.

"Do you know what that is? Do you?" She stamps on it ineffectually. Words are more satisfying. "Do you know what that filthy Alessandro gave us? Do you know what I had in my hands, what I painted with my own hands?" She grabs a paintbrush and snaps it in two.

Chiara hopes she is soon going to tell her. She can hear Orazio crossing the courtyard. She does not want to bear the brunt of the anger of two.

"Do you know? Do you know? That filthy piss rat, that disgusting, scum-encrusted, toad-necked, pig-arsed Tassi. Do you know what he sold to Alessandro? What Alessandro gave me?" She bends down and picks up the urn. She holds it out at arm's length, her hand shaking with rage and her mouth turned down like a child's about to cry. "It is the sexual organ of an elephant."

Chiara understands only that this is the point of outrage, the culmination of whatever she is hearing. She looks at once to Orazio. He is trying not to laugh.

"Give it to me," he says quietly. "I'll take it away."

Sofonisba makes a motion as if she is shaking a wasp out of her hair. She kicks the pot toward Chiara.

"Bury it." she says.

While Chiara digs in the small rectangle of hard earth under the peach tree by the wall, Sofonisba watches.

"Well? What would you do with it?"

"I would serve soup in it."

"To your enemies!"

Sofonisba's laughter salts her mouth with vicarious malice. It tastes good. She likes to think of the blue and gold and scarlet in the darkness under the earth trying to flare.

Chiara, walking back, brushes the dirt from her hands onto her dress.

Sofonisba returns to her work. The Christ on his cold bed is all but finished. There are only the highest of the lights to place, on the linen across his loins, on the opened skin of the five wounds and on the surface of the water in the bowl that was used to wash the body. Sofonisba's anger, though it is real, is soothed by the repetition of the brush strokes. Alessandro is a dolt and not worth her time. And Tassi? It is obvious that Tassi was behind it all, but his uncouth tricks are nothing. She used to see and hear worse when her father's friends came to visit. For Sofonisba, anger is not a sin to be confessed like guilt or envy. Anger is to be enjoyed. It roars into her like a wind down from the Mugello and catches the very centre of her being, sweeping her up in its power. For Sofonisba, anger *is* power. To watch fear, however slight, creep into another's eyes, to watch the body realign itself for its own protection — it is something to savour. And yet she cannot stay mad with Tassi for long. It would not be amusing. More amusing is to wait for the ripe moment, like the peach about to fall, then return the insult tenfold. She can do that. Where would she be without Tassi to play with? He is her ugly rat and she the cat — and she loves him in the same way.

In a little while she has forgotten Tassi altogether. There is only the dry, slightly earthy scent of the tempera in her nostrils, the small, small resistance of the paint as it pulls from the sable hairs of her brush. She will see Tassi again. Today will have been no more than a round lost in a game. And Sofonisba is always ready to play another round. But for now there is only painting. She can taste the water in the bowl. She can taste its tang of iron on her tongue, and time does not exist.

CECCIO, WITH HIS EYES WIDE as saucers, waits at the stand of moonlit poplars just outside the Porta alla Giustizia, as arranged. Beyond the poplars a low-lying tract of ground stretches away, scrubby and forlorn, home only to dogs and crows. It is a place where mists hang even on a clear night. It is not a place where Ceccio, down from *La Castagna* with Paolo, would have hoped to find himself and yet he is here by his own consent. How easy it had been to impress lanky Alessandro when he came to him with a tale of woe. How easy to let the phrases that roosted in his mind flutter from his mouth just when Alessandro needed to hear them. Lanky old Alessandro always needing something, this time demanding it, offering him money, offering him more, even suggesting he was ready to spill his, Ceccio's, store of secrets to Maestro Paolo if he didn't help him. It had been easy to take his money. And oh, how easy to regret. Ceccio is afraid now to turn and look back at the walls of the city, sure as he is that he will see there a murder of scraggy crows with not a straight beak among them.

But all the regret in the world will not get Ceccio out of this agreement.

Alessandro waits here, too, in the darkness of the wall with his hood drawn over his face. He is dry in the mouth and his bowels seem to have acquired a life of their own. This is the place they call the Ley of the Damned, the place they bring criminals to lie for all eternity beyond the shelter of any church. The men he is to meet here would cut his throat for the gold — gold he has embezzled from his own father — sooner than dig. But Ceccio is Alessandro's safeguard. Ceccio is preserved from these men by his uncle who employs them, and by the long shadow of Giuliano, belonging as he does to Maestro Paolo. There is justification for Alessandro's conclusion — which he would have reached anyway through sheer cowardice — that when all is said and done it is safer by far to stay out of the way. Let Ceccio deal with these unsavoury men. Give *him* the purse of dangerous coins. He has instructed the boy to give the men one fourth of their payment for the task when they begin, the rest on completion. As soon as he handed the purse with the quarter payment in it to Ceccio, Alessandro felt better, safer; less nauseous, once he had handed over the knife — a curved blade like the one that Paolo uses — and the empty sack he carried.

Ceccio wraps the sack around the knife and rests it now on his shivering knees, where he crouches in the shelter of the trees.

The two men take Ceccio by surprise, approaching him from behind so that he startles. Alessandro concealed in the darkness does not make a sound. The first man, short and wiry with a battered look about him like an old nail, speaks sharply and puts out his hand for the money. Ceccio, shaking, tells him quickly that his master is close by with the rest. The man looks out into the darkness and is suspicious. He assumes that Maestro Paolo is out there somewhere with a servant or two and the comfort of hefty cudgels or, it is not unlikely, knives. His anxiety runs so high that he bears himself like a man about to be attacked, every inch of him alert, every nerve awake and a look of concentration on him as if he is wholly occupied in suppressing frenzy. He is a man about to crack out of his skin and he alarms Ceccio almost more than the thought of the act they are about to perform. He reaches up to his companion — a bigger, older, simpler fellow — and draws his hood down over his head before he sets off for the Ley of the Damned. Both Ceccio and the second man are forced almost to trot to keep up with him.

The two-day-old grave is easy to locate. When he arrives Ceccio does his best to play the master and begins to hiss instructions, but the skinny man is not listening. He lays out a length of oiled hessian beside the grave and begins to dig the earth out onto it. He starts to swear, makes the second man come and help. The big man digs fast, as if he is digging for treasure in a ruin in the hills. Long strings of spittle swing from his lower lip as he finds a rhythm. The first man continues to curse. Ceccio's stomach is knotted with fear. He retreats to crouch at the foot of an elm, deriving less comfort from the wine he gulps, forcing it down, than from the solid trunk at his back. It is not long before the skinny man pulls on the other's arm. He has to take the shovel and throw it down to make the big man stop. Then, still cursing, he spreads a second piece of cloth on the other side of the grave and jumps down into the hole to work at uncovering the corpse. Ceccio stares from under his long lashes. The big man backs away, whimpering. He shakes his head from side to side, the action originating from the shoulders so that the upper part of his body also rocks, like a child's. After a barrage of curses from the first man, he returns to the graveside and helps to manhandle the corpse in its soiled sacking up and out of the grave. Now he is all curiosity but he holds back. The ambassador from the dead is propped, inside his sack, bolt upright on stiff legs against the earth, so that the top half of him sticks up above the grave. Still in his muddy funeral boat, he is back from the land of the dead to report on the favourable conditions there for commerce, everyone in the underworld greedy for eyes, teeth, lips; everyone prepared to barter memories and loves and lies.

"Get over here," says the skinny man to Ceccio. But Ceccio is feeling queasy and is slow. He arrives in time to make only a gesture toward helping the stiff legs out of the grave.

The skinny man slits the sack open with a knife from his belt.

"Get on with it."

Ceccio has a peculiar look on his face. He finds that if he keeps his teeth together and his lips pulled back — his mouth dragged down at the corners as far as it will go and the strings of his neck standing out like cables — he can hold down his stomach almost indefinitely. His breath hisses through his clenched teeth.

Ceccio knows exactly what to do. He has watched Paolo Pallavicino six, seven times. Neither the hanged man's open eyes, nor his dark face upset him, nor his thick tongue filling the mouth cavity like a dark boulder. All this he has seen before. What upsets him is that there is no one here to give him permission to do this thing.

"Hurry up." It is the skinny man hissing again. "Get it done or I'll break your head." Which seems to be no idle threat. He has the shovel raised and ready.

Ceccio tries to claw back some authority, says, "Cut that sack right open."

He moves forward. His mouth is still distorted in an effort to retain control over the contents of his stomach. He kneels down beside the corpse and unwraps the knife, laying it down beside him, then takes out a small black flint from a leather sheath. Remembering Paolo's commentary, he presses it in the hollow of the neck to break the skin then draws it hard over the ridge of bone and down the centre of the chest to the navel. In the same way he scores a line from the end of the collarbone down past the arm to the waist and another, starting in the same place and running in toward the neck. He does the same on the other side of the chest. Like a tailor he has marked out his design. When he takes the pressure off the flint his hands will not keep still. He turns his face up once to the moon, pulls his chin up with a screwing, turning motion as if he would like to detach his head from what his body is doing. In its misery his face is almost unrecognizable. Only his curls identify him. He cuts under a corner of skin with the flint, making the flap he needs to get hold of, and then he takes up the knife, sliding it under with one hand and pulling the flap taut with the other. Now the work is easier, for he can slide the knife under and right through to the muscle itself, angle it just so and maintain the pressure. He hears the familiar tearing sound as the skin lifts away.

The man tells him to shut up and Ceccio realizes he is praying, still with his mouth pulled out of shape, louder and louder, asking Our Lady for help. He is a leaden soul, poor Ceccio, and there is little hope of his becoming otherwise. It does not occur to him that the Queen of Heaven might not want to soil her hands in this fearful business.

The three men turn the hanged man over.

When Ceccio has finished, his hands are greasy and slippery. He has three pieces of the tailor's pattern in his sack and the hanged man is clad in his own undressed flesh, which glistens. From Alessandro's vantage point he looks as if he is wearing a tight doublet of something shiny, something finer than his hairy arms and the blue-black skin of his face.

Alessandro approaches with the rest of the money while the skinny man and Ceccio are bundling the cadaver back into the grave. The other man, the big man, is doing nothing to assist. He is weeping and weeping into the hem of his shirt.

PART II

SIX

The festaiuoli have declared, as they do every year, that this year's celebrations for the feast of San Giovanni will surpass those of any other. They are meeting in a recently refurbished room in the Palazzo Vecchio. Cosimo's touch is everywhere. The room is itself an exercise in theatre. The solidity of its furnishings, though new, announces permanence, their richness, power. Every material element — from the carved marble lintels to the gilded lilies on the wall — contributes to Cosimo's projection of himself and his position in the grand order of human and cosmic affairs.

Paolo is at first dismayed to see that although the Duke himself is not present, Arcivescovo Andrea is. Andrea's appetite for self-aggrandizement could turn even a civic event into a celebration of himself. Andrea, however, shows great restraint as the meeting progresses and defers at all times to the guildsmen and seasoned *consiglieri* who make up the Board. He is in town to hire his painter, not to take on onerous civic duties. Nevertheless it does no harm to sit in on the proceedings. Doing so allows him to learn in advance what opportunities there might be to assume a position of prominence in the celebrations.

The *festaiuoli* look forward to their moment of benign power. They delight in making provisions rather than prohibitions, as they do in their respective guilds and council chambers for the rest of the year. All commerce shall be suspended for three days. New awnings shall be made for the *Battistero* in cloth of blue and gold, to be extended on each of the eight sides. Stands shall be erected in Piazza della Signoria and as well as Santa Croce, for, in addition to the *palio*, which will be run as usual, there will be a display of men at arms. Pageants and displays will entertain the city over the course of three days, beginning with a procession from the cathedral of Santa Maria del Fiore to the great church of San Pier Scheraggio. And Paolo Pallavicino shall be *direttore*.

Paolo has his wish. He will oversee the procession. He outlines his plans again for the Board. The procession will culminate in a lighted pageant performed for the guests of the city inside San Pier Scheraggio at the hour of compline. For this he has commissioned the help of his friends. It is to be a representation of the death of Santa Margherita. There will be a dragon. There will be wings *and* there will be clouds. The clouds will not be the customary shaped and painted wood, but will be formed of wool so finely teased they will appear to float upon the air. Paolo sees them suspended on wires hung from the rafters high above the altar. But here is the thing that will make it beautiful . . . Paolo makes a note in his book while the *festaiuoli* wait: *Let the paste have the addition of some pigment.* The clouds will be pink and blue. He is pleased with this sudden thought that came to him like a gift. *Boys below to bear torches and move to and fro casting light on the floating clouds.* Yes. The clouds will appear as the first blush of dawn. *Smaller boys to be concealed within the nearer clouds.* Santa Margherita will be praying in a painted glade at the foot of the altar. The dragon will enter from the door to the Via della Ninna. Santa Margherita will turn only when the dragon is upon her. She will fall. The doors at the back of the church will open — *Let the attendants cry ho!* — and a horse — *White!* — and rider will appear in the doorway. *Procure the horse.*

Some of the board members have less than nimble imaginations, but Paolo has the mind of a necromancer. He knows how his spectators will turn away from the altar at the crucial moment and look toward the door. When they turn back — *Oil for the pulleys!* — ropes will have let down the foremost cloud. The Holy Trinity in all Its glory will be revealed. The Son will be standing on a platform that operates independently. At a given signal He shall, as befits the Son of Man, come down to Earth and receive Santa Margherita, bearing her up to His Heavenly home.

The Board members are clearly satisfied. Paolo's terms are modest. He asks for only two carpenters to help him, with permission to hire whatever boys they need. He will employ a team of painters to work on a screen that will represent the glade before the altar. He will hire Matteo Tassi. Matteo has energy and ideas. The board members are clearly confident in their choice and promise a contract by the end of the day. They have a large number of other items to attend to but Paolo is still writing.

Paolo only gets up when he has finished his note to himself. *Ask Matteo about the bronze.* As entangled in a project as he might be, Paolo never neglects business.

⌐

THE ARCIVESCOVO IS a man with dreams of greatness. He has a house on Via Porta Rossa near the Porta Guelfa, apartments in Roma and a country house on the road to Galuzzo. His cash boxes overflow with the wealth he has accumulated, but it is not enough. His riches have been acquired in ways that can bring him no honour and are best kept to himself. His dreams of finding himself in high esteem are the product of his waking mind, which is strangely at odds with his mind at sleep. He wakes regularly from disturbing dreams of ridicule or neglect, most of them involving nakedness in public courts. To allay the fears that visit him at night, he has assiduously acquired a gloss of culture. He has found, to his delight, that his patronage of the art of painting not only increases his stature in the city but bestows an unforeseen benefit. A well-executed painting, Andrea discovers, can truly pleasure his senses and, given the right painting and a more intimate setting, his carnal sense in particular.

He has modelled his country house, *Argentara*, on Villa Farnesina in Roma where he once stayed. On the walls and ceilings of his halls he has employed the finest practitioners of perspective to surprise and delight the eye. Visitors to his house are in awe: here a solid wall becomes an open prospect of the hills across the Arno; here the floor seems to join a painted terrace, so that one could step outside the room, could be *in* the prospect; there, at the end of a hallway, a painted door opens to admit a painted valet bearing a dish of meats from the cook; Clarice Strozzi claimed that her dog would not stop barking at the painted dog lying, foreshortened in the painted passage, gnawing at a bone.

In his town house, the painters have been lavish with illusion. Visitors for the first time waiting in the antechamber never fail to duck when, on looking up, they see a painted servant about to drop a pail from a ledge. To work on the Arcivescovo's house is considered an honour. The artists' material rewards, however, are as illusory as the walls, the Arcivescovo being more than a little slippery in matters of money. The prestige is ample compensation.

Orazio waits in the antechamber along with the four other contestants. All assume a blasé, worldly air, as if they are old friends of the Arcivescovo. No one looks up. An officious retainer has taken their completed samples to the adjoining reception room. No one has been told the design the Arcivescovo has in mind but all are hoping for a sizeable commission. Orazio saw two of his rivals at Mass in San Trinità this morning. Andrea celebrates Mass daily, but seldom prays — though his lips form the words. He prefers to negotiate with God privately as he might do with a neighbouring duke. Orazio, on the other hand, seldom goes to Mass but prays hard, especially when he lies sleepless in the small hours remembering good deeds left undone and listening to every agitation of the heart. Seeing the others in the church this morning, he felt suddenly conspicuous in his intentions and stood out of the way of the shafts of light that were striking from the high windows. He made sure to avoid the eyes of his rivals, who in turn did their best to look nonchalant and customary, praying hard for their own success. It was all for nothing. The Arcivescovo chose that morning to keep to his private chapel in the palace.

In the anteroom no one mentions Mass, each man pretending that he stands on invincible turf and has not thought of supplication.

The retainer is ready for them to come in. He has arranged the five panels — one for each artist, including Sofonisba — around the room, leaning them against the walls strategically to catch the morning light from the high windows.

The Arcivescovo comes in without announcement, eating oranges and breasting the air before him with a brilliant white napkin tucked into the neck of his gown. He pauses briefly in the middle of the room and acknowledges the painters with his mouth full of pulp. He picks a fresh orange from the bowl that a serving boy carries and takes a bite out of it like an ape. He walks across to the first painting where he sucks on the orange and deposits the collapsed peel in a bowl carried by a second boy. *A Last Supper.* Drear, thinks Andrea. He has seen this done before. The disciples strung out in a row like that. Nothing magisterial about being betrayed. He moves to the next without offering an opinion. A somnolent *Madonna* with not enough life to detain him. The *Dead*

Christ stops him in mid-stride. He is staring straight at the Christ's closed face. But what is more remarkable is that he is staring straight past the soles of the feet which extend off the edge of the bier and seem to be protruding into the space in which he stands. Their wounds stare back at him like open eyes. His own eye travels the horizontal length of the dead Christ's body from the soles of the feet to the dark curly hair on the headrest. There is a mysterious quality to the face, unmistakably dead yet sentient. Most mysterious of all, at the left side of the painting is a bitten peach on a ledge, its juice lying in a small raised pool. A serving girl is reaching hurriedly to remove it. Andrea knows that this is the painter he wants, but is wise enough to spend a brief moment in front of each of the remaining panels. The last thing he needs is a petulant squabble, accusations of unfairness on this most fair morning. He lingers over a portrait of a bony Sant' Antonio, — starved-looking! — from old Fra Bartolommeo, who will never know how to please, and another *Last Supper* almost identical to the first. He goes back to the somnolent Madonna, pauses as if considering. He is thinking of the *Dead Christ*. The artistry of the picture is altogether astonishing. The figure might almost be expected to rise and draw a resurrectionary breath. Except that it is well past Easter. Andrea tells himself that is a pleasingly clever remark. He will remember it for dinner. He leaves the *Madonna* and moves back to the *Christ*.

"It is this one," the Arcivescovo says. "This is the man who will paint my delicious walls."

He turns to Orazio. "It's yours, isn't it?"

Orazio bows. "I have to say, most reverend *Monsignore*, that it is, in that the hand that painted it both belongs to me and was schooled by me. For the presumption to include in this assembly of candidates the work of my most simple and obedient daughter, your servant, Sofonisba, I most humbly beg your indulgence. Though my method may seem to you unconventional, my motives, *Monsignore*, are pure. Sofonisba is a painter whom I myself have brought to the highest degree of excellency and to such a degree of skill —" Andrea leans close and whispers loudly, emphatically, through juicy lips, "I *said* she is the one. She will start at once. You too. I shall have my secretary draw up the details of the contract."

On his way home, Orazio congratulates himself on his own boldness, thanks God briefly that it did not bring down a heap of invective on his head.

Andrea, now on his seventh orange, congratulates himself. It is a move that could considerably enhance his reputation as a patron. He is thinking of the arrival of the ambassador from the new English Queen. Everyone knows that Pope Clemente some years ago asked for Properzia of Bologna, hoping to appear as discriminating as the Spanish King. It was common knowledge at the time that the Spanish King was himself besotted with a lady painter. Andrea has seen her work. The Spanish ambassador when he was in Roma had a sample. It made its way eventually to Cosimo's house in town where no one could stop talking about it. Cosimo himself then took a sudden interest in yet another, this one named Lucrezia, and it was suddenly the fashion to employ a woman painter. No doubt the English court would like to keep up. Perhaps the capricious Mary would remember his gift more readily if it were painted by a woman. He will have Orazio agree to the painting of a panel as well as the decoration of his wall. But this is all speculation. What is a real pleasure to Andrea, what is indeed a palpable pleasure, is the excitement he derives when he thinks about his own project and the fact that its painter will be a woman. It most admirably suits the design he has in mind. In his bedchamber he will have a curtained wall; behind the curtain and revealed only to his most private visitors, will be a scene of the utmost intimacy, a scene of seduction, tastefully executed of course, and in keeping with his rank in the church.

He has seen a rendition of *Susanna and the Elders*. It hung in the

Palazzo Branconio in Roma and, while he was there, he could not keep his eyes from it. He sat with the papal notary to discuss the health of the Pope. The figure of Susanna, handsomely rounded out with flesh of the freshest pink, occupied one half of the entire picture plane. She sat at her bath on the edge of the stone pool, the lower half of her body in profile, the farther leg raised up on the side of the pool and about to dip into the water, the upper half of her body in the act of turning as she caught a sound behind her, so that her breasts were exposed full to the beholder while her face looked away toward the elders. Listening to the details of the Pope's digestive disorders, he had found his glance straying back to the *Susanna* so that he shared with the elders the excitement of catching the woman unawares. He found himself agreeably aroused. It would be the perfect subject. Only with this difference: his Susanna will be caught as she climbs *from* her bath. The elders shall have seen her most private moments, the viewer her most private place. He does not acknowledge even to himself the pleasure he feels in anticipation of watching a woman's hands paint a woman's body.

WHEN THE CONTRACT ARRIVES, Orazio sees that the commission falls into two parts: the first is for the painting of a wall in the Arcivescovo's bedchamber at his country house; the second for the painting of a panel, a Madonna, to be sent as a gift to the Queen of England, in token of her loyalty to the Church. The payment for each is fixed, as are the subjects and the dimensions of the finished works. Orazio reads on. Every detail is laid down, even the colours. There is a great emphasis on designation: whose hands should paint this, whose that. Sofonisba, he sees, is assigned the most significant portions: the figure of the Madonna and also the child for the panel, and the figure of Susanna for the wall. He is assigned the respective backgrounds and the elders for the wall, "one leaning, one whispering." There is not even enough time allowed. Seven weeks is not sufficient unless they hire help. It does not matter. The Arcivescovo is well connected, the potential for advancement real. Orazio signs.

That evening Orazio instructs Sofonisba to prepare a panel. One is already distempered and needs only the *sottile* to receive the paint.

He sits in the corner of the workshop on a stool and leans back with his eyes closed while he describes the commission.

Sofonisba rolls up her sleeves. She has Chiara rekindle the fire to warm the glue and make the lamps ready for lighting while she prepares the plaster. The panel will need several coats.

"It would be so easy," Orazio says, "if we could simply divide the work, you to the wall, I to the panel. But he's a stubborn man, Andrea. A donkey, if you must know. And he has the purse strings. He wants you to paint the female figure in each. Insists."

"That pleases me."

"Better if you could do the whole wall. You know how I ache."

But Sofonisba is content. Nothing would displease her more than to have to paint the disagreeable elders, secretive and salacious, feasting their eyes on Susanna. She has seen a depiction in the church of San Stefano. She has never liked it.

"And the colours for this panel?"

"I'm tired. Here." Orazio hands her the contract. "You can order from Alessandro tomorrow. Meanwhile you can be attending to the design." He asks her to kiss him goodnight, though it is not yet dark, and goes away to his bed.

Sofonisba mixes her plaster with a small amount of warmed size and stirs it to a silky smoothness. Their eyes on Susanna's smooth skin. The workshop fills with the familiar fish smell of the *sottile*. She leaves Chiara to stir until it cools. She will use Chiara for the Madonna, but she will have to use Orazio's pattern book for the child. A painting of a painting.

When the preparation has cooled, she lays the panel flat on the floor. She has Chiara tie her rolled sleeves to keep them in place and then she wraps an apron tightly round her middle to keep her skirts from spoiling the panel. She kneels and applies the first coat, pleased at the way it flows and disappears smoothly into the coarser ground beneath, like water vanishing on terra cotta.

The next day, Orazio is up at dawn, although his bones protest, and setting out for *Argentara*. He takes the boy with him and wonders about hiring another assistant, perhaps insisting on lodging while he is working out at the villa.

Sofonisba, too, has been up since dawn. She has taken the pre-pared panel, white and flawless, and set it up in the reception room upstairs. She will not paint today, but the unmarked panel will serve to fix the working area in her mind and shape her composition. Chiara sits on the stool a little to the right of the open door. She is wearing one of Sofonisba's gowns and a mantle of crepe edged in silk. Sofonisba settles her and arranges the cherry-coloured satin of the gown in heavy folds. She gives Chiara a bundle: a linen towel folded and loosely rolled and wound with linen bands. She arranges the bundle, the swaddled baby, on Chiara's lap and has her support it with the crook of her arm. Next she gives her a handkerchief and bunches it in Chiara's free hand, making the hand a fist with the point of the handkerchief sticking out of the opening at the thumb. This is the finch that Chiara must show the Holy Infant.

She emits some mildly lunatic noises, baffling to Chiara until she realizes that her mistress is cooing to the towel baby. Chiara laughs and coos and Sofonisba reaches for her drawing book and begins to sketch with a piece of red chalk. She makes drawing after draw-ing, falling gradually into silence. Chiara talks to the towel baby, says, "*Bello. Bell' uccelletto. Bambino bellino.*" Sofonisba works as fast as she can, never quite satisfied that she has caught the look in the eye, the movement round the mouth. The black mapping of Chiara's face, its white dove, are distracting. She wants to catch the essence of the flow from mother to child. Sometimes she rubs at the page with a piece of dry bread and erases what she has recorded.

Suddenly, from nowhere, a lullaby is in the room. Chiara is singing in a language Sofonisba does not understand. The melody is very simple, very beautiful. Chiara's face is suffused with love. The black and the white have disappeared and Sofonisba, herself overtaken by a swift and indescribable tenderness summoned from another place, sees only love. And she captures it. Chiara falters and stops. When she begins again, Sofonisba continues to make her notations. The panel and its terrifying whiteness are forgotten. The room is very quiet.

Sofonisba attends to her drawing, brushing away the fly that lands repeatedly on her bare neck. Again and again she brushes it away without taking her eyes from Chiara, except to glance quickly at the page. Though her hand makes a switching motion like the tail of a horse, Sofonisba herself is oblivious to the fly. She is not there.

"Monna Sofonisba!"

Sofonisba's chalk skips across the page. She jumps up and laughs and beats Tassi on the shoulder as he bends down to pick up the chalk. Chiara has crumpled the towel baby.

"The shop was locked," he says. "The cook next door let me into the yard. She said I was to go on up." He turns and grins. "By myself. I have come to congratulate you."

"Thank you. You heard."

"Of course. But not what he wants of you —" His voice a whisper, hoarse. But Sofonisba is too engrossed in her work to respond.

"I am planning this Madonna and Child as you can see. His gift to the English ambassador. For the Catholic Queen."

"In?"

"In colours tempered with walnut oil. That is his request. To withstand the dampness of the winters, he says. I like that way of working. It takes long to dry. It will still be able to be worked if I am called away."

"By your father."

"Of course."

"You are the perfect daughter. You will make the perfect wife." Tassi reaches for the drawing book with an insincere, "May I?" He will look anyway.

Sofonisba can smell the wine already on his breath and is cross for having answered him so diligently, so earnestly.

He scrutinizes the page with one eyebrow raised in a show of superior judgement.

"Of course," she says. "I am the perfect woman."

"The perfection of humility too."

"Oh, you could teach me that, Messer Matteo, with your modest and retiring manner. We hardly know when you are in the room, do we, Chiara?"

Chiara shakes her head, though she has not been listening.

"But I intend to be the perfect painter."

"I could teach you that, too."

"No, sir, you are many things but not a painter."

"Nor have I wished to be. This fascination for illusion on a single plane when a man can work with many . . ."

"It is because on this single plane a painter can make manifest all manner of things impalpable."

"Oh, 'impalpable!' Think of the sculptor! Think of joy, grief! Pride! Conquest!" He flings his arms about to illustrate his thesis, looks a little off balance. "Desire! Beauty!" He is leaning over her. Sofonisba pushes him in the chest with her elbow.

And yet she wants him to continue. She knows his words are sodden but there is no one else she can speak to in this way, certainly not her father who talks only of expenses and agreements.

"No," she says, "Stone itself cannot convey great distance. Not the coldness of the stars or the heat of the sun. Not sunlight itself or darkness. Or transparency or luminosity or reflection. And not colour certainly."

She takes back her book, says, "Here is the thing that is most difficult. The Child. The Mother is nothing. Love is easy. But Innocence and Majesty . . . It is not possible. They deny each other. And Innocence and Mercy, too. Pure Innocence cannot know evil. Cannot then recognize suffering. Cannot extend Mercy." She is winding her hand round and around a corner of her apron. "Innocence might be a monster."

"Well, your towel is all innocence I can see that." He wanders over to Chiara. "Not a thread of majesty in it. Mercifully."

Absorbed in her problem, Sofonisba ignores him. "If I could find the gesture . . . It is the child's arm here, the hand you see, that is the difficulty."

"It is a difficulty to see any hand at all. I have never seen a child swaddled so tightly."

Chiara turns her shoulder to keep him from taking the towel baby.

Sofonisba looks at the page again, dissatisfied. "But Innocence and Majesty. How to reach for something with the same hand that created it? How to show desire and at the same time consummation? How to indicate that the bird the Child reaches for, desires, is already the perfect fulfilment of His desire as Creator?"

Tassi feels himself excluded. He has struggled with angels of his own. There is no room in the struggle for observer or mentor. It is a private combat from which the creation emerges, leaving the creator breathless and broken until next time. Tassi, though he does not know it, is envious. He tells himself he is looking for entertainment, diversion, not debate.

He says, "But perhaps the Creator's desire is not always 'perfectly' fulfilled. Perhaps the Creator is sometimes surprised. Look at the material, the substance, look only at that and the immaterial will follow. Look at your model."

He stands back, arms akimbo, head cocked, and appraises Chiara. He makes an elaborate show of looking at Sofonisba's work on the page and comparing the seated figure there with the girl at the window.

"Too much drapery," he says. And now he is down on his haunches in front of Chiara like a tailor, moving with a bobbing, simian motion to rearrange the folds of the gown at the floor. "Excess of weight here will unbalance your composition, deflect the path of the eye from its true destiny which is much higher in the picture plane, which is of course —" he gets up and stands back again, resumes his pose next to Sofonisba, tilts his head again critically, then turns suddenly to look Sofonisba in the eye, "— the breast."

Sofonisba is all attention. She is ready to learn.

Tassi loves this look which he can overturn in the blink of an eye.

"The finest Virgins," he says, "will always be those who offer the breast. There is no more tender moment." Sofonisba's expression is curious, inquiring.

"No moment more mysterious. Think of it: the Lord God of Creation at the breast. By attending to the material, you will achieve the immaterial." He holds a cupped palm at his chest. "And don't you think she might have beautiful breasts? The girl, I mean."

He turns smiling to Sofonisba, and she begins to see what he is at. He is close now, his hand reaching, "Like yours." She cracks him on the hand with the edge of her book. He snatches his hand away but she reaches out and does it again, hard.

"I am serious," he says, though he is grinning broadly, his eyes brimming with laughter for the response he has provoked. "But you saw for yourself. You know she has fine breasts. Why not paint them? One anyway." He walks slowly over to Chiara and both women know that something is coming at them.

Sofonisba wants to tell him not to disturb anything else but her tongue refuses.

She watches him bend to Chiara, watches him murmur, lewdness surely, in her ear, unlace the front of her gown, *her* gown, reach inside and draw the breast up, rolling his palm so that it turns out of the dress and is exposed to view.

And Sofonisba feels herself obscenely stirred, and absurdly jealous.

On his way out, Tassi laughs to see that his knuckle has begun to bleed. He puts it in his mouth.

SEVEN

P AOLO PALLAVICINO RETURNED from Firenze with a sheaf of new notes. He took with him a small crew of workers hired from the *Calimala* and the *Ragattieri*. In two weeks he was ready for his friends. And they, for reasons all their own, were ready to make the journey up.

Although he has not once been accosted on the road in the all time he has known Paolo, Orazio says it would be advisable to travel with Alessandro for common safety. Sofonisba thinks it would be entertaining to travel with Matteo Tassi. She sends a message to his shop so that he is sure to know the hour of their departure. And of course she cannot travel without her Chiara. They meet at the Porta al Prato in the soft pink breaking of a May dawn, the five of them performing an unwitting pantomime for the watchman, who has glimpsed the face the *schiavetta* tries to keep concealed. He sees how one man greets her warmly, another spits on the ground and takes out a handkerchief to cover his mouth when she comes close. He sees how the gesture was intended to be observed, and how the others, busy with their greetings, miss it.

"It is pleasant to ride out at this early hour, leaving the sounds of the city behind us."

No one responds to Alessandro's statement of the obvious. The ride is only marred by his conversation. The air is fresh and good. The signature of each tree's leaf and flower can be read on it. It bathes the sleepy skin like cool water. No one has thought to tell Chiara, who walks behind the horses, the nature of the journey, whether or not they are to return. She looks back at the city and sees the tops of its towers rising pink and gold from a pool of shadows.

After the first hour of reining back his horse to keep pace with the rest, Tassi loses patience. At the halfway point he takes pity on Chiara and gets her up behind him on his horse. A little later, when they reach the place where the road flattens out before its ascent to *La Castagna*, he can resist the joy of the morning no longer.

Sofonisba watches him urge his horse into a run. It is all Chiara can do to cling on. The dust from his horse's hooves hangs briefly like puffs of cloud before it vanishes. She on her horse should be running beside him.

In a little while he slows down but still his horse puts more and more distance between them. Chiara is hers. He can only mean it as an affront. He has no right.

"Ah, the mottled one." Paolo smiles as she gets down.

"She would have worn all the skin off her feet, walking all the way up here. And it would have taken us until next week."

"So now you are going to tell me you have ridden so hard you are starving."

Paolo calls Ceccio and tells him to go with Chiara up to the kitchens at the villa and report that Paolo has guests who are hungry.

Ceccio pouts like a fish and receives a clip on the side of the head. He takes the path up to the villa and Chiara, whom no one has thought to direct, follows at a distance.

"And the work on my bronze, Matteo?"

"Progressing, Maestro! Progressing!"

"It is cast?"

"Cast, but not divested."

Paolo accepts Tassi's word but keeps his own opinion. The thing indeed is not cast. Tassi delays. He always delays. It is one of the many stations on the way to creating beauty and it is inhabited by fear and desire both.

"You know I want it soon."

"I know that. And you shall have it."

The cook up at the villa is shaping dough with his warty hands. When Ceccio begins to speak, reciting Paolo's message verbatim, the man turns his head. A crop of warts flourishes on his face. While Ceccio delivers his message, the man keeps his eyes fixed on Chiara. His face darkens. Slowly, slowly, he shakes his head, his eyes still on Chiara's face. His mouth is turned down.

"Not in my kitchen," he says. He jerks his head toward the door. "Get her out, the filth." His voice is very low. He is known for his volcanic eruptions and for roars that can cause landslides on the hill, but this is slow distant thunder and Ceccio is truly alarmed. He turns on Chiara and yells in her face, "Well, get out! Get out, filth!" so that the others in the kitchen take notice and begin to flail the air and join their shrieks with the cook's low grumble, forming a strange choir of mad men and women, an unmusical entertainment for the twenty-seven rabbits hung in a row from hooks on the pole along the wall, their paws benignly crossed.

Chiara runs before anyone thinks of throwing things. Knives, for instance.

When his other guests arrive, Paolo settles them at the trestle that Tassi has set up under the crabapple tree beside the house. Alessandro, stiff and awkward, watches Tassi constantly. Matteo Tassi has helpings of vulgar charm for everyone: Maestro, *you are the prince of pleasures. And we are in Paradise!* And a huge sigh as if he prefers country air to strong wine. *I'm coming to live at your house!* His voice addressing Messer Paolo, his eyes all over Sofonisba. *Here my lady, take this place in the shade!* Aping the courtier: *I insist!* Matteo Tassi, the welcome guest, yet somehow taking upon himself the reflected glory of the host. It is a puzzle.

Tassi gets up when Ceccio comes back, helps him off with the tall, lidded basket.

Ceccio tells the story of the cook. Only Alessandro laughs.

"And?" says Sofonisba.

"And what?"

"And so where is she now, boy?"

Ceccio points. Chiara is sitting on the ground with her back against the wall of the house.

"Good, then." says Tassi, "She can eat with you when we are finished. But don't keep your master waiting. His guests are hungry." And no one protests the way he has appropriated slave, house, servant, breakfast, all. He begins to unpack the basket, handing items to Ceccio to set out. There is bread and white buffalo cheese and three roasted pullets. There are cooked quails' eggs and radishes and fresh green herbs from the cook's own garden, washed and ready to eat. There is plenty of good green oil and salt and there are dried figs and mouth-watering dates from Arabia. Paolo asks Matteo to pour the cool sweet wine. It is the colour of honey.

Orazio is tired after the journey and eats in silence. Tassi has not eaten since the afternoon of the day before. He says, "Breakfast is the finest meal," and does not hide his enjoyment, but it does not stop him talking, as Alessandro wishes it would. Maestro *Paolo, this is a feast indeed! You treat us like princes! . . . And Madonna*

Sofonisba providing sweets for the eyes! What pleasure! . . . More cheese, Messer *Orazio? Here let me help you.* He even has a kiss on his lips that no one sees and that he mouths on the perfumed air toward Sofonisba.

The day is quick to warm; the wine Paolo serves is of the best vintage and Tassi is liberal with it. It is indeed a rich pleasure to sit with full bellies, with bees working the blossom overhead, the subtle apple almost finished and the heady lilac sweetening the air. But Paolo Pallavicino does not want to sit. He is impatient to show off his creation. He tells Ceccio, who has come to clear away the remains of the meal, to go straight to the workshop once he has taken something to eat. The indefatigable energy of the man! When Orazio himself would like to doze.

"Ready?" asks Paolo.

"Eager as an ant," says Orazio with transparent reluctance and hauls himself slowly off the bench. Sofonisba gets up to follow and calls for Chiara. Alessandro fusses. He says the slave would be better left where she is. That she is afflicted and will bring bad luck on the work. Solicitude, he thinks. That would be the thing to impress the old man. Both old men.

Paolo, with a sidelong stare at Alessandro, says the difference between fear and superstition is sometimes barely discernible. Like the line between superstition and stupidity.

Paolo takes his guests round to the granary he uses as a workshed. Two youths are working on an airy wooden structure, a form with ribs, like the skeleton of an inverted boat. The two young men acknowledge Sofonisba with awkward bows. There is a heap of fine linen on the floor, most of it painted, and two tall circular cages, not much wider than a man, curtained with the same.

"Here," Paolo says. "Watch!"

With the two youths, he lifts the painted linen and slides it like a new skin over the framework. Sofonisba is the first to see the dragon and applauds. Its head lolls sideways and shows a gaping mouth. Paolo walks them round the body and explains the technical challenge of keeping it steady and yet light enough to manoeuvre once it is erected on the 'legs,' the two cloth-covered structures that will bear it aloft in the procession. It will require, he says, a number of assistants who must also be artful performers, for their work of supporting the structure will take place under the guise of enactments in the story that is to be portrayed. The dragon will leave the cathedral and walk out into the square. It will circle the *Battistero* for all to see before it turns and enters Via dell' Arcivescovado. Paolo describes the exact route the dragon will take before it makes its approach westward along Via della Ninna to the church of San Pier Scheraggio. All the way, he says, the performers will seem to be goading or attacking the dragon while they are in fact unobtrusively supporting it.

"It is a long way for such a heavy structure," says Sofonisba. She asks Paolo about the combined mass of the materials and Orazio yawns almost as wide as the dragon. He does not want to listen to Paolo's discourse on willow and alder, his detailed comparison of oiled paper and cloth. He would just like to nap.

"Well, then, let us see this marvel in action," he says and rubs his hands together in what he hopes is a conclusive kind of flourish.

"We shall need two more assistants," says Paolo. "Ceccio, you and the girl."

Alessandro protests again, says, "It is wise . . .?" and "Do you really think . . .?"

Paolo ignores him. He directs the youths to pull the dragon upright so that his guests can inspect the beast themselves. Its skin is linen painted red and green with tempera which has yet to be varnished to protect it from moisture in case of rain. It has been ingeniously cut over its surface to give the illusion of scales when the creature walks. Paolo has given it a crest of linen stretched between battens along its spine. Its eyes are hollow. From its mouth, which is protected with finely beaten copper, will hang a heavily oiled cloth. Set ablaze it will produce a quantity of smoke and flame, a lashing tongue. He wants, he says, a monstrous creature to tower above the crowd in the manner of the *giganti* and the old *spiridegli*.

Chiara lets Paolo take her to one of the support columns. Inside the cloth, the framework of each cage is fixed to four casters at the bottom. At the top, a series of inner rings, closely set, forms a tube attached inside the semicircle. Chiara is made to step into the cage. Paolo has a rope thrown over a beam and attached to a sling. He passes the sling under the dragon and with the help of the youths hauls up the body to hover precariously above Chiara's head. Sofonisba sees how the small weighted forelegs acquire vitality with the motion. Ceccio takes his place inside the second pillar and shuffles, pushing it into position. Slowly Paolo lowers the body of the dragon. He hands the end of the rope to one of the youths and tells him to lower or to stop according to his directions. When the projections for the two hind legs are engaged in their sleeves inside the columns, Paolo says, "One thing more." Chiara waits with her eyes closed.

Paolo goes to the side and comes back with a long pole which he fits into a socket under the dragon's muzzle. The dragon now assumes a life of its own and begins to cast its eye about the work-shed in search of food. Tassi at once responds and offers it his hat.

"Now we walk," Paolo says. He shouts as if the two servants inside the legs are a great distance off. "You, Ceccio! Walk, walk! Stop! Chiara you! You, Chiara —"

It takes Chiara, in her darkness, a few moments to realize she is being addressed.

"You! Walk! Push, push! Walk! Stop!"

"'Cio! You now, walk! Walk! Stop!"

"Chiara! . . ." The dragon appears to be limping.

When Tassi begins to goad it for the entertainment of Sofonisba, Orazio stifles another yawn.

"And now, Maestro?" he says. "You have more to show us?"

When the dragon is dismantled, Paolo takes his visitors up to the stone byre to discuss the wings they will be painting. Fourteen pairs hang from hooks in the rafters. Paolo says the cloud supports for the angels will be constructed at the cathedral workshop but he has been able to advance the construction of the wings with the help of two brothers skilled in working with canvas. For the wings they have used linen as fine as muslin. They will carry the light within them. Paolo has marked out one pair with a design to serve as a pattern for the rest. They are to be resplendent in red and blue and gold. Alessandro has brought the order, a small quantity of choice red lac — to be prepared in the old style, with gum, and to be used with blue for producing a fine violet — a quantity of vermilion finely ground, even more of German blue and a good quantity of white lead. The detailed instructions call for a great deal of gold leaf, for which yellow tin will suffice, provided it is worked up nicely with the lead and with orpiment too, if necessary.

Sofonisba looks at the wings, each pair identical to the one before.

"I think we should begin at once," she says. Orazio, too, is daunted but says he must relieve himself and will be back shortly.

Paolo says, "I'll leave you with Matteo then. He can show you how to begin.

"And Alessandro you can come with me and help finish the linen for the dragon. Then you can get back to your father. There won't be any more for you to do here."

On his way from Paolo's house to the road, Alessandro sees a grey cat sleeping in the low sun. Orazio was nowhere to be seen when he left. Matteo Tassi and Sofonisba Fabroni were painting together.

He bends down, picks up a large piece of rubble and hurls it with all his force at the cat.

Paolo has decided that the forty sacks of wool should be delivered straight to the cathedral where the tinting and starching can be carried out in one operation when the wool is teased. The painters have only to take care of the brushwork on the stretched linen of the angels' wings. Tassi struts and inspects and corrects while Orazio dozes in the sun. Sofonisba sits patiently — for who would take orders from a woman? — and paints in blue and red and violet and white, aligning long, unlikely celestial feathers. When they are dry they are picked out in king's yellow, tipped with gold. The wings will be the most beautiful the congregation has seen. The angels will remain hidden until the signal. Then they will emerge as one with their backs to the church and display the glory of their extended wings, while the choir sings a *Gloria*. There are fourteen angels. Sofonisba will be bored before she has finished the second pair.

CHIARA KEEPS THE LAMPS trimmed for Matteo and Sofonisba in the byre. They have painted all day and will continue until the wings are finished. Chiara is to see that they have enough light. Her task would be easier if only they would work on the same side of the byre, but tonight their friendship is acid. It has passed through familiar banter and rough teasing into insults and offense. They have infected Orazio and Paolo with their anger and now they work in silence. Orazio said that to be in their company was like being in the company of unruly children: they disturb the peace and then they sulk. He went away to sleep in the bed that Paolo had given up for him. Paolo went back to the house to work in his *studio* on a new design for the counterweights.

It is almost midnight and there are still wings to paint when Chiara falls asleep. The silence fills with possibility, with impossibility. Sofonisba has done her best to wound Tassi for the insult of riding off with her own slave and leaving dust in their faces. She has defamed his name and discredited his work. She has blackened his intentions, saying all he wanted was a share in her father's business. She said, hissed, that his true home was the brothel and his companions were gallows birds. It was the reference to the hanged woman that offended him most. Quietly she puts down her brush and goes across to where Matteo is painting. She bends down behind him, asks forgiveness in a whisper, and then they are clasped to one another like shipwrecked mariners rocking in the ocean's night and would drown in it splendidly, but Tassi wants to savour this surrender. He would like to see how the soft light of contrition might look, that tastes so sweet. He leans away, lifts a strand of her hair. "My beautiful penitent. My slave."

Sofonisba glances at the corner of the room where Chiara is sleeping. She is suddenly afraid of being observed. What if Maestro Paolo should come back? She tries to quiet her breathing.

Tassi draws her face close again.

"The slave might wake, Messer Matteo."

"The slave might enjoy it. I should wake her." The joke means nothing, is merely spice for the banquet Tassi has in mind. But Sofonisba pulls away.

"And you? Would you enjoy it, Matteo? Perhaps you should have the slave."

She cannot help herself. She stands up angrily. Waking Chiara, smoothing her dress, she picks up a lamp and leaves. Chiara has to hurry to keep up.

In the kitchen down at the house, Ceccio is sleeping on the table, lying with his limbs sprawled and his beautiful face turned away as if he had been struck and had fallen there. Sofonisba wakes him and tells him to take her to a bed. He snorts, coughs and, looking not at all beautiful, breaks wind; then he shows them to a small upper chamber and stands holding the door open with one hand while he picks his nose with the other.

Sofonisba does not tell Chiara where she is to sleep. She gets into bed and tells her to return to the byre.

Chiara looks longingly at the floor beside the bed. Her feet are cold and wet. She would gladly curl up without even a pallet rather than return into the night. Sofonisba mistakes her hesitation.

"Go now. Messer Matteo wants you." She tells her to leave the lamp and take one of the candle stubs from the chest.

In the byre Matteo Tassi is painting like a madman. He has lined up the remaining wings against the wall and is working from one to the next along the row and back again. Chiara in the doorway makes him jump. He paints on, says, "Well?"

Chiara says, "My mistress sends me to you."

She stands there shielding the guttering candle, her eyes wide, unsure.

"She does, does she?" He paints on in silence. At last he says, "Well, I can use you. You can move the lamps for me. Or, let's see if you can paint. You'll be no good to me falling asleep." He puts a brush in her hand and has her follow behind, showing her first which feather to paint, the same on all. She spoils the first with drips, has learned how by the second. Tassi stops after a while to prepare the powdered tin and the gold which will finish them. Chiara paints on as he showed her and then he says she can rest. When she wakes, Tassi is surveying his work. The last pair of wings is on the table in the middle where the cleaver and the saws hang. Thirteen pairs of wings in red and gold and blue and violet hang from hooks around the walls, a plague of giant moths from somewhere larger than the sky.

Tassi is pleased. He tells Chiara to take a lamp and fetch Maestro Paolo from the *studio*.

It is still dark. Chiara makes her way back down to the house, the night air striking her face, the grass sending needles of cold between her toes. The lamp is a comfort. There is a light burning in the *studio* but Paolo does not answer her knock. The darkness is at her back. The old man's anger is preferable and she goes inside.

Paolo is not there but he is still working, for he has set many candles by his notebook. Chiara looks. There is a drawing of the small dragon in the menagerie. It is covered with little leaves. Marks on the page indicate light bursting forth. On the opposite side there is a drawing of the machinery for the clouds. It is drawn over many times and covered with writing like the tight tendrils of a vine. She turns the page and frowns. She cannot say what she sees there. There is no name for it; an angel, but unclothed in the way that demons are. And yet its wing, the one that is shown, is not leathery but large and feathered. Its face, too, is the face of an angel, beautiful like Ceccio's. It gazes on something that is not visible, that is just behind the viewer's own gaze, something that it shows by its expression to be beautiful beyond measure. But what holds Chiara's gaze is that there is no way to tell if this angel be man or woman, for it is neither — or rather, is both. Below its neck and shoulders, Paolo has shown the full breasts of a young woman and beneath them the smooth and hairless belly of a girl, but with no plumpness or roundness beneath the navel. And then there in the groin, to confuse the eye and overturn the mind, from a nest of tight hair rises its male member, thick like the shaft of a donkey and sticking up at an angle like the flag poles on the wall of the Palazzo Vecchio. Chiara, dizzy with looking, laughs out loud.

At the sound of Paolo's footsteps she moves back quickly to the door.

"Messer Matteo is finished and asks you to come."

"Good," says Paolo, "Is he? Yes. Good." But he sits down again at his desk and she leaves him there, drawing over his drawing, his back bent, his head inclined.

Sofonisba turns over when she hears the door creak open.

"Chiara?"

"Yes." Chiara squeezes the door shut as quietly as she can and goes to get the blanket that has been left for her on the chest. She takes off her gown so that she can roll it for a pillow, then wraps herself in the blanket and lies down behind the door. Sleep is a warm wave and it is easy to slip under. But in her bed, Sofonisba turns and turns.

Eastward along the valley, a thin line of lemon-pink light marks the place where the dark hills meet the sky.

Matteo Tassi, seated on the floor of the byre, has fallen asleep waiting for Paolo with his knees pulled up and his head resting on his arm.

EIGHT

In his room, with his door locked, Alessandro lays out the pieces of skin. They have a parchment feel to them still. Nevertheless he cannot wait any longer. He has waited weeks, keeping his door locked since he acquired them, taking the key with him whenever he went out so that no one could come poking about, and lying to his father that the old woman who cooks for them can't be trusted, that things have gone missing. He kept the skins soaking in a bucket of lime inside a wooden chest. After the first three days he took them out, wrapped them in an oiled cloth and carried them to a secluded part of the river. There he took a blade and scraped them clean of shreds of flesh and hairs, stretching them out, shearing away the tiny withered puckers of nipple. The skins had a repulsive look and rancid smell about them like old tallow. He rinsed them off, cleaned the cloth and wrapped them up again. In the town, he purchased a small quantity of oak tan and took it home. First he spread the skins to dry on the floor of his balcony where the afternoon sun played. He left them out for the next five days, bringing them in at night in case of rats. They stiffened as they dried. When he judged them ready, he made up the bucket of oak tan. The skins have been soaking in it in the locked chest behind his locked door for more than two weeks. Long enough to colour them a little, but not long enough to make them truly supple. There is still a certain stiffness when he picks them up. Nevertheless, he cannot wait. Today when he woke he burned with jealousy at the thought of Tassi and Sofonisba in each other's company up at the villa. He can still hear Paolo's voice: *You can go back today. We have all we need now to finish the task*. We. And Tassi not even a painter.

Nor are those the only words that Alessandro hears. *What you most desire shall come to pass*. He hears Ceccio's voice too, strangely dressed in the rhythms and the timbre of Maestro Paolo. The words were what kept him there, standing in the shadows when his feet wanted to tear away. *What you most desire*. What Alessandro most desires is to lie down with Sofonisba and her impressive shoulders, her magnificent breasts. *What you most desire shall come to pass*. And now that Matteo Tassi is trumping him at every play, he desires her more than ever. Alessandro is ready to believe.

He trims the ragged edges of the skins, takes a stout needle and a narrow leather lace, and begins to sew. The stitches are small and evenly spaced. He sews the shoulders together along the top and then the sides, starting underneath the armholes. A vest for a ghoul. He makes eight small holes, four in each of the open front edges so that it can be laced closed. Perhaps to put off the next moment, or perhaps because he finds the repetitive action soothing, Alessandro oversews the raw edges: down both sides in the front — he has to interrupt his work to find more laces — around the bottom, the armholes, the neck. He takes off his doublet and his shirt and slips it on. His own flesh recoils spontaneously. He lifts his shoulders and rounds them so that the vest falls away from the skin of his chest, but then he can feel it against his back. His stomach drives itself up under his ribcage and he has to fight the urge to retch. His whole upper body is twitching, flinching from each point of contact with the skin. He twists and lets fall one shoulder, shakes himself out of it and reaches round to pluck it off the other. He flings it onto the table. Now he seems suddenly to need to draw giant breaths. He tries again. He picks it up, holding it out in front of him by the thumb and forefinger of each hand. He holds it up by the shoulders. He likes the look of it now. Yes, the very thought of it pleases him rigid. Still breathing deeply, calmly, his mouth shut tight, he puts it on. He will not let himself look down. He struts about, enjoying himself to the full. This resurrection of the flesh is a benefit he had not anticipated; it is surely a sign. The world is his. He opens his shutters and stands at the window, looking down into the street. His father's friend, Domenico, walking on the other side of the street and hearing the shutters as he approaches, looks up and waves in greeting. Alessandro's erection is all but crippling. He closes the shutters and deals with it and then he takes himself down to the street. It gives him the greatest pleasure to walk about like this, clothed in a secret power.

⌒

TASSI SADDLES HIS HORSE for the ride back. By the time he reaches the gates of the town, the road behind is dotted all along with travellers. Every day more come in from the surrounding country-side in anticipation of the festivities. The black and white marble *battistero* of San Giovanni is transformed to a gay pavilion by awnings of blue and gold extending from each of its eight sides. The colours are echoed over at the *campanile* where, just beneath the carved saints, the lower walls have been hung with blue and gold gonfalons. Everywhere there are workmen, even at this hour. Farther on, the piazza in front of the Palazzo Vecchio is crawling with carpenters erecting stands and platforms in front of the buildings. There are stands even against the façade of the Mercantantia and a platform jutting out over its door. The Palazzo itself has been hung with flags on every side and last year's tapers have been carried down from San Giovanni and piled under the great platform, the *ringhiera*, ready to be brought out and burned together in a spectacle of light.

Tassi ignores it all and goes straight to his workshop. He is angry with Paolo who kept him waiting half the night. Who looked at the wings that he'd gone half blind over and said: "They could be brightened, I think, with a touch more gold." Who turned suddenly and said, as if only then remembering he, Matteo, existed: "And the bronze? Tell me again. It will be ready when?" Well, he'll show Paolo a bronze. He'll show him infernal perfection.

But it is not only Paolo. It is not Paolo at all. It is Sofonisba. Sending the girl to him at the dead of night. For an insult? For a joke? Had he cared to search long enough he would have found the sore: to be offered *as an insult* the very slave that he has enjoyed, that he does enjoy. But Matteo is not a man to pull apart his own innards and inspect them when they gnaw at him. He acts — which is why he is heading now for his workshop.

Something draws Tassi in a direct path, like a pigeon to roost. It is a force he recognizes and it always begins with a longing in his belly like hunger and spreads to the roots of his teeth, like the urge to bite. On the way down from Paolo's, it spread from his jaw to his neck to his shoulders, his chest, his arms, hands, fingers. The Devil take Paolo with his carping and his nagging. The Devil take him with all his elaborate mechanical wonders and all his artifice. And the Devil take Sofonisba too, who makes him think she is his then turns aside, offers the slave instead. The slave is his own creation. Chiaroscuro. Shadow and light.

But enough. To work, to create.

Paolo expects his bronze. Despite his preoccupation with the *festa*, he does not forget. He wants to have the bronze in his hands, wants to be able to choose the perfect moment to present it to Giuliano. Well, then, give the old man what he wants. With a pouch full of the city's coins to buy this, to buy that, to pay these, to pay those, the old bugger might even pay for it on time.

Tassi's boy is glad to see him back even if it means an end to leisure. Tassi sends him to take the hand cart and find wood. He will need a great quantity and will have to make several trips. He is to beg it if necessary in the name of Paolo Pallavicino and *Signor* Giuliano. "Never mind if they think it's for the *festa*," he says. "They'll be only more willing."

The one thing that matters is the indescribable beauty of the flawless — and Tassi has it, or anyway its possibility, encased in its jacket of dung and clay and waiting to be revealed by fire.

When Tassi is casting, as he is today, he works in the courtyard, where a shelter of wood projects from the back wall of the narrow house. He builds his furnace in the centre of the yard. His landlord is an old man who sleeps the day through in his aerie on the top floor. He would like to forbid the building of these fires but he has never yet woken in time to stop one before it is well underway, and then it is too late. He is always overcome by Tassi's brutal bonhomie and his unanswerable assurances, and Tassi can always prove beyond a doubt that the fire presents no danger at all, for you see, sir, your house is clearly standing. Have a drink.

Tassi constructs his furnace with loose brick around the mould and starts a fire with the pine wood he has on hand. He leaves it to draw out the wax from the mould and digs out his casting pit beside it. As soon as the boy returns with the first load of wood, he feeds the fire. It is good dry oak and burns fiercely. It cooks a sausage resting on the brick, a reward for the boy, in no time. As Tassi expects, he is interrupted by his gummy-eyed landlord, who, when he finally wakes, comes down to sputter weakly about eviction. But it is a half-hearted complaint. His attention has been caught by the delicious aroma of the sausage. Tassi sits him down with lies about the statue — which he says is a Christ child for a nativity group — lies about his payment in advance — which he says will pay his rent in arrears — and then distracts him with a tale his friend Lavinia told about a well-known *priore*. When he tells him he may take the sausage away, the landlord leaves.

While the boy tends the fire, keeping it hot enough to bake the clay, Tassi prepares his crucible, filling it with pigs of copper and tin and fragments of former castings. Now there is nothing more for him to do. He must wait for the firing of his mould to be finished. This is the moment of lack, of highest expectation. It is the moment he loves, for lack is the essence of true beauty. This is the tension that drives him forward to create anew. He both lives for this access of desire and finds it unbearable. He snatches up his velvet cap and gives the boy a coin. Enough of dedication, enough of work. The whole of Firenze is at his disposal.

Out in the town people are still about. The sound of hammering echoes from the walls down at the piazza, where the carpenters are still working against the fading light. Anticipation is in the air and Tassi knows how to turn it to excitement. He makes his way northeast along Via Bufalini. It is not long before he has caught up with Bianca who is dining at the Pucci house and who could charm the locks off a prison door. In a little while he is as well-fed and as drunk as they are. When someone reports that there is movement on the road down from *La Castagna* he entices the entire party out into the night. They make their tipsy way through the narrow streets, the tops of the houses seeming to lean toward each other over their heads like sleeping soldiers. At the Porta San Gallo they bully the watchman and climb the stairs to the top of the wall to view an unearthly moonlit convoy lurching and swaying down the hill. They can see little at first but an intermittent gleaming where there should be none, and then they make out the lanterns and then the shapes of white oxen plainly visible now, the dark bulk of the two carts they draw, and the shapes of laden mules. As the convoy approaches they can see it is accompanied by some of Cosimo's own guard from the city. The moonlight glances off their helmets.

"What is in the carts?" Bianca does not know why she is whispering. Tassi whispers back. "Pieces of Heaven come to assault the town."

A messenger has instructed the watch at the gate to open and admit the convoy on demand so that they can make their way, as quietly and as quickly as two wagons and a number of mules will allow. Nevertheless, the road from San Lorenzo to Santa Maria del Fiore has begun to fill with the curious who defy the curfew and come in numbers to speculate on what new astonishments might lie under the canvases.

When Tassi gets back in the morning, the fire has died down as he knew it would, and the boy is dozing in its generous warmth. The real work begins.

Together he and the boy knock away the bricks and transfer the mould to the pit, standing the crucible in its place and rebuilding the furnace round it, packing the space between with fresh wood. While the boy keeps the fire high, Tassi fills in the pit and tamps down the earth and sand until only the vents and the casting mouth are exposed. He is constructing a pouring channel to the mouth of the mould when the grumbling landlord reappears. It takes the promise of half a cheese this time to make him go away.

By the end of the afternoon, the crucible inside the furnace takes on a dull red and the boy at last sees an end to his trips for loads of wood. The heat now is so intense that Tassi has to put on his leather apron to protect his legs when he checks the metal. Finally, at about the hour of the evening angelus, the crucible begins to glow more brightly and the pigs of metal begin to soften and slide inside. Yet still they refuse to liquify though the light from the heart of the furnace is like a small sun rising. In desperation, Tassi sends the boy into the house for two of his pewter plates and, when he returns, flings them into the crucible. It glows steadily brighter, and at last sparks fly up from the vapours as the metal melts into itself. It is difficult to approach. Tassi stirs the cake of metal with a long rod wrapped about the handle end with leather and tells the boy to bring the pouring ring. He makes him stand aside while he knocks the bricks of the furnace down. With his long apron he might be a demented baker. Now the crucible stands, glowing the sunset orange of a pumpkin in the field. It is a thing alive, making liquid burps and belches. It is almost unapproachable. There are two iron handles that hook into the rings on the side of the crucible. Tassi wraps the boy's hands and arms with rags for protection and gives him one of the handles. Together, carefully they lift the crucible out and onto the iron pouring ring. Tassi stirs once more, making this strange substance, part fire, part earth, spit. They lift the crucible and carry it to the mould, wizards at an inscrutable rite, and they pour, confounding the elements. Earth, water, fire is all and is none. Tassi's eyes flick to the boy's face. The boy's tongue is jammed between his teeth. Tassi grins and feels a surge of warmth within as the mould receives the bronze.

That evening at the tavern, he is a wild man.

NINE

Paolo pallavicino is in the great church of San Pier Scheraggio. The angels' wings and the parts for the clouds have been transported safely, while the dragon lies on the floor of the Cathedral like a ship that has sailed onto the stones of the city. Paolo has gathered his team of workmen in the nave of San Pier. Some are already constructing the screen which is to stand in front of the altar. When it is ready, the painters will work on it to create the illusion of four great pillars of stone, between which will be glimpsed not the altar, but vistas of distant country painted on the three panels, scenes of mountain and rock, tree and stream and cave.

Paolo's vision expands continually. He has spread out his plans and his notes and is describing to a sceptical carpenter how the Holy Trinity will at first be concealed in Their cloud above the rood loft. They will remain concealed while the dragon enters and will not be revealed until the moment that it is slain. Then the horns will sound, rending the air, says Paolo, so that the heavens part. It will be a scene of great terror, revealing the glory of God. It must be done, he says, with the greatest possible ease so that the spectators detect no artifice. The carpenter looks doubtful. Paolo Pallavicino is asking him to work at a very great height. He says the scaffolding will have to be of double poles to support its own weight. Paolo Pallavicino bears objections well. He is used to them. Patiently he points out the indication for temporary scaffolding to take lines up to the rafters. He explains that the structure is to be built on the ground. A system of pulleys will raise it to its proper place under the tie beams. The arrangement is not only practical but essential to the unfolding of the drama itself, for the same system of pulleys will be used to raise and lower the players. He leads the carpenter back to the plans and shows him again.

"We'll need some good lengths of rope," says the carpenter.

"We shall indeed." Paolo taps his finger on the scribbled calculations. "Twenty-seven hundred and fifty-eight *braccia*, to be exact. Twenty-seven hundred and ninety-eight if we allow forty for any shortfall."

Paolo has his work space in the north transept. He has had the door to the Via della Ninna closed off and screens constructed to fence off the area from the curious, who have already poked holes in the canvas so that they can be the first to see what is being prepared. Rumours abound. At first Paolo was hampered by frequent interruptions from citizens who heard talk of a representation of the Godhead and imagined their personal apotheosis in the role. Paolo let it be known that he would stop work for no one. He would make his selection of players on the Thursday morning at the hour before the angelus.

At the appointed hour, forty-six men, all of whom call themselves players, arrive for the selection. Twenty-seven wish to play the part of God the Father. Paolo tells the workmen they must get on without him for a while. Nineteen have asked to play the Son. The Holy Ghost is easy. Paolo selects the smallest youth, Asciano, a lad of ten or so who is undersized and very light. He will wear the costume of a dove. For the Saviour he chooses Stefano, the unruly son of the sacristan over at San Lorenzo. Because his ribs show prominently giving him a convincingly agonized look, Stefano has been crucified twice before. There are protests. Others would like the opportunity to be exhibited to the public gaze. One, an old and dissolute wool finisher with painful, weeping ulcers on his neck, tries tears and histrionics. He had hoped that to play the part of the Saviour might somehow save him from the torments he feels certain are in store, that have, his skin can testify, already begun.

Paolo ignores him and surveys the hopeful Fathers. Several old men have come forward. He is in the process of dismissing them when the west door opens and a retainer announces a *Signor* Ercole. Paolo's heart sinks. He has already received a letter from Arcivescovo Andrea declaring his wish that this Ercole, presented as his nephew, take the part of God. Ercole, as everyone knows, is not the Arcivescovo's nephew but his son, a man of considerable influence with connections reaching to Cosimo himself. "*Monsignore*," Paolo says, "We are honoured." Ercole, he notices with annoyance, is standing on his design for the pulleys that will raise the platform.

"Maestro Paolo. You are always up to something new. Show me what you have."

Paolo suppresses a sigh and tells the workmen he will be a little while still. His crew wander off outside, in search of something to refresh themselves or simply to piss against the wall, while Paolo goes over the outline of the performance, without, he hopes, giving away precisely how it is to be achieved.

"A revelation of glory," Ercole pretends a consideration of something that has not occurred to him before. "Requiring, no doubt, a prominent public figure of sufficient standing?"

So here it comes again, this disgraceful, time-consuming, soul-rotting need to fawn, to walk again on eggs.

"Were it to be a symbolic representation, yes, *Monsignore*, but our performance is an entertainment, I fear to say." How he wishes he were deaf to the drivel that is coming from his mouth. "Our modest distraction will not support such grandeur. It is all illusion. Behind the apparitions stand the lowest, most dissolute and scurvy actors who make their meagre living in this way."

Ercole is frowning. "Who, then, will play the parts?"

"Asciano over there — whose mother is the whore Lucrezia — takes the part of the Holy Ghost (may his soul be washed clean of his mother's sins in time). And Stefano plays our blessed Saviour (Stefano who, as you know, came out of prison this last month . . .)."

"And —"

"And God the Father —" Paolo Pallavicino makes a quick decision and points toward the most frail of the old men. "We have to keep the load as light as possible."

Ercole looks from one to the other of the Holy Trinity, his eyes flicking restlessly between Father, Son, and Holy Ghost.

He draws a breath. "Good. Excellent. And there will be, as you said, a raised platform for viewing?"

Paolo almost bites his tongue.

"Certainly, *Monsignore*. There will be a raised platform. We shall have it adorned in the colours of your desiring." He makes a mental note to send for additional funds.

⌒

IT HAS BEEN AGREED that until Paolo is ready for the painters in the church, Orazio will begin the preparation of the wall at *Argentara* and Sofonisba will remain at the shop to work on the painted panel.

Chiara sits again for the *Madonna and Finch* while Sofonisba, her eyes accustomed to her markings, blind to them, works in silence. Chiara has become an accomplished sitter, not restless, able to speak without moving. Her position in Orazio's house — and in Sofonisba's own life — is becoming increasingly complex. She is both maidservant and model, ally and companion; she can laugh, providing Orazio is not present, as loudly as Sofonisba at the bad-tempered or the foolish. But since the night at Paolo's she has taken on some other colour that Sofonisba cannot name. In her response to it lies the possibility of execration. It is always possible to revile the powerless, not for themselves (nor even, in Chiara's case, for the way she looks), but for simply being there when rage and disappointment strike. Sofonisba knows that it is the fate of the lapdog to receive the kick when the reverses of the world afflict the house. But this morning it was something more, like a colour caught out of the corner of the eye.

Sofonisba had woken that morning with a longing like an ache between her legs and deep inside. She had been dreaming of Tassi and she was both herself and Tassi together, seeing her own body displayed for his pleasure, she one of his prostitutes. Awake, she could still feel his nose and mouth at her neck in the place he has nuzzled before, but now in the memory of her dream it gave her pleasure so intense it could hardly be told from pain. She tried to hold on to the picture, tried to relive the dream and moaned softly as it faded.

She kicked Chiara awake at the foot of the bed.

"Tell me again what you told me about Matteo." Her voice was thick and strange to her. For a few moments, Chiara, just waking, didn't answer.

"What you told me yesterday."

"What Messer Matteo told me?"

"Yes."

"About Bianca?"

"Any of them."

Chiara's mouth made sleepy, unintelligible noises.

Sofonisba said, "Tell me."

And so Chiara repeated what she had already told Sofonisba, the stories Matteo Tassi had told her in the early hours of the morning up there on the hill; had told because he knew she would repeat them, licentious whisperings only fit for a slave. They fell, as Tassi had known they would, like inflictions on Sofonisba's heart. She wanted to receive them again.

"He said he came upon Bianca lying with a woman and her face was where his prick should be."

"Go on."

"He said Bianca laughed and made room for him to try it."

"And?"

"And he did."

"Tell me."

"What?"

"Tell me what he did."

"He put his face there."

"Where?"

"Between the woman's legs."

Sofonisba ached everywhere with desire. Even her arse ached. She would have liked to kick Chiara to make her carry on, but her hand was between her own legs. She did not want to move.

She looked and looked at the image behind her eyes. She hated Chiara for it yet she wanted it sharpened.

"Tell me."

"So he put his face there and Bianca went round behind him and put her face to the place where he sits."

Chiara burst into explosive laughter.

Sofonisba was grateful for the sound which masked the noise coming from her own throat as something deep inside her gathered itself for release.

She said, "You'll go to Hell. Get out."

Sofonisba is painting Chiara out of existence. She arranges her draperies to match the painted pose. The figures of both the Mother and Child are blocked in on the panel in *verdaccio*, the details of their features picked out in *sinopia*, the Virgin seated with the mantle now covering her head and shoulders so that only her face and part of her neck are exposed. This time it is the Child on her lap who holds the finch. The figure of the Child has assumed for Sofonisba the vitality of poise and gesture that she was seeking, a perfect balance between desire and release, the hand that holds the bird keeping it close even as the arm moves to set it free. This is the real work and Sofonisba knows she has achieved her purpose. The rest, the colouring, the modelling of the forms, is merely finish.

She has worked up her colours for the drapery. She has a row of little dishes nearby. They contain the lac, carefully prepared in stepped values from dark to light as her father has taught her. She loves the rhythm of this way of working. She likes the way the predictability of the method can still yield surprise; she likes the fact that just five little dishes can mimic the endless ruses of the light upon a colour, the infinite variety of Nature. Most of all she loves the way her thoughts disappear when she attends to the technique she has learned. Her hands replace all thought. Her hands become the work and the work becomes herself. It is a charmed circle none can enter, as long as she is painting. And when she has finished . . . there is the paradox. The painting becomes a thing in itself. It leaves her hands and it enters the world. What was part of herself leaves — and yet when it is gone nothing is lacking; she is already heavy with the next.

Tassi wakes to a morning shining with possibility. The day is different from every other. The world today will be changed from the world of yesterday by a new presence. The same deep and private excitement that drives the woman in labour, the same steady sense of desire, drives Tassi.

He gets up, relieves himself in the pot. He passes the palm of his hand over his face as if sleep is a web that has covered him in the night. He rubs his scalp briskly with a towel to restore thought and then he dresses, pours water from the pitcher and drinks like a man in a hurry.

The boy has not woken. Tassi leaves him to sleep a little longer.

Out in the yard, the excitement in the pit of his stomach is intense, is almost pain. He digs out the mould. It is still hot like a loaf fresh from the oven. Tassi carries it to the stones in front of the bench and sets it down. He knocks away the iron bands with a hammer, then he aims a careful blow at the mould itself. A chunk falls away and then another. He continues to strike the mould methodically, turning it, careful not to strike too hard. His blows diminish in force as the pile of fragments grows. He chips through to the bronze itself using a small hammer and a blunt chisel, working delicately. The thing is intact. The figure begins to reveal itself and now he can pick away the rest. Here is no beauty but a swollen crusted bug, the tributary sprues like legs which cling to the twig of the main sprue. The heads of the pins stud the bronze like warts. The surface itself has the texture of bark. Everywhere the remnants of the clay jacket distract the eye. But Tassi is smiling. It is complete. He is the mother who has counted the toes of her infant.

"Food!" He roars through the door to the shop. "Get up boy and get us some food!"

By the time the boy appears with a dish of black bread soaked in broth and a piece of sweaty cheese, Tassi has sawn away the sprues and is starting on the pins. The bug now has lost its legs and is looking strangely human — and strangely inhuman. The boy offers his opinion that it is an ugly little sod.

"You have no eyes to see," says Tassi.

"Where do you want this?" the boy asks, and Tassi says, "Right here," nodding to his left but not looking up once from his work. The work of his hands seizes his soul. This is the work of breaking out beauty. Time no longer exists. Tassi no longer exists.

He works all day and eats only once. When a message comes from Paolo he tells the boy to say he is not at home. By the end of the day the figure is divested of all traces of the vents and pins, cleaned of all remnants of the clay that had adhered between its fingers and toes and in the folds of its small limbs. Its surface is imprinted with a delicate tracery of imperfections from the *luto*, as if the marks of its own caul remain. It is as if the bronze child within the furnace had drawn a breath and held it, exhaling when the skin on the cooling metal began to form so that it wrinkled a little here, there pulled away in delicate flakes. Tassi does not want to leave this work. It is clean enough now to see that beyond this surface the body itself is perfection. He will work through the night. He will polish the skin to rose petal smoothness. He will incise the indentation at the base of every finger nail, the space between each eyelash. He will light a blaze of candles and work until it is done.

And he will not give it over to Paolo and his callipers.

～

WHEN THE NEXT DAY DAWNS, the bronze child sleeps in immaculate stillness on the bench.

The child is beautiful with its strange blunted features, the head that is too big, the eyes that bulge slightly. Its arms are crossed over its chest, the outer hand tentatively open, the palm down at an angle, almost a gesture of refusal, or deflection. The hand on the inside is curled in a fist as if it beats its breast for all the sins of man. It strikes Tassi with pity and with wonder and he does not want to let it go, as if the child had brought to him some inkling of its origin.

It is a mystery. If Paolo were to take his callipers to this child, its beauty would defy him, its imperfection defeat him. The proportions will not do. Here is no geometry of perfect circle, perfect square. This is some errant mean, some hidden rule producing glory, unseen yet apprehended.

There is still work to do. Tassi knows he is not going to give this bronze to Paolo. If he gives it to anyone it will be to Sofonisba. He does not need to finish it. He leaves it and goes through to his bed where the boy is sleeping spread-eagled in unwonted luxury. From the chest at the foot of the bed, Tassi takes a piece of velvet the colour of lapis. He goes back and wraps the bronze and returns the bundle to the chest, stuffing it in as if it were nothing. As if this act of concealment were itself nothing, of no consequence to him and no significance in the world at all.

But no action, however heedless, can be truly bare of consequence. Our deeds stick in the flow of things like rocks in a stream that cause the flood to turn. Only looking back from a great distance or down from a great height might it be possible to see how some that were meant for ill might be turned to good, as the stream itself might turn the rock.

All his life Tassi had obeyed no laws but those his nature dictated and they had served him well, whether he had flesh or crusts to eat, whether he had wine or water to drink. Lusts he may have had in abundance, appetites without limit, but never narrow pinching greed, never, until now, this desire to hold secret what is good and keep it for himself.

Down at the church of San Pier Scheraggio, the watchmen are extinguishing their fires. At the doors of the church, Tassi pauses. The walls are ringing already with the sound of hammering inside. For what? For an illusion, an impermanence to be forgotten like a dream. The bronze is material, is as real as the blue vein that runs obliquely in the bend of Sofonisba's elbow, as real as the white dove on Chiara's brow. He can hear Paolo's chesty voice. For the first time he detects the resonance of a desire for renown.

By mid-morning the interior of the church is swarming with carpenters and painters and the boys who assist them. Tassi paints assiduously. He has been painting for several hours when he finally stands back from his work.

Behind him, in the south transept, the wool for the clouds has been carded and combed and is banked up high in a side chapel. Only Paolo's stick keeps the boys from jumping in it. They are taking it in great armfuls and dipping it into the starch that stands in two great vats. The boys lift the wool, sodden and dripping, some pink, some blue, to empty vats to finish dripping before they lay the pieces on the floor to dry. One of the boys mops up the trails and puddles. Others work at the tinted clouds, teasing them to floss again before they dry. There is not a boy that is not pink or blue or both.

"Matteo," Paolo says. "That is where we shall need you tomorrow. Orazio will be here to paint, and his daughter too. For the clouds I need a man who can work without a plan."

Tassi goes back to the altar screen with renewed vigour, but he makes certain that at the end of the day he has left many places to be painted, enough to keep at least one person — one woman — employed all day.

Outside, the city is transforming. The side of the church of San Pier that faces toward the *Signoria* is hung with red and gold banners. Stands and benches have sprung up at vantage points. Fences of wattle are stacked ready to close off the piazza for the hunt. The dragon is to be driven out into the square on the day after the pageant in the church and set among mastiffs and bulls for the entertainment of the people. If the dogs attack, which is not expected, the men inside the legs will be ready with sticks. The bulls will prove more difficult. They will most certainly run at the dragon, but only when they have become sufficiently used to the sight of it. The men inside and the two at the head must be ready to abandon the dragon and scramble to safety at that exact moment.

Tassi's doubts about the validity of the *festa* fall away. It is excitement. It is alive. And Tassi is always on the side of life.

꙳

ALL NIGHT A WATCHMAN TENDS the fire under the cauldron of eel skins that are melting slowly to glue. In the morning the air is stewed with the smell of fish. Paolo takes Orazio outside to Via de' Leoni to talk. He keeps an eye on the doorway, his mind already halfway through the morning's affairs. The body of the dragon must be reinforced so that its own weight trailing behind does not tear it apart. The painted screen for the glade has to be secured with wires extending in four directions to iron pins in the flagstones. And he must have his assistants practice raising and lowering the clouds until they move seamlessly.

Orazio can see that all this is leading only to aching limbs and a sore back.

"And you, Orazio . . ."

"Paolo, my dear friend, I will paint for you this morning and then I must be back at *Argentara*."

"But I need you to supervise the decoration. Two cartloads of pine boughs will be arriving. No one else knows how they are to be strung."

"My contract is with Andrea."

"Though your word was to me."

Orazio shrugs. "My dear friend, as I said, I will paint for you this morning. I need no fee. And then I must be back at *Argentara*."

Ensconced comfortably, thinks Paolo, in some silk-hung apartment of Andrea's.

"And look," says Orazio, who it seems will do anything rather than engage in physical labour. "Ilario will be back today. You can have his services." He also says that he will allow Sofonisba to stay and paint despite the fact that the church with its swarms of workers is almost as public as the street.

The work is a welcome relief for Sofonisba after the demands of the *Madonna*. It is work for apprentices filling in the colours ordained by the designer, Paolo. She understands why Tassi left his place to join the boys — still pink and blue some of them — helping with the clouds. She cannot ignore the laughter, sees, when she turns, Tassi throwing himself into the pile of leftover fleece. Beside her, Chiara laughs out loud and the next moment has left the little dishes of colours and is over there too. Sofonisba tries to continue painting but has to look. Just as she had anticipated there is her slave falling backwards with Tassi into the fleece, their hands joined. It is a trap. She has no doubt. It is designed to make her leave the panel and go over there. She paints furiously, thinks of striking Chiara for her lack of obedience, except that no one told her to stay. She has succeeded in painting herself out of the church and into the wilderness of rock and stream when she feels warm breath behind her ear and hears through her bones themselves Tassi's voice.

"I have brought back your pied pony. She is too much for me."

Sofonisba looks over her shoulder. Her eyes at once catch the position of Tassi's arm out to the side, circling Chiara, his hand on her shoulder, drawing her closer while ostensibly ushering her forward.

The man is a monster. What can she say but thank you?

"You don't have to thank me."

When she would gladly stick him with a knife.

He lets Chiara go and the girl bends at once to the dishes, pulling her hood farther over her face.

Sofonisba draws it back. "You don't have to be afraid in here. Not unless you are in sin." She turns to catch Tassi's eye but he has gone. Paolo is calling for him over near the altar where he is showing Alessandro and some others how to operate the pulleys.

Sofonisba understands their game has changed. It was once herself and Tassi against all the old men of the world. Now they are pitted instead one against the other. Well, she can take up any game he chooses to play — and win.

Sofonisba's assessment of herself is as sharp as cut stone.

"Chiara?"

"*Madonna?*"

"Go and see if Ser Matteo wants some assistance."

He is looking directly at them while Paolo is talking to him. Sofonisba leans sideways to Chiara, puts her hand out and draws Chiara's face closer, all the while keeping her eyes on Tassi, even as she turns her own face and puts her lips to the dark cheek.

Alessandro sees it all. It is not long before Tassi is back at her side.

"Come. I've something to show you —" He takes Sofonisba's hand and leads her over to the altar where the clouds stand, starched and airy cages of fleece, one or two already glued to their supports under the forest of ropes. Paolo wants a demonstration.

One of the clouds is ready for a trial, and Ceccio is made to stand inside it on the platform. Tassi has cut an opening in the front of the fleece. Still attached at the bottom edge, the wool can be pushed out from inside to fall open like a trap door, allowing the angel to appear to be standing on the cloud, framed in its tinted fleece.

Alessandro hauls on the rope and the cloud ascends just as it will descend on the day of the *festa*. When it is just above their heads, Paolo calls to Ceccio to show himself. The fleece at the front of the cloud falls forward and there is Ceccio, very pleased with himself and grinning. He sticks his leg out and pretends to fall. Even Orazio laughs. Paolo Pallavicino grimaces, his mouth still turned down. Ceccio turns round and waggles his behind.

Paolo says, "Teach the boy a lesson."

Tassi says, "Here," and takes the rope from Alessandro. He takes the cloud higher. Ceccio turns round, waving. Tassi hauls again and this time Ceccio holds on tight. He is almost at the rafters. When he calls out in fear, Tassi brings him down so quickly the blood rushes to his face and falls away again. White and limp as a daisy, he looks as if he might be about to faint. As he steps from the cloud, he lurches forward and is mightily sick over Alessandro's feet. For this Paolo beats him about the shoulders and calls him names. Then he turns round and starts on Alessandro.

⌒

FOR THE LAST SEVEN NIGHTS Alessandro has slept with the jerkin next to his skin, each night wishing for Sofonisba, consoling himself with his hand in the morning. The charm has had no effect and his chances of success seem daily more remote. He is no closer to his goal, his dream of thighs and lips and all their permutations of warm and soft and moist that will comfort him forever. On the contrary, he seems to be sliding inexorably to utter defeat. Today in the church his humiliation was complete. His yellow hose, draped over his windowsill to dry and giving off the reek of Ceccio's vomit though he has washed them twice in the bucket, have become the emblem of his ignominy, the standard of his failure. The smell of his disgrace smothers the secret power he had hoped for, and the stockings hang there pitifully like the arms of one who has given up calling for help. But Alessandro has not given up. Just as he is falling asleep, an idea ignites like a coal in a sudden draught. He comes fully awake, saying to himself, "I have it," without quite knowing what "it" is. The light of his fleeting inspiration is dimming. It flickers, flares again and there it is. He does have it: he will *give the jerkin to Sofonisba.* He does not have to tell her what it is, only that it possesses extraordinary, arcane power. In this way, as the recipient of the gift, the gift that he has worn next to his own skin, she will be joined to him, skin to skin *through* the skin. They will be united by its power. It is a logic that to Alessandro is as good as any. Content, he sleeps.

In the morning, the sun seems to bless his undertaking. Still, just to be sure, he performs a small ritual taught to him by Ceccio, who learned it from his uncle. He lights a candle and takes two lengths of cord and two small pieces of cloth. On the first piece he spits once for "yes" and ties it on the end of a cord; he spits twice on the second piece for "no" and ties it on the second cord. Then he picks both up in one hand so that they dangle over a pewter plate and he lights them to see which will burn first. He burns the hand that holds the cords. It happens every time: he burns his hand, the pieces fall on the plate, and he forgets which is which. He decides that "yes" would have been the answer.

He thinks about it all the way to Via del Cocomero with his cloth-rolled parcel close under his arm. He has no idea how to approach Sofonisba, but he is relieved to learn that Orazio is not home. He thinks that at last the face of Fortune has truly begun to smile on him.

He waits nervously in the shop while the boy goes into the back to fetch Sofonisba. While he waits, Alessandro yawns uncontrollably with nerves. He puts the parcel down on the edge of the desk, changes his mind and picks it up again. He is counting on Sofonisba's curiosity. He has said he has something for her. Sofonisba likes gifts. She will surely come out of the workshop.

Even better, she asks him to go in.

She is wiping her hands on a rag. The girl is there too, sitting without a stitch, exposing her entire extraordinary body to the world. He has difficulty keeping his eyes from the sight. He holds out the parcel to Sofonisba, nods toward it.

"Madonna." It is all he can manage. The hangman's rope has somehow tightened on his own neck.

Sofonisba takes the parcel and waits. She is no help at all.

"To humbly beg your forgiveness for an affront I did not intend." How he wishes the girl were not present. Sofonisba purses her lips to show how close her tolerance is to impatience. "I have brought you a gift."

"Is it as ignominious and stupid as the last?"

"It is far from stupid. You have never, *Madonna*, received such a gift."

"And that should guarantee its worth?" She has unrolled it from its cloth and is holding up the vest by the shoulders.

Alessandro's heart begins to pound. He can hardly hear his own voice.

"It is beyond value," he says.

Sofonisba is unmoved. "Am I to thank you?" She swings it round to look at the back and then holds it out again. "It looks like one of your cast-offs. It would not even do for Chiara here." She puts it down and begins to turn away.

Alessandro laughs out loud, making her turn back in surprise. In exchanges with Alessandro she is supposed to be the one who does the laughing.

"'Cast-off.' Very good," he says.

Sofonisba folds her arms. "Haven't you got a servant of your own to give it to?"

Alessandro recovers. He shakes his head. "With respect, gracious lady, you do not understand. This is a very special garment. Very special." He strokes it as if he is gentling an animal.

Sofonisba sits down. The man is a simpleton. Why must he prove it daily? She folds her hands in her lap in a parody of demure attention and puts her head on one side, waiting.

Chiara reaches for her gown and covers herself.

Alessandro lowers his voice. "If you wear this garment next to your skin for three months," he thrusts out his chin, "the world will lie at your feet."

"And you will be Pope."

"No. Only if I were to —"

"Oh, you are tiresome. Put the thing away and be quiet. It has an unpleasant look." Even as she speaks, an unwholesome thought comes to Sofonisba. She stands up. "Where did you get it?"

"I can't say."

"Say or I'll take the thing —" She snatches at it and misses. "I'll ask everyone I know."

"You don't have to. I got it from Paolo Pallavicino's boy. His angel."

"He's as stupid as you are. Where did he get it?" But the vision has rooted her brain and will not be dispelled by her own voice. Her question is already answered. She can see it all: the table in the byre, its strange burden. She can see the bucket underneath the table, see the folds upon folds of pale skin. The same thought that had come to her as she was standing there returns: that the man, the unlucky pauper, had somehow been sucked away, had vanished when the skin was torn from him; that the thing on the bench bore no relation to the man and his idiot dreams; that the only sign left of him could not possibly be the revolting pelt lying limp in the bucket like a cast off costume after a pageant.

She stares at Alessandro. What was he thinking to have brought her such a thing? Not only is it in itself an object most vile and abhorrent but the notion of it, the conception . . .! Her whole being recoils at the idea of it, never mind the loathsome thing itself. And here is Alessandro still trying to say something about its magical properties. She wants to scream him into silence, wants to throw something at him as she would at a filthy cur to drive it from the courtyard.

"And if a man — or a woman — should wear this garment . . ."

Sofonisba flinches and the words, "Get out!" are on her lips when suddenly she stops. From nowhere, a thought has come to her, an idea as perverse and base as Alessandro's. In her mind's eye she sees Matteo Tassi smiling the smile she knows so well. She sees him naked to the waist and she is smiling too, walking toward him with the unspeakable gift in her hands.

"Leave it," she says quietly. Alessandro senses some change in her as when the wind shifts over water and troubled waves come reaching. She is looking at him with such directness that he is confounded.

"Leave it with me. Leave it for as long as I wish and say nothing, or I will tell where you got it, the same place no doubt that Maestro Paolo Pallavicino sends his men to for supplies."

Alessandro has never before been looked at by a woman with such an unswerving gaze. She is looking straight through his eyes into his most private core and holding a light to what she sees there, his most secret hopes and dreams lying in the darkest corners with his sin and his shame. He hesitates for no more than a breath. She says again, "Leave it," but he is already walking toward the door, the jerkin still on the table.

Sofonisba pushes it onto its cloth wrapping and covers it over. She will find a use for it. She is not sure exactly what. She knows only that, as things stand, Matteo Tassi is ahead in their mysterious, unspoken game, where the rules of play are always a surprise and if she falls behind, she is almost always hurt.

Sofonisba picks up the bundle and takes it upstairs. By the time she has come down and resumed painting, she has thought of a use for it.

"Would you lie down with a dead man, Chiara?"

"Would I . . .?"

"You heard."

"Lie with a dead man?"

"Yes, with a corpse. Would you lie with a corpse?"

"There would not be any point, would there?"

"Oh, very good, Chiara, very good. We could send you to *Careggi* and they could have you at table there for their amusement. You'd fit very well with their peacocks and dwarves and monkeys." She laughs. "But answer the question."

"For money?"

"Well certainly not for pleasure. I hope not for pleasure."

"It would have to be a very great sum."

"I would not do it for any. There is no price to match such an act."

"Who asks you?"

Sofonisba laughs. "No, no dead men have asked me. Though some are as good as corpses, I allow you that. And then, too, they are all the same when they are drunk, dead or alive."

She paints on in silence, appears wholly absorbed in these studies for the *Susanna*. She is absent from her eyes when she looks at Chiara, a ghost in her own garments, until she begins to speak again.

"What would you do to help me put Messer Matteo in his place?" As if Chiara — whose only concern is to avoid pain — might have a plan.

"Anything."

"Anything?"

"If you ask it, *Madonna*."

"Would you lie with him?"

"What for?"

"Come, you are not that stupid."

"Messer Matteo would not want to lie with me."

Sofonisba wonders if the reply is disingenuous. Messer Matteo would lie with a leper.

"Well, that goes without saying."

Chiara does not respond. Her gaze has the perfect artless, unwitting quality that Sofonisba has demanded for the painting.

"Well, would you? Think of it, Chiara. Messer Matteo. Strong as a horse. Perhaps better. Better certainly than the feeble old rake who looks after the horse."

Chiara turns her head, laughter in her eyes. This morning the old man had taken a beating from Orazio for letting his horse piss long and slow in the middle of the courtyard.

⌐

SOFONISBA'S OPPORTUNITY FOR mischief comes calling late in the afternoon in the form of Matteo himself, drawn to Via del Cocomero by Orazio's absence.

Not much more than an hour later, she is at her door applying the finishing touch to her scheme. She is berating a skinny and bewildered boy, Tuccio from across the street, who sometimes runs errands for her. He is twelve. He has a lazy eye, a broken tooth and stiff, dirty-looking hair, none of which softens Sofonisba's heart or deflects her wrath. "Stupid, stupid, stupid!" she shouts, shoving his shoulders alternately right, left, right. "Now go. You go back to Messer Matteo and you apologize to him. You tell him every word I just told you, understand? Every word! You little donkey! You get the package back and you take it to the right place this time. To Messer Alessandro, understand?" She cuffs the side of his head for variety: "*Ales-sandro! Ales-sandro!* Understand?" But she receives no answer because as soon as she releases him, the boy turns tail and is gone.

She smiles and goes back into the shop.

The trick is delicious. She feels buoyant with the mischief of it. She only wishes Chiara were here to share the sweet anticipation of a reaction. But after her overblown pantomime of disgust, Chiara has run off somewhere and is hiding.

She had run out into the yard just when Sofonisba was most enjoying the moment. She had run out and torn off her gown; had sent the bucket clanking down into the well, drawn it up again in a frenzy, stark naked and looking like a mad devil in Hell, pulled it over to the side and tipped the whole lot over herself, falling on her knees like a lunatic, her crazy piebald face up to the sky.

Sofonisba had tried to get her to come in, but it was no use. Chiara had picked up the gown and rubbed at her breasts, her neck, her shoulders. She rubbed hard as if she would erase the very markings on her skin. Angry red tracks began to suffuse the surface. There was a flake of sky in the puddle where she knelt. She scooped it up and splashed it on her face; then she stopped, breathing hard, and shuddered and spat. Sofonisba left her kneeling on the wet stones. She was sorry Chiara had not been with her to witness the boy's confusion but so be it. She would only sour the victory.

⌐̲

CHIARA, WHO HAS A LOCKED room of affliction and sorrow beyond imagining in her heart, has not until now experienced betrayal. If she had, she might have caught some warning tone in Sofonisba's voice, like the shadow of a small cloud across the warmed earth.

"Listen carefully," Sofonisba had said. "Messer Matteo is in the shop.

"You are to go into the far room upstairs. Pull the shutters closed. Take off your gown to the waist. Alessandro's gift is on the bed. Put it on to cover your breasts and lie down on the bed and wait. I will send Messer Matteo up to you. When you hear him at the door you are to tell him to come in."

Chiara had stared.

It could only end in a beating, if not from Tassi, who would feel himself mocked to find her there, then from Sofonisba, who would be jealous if he stayed. And if not from either of them, then from Orazio himself, who might return at any moment and even if he didn't would be sure to find out, turning purple at this conduct in his house and lifting his heavy hand to her yet again.

She had dragged her feet as she climbed the stair.

The sun was streaming into the room at the end. A bird that had been pecking worms from the rafters flew out suddenly as she entered. The jerkin was on the bed. Chiara examined it. It was indeed an ugly thing, rough and unfinished and big enough for a man. It had the sallow waxy look of oiled parchment in a window pane. When she held it up, the sunlight seemed almost to slide through it.

She closed the shutters and went back to the bed. Then, just as Sofonisba had instructed, she unlaced her gown and pulled it down to the waist, picked up the curious garment and put it on. It did not fit snugly even when it was laced with the leather thongs. She gathered her skirt about her and lay down on the bed, looking as wretched as she had begun to feel.

For what seemed like a long time she lay on the bed. The room, with no breeze to pass through, began to feel warm. She watched two flies with heavy blue bodies make loops above her head, crossing and recrossing, winding her as on a spool to the edge of sleep.

The creaking of the door roused her. It opened and Tassi stood for a moment, opening his eyes wide to the darkness of the room.

He said something she didn't catch. Whatever it was carried no indignation or affront. He closed the door and turned the key.

"She was right," he said. "You are here."

Chiara sat up.

"No, don't disturb yourself," he said. "Lie down. Monna Sofonisba tells me you are taking a remedy."

Chiara had no idea what to reply.

"She says you wear a garment that has been invested with powers to heal the skin. By a friar." He touched her cheek with the back of his hand.

"But it won't work with all this." And his fingers were at her waist and he was pulling the gown down and off over her feet.

Chiara closed her eyes. Tassi was taking off his own clothes.

"And now," he was climbing on to the bed, "now my remedy. You take the body of a smooth-skinned man —" was kneeling over her, "and all you have to do —" was opening her with his fingers, "— is receive its vigour. Through the power of the Father —" was in her, "— the Son, and the Holy Spirit. And all the holy *spiriti* in Heaven and the *spiridegli*. And the *cherubini* and the *serafini*." He drove deeper with every word. "*Sacerdote, becchino, diacono, arcidiacono, vescovo,*" Chiara's head was knocking against the wall, "*arcivescovo, papa e Sua Altezza il Santo Pappagallo con il suo santo becco stesso.*"

There were no more clergy, real or invented, to add to the list. He had finished.

And Sofonisba did not come in.

He looked down at Chiara. For a moment, her face wore the expression of one dragged from a river, and then she smiled. Tassi lifted himself and eased her down beneath him. He pulled the jerkin away from her skin and peered inside.

"It is still Chiara," he said. "Even the Holy Parrot couldn't help." But Chiara didn't laugh. She looked down at her arms as if for the first time and turned her face away with her eyes closed.

"Too bad," said Tassi. He smoothed the jerkin out under him and lay against it. "Too bad." In a little while, he kissed her gently, straightened his clothes and left.

A slave could know worse. Better to be bedded than beaten. For now, anyway. Chiara removed the jerkin and was dressing again in her own clothes when Sofonisba came in. Sofonisba looked at the bed.

"You're too late," Chiara said.

"No. I heard you." To Chiara's surprise she was smiling broadly.

"But Messer Matteo has gone."

"Good. Good. Let's hope he went home. We'll send him a mysterious packet." Sofonisba picked up the jerkin. She was still smiling.

Chiara shook her head as a mother shakes her head at a babbling infant and turned her attention to the fallen bed cover. But Sofonisba's next words caught her off balance.

"He will be beside himself," she said, "to have lain with a dead man."

Chiara turned and looked at her. Sofonisba was holding the jerkin out. It hung from her fingers as from pincers. The skin around Chiara's nostrils and lips began to feel strange. Sofonisba held the vest at arm's length, with the little finger of each hand raised like tiny horns. The creeping at the side of Chiara's nose made its way down beside her mouth and along each side of her neck to fan out across her breast where the vest had been. "Come with me and you'll understand."

Chiara followed in silence.

Downstairs, Sofonisba wrapped the jerkin in a piece of waxed paper and tied it round three times with a thin cord. Then she sent Chiara across the road to fetch Tuccio. She gave him the parcel and told him to take it to Messer Matteo Tassi.

"He lives in his shop in Via Rosaio," she said. "Tell him you have instructions to return this garment to him, with thanks. Then come straight back here." She gave him five *soldi* and said there would be five more when he came back and told her it was done.

"So now we'll wait for him to come back."

"And —" Chiara knew there was something more.

"And when he comes back we'll be so nonchalant. *Why, Tuccio! Back already? And was Messer Alessandro pleased to have his jerkin back?*" Then Sofonisba aped the boy, making her voice hoarse and rasping, "*Messer Alessandro? Madonna, if you please —*" her voice squeaking and plunging like Tuccio's, "*you told me Messer Matteo . . .*" Now she was a player. She swiped the space in front of her with the flat of her hand, grabbed two fistfuls of air and shook hard as if it was the very boy she had hold of. "*Messer Matteo Tassi! You stupid boy, you took it to Messer Matteo? It is Messer Alessandro's. I told you take it to Messer Alessandro, son of Emilio. Alessandro. You stupid, stupid boy!*" Then, a player with a new part, she put out her arm suddenly, as if round the shoulders of the invisible boy, and dropped her voice. "*Go back to Messer Matteo. Tell him you made a terrible mistake and your mistress will beat you black and blue if he does not return the packet. He will probably refuse. Tell him —*"

Chiara was barely breathing, she was listening with such attention.

"*Tell him it is a rare and curious thing and belongs to another, to Messer Alessandro, the apothecary's son, and it would be cursed ill luck for him to keep it.*"

Chiara frowned and closed her eyes.

"We don't have to tell him — not just yet — that it was flayed from the corpse of a hanged man. I want to see his face when he learns it. For now, his ignorance is a fine amusement."

Sofonisba looked at Chiara for affirmation, but Chiara was already backing away before she turned and ran.

In the dark storage room next to the kitchen, Chiara draws her hand down over her eyes and across her mouth one last time, her features calm as death. She gets up slowly. There is no one now. She is on her own on this path to Heaven or Hell. Her loneliness is as cold as the brook water, as clear. She draws a deep breath and exhales in one long sigh. Since the boat, the time she thinks of as the beginning of her life, she has been like a leaf in a stream, attaching here to a rock, swept on, sticking there. Perhaps she thought that she had come to rest, come to something like a home in Orazio's house. Sofonisba owned her and she had no complaint. For the converse was true: she belonged. But she is not Sofonisba's creature. She has been betrayed. Chiara does not exist. She is of no worth to anyone whether she lives or dies.

Whoever she is, she is still standing naked on the barrel at the docks. She is still watching the buyers stare and move on. She is still alone.

She is frightened now, whirled back to the beginning of her life here, everything before it a darkness, an unremembered dream. Everything that came after it lost. Ill luck and it won't wash off. A veil of ill luck has fallen over her. She has been clothed in it and it cannot be removed, nor peeled away like the hanged man's skin. She has seen how ill luck attaches to a man or a woman and spreads like a plaguey skin. She wants to cut herself away from it and does not know how. She prefers her own flawed skin to this. Miserably she dresses and it seems to her as if her every action exists only to point to her misfortune. Even the sky is confirming her intuition and darkening in the east where the clouds are piling up.

～

TASSI'S SUSPICIONS ARE AROUSED. There is something not quite right about what the boy is telling him. Something of the look that was in Sofonisba's eyes when she said to him, "She's up there now. Waiting." God, he loves her, but she knows how to throw him into consternation. He thought he had discovered an infallible means of capturing her attention: a little well-timed dalliance with Chiara, who always obliged by laughing, especially if he told her to be quiet. It was never wasted; Sofonisba's eyes always darkening, the flash of jealousy striking like lightning. He knows when he sees it. He liked to think it meant she wanted him, perhaps ached for him and wanted him in her bed the way he sometimes, when she is in a certain light and holding her head a certain way, ached for her. And though these games never won him entry to the place he wanted most of all, they made the nights he spent with Bianca all the more satisfying. It was a rich and rewarding entertainment, and he was master of it all — until today when she offered him Chiara, and changed the value of every card in his hand.

The jerkin is still there on his shop counter where he unwrapped it. The boy is still waiting.

"You take your short legs back to your lady," he says, "and tell her Alessandro has his vest."

The boy begins to protest.

"What might help," says Tassi, "a box on the ears or a few *soldi*?" He roars with laughter when the boy answers him in earnest. "All right," he says, producing a couple of coins. "But you had better be convincing."

When the boy has gone Tassi rewraps the bundle and goes down to San Pier Scheraggio, where he knows Alessandro will be, still trying to ingratiate himself with the world.

He finds Alessandro with his arms folded in front of him, one fist making a rest for his chin, in a pose of earnest, intelligent attention while Paolo instructs him in the handling of the ropes.

Tassi claps him on the shoulder from behind, making him jump. He tries to move away but Tassi, though shorter than he is, sticks like a limpet, says, "I'll wait. Please go on," and bows to Paolo.

Paolo says, "I know why you stayed away today, Matteo. The bronze is spoiled."

Tassi thinks quickly. He says, "Sir, I haven't forgotten my charge. There were difficulties in the pouring. Only have faith in me and I shall solve them and cast another. It will be even better."

Paolo grunts his disapproval and carries on until, noticing some small crisis across the church, he shoves the rope into Alessandro's hand and shambles away.

"Leave that," says Tassi. "I have something for you. Here."

Alessandro knows better than to thank him before he knows what the gift is. He unties the cord on the parcel and pulls back the oiled paper. He sees the vest and quickly covers it up, jamming it out of sight under his arm and colouring like a young girl in a sudden violent blooming of bright roses on his neck and cheeks.

This is a more amusing reaction than even Tassi could hope for.

"An undergarment? A gift for a lady? I have seen a lady in it. Lying in it. She looks well. I mean she lies well."

The roses have darkened to purple, blown with anger.

Outside, it is beginning to spot with rain. Tassi is still not sure what Sofonisba is contriving. He will think about it over a jug of wine.

That night the rain battered the city and thunder broke in the surrounding hills. Parents hushed crying children, told them it was only the giant walking in the mountains, stamping on the top of every hill. He would not come down, they said. Across the river the children who lived in the houses at the foot of San Giorgio were not sure whether they were to take comfort in this. They were not sure the giant was all they had to fear. The noise of the rain was tremendous and it made them think of soldiers, the feet of a thousand soldiers clattering through the streets, a thousand soldiers' hands rattling at the doors and the shutters. Their heads filled with the rain's drumming on the roof tiles, its splashing as it fell in sheets to the cobbles. Some of it forced its way into the houses, running backwards with the wind up under the roof tiles and down through the cracks. It trickled in under sills in Via Bardi. Cobblestones gurgled like the blood-choked dead and no one fell asleep until the storm abated to a watery quiet. Over in the centre of the city the rain had collected in the awnings around the *battistero*, making them drag at their anchors. When one of them tore away, it sluiced the paving: the giant's wife washing her courtyard. But it was the small hour of the night and there was no one to see or hear. The giant's footsteps had receded and the rain now was thinning softly and woke no one.

TEN

THE DAY OF THE *festa* dawned like a miracle, blissfully fair. A stiff breeze made the flags stand out and rustled the pennants strung above the Via del Corso. There was not a soul who could have seen how the day would end when it began with a sky as blue as any Heaven. Citizens who had woken in the night to curse the heavy rain and mutter to their sleeping husbands, their sleeping wives, about former years, former catastrophes, smiled now to hear the single drip-dripping from the corner of the roof and opened their eyes to sunlight sliding through the cracks in the shutters. When they threw the shutters open and looked out, a dazzle of light rebounded from the wet tiles. Stone sparkled; roofs gleamed. The city was new. To walk abroad now in the city was to see it primed and ready for the festivities. The day held out its gifts. Only the *festaiuoli* continued to fret, to send messengers here, carpenters there, and boys over to the *battistero* to lift the canvas awnings with long sticks and release the rain. And even they felt no ill wind.

Over in the *duomo*, the parts of the dragon lolled in an unlikely welter inside the south doors where they had been carried from the workshop. At the appointed time, it would be assembled and lumber forth into the world accompanied by drummers, pipers, and a host of dancing devils.

The great doors of San Pier Scheraggio were closed and barred and would not open again until evening. Only at the south door would the workmen be permitted to come and go, letting in the carpenters' boys to sweep up the last of the wood shavings and the scraps, and the actors to practice ascending and descending on their platforms.

Perhaps Tassi, on waking in Bianca's bed, pressing the heels of his hands against his aching eyes, might have felt the weight of what they were to see that day, but he recognized only the familiar pain of a night's drinking and a head full of vapours. Paolo too might have been granted some portent, waking in the room assigned to him in the *Signoria*, surrounded by a whole collection of signs and wonders in paintings from a hundred years ago. But Paolo's head was too full of his own projections to accommodate more.

As for Orazio Fabroni over in Via del Cocomero, he greeted the day as he greeted any other: with resistance.

He sighed almost as soon as he was awake. He had seen one San Giovanni too many. His whole body temporized. He would have liked to be back at *Argentara* where he could work on the wall and rest as he wished. There he laboured slowly and grumbled constantly, but still the work was preferable to the messy collaboration of this pageant where one man garnered credit for all. He knew that the paintings he — and Sofonisba — completed at *Argentara* would puff his reputation. His name would not go unnoticed by the English ambassador, as it would here in this *stufato* of entertainment for peasants. Orazio had found himself, lately, thinking more and more of fame. What a sweet coronation of his work it would be to paint for the court of a foreign monarch. On his return there would be no equal in all the city. This, the pageant, was an interruption, an unnecessary distraction. As a young man he would have thrown himself into the work with enthusiasm, carousing and revelling to keep his spirits high. But he was no longer a young man.

He dithered and shuffled about the house. Sofonisba was impatient to be out among the milling crowds. Outside, there would be street vendors to offer distraction, musicians to lighten a heavy heart. Sofonisba knew she had trumped Tassi with her move the day before, perhaps had won the game. But what then? Enjoy the victory all alone? Savour the taste of her own power? The house was oppressive, the air heavy with her own misgivings, self-recriminations made worse by Chiara's silent reproach. The girl had not shaken off yesterday's foolery. She ate nothing, spoke scarcely a word. When Sofonisba put an arm round her shoulder and asked her what was the matter, Chiara would repeat only one word, *sfortuna*. Ill luck. As if she were not unlucky enough already in her tainted skin.

But even plain-speaking sibyls go unnoticed when affairs of the heart occupy the mind.

The festivities unfolded just as Paolo had planned. A Mass was celebrated in Santa Maria del Fiore, the Arcivescovo like a princeling in the light of a thousand candles, the soaring voices of the choirs ringing glory all around him. The banners of the Guilds were given his blessing and the dedications made. Then, God's tribute duly paid, the cathedral was cleared and the dragon assembled for its walk.

When the main doors were opened, a great shout rose from the square to greet the towering monster. It filled the dark portal, and when it manoeuvred awkwardly through and lifted its neck, its head rose higher than the doors. It walked forward to the first step and stood for a moment while the Guilds assembled in the nave behind, the reds and golds of the banners just visible, jostling for place. Two boys with long poles turned the dragon's head to one side and the other as if surveying the crowd. To more cheering, a dozen black devils with pitchforks appeared and danced beside it with lashing tails as it lumbered and swayed down the steps.

The dragon took its long walk from the cathedral to the church of San Pier Scheraggio. A path had been made for it with wattle fences. Once they had seen it pass, many of the crowd ran along behind the fences, knocking them down in some places, to see it from a new vantage point. The noise of its approach, with drummers and horn players and every dog in the city barking, could be heard long before the monster came looming into view. In Via Baccano it passed close by, nodding above the heads of the crowd and making the children scream — no one could say if it was in terror or delight. And if a person had a trouble of their own that day, there was no space to contemplate it, for the whole mind was taken up with spectacle.

At San Pier Scheraggio, the dragon was taken to the west door and blessed again for good measure before being taken inside. The Guilds' men and women received their blessing on the steps, before dispersing with the crowd to amusements in other parts of the city. And no one thought to discuss the piper who was bitten by one of the dogs or the woman who was taken with a fit when the dragon passed, though tomorrow these things will flap on every tongue and it will be suddenly remembered that the priest's font was empty and had to be replenished before he could bless the congregation.

About two hours before compline, when the sun was beginning to go down, Sofonisba and her father made their way back to San Pier. A watchman at the sacristy let them in.

Inside, the church was transformed. Sofonisba watched Chiara's face. She had forgotten her hurt. The altar was shut off from view by the three great panels of painted hills and rocks. Low screens of blue and silver cloth fenced the nave on either side. Boughs of cypress, strung on wires above, represented the forest. Dark vines, threaded with white flowers of jasmine, wound around each column, signifying the soul's ascent to Heaven. Overhead, like the stars themselves, myriad candles shone from the great wheels of tin suspended from the rafters. Orazio said Chiara was not to make herself so known, but was to stay out of the way. He pointed to a niche beneath the font close to where the dragon was to be slain. He said it would not do to have her interfering while the pageant was underway, but when the Ascent into Heaven was over she could stay there and help the players out of the dragon so the carcass could be borne away like a dead thing.

Tassi worked with the operators of the platforms. He was committed to his task, serious and unsmiling. A boy who tried to joke with him made a face behind his back when he did not respond. It was inevitable that Sofonisba and he should find themselves face to face across some shedding cloud, some damaged wing. It was a wing that would not open. Tassi bowed slightly and Sofonisba, expecting the long direct gaze that balanced on the edge of insult, felt as if she had stepped unexpectedly to a cliff edge.

When the bell began to sound the hour for compline, Paolo and Tassi supervised the raising of the clouds, which, with their angels inside, were taken up to hang at various heights above the space in front of the screen. Alessandro and two assistants operated the clouds that were to form the Trinity, taking them up to a great height just below the rafters. Alessandro strutted with importance; he was operating God the Father, unaware that no one thought him capable of mastering God the Son.

At a signal from their director, the choristers began a *Jubilate*, and the doors were opened to admit a great press of people, men going to stand on one side, women on the other, behind the divisions of blue and silver. Those at the back took places on raised stands positioned at a slight angle, the better to see the entrance of the players. The people entered in a steady stream, taking whatever places they could find, under the choir stalls, along the west wall and in the side chapels, too. Boys climbed on the scaffolding that stood to the side and on the pillars and on the tombs and soon all effort to make them come down was abandoned. It was all the sexton and his men could do to keep the space clear in front of the painted altar screen.

In a little while the singing stopped. A drummer began to beat the drum at the doors of the church and all turned, their own hats a spectacle of pivoting colour, to see a procession of *spiridegli* on stilts, very fine and strange in antic costumes, entering the church. They came down the nave and out again through the side doors, followed by a solemn procession of saints, each preceded by a youth bearing a banner and each of them carrying the appropriate sign of patronage: San Giuseppe, his saw; San Sebastiano, a quiver. Santa Lucia carried a tray bearing her own eyes, exquisitely cut from opal, though only she was close enough to see them. The company slowly ascended the stairs to their assigned Heaven, a loft beside the altar. Then came the priests and the chaplains of all the churches with their banners, and the tertiaries and the friars, and the monks from Castello and the nuns from San Frediano and Santa Caterina on the Piazza di San Marco, all of them more solemn than the saints, some pale and dazed as if they had just been woken from their devotions, and some of them looking as if they would rather not have been there at all. And indeed for two of them, an old nun and the novice who accompanied her, it would have been better had they stayed away. The last of the clerics was Arcivescovo Andrea himself, resplendent in green and gold.

When the clerics had all taken their places, the trumpeter sounded a fanfare, and the Gonfaloniere and the priors entered the church, followed by the Duke with the English ambassador, and the Duke's family and attendants. They might have rehearsed, they were so closely in step. Only Ercole paused as he ascended to his place, a barnyard cock displaying his finery.

Once more the trumpeter sounded and the lutes and recorders began. The doors of the church were flung open again, and a friar in black burst in, denouncing levity in the House of God. There were cheers for his flailing arms and wild eyes until word was passed that the man was not a player at all but a follower of the teachings of Fra Girolamo, who had been burned in the square. He was turned away, still raving, when the pipers heralded the entrance of Santa Margherita. The skinny hairless youth chosen for the part walked most devoutly down the centre aisle, carrying an apron of flowers for purity, which he cast before him as he went. A procession of children with lighted censers filled with sweet herbs followed, showing that the air was perfumed with holiness. The skinny Santa Margherita minced along in his red dress and knelt devoutly in the glade before the altar while the choir sang a canticle. One by one, the clouds descended into the light of the torches and opened exactly in accordance with Paolo's design. Their angels, stepping forward and rotating to display their wings, tried not to let their tongues protrude in concentration on this difficult task of revealing glory. Then the drum at the back of the church began to beat again, but more fiercely now. Amid great uproar, the dragon entered. It lurched and swayed like a sick and raging animal, and fire issued from its jaw. Those nearest the screens could plainly see how it was done, yet they moved back instinctively as the dragon lunged and threatened. But for all that, there was not a soul who did not secretly want to feel the grip of terror. The devils danced. The dead appeared dressed in the bones of the grave and holding their heads in pain and grief. Then even those who had laboured to create the illusion allowed themselves to believe.

Santa Margherita collapsed, just as he should, in mortal distress before the dragon. San Giorgio entered, just as he should, mounted on his white horse and gleaming heroically in his soldier's armour. The boys extinguished their torches, San Giorgio extinguished the dragon, and the Holy Trinity miraculously appeared, suspended high above the drama. Paolo Pallavicino said afterwards that those who saw the first flames took them for a device representing the dragon's last fiendish attempts to overcome the Saviour. The people, he said, were as children, unable to distinguish between the representation and the real. Perhaps the dragon, breathing its last, caught the teased and airy floss of the descended cloud and caused it to smoulder; perhaps one of the torches, imperfectly extinguished, reignited to do the damage. Those closest to the action were too busy with the ropes or with the hindrance of their costumes to notice. Santa Margherita and the Saviour were wholly occupied with securing their places on the platform of the cloud, ready for their ascent, and the cloud's operator was in the throes of his own struggle to keep hold of the Saviour's rope, which Alessandro had decided to contest. In all of this, the trampling, stony hooves of the horse were rearranging ropes and robes and the attention of everyone until the animal was led away. By the time the cloud was hauled aloft to rejoin its celestial partner, the draught of its motion was enough to fan the glowing wool to flames, yet still some watching believed it was all intended.

Those who were alert to the danger called out to the men work-ing the pulleys to bring the thing down. Then all might have been saved had not a rope that should have run freely snagged on the iron work of the grille at the top of the altar steps. The panicking hands only caused it to become more hopelessly entangled, jam-ming it tighter and leaving the cloud hanging there burning above the heads of the crowd, with Margherita and the Saviour calling out, "Save us! Save us, for the love of God!" Pieces of flaming cloud came away and floated down, some to be stamped out, some sailing off to catch in the foliage decorating the pillars. The green-ery, being full of resin, began to crackle and spit, and in no time a tongue of flame shot up to a banner and then that too was alight. The screaming began in earnest as one of the ropes holding the cloud burnt suddenly through. The platform lurched and tipped, hurling the Saviour to the floor below. Margherita struggled to free himself and hung for a moment above the dragon, before he, too, let go and fell into its carcass. The platform fell only moments after, narrowly missing the players. Now it was plain that the fire would not be easily contained. The water that had been quickly sent for slopped hopelessly in buckets outside, while the doorways clotted with those trying to get out, some stumbling and falling in the attempt. There was trampling and fighting, conduct that could not afterwards be remembered with pride. Meanwhile, the fire continued among the foliage, creeping about until the forest was alight and part of the screen, too. Some brave souls stayed to let down the angels. The young novice stayed and tried in vain to help her Mother Superior abandoned by her more sprightly sisters. The old woman gasped and clutched at her breast but would not rise from her place and it seemed to the novice that the fire was sucking the breath from the toothless mouth. The worst was to come, for with the screen alight there was nowhere to bring down the cloud that carried God the Father and the Holy Spirit. Tassi — for Alessandro was nowhere to be seen — and two others brought the cloud as low as they could, and the Holy Spirit leapt to safety. But God the Father, being frail as he was and unsteady, had been bound in his place for his own safety and could not free himself before the rope itself burned through and he fell, crashing amid a tangle of wreckage. They said afterwards it was a mercy his neck was broken. But the words were whispered only. For who would say them aloud?

IT IS PAST MIDNIGHT. Paolo sits alone in his room in the *Signoria*. His ears are still ringing with the old man's screams. He knows he is lucky that he did not bow to Ercole's wishes and that it was the old man and not the Arcivescovo's son who burned. But the cries are terrible and will not abate, though he is sitting in silence and has asked to be alone. There were others who were hurt, some who fell in the scramble to escape, an old nun who died of fright where she sat, a young novice whose hands were burned. In the assembly hall on the floor above, he had listened while the priors, the Podestà, the Gonfaloniere and the Duke tried gravely to apportion blame, but it was like a slippery eel they tried to pass from hand to hand. It would not be still. Paolo has no interest in blame. Paolo Pallavicino, director and architect of the festivities, wants only to know how to make these cries diminish. Like God, he has no one to turn to. He would like to forget the old man's face. He would like to be as a young man on a horse, able to gallop away, the cries fainter and fainter behind him.

He sits and stares into the flame of the candle. From where he was situated in the church, he did not see the old man's face in its agony, but for Paolo's imagination that is no obstacle. He remembers the look in the old man's eyes when he said, "And this, *Signore*, this is the man who will play the part of God the Father." He remembers the swift passage of terror, gone almost before it could be registered, like a flash of darkness, a wing across the sun, no more. And then the old man had smiled.

By midnight, Orazio too has shut himself away. After the accident, he had turned his back on the devastation and hurried straight home with Sofonisba and Chiara. He did not like what he had seen amid the confusion in the church, a young man trying to get past a press of people and pausing to strike Chiara, accusing her of starting the fire. He would have left her there to her own devices, except that Sofonisba went to her aid and led her away from her assailant. Nor did he relish the opinions he had heard bandied in the square outside as darkness fell. Everyone had a view as to the cause, a name for the culprit. He heard his own name more than once in connection with the girl. Heard himself named as the overseer of the machinery. He does not want to hear more. When the citizens are roused to anger, it does no good to argue against them. Safer to be out of the way altogether. He has seen how quickly things can turn bad. Look at the monk that went out to Caiano last year. He went with a warning for the Duke's family, and where did it get him? They turned against him. Burned the skin off the soles of his feet. Held his feet over the fire until the fat dripped, they say. And he from a religious house within the very city. And there is Sofonisba to consider. She has no business at such ugly scenes. A hanging is one thing — an orderly administration of justice — an unnatural accident quite another. The body of the old man was still there on the ground, the boys like flies around it, though none dared touch. There was already talk of the Devil's work. Regrettable that they had ever taken on the piebald girl. All her muttering of ill luck spread now like a plague to the people outside. It reflected badly on Sofonisba. Everyone knew Sofonisba had been working inside the church, and there were plenty who had already voiced their opinions on the matter, saying that they had been against it from the start, that it could only catch the attention of the Devil, summon God's wrath. Bring down the roof.

Orazio says he is going to *Argentara* tomorrow to continue working. Sofonisba must keep herself to the house. With the doors locked.

⌇

LIKE INCENSE FROM A THOUSAND MASSES, the smoke from the fire hangs in darkness above the rafters. The last of the people on their way home in the dark cross themselves and thank God there are still rafters, still a roof that has not collapsed. In a corner of the church, the guards appointed by the Bargello to watch for timbers reigniting are picking through the heap of garments that have been swept there — shoes and hats, jackets, even tunics, torn off in the rush for the doors. The floor is still littered with leaves and twigs from the foliage that was pulled down to avert the spread of the fire. Everywhere there are fragments of charred and splintered wood. At first it had seemed as if the fire must take hold of everything that could burn, until Tassi and some of the others saw that the quickest way to outwit it was to remove from the church all that was burning and that could be moved, leaving others to throw water on all that could not. The scaffolding was wheeled into place, and a great crowd of men, like ants from a nest that has been kicked apart, scrambled up and down with buckets to throw water on the places where the rafters had begun to catch, while others worked below to save the choir stall. To a monk looking back from the doorway, the church resembled the pit of Hell itself, with every man gone mad, coughing, shouting, calling to every other in the smoke. They climbed, they ran, they fell on the slick floor, every last one of them desperate to quench the flames. All that was alight was cut down. Tassi and others with him used broken timber and whatever they could lay their hands on to push the burning clouds to the doors and out onto the piazza.

Men with smeared faces and eyes that won't stop running sit spent now, slack on the steps outside. Inside the church, two of the cloud structures are still hanging in mid-air, the sodden floss reduced to long twists of greasy wool, the hair of a distraught giantess torn in grief.

PART III

ELEVEN

IT IS THE SECOND day following the accident and Alessandro, wearing his vest for protection, walks among the crowds, alert for any mention of his name. Though the entertainments have been cancelled by order of the Gonfaloniere, the streets are alive with people who yesterday all day long were gathering the news and working on it. First came the appalling mischance of the fire and talk of who predicted it, who did not give voice but saw it coming, who was first to sound the alarm, who to relay it, the greatest prestige accorded as always to those who were closest to the terror. Those who could claim to have seen the old man spit a tooth in his grinding agony stood almost as high as those who could show the hairs of their arms singed by the heat of the fire. In the tapestry of their telling the people pulled threads and looped them, they gilded and embellished the work, twisted it and stretched it. The horror of the crashing fall and the panic that ensued became less painful to think about as the words for them were found in the telling. There was the brave rescue and who ran to assist, who fled the scene to save himself, and — here the names come thick and fast — who was hurt, who not, who helped, who tried and failed, would have, could have, didn't. Arguments and contradictions followed. The six nuns rumoured to be dead were found — disappointingly — to be only one. The heroism of her young companion helped compensate for the loss of excitement. To some the body of God the Father lying dead on the cold stones of the piazza was as sad and familiar as their own grandfathers dead in their beds; to others every remembered detail of the day, especially the piebald girl, became a portent, an omen. The very naming of God the Father caused them to cross themselves: here was no unhappy mischance but a terrible symbol of the speechless judgement of Heaven. It was like the famous painted rooms in the Arcivescovo's house: stand here and you behold a magnificent view from a portico; stand there and the pavement will seem to tilt, the marble columns to lurch.

It did not seem to matter greatly which construction prevailed. The important thing was to accommodate the new — even when it was abhorrent. And so they continued to alter and reshape the story and to rework it until there were parts that were entirely their own. And in all of this they might have succeeded — until this morning.

Few this morning could believe the news that flew from lip to lip, the baleful and pointless coda that had attached itself to the terror. Something about a mare that, forgotten in the catastrophe and ignored in the aftermath, had stood tethered all day to a ring in the wall of the Palazzo, watching with her patient eye (too old to be afraid) these swarming humans. There was something about some youths taking this mare last night, untethering it from the iron ring, riding off on it, two, three on its back, the others running along beside. And something about what they did and how they brought it back that was so terrible to hear, so abhorrent, that many did not believe until they saw for themselves the animal still lying there broken on the altar steps. The boys had taken it and ridden it in the dark all the way out toward the *prato*, and it seems they did not come back for hours, and when they did they tore into the church with the hack mortally wounded and with blood running down her hind legs. They drove her with sticks and with pikes, round and round the church, until she fell and lay bleeding from under her tail on the steps of the altar. It was something too hard to comprehend on this bright, blue morning with the doves all burbling and mindless as happiness itself under the eaves. This intentioned cruelty, this carefully managed sacrilege, was worse than any impersonal calamity. It was an arrangement of thought and deeds, never before contemplated, and something that surely, please God, could not have been thought, done, here, now, in this city. For if the report were true, what next? What depravity, what viciousness might follow? The story of the horse seemed to announce a ruinous path the days ahead might take. Just when the people were ready to absorb the outcome of the accident and accept the judgement of God, here came this stark and dire event. Every citizen who heard the story was moved to disbelief, and had to go and see for himself, for herself, the creature still lying panting on the marble steps, until about the middle of the morning a bookbinder came with a sharp knife and cut its throat.

Just as some sights are too terrible to witness and must be obliterated by closing the mind's eye, some news is too terrible for the ears to receive, too difficult for the mind to accept in its entirety. Unless it be closed away forever, it must be dissected, its constituent parts separated and laid out. Each part carefully examined, weighed, and held to the light. Each must be named. Then will it be possible to try to understand how all parts came together. It must be trapped, secured in some tapestry, text or tale. It will be disarmed of its autonomy and kept in a safe place, a created, a finished thing, no dangerous life of its own to enter our dreams.

And so, like a shop full of embroiderers, the people have worked all day on this tapestry again, always trying to incorporate this ugly knot, the stubborn fact of the horse. The fate of God the Father could have been easily accommodated, one way or another, given time: a dire blow from blind Fortune, or the terrible cost of their own sin. In the reworking of the accident, the threads weave an intricate pattern of action and reaction, praise and blame — but all converge and finish at the horse in a tight knot of disbelief, the intractable nub of the wickedness of man.

Today Sofonisba has a toothache, or says she has. She has retired to her room with the door closed against ruin and disorder. This morning someone came, perhaps before it was light, and threw horse shit at their door as if to mark them and — they have since learned — Matteo too. Orazio, in a red-faced fury, railed against the desecration of his house. He did not go at once to *Argentara*, but sent the yard boy to try to find out who it was. When the boy came back, he was so out of breath he was hardly able to speak. He had not discovered who threw the filth at the door, but, he said, a horse had been slain on the very steps of the altar at San Pier. There was filth everywhere. The news seemed to make Orazio feel better about his front door. He said he would see for himself and then he would continue to the Arcivescovo's house as he had planned. He set the boy to watch the door against further trouble and told Sofonisba to remain within. It fell to Chiara to clean the door.

The boy did not stay, of course, but went again in search of new excitements. Sofonisba went to the workshop, but had no heart for work. When the boy came back he was as out of breath as before. He had been, he said, to see what they had done with the horse. It had been taken outside the Porta alla Giustizia where the bodies of the damned are taken for burial. He went to look but there was no horse there. Instead he saw the body of God the Father. He saw it himself. He said it lay there just outside the wall with the crows beginning to tear it. Sofonisba said she had heard enough and would not hear more. There was no end to the ugliness of this feast. She sighed heavily and went up to her room.

Content to comply with her father's wishes, she has no wish to revisit the wreckage of a dream. She heard the people yesterday, a group of monks blaming Maestro Paolo for carrying out the work of the Devil. Paolo retorted that the only devil there that day was the one who was born an idiot and did not have the sense to carry out his instructions, and they did not have to look very far to see who that was. But who can say who is to blame? Her father called Chiara the work of the Devil. But if he wanted to talk like that then why not blame the Devil himself? Surely only the Devil could dream of such a thing. Too much talk of devils. She has a muddied feeling about the heart. She cannot paint. Nothing is right with the world or ever can be. There seems no way forward from the catastrophe of San Giovanni. It has undermined the validity of all their fine endeavours. It is as if they were all — artists, labourers, clergy, *festaiuoli*, even the townspeople whose only role was to be enthralled — mere children, their game kicked apart by an angry father. Their innocent enjoyment is denounced, condemned and all of them are punished. Now the words of the black-robed friar who stood in the doorway of San Pier echo in her room: *Who has introduced these devilish games among you? You feed on vanity and pomp and are rendered dry as tinder for the flames of Hell.* And before that, the young acolyte, hardly more than a boy, who came into the church when they were assembling the machinery: *The wings of devils shall carry you to Hell. And the woman shall go first.* She had laughed that morning with Tassi who mocked him as soon as his back was turned, saying "Lead the way, woman. Carry me to eternal damnation." Yet the words of that thin young fellow and the mad raving Dominican seem vindicated. *All shall end in discord and destruction.* A terrible unease gnaws at the foundation of all she believes — and all she cannot. There is no way forward. Orazio seems not to notice. He has gone just as before to Andrea's house, preferring

to take one step at a time and so get the job done and, more important, receive his fee. Sofonisba has promised to work on the panel
for the ambassador. The young Madonna, her plump Infant and
the tiny bird seem stripped of significance in a world of old men.
Worse, they seem impossibly naïve, wilfully blind to what they
know is to come, stubbornly deaf to the echoes in her head.
Sofonisba professes a toothache. Chiara is no use. She has carried
out her odious duty but she is no company at all. Since San Giovanni
she has worn a stricken, dreadful face. She will barely speak except
to repeat "*Sfortuna.*" and sometimes to point at her heart. Sofonisba
has her straighten out the bed, not caring about the dung crusting
her fingernails; she lies down on top of the smooth sheets and
exhales slowly and softly as Chiara goes out and closes the door
behind her.

Downstairs in the yard, the boy Tanai, who has lost the most dis-
cerning half of his audience, continues regardless as soon as Chiara
reappears. The *Confraternita della Misericordia*, he says, had taken
the body of God the Father, like that of any destitute, to the *Bigallo*,
since the man had no family and no one had come forward to bury
him. But in the night, some of the friars from San Marco had
arrived and demanded entrance there. They had protested loudly
and had taken the body away themselves, saying the citizens gave
good gold to the *Misericordia* to attend the remains of the Faithful,
not to carry out the work of the Devil. They carried it through the
streets in darkness and left it outside the Porta alla Giustizia. Now
no one will touch it, the boy says, for fear. He says this morning he
climbed the tower at the gate with some other boys and threw
stones down at it. He says the skin was black and shiny.

Tanai repeats everything he has heard in the town: that God let
the Devil take the old man for his sin of pride in ascending on the
cloud; that the fire was hellfire and that is why there was no stopping it; that there was a strange disfigured girl in the church — he

bores his eyes into Chiara's. When he asks her if she wants to see the charred God she of course says yes.

With Monna Sofonisba shut in her room in a black despair that she calls a toothache, the boy is happy to leave the shop and run with Chiara out to the Porta alla Giustizia.

They climb the stairs of the wall to see. There are crows flapping heavily to and from the tower. Outside, on the scrubby ground where the carcasses of mules are left to be picked clean, the body is stretched out. There are people about on the road, coming and going at the gate, a group watching from a little way off, but the body is all in its own space, except for a friar digging beside it. Chiara climbs down again and makes her way through the gate, though the boy advises against it. Some, recognizing her for a slave, make to stop her. She turns her face toward them and they let her continue, her skin its own protection. Her legs shake uncontrollably but no one follows her. She goes over to the friar where he bends to his work, his brown hood pulled up over his head. He has a small spade of the kind that is used to dig for onions, and the ground is very hard. Still, he has dug a hole sufficiently long and deep to the level of his hips.

"God is all burnt up."

The friar starts and looks back over his shoulder. He crosses himself then bows his head and goes on digging.

"No one wants to help you bury God."

He slices at the walls of his pit.

Three dogs lie waiting in the shade of a low broken wall, their paws stretched innocently in front, their heads erect, alert.

"I can dig."

Only then does he look up. Above the kerchief that covers his face, the sweat runs into his eyes, runs from his eyes. He makes the sign of the cross in the air between them and goes on with his work. The boy is calling from the wall.

Chiara crossed herself too. She has seen the body of God the Father and she has seen his skin. She has seen it plainly. A torn black sheet was thrown over the corpse, but she could see a leg and it was just as the boy had said. It might have been a tanned hide. It might have been something Maestro Paolo had made, something from the skin of a pony stretched on sticks. A dragon. A devil. Perhaps because his back is turned to her, or perhaps because there is no one else to hear, she begins to tell the friar as best she can about the hanged man's skin and Matteo Tassi and her own ill luck, for it seems they were all bound as one with the blackened God and no one can untangle them.

And then the first stone hits her, and there are the boys that Tanai has tried to warn her about, six or seven of them a little way off, and every one of them with a stone in his hand.

AT FIRST ALESSANDRO is careful. He attaches himself loosely to this group, to that, to test the winds of opinion. He hears his own name once in reference to the fire. He does not hear it mentioned in the same breath as the horse. No one breaks away from the conversation to point. No one shouts: "There's one of them!" He judges it safe to stay about, and eventually finds himself descending the steps of the tavern.

Tassi is there, drinking heavily. It is obvious from the way the others at his table are positioned, just as it is obvious from any two-a-penny Last Supper, exactly who is the centre of attention. Tassi was working nearly all day at the church. All of the debris has been carried out, and the carcass of the horse dragged away. The pillars have been cleaned of smoke. The blood and the stains of the horse have been washed from the marble paving, and the altar steps have been scrubbed.

At noon the *Arte del Cambio* sent baskets of bread and jugs of wine to sustain the workers. By the middle of the afternoon it was done.

The men left the locked church and went off to their families or came here to the tavern on the Via Baccano to do their share of the telling of the tale. They are thirsty and the taverner is liberal with his wine. The city has its church restored and these men are heroes.

No one notices Alessandro come down the steps, least of all Tassi the brave, Tassi the heroic with his stock of tales replenished and brimming with details that only the first on the scene, the nearest to the action, could supply.

Inconspicuousness is a double-sided coin. Sometimes to be ignored can be a blessing, sometimes a wound keenly felt, an affront that can never be answered.

Alessandro approaches the table, sees a spot on the end of one of the benches, understands as soon as his cheeks settle there why it is empty. It overlaps the bench that runs at right angles along the adjacent side; any one who sits there is facing away from the centre of the conversation and has nowhere at all to rest his cup. It is lucky for Alessandro that he is too dull to see how it suits his place in life. He is not, is never, thinking of the meaning of things. Right now he is fully engaged in trying to enter the conversation, or at least the outer edges of the drinkers' awareness. He turns his body, he looks toward their faces, he dutifully follows the conversation and duly interjects with, "And I, too . . ." or, "So it was . . ." or, "I saw, myself . . ." But no one turns in his direction until at last Tassi catches sight of him out of the corner of his eye.

"Alessandro!" he says and bangs his cup down, the wine jumping from the earthen vessel in surprised drops.

"What are you doing hanging off the end there? Get in here, man." He makes room. Is in such a mind for revelry he would make room for the entire Guild of Apothecaries if they now appeared. He calls for drinks. Says, "Alessandro will buy one for all," slaps him on the back. Alessandro barely moves a muscle, does not reply. It is then, leaning forward and turning so that he can look him in the eye, that Tassi catches sight of a slip of pale kidskin or something like it at Alessandro's neck, beneath his shirt. It is bound at the edges with a leather thong. He recognizes it at once. Reaches round and hooks a forefinger under the edge of the jerkin. He gives it a tug.

"Not feeling yourself, ha? Touch of the French disease?" He leers.

Alessandro pulls away, adjusts the neck of his shirt, closing it with a womanish gesture as if he is driven by modesty.

"Yes, hide it. It's a poor-looking thing. On you anyway." Tassi takes a swig of his wine. "Though I have to say," he leans close and lowers his voice, "I told you this before: it looks better on a woman." He can tell by the sharp movement of Alessandro's head that he has struck a nerve. He smiles and looks Alessandro in the eye, nods. Yes. Whatever you're thinking, yes, you're right. He jerks his chin, signals Alessandro to come closer, hear more.

"On a woman's breast. On a woman's splendid, naked breast even a pork rind looks beautiful."

Alessandro is on fire. It begins at his cheeks as if someone has opened the door of a furnace in his face, and it spreads like molten copper. His chest is tight and his head feels as if it will explode with the pressure of his anger. His eyes are blinded by the vision of Tassi with Sofonisba naked beneath him but for the charmed vest. He would like to strike back but all he can say is, "Pork rind?"

"Donkey. What you will." Tassi puts his two hands suggestively to his chest, leers. "It is what is underneath . . ."

Alessandro now would risk his life to hurt this man. He sees the only option left to him and takes it.

"Skin of a hanged man." He says it quietly, almost under his breath and Tassi is stopped like a bird in mid-flight struck by a stone. He snaps his head round to catch the words. "Again?" And Alessandro, quieter still, obliges.

"Skin. Flayed from the corpse of a hanged man. That's what it is." It is Alessandro's turn to look his listener in the eye and nod, but Tassi already knows without a doubt that it is true.

He knocks back his cup of wine, punches it into Alessandro's chest and shoves his head down toward the table top as he climbs out of his place on the bench and turns for the door. He wants to hurt someone now. Now see if desire can be denied. It wells and inflates his chest, pressing at his ribcage with every breath. And how his chest itches! He scratches at it furiously, beside himself with incoherent rage at the vileness of women. The filthy little wretch. And her whore of a mistress. He pounds up the stairs to the street, bangs the door open, would be happy if it were a thing alive that could shriek in pain at his touch. He begins to stride, covering twice his usual ground at every step, swearing in his head and through his teeth. Christ's bloody bones. Christ's bloody, bloody bones. He does not know what he is going to do. Anything. Just let him do anything. His whole body itches. He has no thought in his head that could make sense with any other, no words except curses and foul abuse running on his tongue. He has no plan or strategy but to confront the author of his humiliation. He knows only that his hands ache to inflict pain.

⌐⌐

IN THE EARLY AFTERNOON Sofonisba came down to the shop, deciding that she did not after all want to be consumed by her dismay. She had heard Chiara leave and then return, sobbing for some reason of her own. She had no energy to play the mistress, only enough to begin to sweep the broken pieces of the last days aside. She looked at the work. Her heart was not with the *Madonna and Finch*, not yet. There was a panel in oil begun many months ago for the nuns of Sant' Ambrogio. It was to be *St. Peter Receiving the Keys of the Kingdom*. She considered the subject monumentally dull, too overtly didactic for her taste, and she pitied the nuns who would have to look at it. Working on it today would be suitably penitential. The composition was laid down and the colouring begun. She does not need Chiara, does not care at all that the girl sleeps away the afternoon in a corner of the locked shop.

It is almost evening when Chiara wakes to hear knocking at the street door. She inspects her bruises before she moves. Four or five stones had hit their mark. She is lucky there were not more, lucky she is fast on her feet, lucky Orazio's boy did not abandon her, but she does not feel lucky.

Sofonisba is eating a dish of cream and almonds outside in the courtyard. She is sitting on a low wall in the last patch of sun before it dips below the roof. She does not hear the knocking. The air is filled with a riot of small noise issuing from the vine beside the stairs. Every leaf has twinned a bird and all might rise up at any moment and be borne away on a thousand wings.

When Chiara finally opens the door, still inspecting her arm, Tassi shoves past her, barely sees her.

"Where is she?"

A few strides more and he is in the courtyard, is at Sofonisba's side, the birds spraying up out of the tree, a broken wave rebounding from a rock.

Chiara sees him from the back door of the shop, sees Sofonisba putting her dish down, getting up. She sees Tassi, as if he is shepherding Sofonisba with his arm, with the side of his chest, pushing her toward the stairs, Sofonisba looking back at him, a smile on her lips, but a frown around her eyes. They go up the stairs together and Tassi's hand is under her mistress's elbow, almost lifting her, and then her door closes behind them. The shouting begins at once.

Chiara knows how to ignore what goes on between her mistress and Messer Matteo, for why risk a beating for eavesdropping or spying on their coarse games? But something here is amiss. There is no laughter; Sofonisba loves to laugh, and Tassi too. They feed each other's appetites.

Monna Sofonisba can shout, she can bellow, she can wheedle and cajole. But this is a voice Chiara has not heard before. It is a protesting, warning voice and it is in earnest without any hint of play. There is a cry. They are fighting. Chiara goes to the foot of the stair. If she could hear just one laugh she would not put her foot upon it. But there is her mistress's voice again, but this time muffled, as if she has her sleeve across her face. There are sounds of a struggle. Chiara climbs, listening at each step. There are no more voices, but neither is there silence, for there is a presence of movement unseen, rhythmic, and of breathing. Chiara knows what it is. She is on the top stair and the sounds of coupling are coming faster now. She creeps past the closed door to the window and holds her breath. She knows if she moves just a little she will be able to see through the gap behind the shutter that stands half-open. There is a sudden release of sound, as of held breath let go, and she looks. The bed is empty, untouched. She moves round the shutter and looks in through the open window, keeping back and hoping naively that if they see her they will think her on her way to the door farther on. There on the floor, beside the bed, on her hands and knees, is Sofonisba. She is getting to her feet. Chiara glimpses her face, red and tight with anger under her fallen hair, her mouth contorted with rage like a man's. Sofonisba brushes at her skirt again and again, spitting insults and abuse at Messer Matteo, enlisting the animal kingdom for her purposes. "Pig. You bastard pig. You filthy dog. You . . . you . . . you . . ." and then in desperation, "piece of bat shit!" But Messer Matteo is not listening. He is kneeling with his back to the window, sitting back on his heels, his legs wide apart. His head is thrown back. His shoulders fall with each breath. It gusts from him, "Ha . . . Ha . . . Ha . . ." at long intervals. It might be the slow laughter of a giant.

Chiara draws back from the window. There is a long moment of silence. When she tries to slip away, her shoulder knocks the shutter. She scrambles down the stairs as fast as she can and the next moment Tassi is at the door. He comes out onto the balcony, and Chiara sees him when she looks back from across the courtyard. He is standing with a fistful of bed linen clutched in front of him and one arm outstretched toward her. Satan himself with his black brows and his black intentions.

Chiara ducks into the kitchen in the hope of hiding until he has gone. She stays close in the shadow of the wall behind the door, so that if he looks in he will not see her. But it is no use. He comes thundering down the stairs and straight to the kitchen like a mastiff that has sniffed her out.

"You!" He grabs her shoulder. "Say one word of this and I'll slit your dirty, little piebald throat."

Chiara cannot speak a word but only shakes her head to show him that she understands.

"One word and I'll break your arms and your stinking little legs."

Chiara looks at Tassi's great square hands. In the taverns, he lays wagers that he can bend iron — and then he wins. She says she will not tell a word. "Good," he says. "Because if you do —" He holds her face under the jawbone. Chiara is too scared to notice that the great square hands apply no pressure at all. He does not finish his thought. "If you do," is all he says, "if you do."

Outside, he knocks Sofonisba's dish from the wall as he passes. Then he tears a lemon from the tree in its pot and hurls it to the far wall where it bursts.

Chiara waits. When she has stopped shaking she goes out to pick up the pieces of the dish.

There is no sound at all from Sofonisba's room.

Climbing the stairs demands courage. Chiara's bare feet make hardly any sound. *Your most loyal servant.* The door is open. Sofonisba is lying on her bed, stretched out like a corpse, with her eyes staring at the ceiling.

"*Madonna?*"

Sofonisba only rolls her head from side to side, her eyes still fixed where they stare.

"*Madonna?*"

"Get out."

Sofonisba lies motionless, an effigy. When finally she rises, it is with a black hollow in her heart. This morning's sense of disorder is as nothing beside it. Tassi has broken into her house and taken what was hers. The gravity of her look could pull a man under the waves of her grief. She has nothing. She looks around the room as if she finds herself in a stranger's house to which she will never return. The bed, the chest, the window, hold no past and no future. They hold only the moment after Tassi pushed her inside and closed the door behind him. She should have known. *I have something for you*, he had been saying as they climbed the stairs. She heard the false note in his voice, suspected only a trick. She should have turned and looked at his eyes. They would have warned her. She saw as soon as she was in the room with him.

You want to play tricks with skins? With a bit of flesh? Try this. Carne vivente. He had pushed her down hard.

She looks down at her body with distaste. With slow deliberate movements she unfastens her dress and pulls it from her shoulders, letting it fall and treading it out of the way. She pulls off all that she is wearing and goes to put on new clothes, taking first a clean towel to wipe down her limbs and rub her body as if she has been splashed with something foul. There are places she works at carefully, as if wiping Tassi from a painting. When she is dressed she gathers up the bedcover that Tassi pulled to the floor and her clothes, too, and takes them down to the courtyard.

She dumps the pile on the stones and goes to the kitchen for a pitcher of oil and a brand. Ignoring Chiara who can sense something extraordinary about to happen and is trying to speak to her, she pours the oil over and lights it. Soon a vast quantity of black smoke is darkening the evening shadows in the courtyard. It is not long before there are shouts and cries from those outside who think the house is ablaze and another night of terror lies ahead. Sofonisba only stands and stares at them as they come to see, pushing past each other through the door that stood wide open after Tassi left, pushing their way past each other into the courtyard: two strangers first, staring at Chiara, and then another with the cook from her lodging next door (once in trouble for starting a fire and never easy since). Tanai appears and then the boy Tuccio from across the street, fearful and ready to run, and then the old fellow who looks after the horse and is disordered in the brain. He asks if the chestnuts are ready. Sofonisba stares at them icily through the dusky, wavering air, her raised eyebrows and her cold eyes asking plainly what business they have there, spectators of her pain.

When the cook says, "*Madonna*, what in Heaven's . . ." she turns a savage eye on her and growls.

"Do you have business in this house?"

Chiara brings the stick she uses to push down the washing in the barrel. Sofonisba takes it. She pushes the clothes with the stick then spins round, suddenly infuriated by the silence behind her.

"Well aren't you a lot of gaping fools? Go back where you came from. Go on." But she grabs hold of Chiara as the others leave and puts her arm round her shoulders.

Chiara doesn't think of moving. She leans into the warmth beside her, feeling its comfort across her shoulders, trying to remember when she has felt this warmth before. She doesn't mind that the heat of the fire is scorching her bare ankles.

On his way home, Orazio is thinking Sofonisba must come with him tomorrow. Andrea is asking for her and, besides, he is getting too old for this. His bed seems the place to be. He will have Sofonisba prepare a soothing balm, and perhaps a little sweet wine, warmed. He has just begun to consider one or two little honey cakes when he sees the crowd outside the house. Tanai has put on some kind of authority, ill-fitting like his father's shirt. He is telling everyone who stops that the fire is being tended and it is only the cook burning some rags.

Orazio dismounts and stuffs the reins of his horse into the boy's hand, tells him to take it round to the old man.

Sofonisba is still standing in the semidarkness with Chiara, staring into the embers. Nothing Orazio says can force her to tell him what she has been burning. He prods the blackened remains but they crumble to ash. He would like to beat an explanation out of her, but her stony gaze is disconcerting. Chiara is not so alarming. He will surely get something out of her, but Sofonisba intervenes, taking her upstairs and out of reach.

The next morning, Ser Tomasso is at the house to tell Orazio in person what is being said in the street. He has considered most carefully whether or not to come. There will be plenty of others to tell Orazio, if he doesn't already know. Why be the butt of his anger? And yet the matter is altogether too serious, and made more grave by the weight of friendship. It is not the job of strangers. He comes as the bearer of bad news and Orazio listens in silence, trying while the room spins before his eyes to salvage dignity in the face of shame.

"Thank you, Tomasso," he says. "I don't want to hear more." He shows him to the door himself.

He takes the stairs as if Jesus Christ himself has taken away his lameness.

He barges through the door to Sofonisba's room like a boar through a thicket, and before twenty words have passed his lips she is a whore, a harlot and a slut. What was she thinking of, letting Matteo Tassi in? When his expressed instructions were to lock the door? And what does she think she is doing now, lying there all this time like a plague victim? Never mind burning clouts! She should have been up and sending the guard after Matteo.

"Because do you know what he did after he left here? Do you? Do you know?"

Sofonisba is shaking her head, though it is more like a tremor, and her mouth is making ugly shapes. She can scarcely breathe.

"I'll tell you. He went straight to the card house and filled himself with drink and told it to every last scoundrel who would listen. The whole quarter knows now, thanks to you, that Monna Sofonisba Fabroni has lain with the sculptor Tassi."

Sofonisba tries to defend herself, but wave upon wave of vituperation break upon her and it is no use. She is not the same woman. Tears are all she can manage.

Orazio hauls himself down the stairs as angrily as he went up, but more out of breath and red in the face. Chiara is carrying water to sluice down the yard and wash away the black from the stones as he has ordered. When he draws level, he grabs her by the hair at the nape of her neck and twists her head round so that she has to look in his face. Her eyes close against the sun, water spills over her feet.

"And you!" His face so dark, so blood-filled. "What did you see? You little dung ball!"

Chiara answers the only thing a slave can answer in the circumstances: "*Niente, Monsignore.*"

Orazio thumps his fist on the side of her head.

"Answer me honestly. *Sudiciona.*" He twists her hair while he drains his reservoir of vile names, a roll call of the lower orders of creation. "*Verme. Serpe. Baco. Scarafaggio* . . . Answer me honestly."

Chiara looks at the fist that has punched her. It is not as large as Tassi's.

"Nothing, sir." Which only brings this fist to her head again, though he has the grace to do it on the other side.

"I repeat. Tell me what you saw."

"A little, Messer Orazio, *Signore, Monsignore*, but not much."
He says, "Tell me then," and shakes her to make sure she will.
"Messer Matteo was in Monna Sofonisba's bedchamber."
"In her bed?"
"No, Messer . . . *Signore*"
"On her bed?"
"No, *Monsignore*. On the floor." Orazio waggles her head as if her words are drops he can shake from a bottle.
"And my lady was on the floor." He shakes her again. "And she was crying." Orazio stares hard in her eyes then jams his teeth together and shakes her as violently as he can with his bent hand. He might be a dog shaking the life from a duck. Chiara can hear the hairs tearing from the back of her head.
"I'm sorry." She says it three, four, five times, and at last he stops.
"And their clothes were in disarray."
Out of breath, spent, Orazio lets go of his hold.
"Thank you." Though he means, *finally*.
"Thank you, *Signore*." Though she means, *bastard*.
Orazio flings on a rag of a cloak, one he wears about the house only on winter days, and storms away to the Palazzo del Podestà.
While Orazio is making a loud and formal accusation of rape, Chiara scrubs at the stones, trying to remove all trace of the fire. A black stain refuses to shift and remains there, a shadow of the mark on her brow, in the shape of a bird in flight.
By midday the guard of the Bargello have Ser Matteo Tassi behind bars, and the Podestà has decreed a trial to take place within thirty-six hours.

⌒

IT IS AS WELL THAT SOFONISBA does not emerge from her room until it is time to leave for the courtroom, as well that she remains ignorant of her father's prevarication, for Orazio, who has spent so much of his life in contempt of public opinion is now, in his last years, consumed by his regard for it. When Tomasso came to him with the sorry news, his first thought was for his business and how his daughter's fallen state might affect present and future commissions. His rage against her and against Tassi was driven by his anxiety. It was as if Tassi had pilfered his shop. But concern for opinion is as strong and sticky as a spider's web, and soon entangles those who fear it. No sooner is Matteo Tassi behind bars than Orazio begins to worry that he is cast in a particularly bad light, as if he and his daughter are wont to associate with common felons. He decides to pay a bond so that Matteo Tassi does not have to wait in the dungeon of the Palazzo for his trial. He thinks it will not hurt at all to have Matteo know that he is indebted to the family he has injured.

The Sala della Giustizia is a hall built for giants, the glazed windows so high that nothing can be seen from them but a corner of roof nearby and a sky so blue it might be the floor of Heaven. Above the windows, the walls are plastered and painted with allegories of Justice and Mercy; below, their grey stone is unadorned except for the coat of arms of the magistrate, the Podestà, which hangs behind his chair at the far end of the room. The Podestà sits in his red robe at the centre of a long table with his officers in their clerical black on either side. Two guards wearing breastplates and helmets over their uniforms stand with pikestaffs at each of the doors and two more stand behind his chair. In front of the table two scribes sit at a small desk bearing ink and parchment. At a second long table to one side, men in long black gowns seem to be conducting some business all their own. Matteo Tassi stands to the left of the Podestà. He has washed and scrubbed for the occasion. He has borrowed a clean shirt and a doublet in green velvet with silver clasps, put on his best woolen hose and his best black breeches trimmed with ribbon. The sleeves of the shirt are too extravagant, the linen is too white, too bright. They shout across at Orazio and Sofonisba, a partnership of sobriety and modesty sweltering in their long surcoats of black and brown, their own sleeves denoting nothing but restraint. There is some question about where the slave should stand. An officer leans back and whispers to the guard behind him and Chiara is taken away to the side of the room.

The Podestà calls first on Orazio. Orazio tells how he came upon his daughter distracted and tearing her clothes. He tells how she wept and wailed and burned her garments in the middle of the courtyard, how he determined then that she must have been driven mad, stricken with some wild affliction — which proved, he says, as matters unfolded, to be true. He tells them how, in a little while, on his kindly questioning, she told him all the matter. In this way he learned that Ser Matteo Tassi had violated his daughter in his very house on the day that he himself was away, occupied in the house of a most holy man of God, a most just and righteous man. He speaks at length about his daughter's spotless soul and how it is now trapped like a pure white dove in a filthy cage. Ser Matteo Tassi has, he says, destroyed her most precious possession, robbing her of a treasure that is irreplaceable. He might speak for longer but one of the guards lets fall his lance. It is a relief to all.

The Podestà calls upon Tassi to answer. Tassi sighs audibly to suggest the difficulty of the task ahead. He looks around the room, meeting every eye, steps forward, folds his arms across his chest and looks down as if consulting the flagstones for an answer. Tassi, who loves to entertain his friends, play the showman, the clown, has no difficulty capturing the attention of the court. If Orazio before this moment had any hopes that the pains he took to secure bond will be rewarded, he is swiftly relieved of them.

No, Tassi says, he will not deny the charge that he enjoyed an intimacy with the lady Sofonisba. But he will resist to the death the charge that he enjoyed it against her will. On the contrary, he says, the lady Sofonisba opened her arms — and here one of the guards, perhaps the same one, interrupts with a fit of sarcastic coughing.

Opened her *arms*, Tassi repeats — ensuring that every man in the room, hearing this emphasis, will now think "legs" — to his advances.

It is not the testimony Orazio expected. He stands with his bursting, ruddy face and bellows like a bull across the room. One of the guards steps forward and puts a hand on his arm. The old man is so incensed that he flings up his arm, shoves the guard aside and lurches over to pound upon the table of the scribes. The ink in the pots spurts up in miniature black fountains that sprinkle all the papers.

Orazio shouts, Tassi shouts, the Podestà shouts, and the whole affair ends in disorder when Orazio says he is leaving. Some of the men turn and shout at Chiara and everyone goes home in a vile temper.

Sofonisba shuts herself in her room. She has no wish to speak.

THE NEXT MORNING WHEN ORAZIO wakes he is not refreshed. He has not slept more than three hours since the conflagration. This whole business is an unwanted intrusion in his affairs, disrupting his work at the worst possible time. Yesterday in the evening a letter was brought to him — with less than perfect timing — from the secretary to the English ambassador. It contained an invitation to return with him to the court of the English Queen along with a number of distinguished artists and thinkers. The Court of England. How could a person manage such affairs in the midst of this domestic turmoil? Orazio went straight to Ser Tomasso.

He arrived at the notary's door, blowing through his teeth with exertion, his hands clenched in fists of frustration. Ser Tomasso prepared himself for a long night. They sat together with glasses of sweet wine.

Ser Tomasso listened and, as usual, saw matters clearly, like objects on a table. He immediately proposed a simple remedy for

Sofonisba's plight.

"You have known the man too long."

"Scoundrel," Orazio corrected him.

"Scoundrel, then. But not worthless. You've known him too long. You can't see the wood for the trees."

Orazio made a movement with his head, like a horse refusing the bit.

"Tassi may not have much —"

"Nothing."

"All right, nothing in the way of assets, but that is because he lets money pass through his hands like water. But a great deal of money, I might point out. And his reputation is growing. He works closely with Maestro Pallavicino. He's admired by the Duke. He's even completed a commission from Roma."

"A small one."

"You're not attending. I'm telling you that an alliance with Messer Matteo would be no bad thing. Your business would only expand."

Orazio reached for the jug. If he was going to accede at least he could feel good about it.

"You'll be saving Sofonisba's name, saving further scandal, gaining a partner and an heir (who has only the best interests of your daughter at heart), and expanding your business. What more could you ask?"

Orazio drained his cup and Tomasso knew he had won. "Demand a marriage of reparation," he said. "Tassi will jump at it. You don't need the Podestà." He waited while Orazio stared into his cup.

"Agreed?"

Orazio raised his eyebrows and let his lower lip jut. Only a friend as close as Tomasso would know it signalled his morose assent. Tomasso called one of his boys and, despite the hour and the risk, sent him to Tassi's house with a message.

"Now," he said. "You see how the solution to one problem may also provide the solution to another. This invitation. It is safe to surmise that the English Queen would not be interested in the services of a woman painter. Would prefer most likely to keep all fascinating creatures far from her Spanish husband. Good then." He got up and went to his writing desk, keeping his movements as small as possible, as if disturbance in the room might stir his friend to new anxieties. He dipped his pen.

"You will seal the marriage contract with Tassi; you will leave your capable daughter to finish the work for Andrea — which in any case is just what he wants — and you will reply to the English ambassador as follows."

With his mouth still sour from the night, Orazio goes to speak to Sofonisba while she still lies in bed.

"Daughter," he says, kissing her, "I could see this would happen. Matteo and you. It was bound to be. But he shall marry you. We shall see to it without a return to the Podestà. I have asked Tassi to come here this afternoon. I have told him I'm prepared to be reasonable."

Sofonisba turns her head and stares, as incredulous as if it were the doorpost speaking to her.

"You can make peace with him. He will come round."

"'Come round?'" She cannot believe what she is hearing. "'*Come round?*'"

"Yes. *Nozze riparanti*. It is the only honourable thing for him to do."

"*Nozze ripugnanti*."

Orazio takes a deep breath and continues as if he hasn't heard. Sometimes it is as well not to hear the things a daughter says. "He cannot refuse. What you take with you is worth far too much. There is of course your endowment of five hundred and fifty florins together with two new chests which shall contain your linens and clothes to the value of seventy-five florins, in addition to the value of Chiara at, let us say, thirty-five since she is flawed. I have kept Ser Tomasso up all night setting a figure on your worth as a painter's assistant, which with current commissions, future commissions, work on hand and materials amounts to almost one hundred and ninety-five florins more. And that is before any discussion of the distribution of my assets after I am gone."

Orazio is waiting for a response. A fly is buzzing round his beard.

Sofonisba smiles at last, says, "I am surprised you are so ready to let me go."

"Oh, I am not, I am not. All this is on condition that Tassi come to work for me. Now —"

Sofonisba sees no sign on her father's face that the discussion of this proposed marriage is at an end; Orazio is simply moving to the next subject for consideration. "I received," he says, "only last night an invitation of the greatest importance."

As he continues, it becomes clear to Sofonisba that Orazio has already drafted his letter of acceptance and expects to be on his way in the next few weeks. She can see that her father has his heart set on England. For him, there are no impediments, only easily managed details.

She can, he says, complete all unfinished commissions, starting today with the *San Pier* for the nuns of Sant' Ambrogio. He meanwhile will have the wall in the palace brought to a state of readiness, with the composition traced on in *sinopia*, so that she need only lay on the colour. She can work some sections *a secco*. It will be easier in the absence of an assistant. In this way, as soon as the contract with Tassi is signed, he will be away for Pisa and from there to England. He has every confidence that she will be able to manage affairs in his absence and in any case Messer Tomasso has agreed to cast an eye over the business each week.

It is only when he has left her room and closed the door behind him that Orazio is beset by anxieties of the severest kind. He is an old man and it is against the order of things for him to leave his estate. He is troubled by a deep misgiving, knowing that his undertaking is driven by pride. What if as a result his house should burn in his absence? His ship go down? He will leave instructions to have Ser Tomasso authorize a donation to the *Innocenti*.

SOFONISBA CANNOT BRING HERSELF to paint. She stands in the workshop and stares at the panel begun for the nuns of Sant' Ambrogio. The materials are all there, but her hands will not pick up a brush. They wander over the pigments and the pots, the jars of oil and the little mixing dishes, over the mixing board, the glue brush. They hesitate at the lamp with its promise of flame. In the pit of her stomach, a hollow place remains. It drags at her heart, would pull it in, *will* pull it in to drown in darkness and in bile if she does not do something. But she cannot work. Her hands return along the shelf, the table. They will not pick up anything. She feels as if she is closed within a prison cell. Her father has turned the key. The trial was a fiasco. Her father seems to have forgotten that. It was tantamount to parading her through the streets, standing her naked in the Loggia dei Lanzi like a marble statue and declaring her spoiled. Her father, in pursuing Matteo to court, ensured that everyone knew it, leaving her only one prospect of marriage — Matteo. Whatever she thought of Tassi, she did not think of him as a husband. He was a gambler, a whoremonger, a drunkard who tried to empty himself in her as if he were relieving himself. Now her father was intent on completing the business that Matteo, the filthy Matteo, had started.

Her left hand reaches out and picks up a rag. She dips it in the dish of turpentine and drags it across St. Peter's face.

TASSI SMILES TO THINK of his luck. He is like the inattentive card player who unwittingly trumps the ace. He had no intention, none. When he spoke out before the Court he spoke in anger as a man can who possesses nothing. For in the same instant that he had possessed Sofonisba he knew he had lost her. When he had spent himself there on the floor of her room, spilling himself into his hand because she managed at the very last to pull herself from under him, it had been just that: an expenditure of himself and all that he had. It was his veins emptying. He might have cut a vein and watched the blood drain with the same bleakness in his heart. In that moment his anger turned on himself. He was the man who breaks his most precious marble and punches his fist against the wall. He was still angry when he stood before the magistrate. His game with Sofonisba was over, he knew it. He was not even in the game any more. He did not care who won.

But now. Now a man could not help smiling. This message from Orazio has transformed him. He has stayed up all night. He has a small silver box with a lid, its handle a bird about to fly. It is almost finished. He can negotiate more time from the merchant who ordered it, get a loan for more silver from Orazio, make another, he does not care. This one he finishes for Sofonisba. But what to place inside?

In the hour before dawn, when all that remains to do is to burnish the surface, a new thought arrives. His mind is soothed to stillness by the action of his hands. The new thought floats into his mind unasked and settles like a feather on the surface. As soon as the sky is pink, he is outside. He climbs up on the roof of the shelter at the back of the shop and from there onto the high wall. If he balances carefully, he can reach up and rob the nest under the eaves.

In the workshop he has a small quantity of gold leaf still, a few flakes, but enough. It is delicate work. The blue of the egg is astonishing. He holds it between the thumb and middle finger of one hand and paints it with the clear of a hen's egg. It is the cosmos pinched in the fingers of God. He waits patiently for it to dry, blowing softly on it, humming. It has a gloss now that intensifies the blue. He knows how he will apply the flakes of leaf and waits patiently. After a second coat mixed with a little water to keep it tacky, he is ready. He draws his brush swiftly, lightly across his cheekbone to pick up a trace of oil and then bends his head to the gold. Blowing gently on the flakes to lift them, he catches one on the tip of his brush and transfers it to the egg. He works quickly. His lips, blowing, form a small and tender 'o' as if they are taking a nipple. If a flake is too large, he lays it on a leather pad and pushes it with the tip of a knife against the brush so that it fractures, leaving an uneven edge. He lays on the flakes, leaving a hair's breadth between so that a blue lightning seems about to crack apart the egg.

When it is finished, he is too excited to eat. It is a gift for a queen.

Now it is time to take off his filthy shirt, to rub his face and neck and arms and hands until every speck of grime is gone without trace, to splash his skin with the rosewater Bianca gave him "for keeping me close," to pull her ivory comb through his black tangles, to put on clean linen, to rub his teeth with salt and tear out a stalk of fennel from the base of the wall and chew on it as he sets out. He knows what is coming, and it is all good.

⸺

CHIARA, SO USED TO BEING alternately shunned by the world or singled out for blame, is now convinced that she is a marker for all misfortune. Misfortune strikes around her like a storm circling, drawing nearer. She goes about her duties with a cringing, cowering air, retreats to dark corners when she is not wanted. Sofonisba is too unhappy to notice; Orazio, too preoccupied. When he tells her in the afternoon to open the door to Tassi, she performs the sign of the cross.

But Tassi is all smiles, despite Orazio's solemn, formal greeting.

He puts his arm briefly on Chiara's shoulder as he passes her. She allows her eyes to flit to his face, thinks she sees there some kindness, but is afraid to look longer.

Orazio walks Tassi to the bench by the vine and tells Chiara to fetch Sofonisba from the kitchen. This too is a task to terrify. Chiara treads cautiously, creeps silently in.

"Messer Orazio says Messer Matteo —"

"Matteo?" Sofonisba hawks a gobbet of spit that lands on the table.

Chiara can only point mutely and stupidly toward the courtyard. Sofonisba stalks over to the window and pulls the shutters closed with a bang, drives the bar home behind them.

"Sofonisba?" Orazio's tone wavers uneasily between cajolery and threat.

The next moment he is inside, his voice suppressed, hissing Tassi this, Tassi that, your happiness, our prosperity.

But he only fuels Sofonisba's anger, reviving her resistance to him. Her replies grow louder and louder. She curses like a carter. Outside, Tassi wanders to the far side of the courtyard as if he does not want to hear more. Sofonisba's voice has a tremor in it. Chiara watches Orazio sieze his daughter by the shoulders. He shakes her. When he stops they are both out of breath. Sofonisba says not another word, and they leave the kitchen together to go and sit under the tree.

They sit side by side as if to receive an honoured guest, Sofonisba smoothing her gown, her mouth firmly closed, her eyelids lowered, but her arched eyebrows drawn up high. Tassi stands by uncomfortably. He might now be a schoolboy. Orazio nods to him and he comes forward. Tassi who has never in his life felt nervous, would as soon turn and run. Orazio gets up and moves to stand a few steps away. Tassi leans toward Sofonisba and speaks softly.

"*Madonna* Sofonisba, I beg leave humbly to offer you this token of my esteem."

He might as well be Alessandro with some crass idea of a curiosity, some half-baked attempt at seduction. She looks at him with
disbelief. He is offering her the box. She takes it without saying a
word and gets up slowly, her eyes never leaving his. She walks away
with the gift, contemplating it, like a nun her breviary. When she
draws level with the well, she stops and turns, smiling, toward Tassi,
whose face is changing even as her arm reaches out behind and lets
go the box over the edge. She pauses only a fraction of a moment
for the hollow gulp to register before she continues on her way. Not
a word then is spoken by any of them. And then Tassi is gone.
Messer Orazio stands a while longer, staring at his own feet.

Sofonisba and Tassi in the same house? If he achieves it, it will
be like thunder and lightning in the same box.

Never before has Tassi been at such a loss for a response of any
kind. He is a man of few words; the eloquence of the body has
always served him well enough: a smile, a curse, a gesture, a look,
a snort of derision, a blow, an explosion of laughter. But not today.
He knows the meaning of the word dumbfounded. He knows how
it feels to be struck on the head. It feels like this. Something blocks
the action of the will that instructs the lips to move. It is difficult to
put two thoughts together. Certainly he cannot answer Sofonisba's
shift. He cannot even describe it to himself. So sudden, so unforeseen. His hand still knows the heft of the box, his eye still sees the
shape of the silver bird, its wings partially extended, still toward
its tail, its breast thrust forward to meet the onrush of air when it
rises. His palm still remembers the almost weightless presence of the
blown egg, gilded and marvellous, so light it was both there and not
there. The junctures of the gold leaf on its surface formed a crazing
of lines as fine as the hair of infants, the blue tracks of an infinites-
imal lightning that held within it all that might be: the bird, his
desire for Sofonisba, suddenly overpowering when she seemed
within reach again; the egg, his promise of fulfilment. It was not the

loss of the box, the silver, that he resented. It was the destruction of what might be.

A new sensation has overtaken his mind. Or is it his heart? It is nothing he has ever felt before. The word does not come to him until he has reached his shop and is again seated at his work bench. Wounded. His heart is as raw and seeping as a wound.

And Sofonisba's heart? Perhaps it, too, was swallowed by the well. Whatever lives now in its place is a stony thing, dry of tears. Each new action of her father's only hardens it more. She is in the workshop the next morning when Orazio comes to her to say that he has arranged now for a new trial. He has come to her in all seriousness and told her she must prepare herself to bear witness to all of Tassi's lascivious advances. How little he understands. She listens to him now telling the same thing to Chiara.

"You are a good girl," he says. "You will be on your oath to tell every word, every action of Ser Matteo's." He even takes her hand in his.

"You would not want to be turned away from this house." He is patting her hand as if it were a mouse or a stoat, something not belonging to her. "Some people in the town are afraid of you," he says. "They say you carry the plague." He turns her hand over in his. "I don't believe that. You are ugly. That is all. But you serve us. And we protect you. And when Tassi is found guilty and the marriage of *riparazione* is ordained you shall still serve us. Nothing will change."

He gets up with a groan and pats her head. "Be a good girl, now," he says and walks stiffly to the door. "Remember, there is no life for you beyond Via del Cocomero."

Why, Sofonisba asks herself, does this feel as if Matteo and her father and even Chiara are aligning themselves against her? Her father, her protector. Won't Matteo be the victor in all this?

Sofonisba waits until he is out of earshot.

"You are my most loyal servant, remember? You will not tell them everything." Her anger is returning and she welcomes it. It comes at her like a rider on dark horse and sweeps her up and then she has the reins, she is the rider and the thundering hooves carry her over every obstacle.

She will not sit in her room and wait for her humiliation. Nor will she work like a cringing apprentice for her father. She bends down and pulls the Sant' Ambrogio panel out from behind another. She turns it over to reveal the ghosts of the two spoiled, faceless figures, just visible in a thin mist of pigment. For the first time in days the promise of a smile shows on her lips.

"Come here, Chiara. We are going to make a new painting. With an entirely new subject." She lays it flat and begins to assemble what she needs for the white ground.

"We shall need several coats." She is mixing the gesso now with all the vigour of a cook with fresh batter. "And while we are waiting," she says, beginning to lay it on the panel in long easy strokes, "I shall tell you the story of how Judith overcame her enemy, the powerful Holofernes."

By the end of the afternoon, Christ and St. Peter are obliterated, the panel already bears some light notation, and Sofonisba's drawing book is filling with sketches for the composition. Chiara herself has become thoroughly acquainted with how Judith steeled herself to enter the enemy camp with her maidservant and with her own sword cut off the head of the Assyrian general who was laying waste her country. She plays the part of both women for Sofonisba, stands patiently to have her head wrapped in a long saffron cloth.

"There will be Judith and her handmaiden." Sofonisba gestures with her palms up toward Chiara. "And there will be Holofernes." She goes to the shelf and takes down the plaster head, lays it, face up, in the basket of rags. "Or what is left of him." She picks up the basket and puts it in the middle of the floor.

"There," she says. "Now bend over the basket as if you are about to lift it."

But Chiara is taken with a fit of shaking and seems incapable of moving.

"It can't hurt you."

Chiara visibly shudders, cannot look at the head nestling in the basket. She bends and picks it up with her face turned away. This is a detail Sofonisba had not thought of. Its authenticity delights her.

"Stay there! Exactly like that!" She takes her book and makes a quick sketch of the turn of the servant's head, notations for the direction of the eyes. She has another thought.

"Now turn toward the door, you hear a sound."

Chiara does as she is asked, and her eyes are wide, fearing the worst.

"Perfect! Now look at the head again . . ." But Chiara keeps her face turned rigidly away.

"Look, stupid! It's plaster." Sofonisba goes over and lifts the head again, her hands cupped at the sides of its face. She kisses it on the lips.

Chiara lets the basket fall and runs out through the nearest door to vomit onto the stones of the courtyard.

Sofonisba, taken aback, shuts the door, leaving Chiara to clean up her mess. She will not be kept from her purpose, whatever it is that stirs Chiara to such an extraordinary response.

⌐⌐

ORAZIO RETURNS FROM his business in the town with preoccupations of his own. The news he has to convey is not pleasant. His imagination fails when he tries to predict how his daughter will respond to it. They are to use the presses. He has been to the Bargello and he has been told that the thumbscrew is the most reliable means of expediting a conclusion. He lodged a protest with the Podestà, but the decision had been made and there was no reversing it. He left with the uncomfortable feeling of having instigated something he did not quite intend.

Ser Tomasso sighs under his breath when Orazio appears at his door for the second time in less than twenty-four hours. He softens when he hears the reason, is glad that he himself is spared the vexations of women.

"Come in, come in. No need to tell it to the whole street."

He settles Orazio with a glass of wine — sensing that as a service to his friend it is at least as useful as his advice — and he listens: Sofonisba is good, beautiful and undeserving of ill treatment; she will never paint again; he, Orazio, is old, ailing and, as Tomasso quickly infers, mortally afraid of a future with a crippled daughter.

"Two things you must ensure," he says, when Orazio has finished. "Firstly, that Matteo is called to the presses first; that they are applied to him before any one else. That way it may be unnecessary to employ them further. Secondly, that if they do use them on Monna Sofonisba they agree to use only the left hand. They are likely to use only the left hand of the slave, since they know her value to you. You can ask at least as much — or should I say as little — for your daughter."

Orazio is considerably comforted by the practicality of this advice. He is about to leave when Tomasso puts his hand on his arm.

"And Orazio, don't keep it from her. The last thing you want is for her to faint away at the most critical moment. Advise her tonight. Let her prepare herself, fortify her will. Prayer is a help."

On his way home, Orazio rehearses the words he will say to comfort and strengthen his daughter. But there is no opportunity to use them. When he tells her the news she says nothing, not a word. He wishes she would protest, seek an explanation. His own words of consolation cannot get past her obdurate calm. It fills the air between them like a block of untouched marble. His words, like dull implements, skip off it without leaving a mark: *It is God's will and He will give you the grace to exonerate yourself. You have nothing to fear if you give a true account.*

"Chiara?" Sofonisba looks the girl in the eye. "Are you brave?"

They are kneeling side by side on the floor of the church of San Pier Scheraggio, where no prayers have been said since the fire.

Last year, Sofonisba saw the face of a witness leaving the court of justice. He had been examined at the trial of a man accused of pilfering the coffers of the city. He was holding his hand against his chest as if he were holding there some precious broken thing. His top lip was drawn up almost to his nostrils showing his yellow teeth and his slippery gums and it was twitching and quivering uncontrollably like a thing alive. Her father then caught hold of her and said, "Do you see that? That is the face of Marsyas. Remember it." It is not a face that could be easily forgotten.

Chiara nods doubtfully.

"Do you love me?"

"Of course."

"And what will you tell the Court?"

"What you wish me tell."

"They are to use the presses. You know that? It will be the day after tomorrow."

She is not sure if Chiara understand what it means. She does not want to tell her. She is still not sure how it came to this.

"They have removed all ornament from this church," she says. "It is the mirror of my heart."

TWELVE

Eᴍɪʟɪᴏ ᴅᴀ ᴘʀᴀᴛᴏ is confirmed in his opinion that a man does not need a daughter in order to be visited by care and woe. He thought about — prayed about — Orazio's troubles with his daughter all morning. He walked to San Lorenzo to offer thanks that her betrothal to Alessandro had been forestalled. His relief to have been spared the shame far outweighed his regret that the union would not come to pass. He spared a prayer, too, for his friend, asking humbly that his sorrows would soon be relieved by a judgement in his favour. He is sorely stung by the fact that while he was saying these very prayers, new evidence was inviting public censure on the conduct of his own son.

He would be doubly mortified to know how quickly the news had travelled. It flew from the doors of the Sala della Giustizia even before the trial was over. In less than the time it would take for ten *Aves*, the details of Alessandro's grotesque doublet and what was done with it had travelled from the Palazzo del Podestà to the stables behind the Palazzo Vecchio, and from there to the Mercato Vecchio. After that, it was everywhere, like chestnut floss at summer's start. Even the strange parti-coloured slave who told it became unremarkable for a while. It displaced the scandalous accusations of one artist against another and almost overshadowed the reports of who was put to the press. In a little less than two hours it was everywhere, settling on the sills of merchants' upper chambers, floating into the open awnings of the tinsmiths and the leather workers, slipping under the elaborate ear pieces of expectant dames, insinuating itself under the very wimple of the abbess up at the priory and returning to arrive — breathlessly — at Emilio's door: *Listen, Ser Emilio, you know what they are saying in the town . . .*

In a mighty rage, Emilio attacked his son, pushing him up against a doorjamb and striking him repeatedly on the side of the head, smacking his arm down when Alessandro raised it to ward off the blows. "You're a fool and a shame on the name of Emilio da Prato," he said, grabbing the front of Alessandro's jacket to drag him aside. He went through to his bedroom, clawing keys from his belt. Alessandro knew what he was going for. In the bedroom Emilio rattled at a lock and banged open the lid of a chest; rifled and banged and rattled again and returned with his will. "Well, then?" he said. "Fire. Bring me fire." Alessandro lit a taper at the shop's brazier and spent a long time doing it. When he could delay no longer, he brought it back. Emilio made a great show of holding the will above the flame. The edges of the document blackened and burned but Alessandro was watching his father's face. Emilio was skilful, managing the whole document without burning his fingers, letting the last scrap drop to burn away on the table. He had done this many times in the last five years, always reversing his decision in the morning when he thought of his fortune ending in the hands of strangers.

What possessed Alessandro to choose this moment to spit out a cherry pit that he had been rolling in his mouth is a puzzle. Perhaps he meant it as a gesture of bravado, a sign of defiance. He aimed for the window and narrowly missed striking the old man on the cheek. He braced himself for a second assault.

"Spit at me? Spit at me, would you?" The back of his hand connected with the other side of Alessandro's head, some small relief. But it gave Emilio's tirade fresh vigour. He pushed his son away and turned his back, striding up and down the room as he railed. Alessandro watched sulkily, winding his father to new heights of invective with his lack of response.

Emilio turned on him. "Look at you!" he said. "Look! Look! It is the shame. More than anything it is the shame. You know who told me? *My own boy.* And you know who told him? The *fishmonger* Pietro Pegolotti's boy."

He stalked away again. "God in Heaven, you are the laughing stock of the city." He turned round. But Alessandro had retreated to the privy.

～

ON THE OTHER SIDE of the city Orazio is suffering in his own way. He has the boy arrange his divan with a basin of cool fermented ewe's milk on each side for his hands. Not, of course, that he has been working with lime — he has not been working at all — but that supine on this bed, his arms extended at his sides, his hands resting in the basins, he feels finally at rest. To begin with, it is a crucifixion, while the anguish and confusion of the trial crowd in on him; but, at last, by the time the curds have settled to the bottom of the basins, his mind has cleared.

The new trial had begun calmly enough. The knowledge that the presses were to be used caused a stillness to descend upon the proceedings. There was no one in the hall who was not attending to this small scandal, made so much more interesting by the presence of the iron instrument mounted on a low block and set in front of the Podestà's table. The application of the press was conducted according to rule. A priest was called in to bless the apparatus, the assembled *signori*, the accused man, the witnesses and the spectators. The blessings calmed Orazio's nerves. When it was time to speak he followed Ser Tomasso's advice, stating his case against Tassi succinctly.

Their Lordships for their part were impeccable in their bearing. They called Matteo Tassi first. They listened with faces as flat as a plastered wall while he perjured his immortal soul and denied the charge outright, but they did not subject him to the presses. They argued that they knew him to be a scoundrel and a liar already. He would retract from his position when he had had an opportunity to hear the witnesses' testimony.

It was when his daughter was called to stand that Orazio's heart began to pound, sending the blood thundering in his ears. But she was a paragon of composure. She stood tall while each of Matteo's responses from the first trial was read back to her, every lewd allegation, and she denied each one. She was asked to kneel and she needed no help. When her hand was put to the press, she barely flinched. It filled him with satisfaction. She answered each of the repeated questions, again denying Tassi's allegations and repeating the charge that he had come to her unasked and forcibly violated her. She was looking straight at Matteo when she spoke. Orazio could see her face. She was deathly pale, but not a single tear fell. He could have felt proud, was not the whole affair so charged with disgrace. She has now a blackened and bruised hand the colour of a ripe *melanzana* and nearly as fat, and her thumb sticks out at an odd angle. The nail of her thumb looks like a mussel shell split in two and is sure to fall, but his doctor says her thumb will return to its place in time. Orazio thanks God Tomasso had the foresight to make them agree not to touch the hand she uses to hold the brush.

All that was as to be expected. It was when they took the girl that the affair began to come undone. It seemed that the whole court was on its feet, and he realized for the first time that it was not only the misdeeds of lovers that had drawn the crowd of people. Chiara, so unremarkable to his eyes now, was still a curiosity. She rewarded their interest tenfold, screaming and writhing between the officers even before they had her at the press. There was something faintly disgusting so that he could hardly watch, and, he noticed, neither could Matteo. She had to be struck several times to be quietened. Even then her arms and legs continued to thrash so wildly that the two men had difficulty holding her still and the court began to fill with laughter. They got one of her hands into the press as quickly as they could, and the Podestà said, "This is not a girl. This is a fish on a hook." The Podestà called for silence because he could not hear her answers but it was even then difficult to make out what she was saying. Still it seemed as if she was supporting his daughter's testimony. Orazio does not really understand why they had to put her other hand to the press because that was when the affair took a strange turn. The Podestà asked her why she thought Messer Matteo would do such a thing if there had been no previous intimacies of any kind. He was leaning forward, trying to catch what she was saying and then he was asking her to tell her story again and there it was garbled and disordered. Something about the skin of a hanged man belonging to Emilio's son and the gift of that skin to the mistress and Messer Matteo flying into a blind rage. Orazio had not been able to believe what he was hearing as the whole sordid affair of the vest came tumbling from Chiara's mouth like spoiled meats. He had wanted to jump up and stifle her on the spot. This was proof that it had been a mistake to take the girl. Countless people had told him she would only mean bad luck. As if he needed more agitation and scandal in his life. But the Podestà had a mind to hear more. He had Chiara released from the press and her face splashed with water to calm her. When she was quiet, he had her repeat her story a third time. Ser Tomasso said that in the end the girl had done them all a service for there was no knowing what lies Matteo Tassi would have concocted if the Podestà had called him to stand a second time as he intended at the outset. As it was, the Podestà brought down his verdict without calling him to stand again, finding him guilty as charged and ordering him to make a marriage of reparation with the lady Sofonisba and, in so doing, to forfeit all dowry whether promised or due.

Finally. Finally after all they had been through. And then what does his daughter — his loyal, his obedient daughter — choose to do? She stands up again. Just when it is all settled. She stands up and she declares in a voice for everyone to hear that she would rather die. Then turns to Tassi himself and says it again. She would rather die! The whole court was in uproar. It was the only word for it. The laughter, the girl Chiara crying and wailing, the officers of the court slapping their knees, repeating what his daughter had said. Orazio feels the blood suffusing his face again just at the memory of it. It could have been the market place and Sofonisba a fool there for their entertainment. Certainly she offended the Podestà, because he said if the two of them were going to enter a fresh dispute they had better go about it outside. The judgement had been brought down, and the terms of reparation pronounced. The court at this time was more interested in pursuing the business as it related to Alessandro and his foul misdeed. He cleared the court. As if they were nobody.

It gives Orazio a headache just to think about it. He is calmer now but there in the street he had been in the grip of an impotent rage that was like an iron band around his chest and throat. The slave beside him, then behind him trying to hide. The people all gawking. The trouble that had come to him since the girl Chiara. Nothing but trouble. And now she herself good for nothing at all, except attracting the wrong kind of attention. She could hardly put one foot in front of the other when they left the court, and that was bad enough, but then she was moaning and whimpering for her hands. There was a crowd around them in no time.

It was a relief when Matteo came out, snorting air and striding off. Half the riff-raff followed him. At least he threw things back.

Orazio groans. He calls for the boy to come and take the basins away and dry his hands. He asks where the noise is coming from. Tanai says it is the girl caterwauling.

What they will do now only the good Lord in Heaven knows. Orazio says his prayers, excusing himself first for not kneeling, and shutting his ears to the slave's racket.

Chiara sleeps, but fitfully.

Sofonisba in her bed, holding her left hand against her breast, pushes awkwardly with her right until she is sitting up. The girl is dreaming on her pallet at the foot of the bed, crying out again in anguish, the words tortured, like birds at the hands of boys. But these are not cries of pain. These are names, Sofonisba is sure of it, and they are called out in despair. Cries of pain would be more bearable. Sofonisba gets up and shakes Chiara.

"Wake up."

She opens a shutter.

Chiara stops and opens her eyes. She seems not to see Sofonisba for many moments. She pays no attention to her hands but looks around her into the room. Sofonisba puts out her hand and lightly touches Chiara's arm. She is glad the girl's hands are bound now and not so alarming. The thumbs had hung like crooked black bean pods, purple where the white should be. Orazio had sent for his doctor. He bound her own left hand with a strip of linen to hold the thumb quiet. Afterwards, he attended to Chiara. Orazio and Tanai held her while he turned her thumbs back to their proper place. He painted them with a foul-smelling, greenish-black tincture.

"Now you hold every colour of the rainbow in your hands," he said. "And they smell as bad as they look."

The thumbs are hidden now, neatly bound against the sides of her hands. Neatly bound but useless.

"Now what shall we do with you?"

Chiara only stares.

"It should have been Matteo," Sofonisba says. "It should have been Matteo."

The pain of the press continued long after it had been removed. Her own injury is not so severe. She had made herself kneel without moving. The pain travelled like a deep incision along the length of her arm, as if an arrow had been let fly within it. Now it comes more steadily, like waves that lap and wash against the pillars of a bridge. But Chiara stares and stares into the dimness of the room. It is as if some other injury has taken her senses.

"The trial is over. No one is going to hurt you again."

Chiara lies down. She curls on her side and her hands lie beside her face on the pallet as if they are not hers at all. Her eyes are open. She will not close them again until the next day's dawn.

⌒

ALESSANDRO CANNOT BE CALLED a rational thinker. Vague remembrances and yearnings haunt his skull and bump into one another in the dark. Sometimes when they collide they fuse, making a new hunger that triggers movement. At this very moment, the space between his ears is filled with a leaping and crackling. He sees the burning clouds inside the church; he hears the crowd outside naming him for the culprit. He feels his own fear, his obscene excitement at the sight of the screaming horse that Ceccio and the other boys are swarming. He sees his inheritance burning in the candle flame, insubstantial flakes of it floating off in the draught. And now he hears Matteo Tassi, the biggest foul-mouthed liar in the city, confirming the words of that toad of a slave, repeating the story of his most holy vestment. And everyone believing him. Alessandro knows himself exposed. He feels as if he has walked the streets naked, the eyes of his enemies searing his own skin like hot coals. The trial could have been Matteo's downfall, could have meant his indictment, perhaps imprisonment. Instead it has shamed and degraded Alessandro, and conferred on Tassi their most contested, most coveted prize: Sofonisba. Remembered humiliations and injuries, his sins too, become an angry mob, rushing back to hurl themselves in his face, like horse dung at Ser Orazio's door.

When he leaves the house, he has a jar of lamp oil tucked under his arm, and a flint and striking steel in his pouch.

Loping through the market, he pulls down a canopy for spite. Many times he is shouted at. He picks up a turnip and throws it violently in the direction of the voices, striking an old woman on the side of the head. Still it is not enough, and he finds himself rounding a corner and turning into Via Rosaio. Three times he walks past Tassi's shop, resentment burning in the centre of his chest like a piece of swallowed bone. But each time his mind projects malice, the image of Matteo, enraged, leaps from the picture. He begins to think of the slave instead. It was the slave after all who let slip the tale of the vest. A slave! To have a slave reveal his most secret business, telling it all, shaming him before his friends, the whole city laughing at him. The third time past the shop he does not turn back but goes on in the direction of the Fabroni's, passing first along Via Baccano and looking in at the tavern where the most dissolute dribble into their wine. It does not take many drinks before he is openly declaring his intention to burn down the house in Via del Cocomero and murder all of its inhabitants. After a few drinks more he is fast asleep and snoring with his head on the table and is no trouble at all for the Bargello's men who come to arrest him.

⌒

ORAZIO KNOWS THAT TODAY there will be no one in the city who will not have heard the scandal of the hanged man's shirt. He has made up his mind. The most important commission he has ever won is at stake. It can take him out of the realm of house painter, church decorator and into the orbit of royalty. It will be like working for *il Papa* himself. The only sensible course of action now is to remove themselves from the city with all speed.

The next day, he is up as soon the shop boys along the street begin to raise a clatter. There is still the problem of his intractable daughter but it is nothing that cannot be managed by the passage of time. He has found a way to think clearly through the knots of his problem: he answers his own questions as if he were Ser Tomasso. It is like putting on a pair of spectacles. What to do about Sofonisba and her rank disobedience? Simple: nothing! He will attend to his own affairs first. She has the rest of her life in which to marry Matteo. No one else, after all, is going to come beating on his door for a second-hand coat. As for Matteo, he is not a problem. He rode away, yes. But Matteo Tassi has always ridden away from difficulties. He will come back. His choice is to marry or face eventual imprisonment. He knows Matteo will marry. It is like a window in a tower, this new view of life's vicissitudes. He is far above them. Still, it will not hurt to have Ser Tomasso beside him.

Orazio spends the rest of the morning at the back of the shop, poring over papers with the notary, arguing and questioning until Ser Tomasso bangs both hands down flat on the table and says, "Who is the notary here?" and Orazio becomes submissive and co-operative, signing whatever is put in front of him. On one point, however, he will not yield. Ser Tomasso would have had him wait, negotiate an allowance for the voyage, but Orazio insists on leaving as soon as possible. He is prepared to sell a little piece of land to fund his voyage. He will do what must be done. After that, the matter is in God's hands.

When the notary has gone, Orazio shuffles along to Sofonisba's room.

"Come down," he says. "Come down. I want to talk to you."

He sits at his writing desk, where he begins to make up another set of instructions for Tomasso.

When Sofonisba appears, he says, "I have made up my mind." He seems not to notice the dark shadows under her eyes, her pale, drawn look. "I shall go at once. I shall take the boy and possibly another. Chiara is no use. We shall send her to Paolo."

"I shall keep Chiara with me in your absence."

"Chiara cannot stay on any account. She cannot work. She is good for nothing except perhaps more of Paolo's endless depictions in silverpoint."

"I should like to keep her."

"After yesterday? She is ill luck. She is a walking plague. I want nothing more to do with her."

"I should like her to stay."

"It is not for you to say."

Sofonisba, though she might have, makes no more protest. She is well aware that there are matters here which might shape her life. Chiara can go to Paolo for the time being. It will make no difference. Her father will be too far away to object when she decides to bring her back.

"Then who shall you provide to assist me?"

"You need no one for *Argentara*. Andrea will have labourers. You are wholly capable. If it cannot be avoided hire Ilario or someone of equal skill and have Tomasso draw up a note to be redeemed on my return. I need all my resources to finance this journey unless the ambassador can come forward with some funds."

"And Matteo?" She does not ask innocently. It will be interesting to hear her father excuse himself from pressing forward with the *nozze*. She is amused and faintly disgusted to see how this marriage, that she did not want and for which she has already been made to suffer, is being so easily pushed to the side.

"On my return. There will be time enough. Matteo Tassi may run to Siena. But he will be back."

"In the meantime you are content for me to live here alone, like a widow?" Though the idea is like the surface of the river in a distant valley. It shimmers.

"That is not the case. The Arcivescovo has generously arranged for you to be lodged in an apartment with a maid at his expense while you are working on his walls." Orazio is unlocking his desk. He pulls out paper after paper. Sofonisba's river gleams as it winds toward the open sea.

"And so my good name will be safe?"

Orazio jams his teeth together against this obnoxious and inappropriate irony. He takes two deep breaths.

"You *have* no good name until you marry."

Sofonisba smiles with the satisfaction of having exposed his hypocrisy, if only to herself.

"And when the walls are finished? I am to conduct the business of the shop with no one to help me?"

"You will have Ser Tomasso. I have discussed that with you." He is rifling through the papers, frowning. Sofonisba is not sure whether he is preoccupied or trying to avoid this conversation. She does not care.

Already she is beginning to breathe a different air. It is like a cool, fresh morning. She can drink it like water. It clears her head. She can see the painting that is waiting for her. It is neither a *Madonna* nor a *Susanna*. She cannot wait for him to be gone.

He is turning back to the letter when he remembers and looks up.

"And your poor hand," he says, reaching out with his own. "How is your poor hand?"

Sofonisba listens to the scratch of his pen as she goes back to her room.

Chiara is still sleeping at the foot of the bed as if she has been on a long, long journey. She has not moved.

Sofonisba slides back under her sheets.

She thinks of Iacopo's wife at the farm, Margherita, who goes beetle-backed between the vines, dragging a basket behind her for the thistles she pulls. She thinks of Antonio the sculptor's wife who, everyone knows, lies upstairs unsleeping while Antonio fornicates with his latest model below. She thinks of the cook from the house next door, who wears the bruises from her husband like new jewels. She thinks of the woman she believed for a time was her mother rolling and shrieking on her father's big bed. She thinks of her mother dying at the moment of giving birth. She thinks of Chiara calling in the night. She knows that it was for her mother that she called. She guesses that the foreign syllables were names.

Sofonisba's world is in pieces. Rage and resentment bear down on her, and still she has not spoken. But she knows now how to tell it, and it will not be in words as they were hoping. She will tell her story. Not like Chiara, spluttering business that ought to be kept within walls, business that might have gone against them had it not been so interesting to the vile old men. No, she has a vision and she will present it in the way she knows best. Two days ago, on the way back from San Pier, passing the Loggia dei Lanzi, as she had passed it many times, her eyes were suddenly opened. There was the new bronze Perseus, fashioned and cast by Tassi's brilliant friend; Perseus, muscular and graceful, balanced in his easy, elegant victory, holding aloft the dripping head of Medusa. An artist might know Heaven, achieving such perfection. Then she saw it as if for the first time. The body at his feet, expended, was not the slain gorgon. It was no monster. Headless, it had been shorn of its mythic identity. It was a young body, beautiful, supine, its female form exposed to the public gaze, disgraced and defenceless, naked, spent.

When her hand was under the press, she bit her tongue to keep it from speaking the truth, which could only harm her. Instead she denied Matteo and every word he said about their "sweet regard," their "common delight." She repeated only those things that would help her case, careful to say nothing that would make the justices deaf to the outrage of his imposition. The Podestà had called his attack "advances." Sofonisba called it molestation — uninvited, protested, and most bitterly resisted. It was a vicious and spiteful assault. How could she answer honestly about former occasions and still have the Podestà believe she refused him on this single day? How could she tell them the things that he did, not then, not in that moment when he defiled their friendship, but in former times when all their amusement and delight were in each other's company? Could she have told them the way he spoke to her, his hand on her hair, her wrist, his voice low, telling her his lewdness was merely a costume put on for the entertainment of fools, promising to discard it and lay himself in all tenderness at her feet? Could she have described how his eyes searched her own while he said these things, and still have them, the stone-faced fathers, believe she resisted him when he came to her, the innocent birds filling that late afternoon with song? Sofonisba's tears at last begin to fall. They fall not for her hurt, not for her humiliation; they fall for all the days of their laughter, their eyes in collusion, their hands and their lips complicit, their tongues. Outwitting the whole grave and stupid world to exchange kisses, caresses. In the swift and ugly action — which, yes, she did resist with every muscle, every sinew, with her teeth — her only shame was that she once loved the man. Because he was her equal. Because he was Matteo. Because there was no other like him. And this was what she bit her tongue to keep from saying, because she knows, just as surely as the stars hang in the heavens, that if she had let slip any of her former affection there is no judge, no priest — even though Tassi had come at her with most vile intent — there is no lord, no city father, who would not have believed him blameless. Believed him blameless and her the sinner. As if she could have yielded to a man who came to her in anger and with his heart bent on blood; for it was not the same Matteo who came at her with his teeth jammed in rage and pushed her down; who spat in her face and covered it over with his palm, smearing her eyes, her nose, her mouth; who knelt on her, pinning her arms; who tore her clothes and turned her over, crushing her face against the floor; who took her and entered her like a stranger, then, when she got free of him, pulled away to his obscene business, saying, "I don't need you."

All the games that they had played — as two princes at play in the wide world — were games no more. She wanted only to deliver the same mortal pain. In the court it was important to deny this new Matteo, refute all his claims to shared affections. With her hand under the press she denied them, kept silence on all the secrets of her heart, knowing that if she spoke, this Matteo Tassi, the one she hated, would go free. There was not a man or woman in all the city who would understand why, if she loved him, her anger should now be so great, no one who would understand how utterly she was betrayed. A little of her anger she reserves for the Podestà and his court, who thought it justice to sentence her despoiler to wed her. The black depths of it are for Matteo whom she believed her equal and her friend. It is for Matteo that she is riven now with anger as heavy as a falling axe blade. She has been forced to lie, to perjure herself, so that others might know the truth. In defending herself against what is now hateful, in striving to win justice for her cause, she has denied all that was dear to her. She has trampled on her own life and is as cold now, as hard, as winter earth opened by the blue plough, her heart a rock turned on the frozen furrow. She is in a place where only hatred can put down roots and all the land she sees ahead is barren.

But she will not keep silent forever. She will show them retribution. She will show them justice. She knows how to do it. If they think that because she is silent she has nothing to say, they are mistaken. But when she decides to speak it will be in the language of her choosing, one that cannot be contradicted, or misconstrued, or twisted back upon itself like a serpent. It will not be in words at all. With no words there will be no gainsaying. The truth she will tell will be more powerful than all the deceits of her silence.

THIRTEEN

Paolo pallavicino watches the little party coming up the hill. They are still a distance away, but it looks to him like the Fabronis. Paolo cannot think why they would be coming up to see him. He has returned in advance of Giuliano and he has no wish for company. After San Giovanni he could not wait to get back to his work. The debacle of the public entertainments has left his self-esteem in tatters and dissolved his interest in such amusements. He sees how, seduced by last year's success, he was led astray from his real work, tempted into distraction, indulgence, by the promise of even greater renown. It is hard for him, the staunch defender of empirical observation, not to see the accident as a personal lesson from his Maker, the direct outcome of his vanity. But it is only confirmation of what he has known all along. This playing at creation is unsatisfactory. It is the construction of toys and trinkets that can only fall apart, models that can never breathe life. The heaped, neglected feathers on his table signal it. A fine, white dusting of lime has settled on them. Lifeless, they represent nothing but their own disjunction and disarray. Art in the service of diversion becomes deception and is an obstacle in the pursuit of truth. He knows this.

No, the way forward is through investigation, through careful attention to what is there. Before San Giovanni, he was considering another dissection. It will please him to return to serious work. He will immerse himself again in the investigation of Nature. It is in the barn and the byre that true learning and advancement will be made. Experience. That is the thing. In experience can Nature be known. In art she can be revealed. It is this amassing of experience, this thorough and rigorous investigation of what is before the eye, that is the principal duty and chief dignity of man. For the duty of man is to know God. And to know God, man has only to look to His creation. By close attention to the creature, its original spark, its secret divinity, may be discovered — and this most readily when the creature lives, which is to say, before its essence has dissipated. One thing Paolo knows without a doubt: that the true beauty of a thing lies exactly here, not in the material shell, but in the secret spark of its existence. He has proven this to himself many times with the simple expedient of a flower cut from the stalk. Within moments, the vitality of its leaf and petal begins to vanish, proving that the beauty of appearance works only to inveigle the perception. Then we believe the bloom to be the flower itself, when in truth the flower exists in its own hidden essence, the peculiar property that courses in its veins for the measure of its life, emanating back into the air only at its death. Again, he has verified his thesis by observing small creatures where the beauty of the eye, the glimmer on the window of the soul, vanishes at the instant that life is extinguished.

And this is why, perversely, Paolo holds depiction to be supreme of all the arts. It is why his drawing of the foetus extracted from the hanged woman was more beautiful than the child itself; for only in drawing and painting can the vital force appear to be arrested in perpetuity, as in the likeness of a man or a woman whose eyes appear to have the power of sight, or in the representation of a brute creature who appears to be drawing blood from another, or of a child who appears to sleep. It will please him just now to return to his investigations.

There is a question that leads him back and back again to the starting place. If this beauty of appearances, this false veil, serves only to hide the true beauty — which is the Lord God of Creation Himself — then what purpose does ugliness serve? Is the same beauty to be found within? This is the paradox that his investigations have revealed to him: if a man looks closely enough at the skin of the toad, the leg of the spider, a beauty beyond imagining flares in his eye, as when storm clouds are rent to reveal the sun. This is truth, this is confirmation that the Lord God of Absolute Good created the world. And yet the argument is fallacious. He cannot deceive himself; he knows that the reverse is true, that he might slit the downy belly of the fawn and find corruption, open the body of the beautiful woman and find the cankers of sin. Here the thought reverses again. Putrefaction, if one only looks with true attention, reveals a strange discordant beauty of its own, forms and designs not imagined by any man and all of them painted from a pallet resplendent with undreamed colours. The argument, he can see, is a twin spiral, an endless figure eight taking him nowhere. As beauty may be struck from terror — the coruscation of the lightning, the leap of flame — so terror may be summoned by perfection.

The work of that night with the unborn child has not left him. It resides now within him the way his words reside in Ceccio, to be recalled whole and in sequence.

He had had his agents leave the woman's cadaver inside the byre and paid them off. He had Ceccio light the lamps, for which special responsibility Ceccio saw no reason to thank him. Ceccio, in fact, was scared half to death and had to go outside to the dung heap once to empty his bowels. He was quick about it. He came back inside, making himself bold with threats and curses to the corpse, calling it a variety of animal and devil names, and accusing it of a number of practices more inventive than the conspiracy for which it had lost its life.

When he saw the woman's condition, he had asked for twice the usual number of candles round the subject's frame. He remembers the boy's hands shaking as he lit them. It was impossible to overlook the allusion to an altar though he tried, as he always tries, to remain detached and objective in his explorations. The boy kept his gaze firmly fixed on the hanged woman's starting, clouded eyes. He burnt himself twice.

The woman was neither young nor old. Her face was not deeply lined. The nose was straight, the brows slightly arched; the lashes that fringed the terrible eyes were unnaturally long. Her hair was matted from her time in prison and the skin of her neck was damaged, yet the trace of beauty was still visible even in the lips now drawn back from the teeth. He covered the upper body and head with linen towels. The pregnant belly then seemed to rise, a pale moon within the room, the skin stretched to silvery tautness.

He was never more alone. Ceccio had taken himself to sit on the floor over by the door as far away as possible. Neither promises nor threats could persuade him to assist in this, nor did Paolo try by force to make him. The knives were ready on the small block beside the table. He reached out and was appalled by the shaking of his hand. Paolo Pallavicino, who was always so sure of what he must be doing, he with his years of slicing and probing at life and death to find its source, years of picking apart his universe, was close to becoming unmanned by the act he was about to perform. Had he been about to enter Santa Maria Novella and approach the high altar, take down the tabernacle where the Godhead hides and pry open the doors, he could not have been more infirm. It was as if he were, with the knife he held, about to open his own breast and reach inside.

He made the first cut from the sternum to the pubic bone on a meridian through the navel, and then a transverse cut laterally just between the seventh and eighth rib, and a third in a crescent across the pubis, below the mound of the belly. Beneath the skin there was no fat. The longitudinal muscle of the abdomen, already thinned in the centre under pressure from the uterus, parted like the opening of a coat. Underneath, the two oblique fans forming the next layer of muscle separated easily, spread fingers unclasping. Paolo worked carefully for fear of accidentally cutting through. As he turned back the flaps to expose the uterus, he saw that the deepest transverse layer had thinned to an unearthly translucence.

With the flesh laid back, he sponged the surface of the uterus, feeling quite plainly the rump of the infant, even the bump of an elbow or a knee, the head as adamant as a rock lodged in the mouth of a drain.

The opened abdomen gave off a familiar taint. He went outside, he remembers, and drew two great breaths of air, driving his fingers into his hair to clear his head, and suddenly it was plain to him how to enter the uterus.

Inside, he took a small curved scalpel and made a careful incision through the wall of the uterus, rather low and to one side, working in the area between the protuberances of the curled foetus, between hip and knee, he guessed. Sawing slightly with the blade, he made a small slit, then changed his scalpel for shears. He inserted the lower blade carefully just under the muscle wall. Working cautiously, he snipped round, probing first with the blunt tip of the blade and then, feeling no obstruction, snipping farther. In this manner, he carefully cut away the anterior surface of the uterus. He could see a confusion of limbs. Though he could not make out how the child was lying, it was there, and it was revealing itself to him as he cut away its dark veil of flesh. He was uncovering a mystery, creating a window on creation. His hand was shaking as he let it touch the small thigh he had exposed. He continued cutting carefully, only once meeting an obstruction. Working with the shears, he was able to follow the contours of the child without disturbing its position, cutting low and around until the entire head was revealed where it rested at the mouth of its passage to the outside world. He made the last, easy passes with the shears, allowing the flap of muscle to come down to lie like an apron in the woman's lap. He saw the child cocooned in its silky membrane. It might have been sleeping. He snipped the amnion and pulled it away with his fingers. He sponged the copious seepage, aware as he did so that a second odour was competing with the first and it was not unpleasant, carried no hint of putrefaction. He stood for a long time gazing at the child, astonished at its composure, ravished by the beauty of its terrible blue, the near transparency of its skin, its perfect eyelids that would never lift on the reciprocal beauty of the world. He felt then as he does before the perfection of the leaf, the wing. He wanted inexplicably to weep. He wanted to apologize. He needed air again. He did not want to leave the thing exposed. He covered it with a towel.

The moon was shining on a bank of white lilies by the stream. He recognized the scent at once and was overtaken by a sudden calm. He saw the child blessed in its perfection and he knew then that apology was due not to it, lifted as it was above pity, but to all infants everywhere and in all times, to him and to Ceccio and to the poor dead woman and to all creation whose eyes open on the loveliness of sky and then must close again. He lay down on the grass by the door to take some rest before working again.

An hour later he was up again to make his drawing. He fetched his notebook and a small board to rest on his knee. He sent Ceccio for fresh water. He trimmed the lamps and pulled the sacking off the woman's belly, leaving her head and upper torso covered. He tried not to entertain the word "desecration" when he looked at what he had done. It might have been the work of beasts despite his care. But the child was intact. It curled in an attitude of quiet concentration on itself. He had an overwhelming sense that it might, if he reached out and touched it, wake — and then for a moment, no more than a moment, an overwhelming desire that it should. He had wanted to cut in and to cut in. He had thought to find some secret, some key to all knowledge but what he saw was only beauty again, beauty that flails at the surface of the eye and draws tears.

He dipped his sponge and squeezed out the water. His fingers were trembling as he reached down to the small mound of the shoulder. It was as cold and hard as a pebble. At once his shaking stopped. He sponged the small form, removing all the traces of membrane and blood, working carefully, conscious of his midwife's gestures, tender. He saw, felt now that the child's skin was covered in a fine waxy substance that flaked away under his fingertips. It was perfumed, making him want to bring his fingers to his lips, to taste, to lick. Paolo Pallavicino who always knows how to manage his desires, found himself overwhelmed. He picked up his pen and began.

It had happened before, this sudden crumbling of all his intellect's elaborate construction in the face of the surface of things. He had cut once into a thief's chest, sawing with shaking fingers through each rib beside the man's breastbone and then in his hurry breaking them away. He had thought to find the heart like a heavy secret laid bare after long years in darkness, had expected it almost to be lit from within, reflecting still the *spiritus vitalis*. But when at last the heart was uncovered, he saw only muscle, smooth and beautiful, compact and dense, telling him no more than the organs laid out on the butcher's stall in the market. He saw only what he already knew, but he sat down all the same to make notes, describing the way the parts were connected one to the other, losing his sense of time and place, losing his need for knowledge itself as his pen followed the lines of the arteries, as his knife cut them away to expose yet more perfect forms, the ellipses of the openings, the tubular branchlets of veins, losing for an eternal instant, within the small concert of delicate blues and purpled reds, the consciousness of his own being.

Paolo sat with the foetus and drew for more than two hours, his fingertips turning white in the cold, becoming a corpse's. He did not stop drawing until the time approached for his agents to return with the barrow. His drawing showed a lily bisected to expose its centre. It was opened out. An egg was nestled within the ornamental frame of its petals. The egg, too, was sectioned longitudinally, within the egg a womb, it, too, opened, the points of its triangular flaps, traversing the outline of the egg, counterpointing the angles of the petals. Within the uterus a child, as if sleeping.

When the men arrived he was wrapping the cadaver in its sheet, winding it round with long strips of linen, binding it tightly. It was not easy, even with Ceccio. He asked one of the men to help.

"Too late for all that now," said the man. "Little bugger's jumped out, looks like. Run away, did he? Punish him too much, did you?"

Paolo turned, unsmiling, to the man. "And you," he said just to make him be quiet, "would you like to be paid or not?" The man said no more, though his boy, as they left with the loaded cart, could not help looking back and back again, and asked, "What'd he have all them flowers for under the table?"

"What flowers?" said the man.

Paolo watches Orazio and his daughter dismount. They have a young man with them, a fellow hired for their protection, he surmises, and the slave up behind him. Paolo sees at once that something is amiss: Orazio's strained expression, Sofonisba's awkwardness, the way she dismounts and uses only one hand, the other bound. The slave with both her hands wrapped. He notes how their burly escort must lift the girl down, the girl neither resisting nor helping.

"You have a lot to tell me, I see."

Orazio shakes his head hopelessly, as if his woes are endless. "Much. Much."

"Ceccio! Come and help these people.

"Come with me," he says to Orazio. "Monna Sofonisba take some rest. Take your girl with you."

"Maestro Paolo, the girl is the purpose of our visit. We are bringing her to you."

Paolo looks at Chiara. Sees her eyes strangely listless. There is an exhausted air about her. And her damaged hands? Burned? He will hear soon enough.

"So." He attempts cheer. "You bring her back to me. The one I cannot give away comes back."

Sofonisba returns a wan smile.

"There is a time," says Orazio, "in every man's life when he must call upon a true friend."

The girl has sidled closer to Sofonisba, half leans against her. Sofonisba puts her hand to her face and pinches at the bridge of her nose, closing her eyes.

"The road is so dusty," she says. And Paolo understands that he is not going to be able to refuse this request for help when it comes.

"Sit down. Sit down. Ceccio will bring you some water. Some bread, too, Ceccio. And some meat for the young man.

"Come with me, Orazio. Tell me what it is you need."

From the bench outside Paolo's door, Sofonisba watches Chiara's face while the two old man confer. She is not sure how much Chiara has understood. She had told her only that they were going to see Paolo Pallavicino. The girl had put on her grey gown and wrapped her head in the saffron cloth, to which she had taken a liking. She had watched Sofonisba roll her extra gown into a bundle along with a clean shift. She tied the roll onto the front of her saddle. Before they were out of the town, she had asked if they were going to stay at Maestro Paolo's. Sofonisba had answered only, "Yes. You are staying." They had not spoken again in all the long ride.

"You really leave me no choice," Paolo says when Orazio has finished. "You compel me to answer yes."

In that moment it seems quite clear to Sofonisba that she will not see the girl again.

A little while later Sofonisba speaks to Chiara in the sun-baked courtyard.

"God have mercy on your soul, Chiara. Remember to serve Maestro Paolo humbly and well and bring no misfortune on him, nor on any man or woman who keeps you hereafter." She turns away to the mare that Ceccio is holding for her, but stops.

"Come here."

She holds out her arm. Chiara goes over and leans into her. Sofonisba brushes her cheek on the girl's hair.

"Be a good girl," she says. "Maestro Paolo is a good man."

When they have left, Paolo looks at Chiara as if she is some new breed of farm animal whose purpose is unclear. He reaches out for her hands.

"They are a study," he says, "and like to be as much an aberration as your pied skin when they are healed." This evening, he will take her into his *studio* and light candles, though it will not yet be dark. He will sit her at the table and position her hands on its surface. Then he will set about to putting them to paper, gazing at them fixedly as if they do not belong to the girl at all. With the bandages removed they will seem more like two dead creatures from the cages, their shape so altered.

When he has finished, he will let Chiara see what he has drawn. He will have shown no colouring, only the shadows necessary to define the form. The skin will be unmarked and her hands will appear as any others, except that they are broken.

After that he will return to the fascination of the surface and its beautiful distraction, drawing her every day, from different angles and in different lights. It will be a form of contemplation, following the contours of her body and overlaying the mapping of her markings.

⁓

TWO DAYS LATER, just before daybreak, out in the Ley of the Damned, a hooded figure is digging in an inefficient, arrhythmic fashion, chopping and smacking at earth that would not yield at all except that it has so recently been disturbed. It is Alessandro, shovelling out the grave of the hanged man. His father watches from the shadow of the wall where Alessandro, months ago, had watched Paolo's agents. The vest lies on the ground ready to be replaced as the Podestà ordered. A Franciscan in his brown robe walks up and down saying his office while Alessandro digs. He is there to see that the penance is carried out and the man's own shirt of flesh is returned to him in proper fashion, just as he was there to see that the body of God the Father was not laid to rest without a prayer. His footsteps are measured, his voice barely audible. His piety has no effect on Alessandro. Alessandro is digging himself into a pit of anger and resentment. He would as soon smack the monk with the shovel. But if ever an action can reach back in time and affect another, perhaps the presence of the monk will be able reach back and lift the stain of Alessandro's tainted actions from his life, for the monk is moved to be there not by any appetite for castigation, but by compassion, which has no equal in the measure of good and ill.

When the job is finished and the earth scuffled into place, Alessandro all but runs back to the city gates. His father takes him directly to Santa Croce to be shriven yet again, and there on the steps of the church, just leaving, is his friend Orazio.

Orazio, too, has been up since midnight. He is surprised to see Emilio, but pleased.

"Emilio!" He holds out his arms. Everyone is dearer than life to Orazio just now. Sofonisba, he says, left yesterday for the country.

He himself departs on the hour for Pisa. He does not mention that he has been stricken with terror at the prospect of the long and hazardous journey, and has prayed for the duration of the Mass, begging with an abject lack of dignity for safe delivery from the perils of land and sea. There is no turning back.

Emilio wishes him Godspeed. He does not tell him where he and Alessandro have been this morning. He hopes he will not notice the dirt on his son's hands.

When Orazio says he must hurry, the two men embrace, weeping both of them, there in the street, their backs to the world.

THE ROOM THE ARCIVESCOVO has set aside for Sofonisba is fit for an honoured guest. A maidservant sleeps in the room adjoining. Servants in the Arcivescovo's house never sleep in the same chamber as those they attend. The windows of Sofonisba's room are glazed and face south to the gardens, where rosemary and juniper have been clipped into low hedges, and lemon and bay trees stand in pots along wide avenues. Between the walks lies a pleasure ground of fountains and statues, hidden groves and secluded seats.

The room is furnished with a curtained bed on a raised platform, at the foot of which is a finely carved and painted chest. The wall opposite the bed is panelled in intarsia; its beautiful and various woods faithfully depict the external façade of the house in scale, as if the building had thrown its own shadow, its own visual echo, back inside itself. Underneath a heavy brocade, the bed is awash with fine linen sheets, satins and padded silks in blue and red and gold. There are three bolsters stuffed with goose down. None of these sumptuous appointments helps Sofonisba to sleep.

At dawn on this first morning of her stay, she stands at the window, looking out on the shadowy forms of the statuary emerging from the foliage. She imagines the figure of her father with the boy behind him. They will ride out with the others in the entourage, strung out along the road to Pisa. At Pisa, they will take a boat to Genoa and from there another to Southampton. She pictures the figures smaller and smaller on the road, and it is as if they are carrying away all her former days. Now she will please herself in all that she does, will answer to no one. She will be alone at least until her father's return. No father. No Matteo. Not even the girl.

WHEN GIULIANO RETURNS AND HEARS about the reappearance of the mottled slave, he closes his long eyelids slowly. What reason is there, without his wife, to be stalking down the hill in search of conflict? Attributing his own qualities to those around him, he finds men and women — if left to themselves — to be peace-loving and amenable; he will not go out of his way to disturb another. His wife is once again at her sister's house. Giuliano believes a little sadly, but not despairingly, that she goes there to avoid his company, though in truth she goes there in the hope that one of her sister's concoctions or decoctions will bring about the blessing of a child on her marriage. Every time she comes home, Giuliano beds her tenderly, lovingly. Lucia remains at home long enough for his attentions to renew her longing for a child, compelling her to return to her sister who will, she hopes, transmute these fierce longings to flesh. She remains at her sister's house until she is sure the decoctions have taken effect, whereupon she makes the long and strenuous ride back to *La Castagna* ... And so the round of absence and return continues, not producing a child, but performing miracles of sweetness and affection between the pair. Lucia is about to miss the most voluptuous time of year at *La Castagna*.

For Giuliano, the months of summer are no time for conflict. They are the time to walk the raked paths of one's garden and breathe in the perfume of jasmine and the sweet outlaw rose climbing the clipped walls of cypress. They are the time to walk through the silvery olive groves and inspect the fruit, sit by the fountain in the evening and listen with closed eyes to the thrush singing from the top of a chimney.

When Paolo Pallavicino comes up to the house a few weeks later, Giuliano brings up the subject of Chiara in a reasonable, temperate manner.

"Is it true, Paolo, what I hear about the slave?"

"She has been with me for about three weeks now."

"Against my wishes?"

"I have been careful to keep her within bounds, *Monsignore*. She doesn't stray."

"I have heard she does."

"Then I shall be more careful with her. Perhaps I can write to Ser Tomasso about what should become of her."

"Let her stay until her hands are healed."

It occurs to Paolo that Giuliano will never, as he had at first hoped, take her back. She is no use to God or man. If they were to stand her now on a barrel at the wharf, who would bid? With thumbs bound to her hands, she was no more use than the dumb creatures in the barn who cannot lift their food to their mouths but must bend to it.

"How many times have you drawn her?"

"Countless. I couldn't say."

"And you have not exhausted your interest?"

"Sometimes I think I may be able to do something for her." The surface of things is not enough. It is a tease, seducing the eye and leaving it looking for more. Drawing Chiara is not enough. Paolo Pallavicino would like to overcome this trick of light and shade and make it all one.

"Fit her with finery, trim her with gems and brilliants?"

Paolo will not be distracted.

"If the topmost layer of skin could be removed . . . We are all flesh underneath."

"You are talking about the fate of Marsyas."

"If there were a means of removing the skin measure by measure without inflicting undue suffering . . ." To see if it is feasible, he has thought of taking a fine layer of black skin from her shoulder and observing how it heals. The thing could be done, he reasons, if she were in a stupor, a state easily induced by the administration of a great quantity of wine.

"Well, if there be such a way, I'm sure you are the man to discover it."

"It would be work of greater value than the provision of spectacle for the people."

"But of benefit to only one. When you provide an entertainment you make all the people rejoice."

Giuliano knows what he has said the moment the words leave his lips.

"Not this time."

"It was a freak of fortune."

"Like the girl."

"The girl is something that perhaps I can put right, a work I can amend."

"*Correct* the work of God?"

Who would not? thinks Paolo, though it is blasphemy to say it.

"Of course not. Who would play God is always brought low."

The two men fall silent, both aware of the bad joke and the remains of the wretched old fellow rotting in the Ley of the Damned.

When he leaves the villa, Paolo goes straight to his workshop, draws and makes copious notes. He works there for the next few days, sleeps there. He sends Ceccio to hunt down by the stream for newts and frogs. Ceccio tells Chiara his master flays them and then eats them alive. He tells her other things she does not want to hear about. She begins to avoid Paolo Pallavicino unless he calls for her.

In time, and because she has no duties, Chiara's hands begin to heal. The thumbs move stiffly. They seem, with their massive joints, to belong to an old, old woman. Paolo still sends for her each day to submit to his salves and tinctures, but he applies them now, in stronger concentrations, on her shoulder also. She submits to these new procedures with guarded attention. The dullness in her eye that he observed the day she was returned to him has been replaced with watchfulness. Yet she stands without moving while he examines her shoulder, only flinching when he takes up his callipers. He places them at the border of the markings, tries to calculate the ratio of black to white. The girl cringes, breathes again easily only when he sends her away with an impatient, distracted flick of the back of the hand. Her company is becoming an imposition. He has taken of her as much as he can take without opening her body: his eyes have feasted all they want on her strange charm.

As the weeks go by, it becomes clear that Chiara has indeed become a problem. The practical difficulties presented by the experiment Paolo has in mind are too great. It is no use trying to send her back to the farm. Iacopo has been demanding payment. He would send her right back with a new request. Giuliano would have certainly had her at the villa were it not for Lucia. Tassi would take her back, he knows that, but Tassi is rumoured to be producing wonders in gold and silver in Siena. Meanwhile here she is still, something now like a fearful bitch. When he passes her, she follows him with her wary eye. It is an imposition. If she sits nearby when he is working, he can hear her cough. Every little while, she coughs, marking the passage of time that should be seamless. When Paolo considers that her markings make it impossible for her to run away he becomes suddenly afraid. His very integrity will be taken from him. Her presence will gradually alter his relationship to the world and to God. No longer God's servant, Paolo, but one of a pair. They will be like yoked animals, like manacled prisoners, like husband and wife. She would make him mysteriously — and unlike Ceccio — in some way less than whole.

⌐⌐

WHILE THE SUMMER SUN blazes down on the immaculate geometry of leaf and stone at *Argentara* and even the statues seem to sweat, Sofonisba works diligently on her paintings. Almost as soon as she arrived, the Arcivescovo changed his mind. The *Susanna*, he decided, would be better on a panel that could be hung above the bed, taken to Roma if he so wished. It could be worked in tempera, but would not be painted directly onto the wall. He had the work that Orazio had prepared plastered over. Several motives governed his decision, and all of them had to do with Sofonisba. The longer she was with him the better.

He has a collection of ancient and modern sculptures displayed in a loggia overlooking the gardens from a terrace at the rear of the villa. A low room at the back, *la sala delle statue*, houses smaller pieces and has been designated a temporary workshop. Andrea likes to visit Sofonisba there while she is painting. He asks her to reverse the relative positions of the legs of the bathing Susanna, making the nearer leg drop to reach for the ground from the wall she is sitting on and raising the farther leg to a bent position at rest on the wall. Sofonisba makes the changes to the composition and begins a painting of her own.

It is not long before Andrea sees how she might not meet his expectations. She declines his frequent invitations to dine or to join a party of guests to ride out. Instead she spends time on her own painting. She is a disappointment. He has known more responsive nuns.

"I had not thought a lady such as yourself would prove ungracious — or ungrateful," Andrea said. "You have the finest bedchamber in the house."

"I am more grateful than words can ever express for the honour to complete a commission for your Lordship. The accommodation your Lordship has so generously provided exceeds my needs. I should have been content with less — and still should be." Which sounds almost like the threat that it is. She can take her work back to the shop at any time. Andrea is too old to waste time cajoling a resistant woman, too experienced to pretend that it can lead to anything but trouble. There are other ways to get what he wants, and there is certainly easier prey. Regretfully, he will allow this one to be lost, enjoy instead a fine platonic friendship with her and prove himself a cultivated man.

Sofonisba is left to devote her time to her two paintings, the *Susanna* for Andrea, the *Judith* for herself.

Her powers of concentration are prodigious. Once the composition for the *Susanna* is mapped and the base colours laid on, the work is rote and not demanding. Instead, Sofonisba makes demands of the subject. When Andrea requests that the piece of obscuring gauze be removed from the subject's lap, Sofonisba has no objections. It suits her purpose perfectly. The modelling of flesh and stone and drapery, the definition of foliage, water and hair are in place by the end of August. What remains is the modelling of the faces, especially the eyes. By the middle of September, the faces have developed a troubling quality. The elders are uncomfortably familiar, disconcerting because they cannot quite be placed in the mind of the viewer. They are of course the irreproachable faces of the Podestà and his two justices, but Sofonisba has been careful to give the Podestà a straight nose in place of his hooked one, a small beard to the justice who had none and bushy brows to the bald one. It is disturbing to know them and not to know them. The finer modelling of the faces, which will pull the muscles into play and show their expressions, will be the last work to be done. Sofonisba knows precisely the effect it will have on the viewer. The lower half of the faces will appear as the faces of the justices in court, impeccably disinterested. The eyes, given license by each man, who thinks himself unobserved, will roam at will over Susanna's flesh. But it is how she will paint the face of Susanna herself that will force the viewer to stand in a spot that is wholly his but that he rarely owns. The eyes of Susanna will function like a finger pointing, indicating exactly where the viewer stands, making it impossible for him to shelter with the elders behind their scenic shrubbery (where in any case he is reluctant to go, not wanting to align himself with such a blatantly dissembling crew). The viewer will be left undeniably marked out; an observer observed. Susanna at her bath will be looking directly into his eyes, returning his gaze moment for moment — and he will always be the first to turn away.

There is a sweet satisfaction to her work on the *Susanna*, but it is the *Judith* that arouses a visceral excitement. She keeps the panel leaning against the wall and covered with a piece of fine scarlet. When she works on it, she paints without hesitation, sure in her mind of the finished look of the composition, each brush stroke only confirming her intuition and itself revealing new possibilities.

It came to her as she lay in bed, impotent with anger, the day after the trial. Perhaps it was the thought itself that woke her, the awareness of it like a sudden fire, rushing from the soles of her feet. It made her heart turn over. She would move the moment of the action of her *Judith* painting back. The two women, the ghastly trophy of Holofernes' head between them, would not do. The subject of her painting — Judith and Holofernes — would be the same but the instant of its reprise would be moved back in time. Her palms burned with it. It would not be two figures but three. Holofernes himself at the last moment of his life would carry equal weight with Judith at the moment of her victory. Her depiction would catch his final breath, the extremity of his agony and the ultimate disgrace of his death. She would paint terror itself and the balm of vindication would soothe all who viewed it.

GIULIANO LIKES TO HAVE Gaetano stand to one side when he has summoned Paolo to his *guardaroba*. Invited. He must remember that word. He likes to think that Paolo is all his. This man of such extraordinary genius, such wide learning. He likes to think that his own mind can engage such a man, that the two of them are intimate, can be equals. The two of them at their leisure, above the mundane affairs that eat up the hours of men of lesser substance.

It would not please him to know that Paolo accepts his invitations with increasing reluctance, wanting, when all is said and done, only to be left alone to pursue his investigations. For Paolo is tiring of his role as artistic adviser. It is as if his patron wants to shut his mind in a cage, or keep it like a falcon close to the wrist.

Paolo has learned all he can from examination of Giuliano's treasures. Every viewing is the same. They sit in the panelled room at the table that Gaetano has covered with heavy black broadcloth and illuminated with tiers of candles. Giuliano will pick up now a newly minted medal, now a coral-encrusted saltcellar of gold. He will turn the object over and over in his long fingers. "Listen, now, Gaetano," he will say. "Mark what Maestro Paolo can teach us." For Paolo, this idle contemplation goes against the grain. What use are these objects to his patron? Shut up in twelve chests? Brought out to be turned in the light, and put away again? What does it matter to Giuliano that he knows the composition of a medal or a glaze, the weight of gold used in the setting of a ruby clasp? It makes Paolo tired. He begins to question the value of his patron's interest and then he begins to question the value of the objects themselves, or, more accurately, the validity of their creation. For if Giuliano's time spent in idle admiration of these things is worthless, what of the artisan's time spent in their creation? Giuliano has taken, and kept, some working notes of his because they caught his fancy, studies of heads he was making to catalogue the vocabulary of man's emotions and come to some understanding of how best they might be forced into service. Giuliano keeps them now in a leather cover on the book table and brings them out for the entertainment of his guests. Paolo wishes he could light the fire with them. It was the same with the small bronze horse that some years ago he had Tassi cast for him. It had served him well as a study of motion and he learned much in its modelling, coming to understand the redistribution of weight that is required for forward motion. He could have melted it down, reused the metal to study some new face of Nature, but it is shut away now in one of the chests, a study of futility.

Today, to Paolo's relief, the black broadcloth is empty, the collection remains locked away. Instead, Giuliano smiles and lays out Cosimo's impending visit for discussion. The Duke, he says, is bringing an important guest from Spain with him and will stay for two or three days before repairing to Careggi. Giuliano suggests that the menagerie — his ark — might be cleaned and purified with herbs for the occasion. He would like to ensure that his guests pass their time pleasurably. He has some entertainments in mind for a banquet and he is stocking his lake with trout so that they might spend an afternoon at fishing. They will of course spend some time here in these very rooms, but there will be hours to fill and he would like Paolo to arrange for a scientific demonstration.

Paolo says if he has enough time he can construct a complete *camera ottica*. But, failing that, he can with very little trouble arrange a simple demonstration of perspective.

Yes, says Giuliano, he was thinking of such a thing himself. But he would like to engage more thoroughly the Spaniard's interest in the marvels of the whole of Nature, not only one part, which is to say the light.

"The action of the bird's wing?" says Paolo, beginning to guess what Giuliano has in mind but perversely waiting for him to ask outright. "I have the feathers still."

"I was thinking," says Giuliano, "of perhaps an anatomical demonstration. We are in this respect far in advance of the English, who are still performing in the old style, using the texts of the ancients and employing the services of whoever offers the sharpest steel."

"Well," says Paolo, "I will see what I can arrange in such a short time." But his tone is icy with resistance. It is a sacred trust, this work of science, and not to be undertaken lightly. His commitment to return to the quiet practice of his investigations, to enter again the holy compact between Creator and created, had not included a performance, another spectacle.

The heat has gone out of the air when Paolo makes his way back to his own house. He takes a walk along the perfumed path toward the menagerie. The late sun enriches the colours of the vetch and cranesbill beside the path and the still air fills with the scent of wild thyme and chamomile beneath his feet. He can smell the stench of the barn long before he reaches it. Giuliano's steward is lax in his supervision, the workers not always conscientious in their duties. Inside, he looks in every cage to see that each animal has water to drink. The lizard with its silver-scaled ruff has frozen itself, splayed, against the back wall of its wicker cage, the silver platelets hanging like a necklace against its back. As Paolo turns to go, he has the sudden and ruinous premonition that these creatures will take their secrets to the grave.

In his *studio*, he lights his candles and settles Ceccio by him while he consults his notebook on previous dissections, checking his drawings against the commentary of Ceccio's prodigious memory. There is a dissection he has performed on occasion to demonstrate that the seat of the breath — that is, of the material life — is in the throat. Paolo intuits a connection between voice, breath and spirit. The demonstration is simple and reasonably swift. He will repeat it for the guests. But he wants to show them something more. Before he goes to bed, he tells Ceccio to sweep the feathers from the table. They lift like snow against the night.

The next day Paolo sets to work at once to prepare the apparatus he will need for the demonstration. Something troubles him as it has not done in the past. He has not lost his conviction that close attention to Nature is the path to knowledge, but what does it signify if the subject itself be destroyed? He would like the subject to reveal itself in a way that reflects the beauty and mystery of its creation. It is with this in mind that he resumes his work on the lizard, his silver-scaled dragon. While the menagerie is being cleaned and decorated for the visit, Paolo spends the days in the privacy of his own room enhancing the lizard's ruff and augmenting the scales until it wears a shawl of silver. It is demanding work for such old eyes, but he has devised a small contraption that holds the creature, and his fingers have learned the quickest and easiest technique of stitching through with the fine wire. It will be a delight for the guests, perhaps a gift for Lucia, who will be home in time for Cosimo's visit. Or perhaps Giuliano will need to be artful in his choice and bestow it instead on the Spaniard. In any event, it will be a marvel to be remembered.

When he is working, Paolo forgets every doubt that ever assailed him. Creating beauty is all that matters. His interest is consumed by the painstaking stitching.

He is so preoccupied that Chiara is almost forgotten. She spends these gentle waning days like the grey cat wandering the tracks that meander down away from the house. She inhales the dry pungent smells from bright marigold and feverfew, picks her favourite leaves, tangy and sweet, and bites into them. Down in the valley a white mist sometimes clings to the river's back. Up here the springy grass is warm and inviting before the sun is halfway up the sky. The Pope himself could not be closer to Heaven.

When Paolo's creation is ready, Ceccio carries it up to the villa in a fine latticework cage, covered with a piece of red velvet. A homecoming gift for Lucia. Paolo takes it from the boy at the door to the *guardaroba* where Giuliano and his wife are seated at the great table, smiling in anticipation. Paolo carries the cage in and sets it down on the black broadcloth square in front of the couple.

He lifts the cover. His hosts at first have difficulty making out what it is that encrusts one of the cage walls. Giuliano remembers the crested lizard, but this is an entirely new creature. It is a creeping thing, transformed by an armoured suit of light. It glints. It shimmers. It is like a crusted rock that lives and breathes.

"What new wonder is this, Maestro Paolo?"

Paolo reaches in and scoops the lizard, places it on the cloth where it seems to turn again to stone.

"Oh, look, will you! Look!" Lucia is delighted. She turns to Giuliano. "You support a warlock, do you know? A sorcerer."

She reaches forward and touches one of the lizard's feet. The foot rises as if on a string and stays suspended like the arm of a statue. She laughs. With a little more encouragement, the lizard begins moving, taking two steps, another two. It stops. Its sides wink and tremble.

Paolo, who had only wanted to create beauty, saw the sudden appetite in Giuliano's face. Giuliano would have liked to see the creature run.

Today, two days before Cosimo is due to arrive, Ceccio tells Chiara she must walk up to the menagerie. He says they have created there a perfumed palace for a mythical beast. She agrees to go only if they take the path furthest from sight of the villa. She keeps a careful watch all the way. At first, it seems not worth the trouble or the risk; it is all as before, the darkness, the foetid air. Neither the vines that garland the rafters, nor the herbs that carpet the floor can exorcize the smell of mouldy straw and piss and plaguey gasses. Only near the far door, where the sun streams in a straight path onto the birds, is there any sense of cheer. But then she sees the cage covered with a red cloth. The cloth is edged in gold braid, a thick tassel at each corner.

"Come on," says Ceccio. "I'll show you."

He darts inside and goes to the cage, lifts the red cloth, beckons.

Chiara cannot believe what she is seeing, this shining creature that has walked out of a dream. Something that cannot be, yet is. She would not believe it alive if she did not see its eye.

"Now get out. Quick."

She runs with Ceccio back down the hill, taking a wide loop of track that keeps them out of sight. They stop for breath a little way west of the byre.

"Want to know what it was?"

Chiara nods.

"*Un diavoletto*. Maestro Paolo bought it from the Devil himself. Want to see another marvel?"

Chiara nods again, but follows at a distance. What Ceccio has to show is always interesting. Once he took her, at great risk of discovery, to up to a small enclosure behind one of the stables and pointed like a proud father to a pair of lambs, undersized and joined at the rump, which Giuliano had kept there since spring. The hind legs of one were shorter and withered and swung uselessly against the legs of the other as it came toward them. But Ceccio is not to be trusted. She has not forgotten how in the height of the summer he took her to see the old man who cleans the barn, drunk and himself a curiosity. He was sitting down against the wall on the side away from the house. When he saw Chiara, he began to laugh and pat his face. He had a single stump of a tooth and it had polished his lip to a satiny purple where it rubbed up and down. When he began to rummage in his lap, she turned and ran.

Ceccio cuts back toward the byre, grinning whenever he turns round. He opens one of the doors and props it back. Chiara waits for him to go right in before she draws nearer to stand at the entrance. On the heavy table beside the wooden block are two planks, each with two holes spaced some distance apart. Across one end of these is another board with a chain dangling from an iron ring. There are rings, too, on each side of the wooden block in the centre of the room, from which the knives and the saws hang. There are rings on the sides of the block and on the floor around it. Some hold lengths of rope neatly coiled and lying ready. Four lamps, positioned to light each corner, hang from the rafters above the table. A broom and a pail stand in the corner. Ceccio motions to her to come in. She knows better.

"See," says Ceccio. "Your arms in here," pointing to one of the planks. "Your legs in there."

But Chiara is not so stupid.

SOFONISBA READS ORAZIO'S LETTER again in the privacy of her room. It has come to her through a papal envoy returning from England and on his way to Roma. For a while dismay and consternation keep her from seeing past the first line. He writes that his health is failing and that she must come at once. She has to read it several times. He writes that she is to abandon all work on hand and leave without delay. She is to use her fee from the *Argentara* commission, and Ser Tomasso is to assist her. He writes that he has sent a separate letter to Ser Tomasso authorizing him to let a portion of their house and attend to all business details, as well as the arrangements for her journey. It is as if her life is a thread being wound tightly in to a spool. Her father has thought of everything, except perhaps the practical difficulties of the journey. All he requires from her is her presence, her "sweet flesh and blood" before his face:

For, my beloved daughter, I am alone and sick and in low spirits. The assistance that is provided me here is worse than incompetent, for the men know little of our way of working, and the major-domo expects too much. I am able to work for only an hour or two at a time, and fear that the monies due to me will be withheld indefinitely. I urge you, my beloved daughter, to come in all haste and assist me with this work. My years fly before my eyes like winter leaves, and there is no one I can turn to for solace.

Sofonisba can barely recognize Orazio in these words. This is not the father who stormed at her and railed at the court. This is her father suddenly old and feeble and a great distance away. The obstacles between them diminish. It is easy to make the decision to go to him. There is no one she must take leave of. Matteo Tassi, she knows, will be coming back. She has no wish to be in the same city. She does not want to breathe the same air. And Chiara? She gives her barely a thought. There is no reason why she should not stay with Maestro Paolo.

The next morning she informs Andrea's major-domo that she must leave almost immediately. Over the next two days, she works to put the final touches to the *Susanna*, the highest lights and the subtlest shades. She sleeps hardly at all. Once, as she lay awake, she heard footsteps in the passage outside, the faintly audible pad of bare feet approaching, and then receding. She was almost certain that she knew who it was. There was no lock on the door but she felt confident he would not come again.

It was a judicious guess. The Arcivescovo, at that moment retreating down the passage with a wilting erection and a sudden urgent need to piss, had had a change of heart. On his way to do the thing he had been thinking of all day, perhaps all summer, he had not even reached her door when the intrusive vision assailed him: Sofonisba undressed and ready to slip into her bed, pausing as he opens the door; Sofonisba pausing and fixing him eyeball to eyeball in the manner of her *Susanna*. Not turning away, not covering herself or crying out in alarm, but staring at him as if he were one of his own servants blundering into the wrong room. Staring him down and demanding simply by her look to know what exactly he thought he was about. Holding his breath, he turned back before he had even opened the door, taking long, careful, ridiculous strides to gain the most distance with the fewest steps. He slipped back into his room with relief. It was a fine thought, to take her just before she slipped out of reach. But he is a busy man. He does not have time to plead the case for his pleasures.

Cardinals, labourers, merchants, diplomats, slaves, and princes have all crossed the path of the Arcivescovo, and he has known exactly where to place them, how to deal with them. This woman is a puzzle, with her withdrawn, intense manner of working, her bold-faced responses and her steady gaze. She has become more troubling as the paintings have progressed. He looked once at the chilling representation she keeps under the piece of scarlet. There was something more than untoward in a woman who could conceive such diabolical treachery. *Judith* and Sofonisba, the created and the creator, were inextricably compounded. And the *Susanna* was no less disturbing. For weeks, he had employed a carpenter to work on a false wall behind his bed, making the inlaid panels that open out now in the manner of a cupboard or a tabernacle. Last week the man had fetched the painting and carried it up. Sofonisba had followed.

It was behind these doors in the wall that the *Susanna* was to be fixed, concealed from sight unless Andrea chose to reveal it. Sofonisba helped the carpenter hold the panel in place for approval. Andrea nodded.

The painting then was returned to the workshop. He went to see it again when Sofonisba had gone walking in the gardens. It bothered him. It was not the luscious treat he had anticipated but he could not determine why. All he knew was that it left him feeling uncomfortable.

To Sofonisba, the silence that followed the retreating footsteps represented more than a simple absence of sound. It opened out to become an expression of space, a broad expanse of washed sky. During the fire in San Pier, she had seen a flame catch at a painted banner. In the blink of an eye, it had shot the length of the cloth, silk become flame. The footsteps in the passage were unstoppable fire, fear made flesh. There was no separation. Gradually, calmly as they receded, her body returned to itself.

She reads her father's letter again. Since she has come to this house without him, without anyone, it is as if the air has opened around her, a space in which her soul, her heart (what is this thing that lives?), can freely breathe. And the more it breathes, the stronger it becomes. She sees her father on the periphery of her space, dressed in his dry, old bones and his thin skin, small and in need. It will be an easy thing to go to him.

PART IV

FOURTEEN

Tassi has been a slower, quieter man since the trial. Tassi, whom nothing could rattle, nothing disturb, feels himself altered.

Chiara had brought him as low as Alessandro with her story of the hanged man's shirt. Even the attendants in the court had sniggered. But what, then, had caused his throat to constrict as if he were suffocating? His stomach to contract as if he might vomit? Was it the sight of her as on a hook, wriggling? Her pitiful hoarse voice? Like the voice of a boy. Tassi, who had stood before bulls with mastiffs hanging from their flanks, their throats; Tassi, who had watched Alessandro shave his head for money and run at a live cat nailed to a warehouse door; Tassi, who had seen Sofonisba herself under the presses, had not been able to abide seeing Chiara squirm or hearing her cry out. They were savage with her. They had the blood running from her knuckles even before her hands were released. And yet, despite the pity that welled in him like tears, his fury was directed not at the judges who were forcing the testimony from her, but at Chiara herself. How it grated to see her loyal to the unbending Sofonisba. Wasn't it he who had first fed her, first warmed her? Wasn't it he who had stroked her pied skin as if it were beautiful, he who had tumbled her, made her smile, hanged man's skin or no, she who might otherwise have never known a man? Yet she stood in the court screaming that he violated her as well as her mistress. While Sofonisba's comtemptuous, beautiful face turned away, not flinching, only to turn back after the verdict and refuse him. A plague on them.

In the court, he had been a man drowning in Sofonisba's unrelenting silence. It spread about him like a sea. There was no one else in the city she had allowed so close. But her silence denied all that had passed between them. It was a lie that negated his triumphs and robbed him of the victory that was his. He had not believed that she would maintain it under threat of pain, and then under pain itself. He had expected her to yield, confess their private pleasures, her admission then a badge, a seal for him to wear before the world. Instead, her testimony — which was nothing but her accusation — was received as a testament to her spotless virtue. There was no rejoicing in the court's order to wed this sterile lily stalk. She was not the profligate honeysuckle he knew, not the riotous, clambering dog rose that could take his breath away.

When she came to him that night in the byre, coming up behind him where he crouched at a wing, breathing a kiss into his ear, letting the weight of her breasts fall on his back, he could have had her in a moment. Their kisses, when he turned, were open, as if mouth would consume mouth, and she caught him between her legs as she pulled him down and onto her. But then when his hands were on her flesh, she was afraid of old Paolo, afraid of waking the girl. She was out of breath. Yet he could have had her even then, but for something he said. A joke. He cannot remember what it was, but in a moment she was pulling at her gown and then was gone. He has wanted that soft mouth ever since. But when he had her beneath him again, he did not find it.

He has been trounced by life, and the demoralizing taste of defeat returns as it has tirelessly all these long summer months. The only time he can mask it is when he is in the tavern. He has pissed away a whole summer of lucrative commissions in Siena. He went there immediately after the trial, taking with him (as if he were some other man altogether) a pathetic dream. He imagined himself returning to Firenze rich and successful, presenting himself next spring when Orazio arrived home from England ready to enforce the marriage. Instead, he is returning early. He has not looked to his affairs. His reputation as an artist has soared but he is worse than penniless. He is in debt. He has a velvet cape, blue like the one he lost to Alessandro, and won last night from an equally impecunious friend. He has a knife at his belt, and he has his tools, wrapped in a leather pouch and tied at his saddle. If he had stayed in Siena longer, he would surely have lost all.

Once he is on the road to Firenze, Tassi's spirits lift. He begins to think of friends who owe him favours. He begins to think more kindly of Sofonisba. She cannot refuse him forever.

The countryside he rides through on his borrowed horse has the warmth of promises fulfilled. The busy green has long since turned to shades of gold. The earth shows sand and dun and ochre against the cloudless blue. He passes oxen pulling wagons laden with baskets of translucent grapes, misty green, red, purple, dusted with bloom. Flocks of starlings fall in skeins like flung net over the vines not yet harvested. In the orchards the apples hang heavy on the bough, waiting for frost.

He will go to Paolo, for whom he has worked so hard. Paolo will remember the bronze and he will think up a new expense — his plates! He will ask for the cost of his pewter plates. It will be a beginning. Paolo may have more work. He will go straight there. When he gets near the city, he will cross the river at Ponte Alle

Grazie and keep to the east, avoiding the temptations of the city. But *Argentara* lies between Tassi and the river. Stuffed with good intentions, he can see no reason not to present himself to Sofonisba.

By the time he rides through the gates of *Argentara*, Tassi has convinced himself that his troubles are over. As soon as he dismounts, two, three attendants are at his side to find out his business. He is taken to a small reception room and waits while one of them darts away into the mazey passages of the palazzo. When he returns he takes Tassi along to the *sala delle statue*, saying that the painter will receive him there. He says he will bring a glass of wine for him while he waits.

Matteo Tassi, who has burned with resentment and shame all these last months, is suddenly absurdly hopeful at the prospect of seeing the woman who most certainly loathes him with all her being. He is churning inside like a callow youth about to see a harlot alone for the first time. He is glad to be able to wet his lips.

Sofonisba, at her window overlooking the gardens, combs out her hair. When she received the message that Messer Matteo Tassi was waiting for her in the reception room, she had been on the point of saying she would not go down. She said instead that she would receive him in the workshop.

"You can remain in attendance at the door," she said to the servant. "I do not wish to be alone." But she knew even then that it was not necessary, that whatever he had to say would slide from her like oil. She would be deaf to him, dead to him, standing beside the *Judith*, her private preparation of his public pain. The painting would speak for her. There was nothing she need say.

She stops to pin her hair before she goes down. For some reason it seems important not to appear dishevelled. Important, too, to walk without haste to the workshop, important to breathe calmly, to stand and wait with dignity. When Tassi comes in, she expects to be stricken with rage and resentment. She will not let him see it.

But Tassi comes in with a step and a bearing she does not recognize. He falters, misses his footing at the door, is on the point of apologizing and then he stops awkwardly. The silence between them is no silence at all. It rings in the stone room.

The *sala delle statue* is ranged with shelves and niches and plinths that hold marbles and bronzes. Sofonisba is standing squarely in the centre in front of the easel that supports the *Susanna*. Another easel stands at her side, its painting covered by a piece of scarlet. There is no sign of her tools, only the finished work.

"*Madonna*!" Tassi bows and when he straightens, extends his hands in a gesture of reconciliation.

Sofonisba watches him warily.

"Ser Matteo."

His gaze flicks toward the painting.

"*Madonna*, I am honoured that you so graciously receive one who has wronged you unpardonably. For your kindness and clemency, I am forever in your debt."

Sofonisba says nothing.

"Let me show you, I beg you, *Madonna*, how I might repair our friendship."

Behind Sofonisba, the rosy flesh of the *Susanna* draws Tassi's eye. She steps to the side.

Despite his nerves, Tassi smiles. He looks at Sofonisba but she does not smile back. But the painting! He has never seen anything like this rendition. The elders! They are lecherous old fornicators. He is suddenly stricken again with love for this woman. Only Sofonisba could paint these men. Ah, but the *Susanna*! Look at her! How coldly her eyes stare back at him. It might be — it is — the viewer who is stripped bare in this ocular exchange. He could laugh out loud at the boldness of it. It does not shame him in the least to be staring between this woman's thighs. Many a time he has enjoyed the sight at the brothel — and returned the favour, in all his aching glory, to any who cared to look. But how, how in Heaven's name can a pompous, pious prelate gaze on this and not feel himself unmasked? Oh, he loves her. How he wants now to restore the conspiracy they enjoyed against the world. All life a joke, a *burla*, a *burletta*, against itself, against the rest of them.

"It is an achievement, this painting, *Madonna*. It is an achievement."

She acknowledges the compliment with an almost imperceptible nod.

"Will you show me the other?"

She extends her hand in invitation.

Tassi, more at ease now, smiles his thanks and goes to the painting, takes the edges of the scarlet between thumb and forefinger and raises it.

Sofonisba watches him. If he were raising a woman's skirts she could not feel a sharper excitement.

For Tassi, it might have been an earthquake, a lightning bolt. The ground shifts under his feet. He sees his own face painted on the panel. His own face upside down, standing his rediscovered universe on its head. It is his own face tilted back toward him, his own head that hangs over the foot of the satin-covered bed. And the woman who wields the sword. Sofonisba has disguised the face but cannot disguise the expression. This Judith is intent and purposeful. She has not hesitated for a moment to strike. The flesh of her face is distended with the exertion of the act. Her eyes are fixed on what she is doing and her jaw is set. The servant behind in the shadows looks in her direction, questioningly. Judith ignores her, and when Tassi looks more closely he can see about the mouth something like anticipation. He looks again at the face of Holofernes. Its — his — eyes roll wildly back in the head in full awareness of the moment, begging him silently for assistance. But the figure in the painting is beyond all help, whether it comes or no, for Judith has already brought down the sword, its blade has already entered his neck, and a jet of blood is springing, describing the same shallow arc as the leaf of the lily, across her breast.

His breathing has become so heavy he can hear nothing else. He lets the cloth fall, looks sideways at Sofonisba, but briefly, looking away at once as if his eyes have encountered a harsh and painful light. He leaves without looking again at the painting.

Sofonisba watches him go without regret. He had come with the intention of winning her back. She has caused him to leave. She is intact. The quality of light and air is unchanged. The prospect of the day is as before. For once their positions are reversed: she has dictated Tassi's conduct — and she did not speak a word.

Tassi has few words for the boy who hands him his horse. He rides back down the avenue of cypress as if he is riding into battle. The stones fly up from his horse's hooves, and birds startle from the dark foliage.

By the time he crosses the bridge, his fury has burnt itself out. He passes the towers of the Porta alla Giustizia, where some miscreant hangs, forgotten by all but the crows and buzzards that circle overhead, and the rats that make the clever, head-first climb down the rope at night. Outside the walls, there is a pack of dogs at work on some intricate ritual of bullying a newcomer. They trot and lie down, rise up singly to make feints and lunges at the yellow beast.

He can hear a disturbance as he passes the jail where some other fellow, some misfit, some unfortunate, is providing the people with a lesson in the law. Tassi has an overwhelming thirst. He passes Porta alla Croce, passes Porta San Piero Maggiore, and, on an impulse, turns in at the Porta San Gallo and walks his horse to the house of his friend Benvenuto, who is sure to pour wine down his throat with a funnel if he will only listen to his outrageous stories. Tassi will not even have to remember what he says.

⌐⌐

THE AFTERNOON IS VERY QUIET. The birds have disappeared into the cool shade. There is a single bee in the bramble over by the wall, intent on an out-of-season, last, perfect blossom. On the ground under the pear tree, wasps frill the hollowed fruit. Nearby, only a fly buzzes. Chiara has been sleeping on Paolo's great bed. She stands now in the doorway of his house, blinking at the sunlight. Paolo has said he will not be back until evening, but the sun is still high. He went up to the villa this morning. He took Ceccio with him. Chiara knows where they are this afternoon. She takes a drink from the rain barrel, has to scoop far down to raise the dark water, brackish with a flavour of green and moss and smoke. She goes away behind the dung heap to urinate. She wanders off to the chestnut tree, where the fruit litters the ground, but she is soon deterred by its spiny armour. There is nothing more to do until Paolo returns. He is at the byre. She knows this. She goes back and sits on the threshold in the sun. The fly persists at whatever it is feasting on, the flagstone. Chiara knows she is going to get up and go to the byre. Ceccio, this morning, took her aside.

"They have been talking about you," he said. "Old Paolo wanted the *Signore* to keep you up at the villa for a pet."

She had waited for more.

"But he wouldn't. He said *Signora* Lucia would never allow it. She said you were not a marvel of Nature. She said you were an affliction." He laughed and kicked dust in her direction, then stopped abruptly and said, "Do you want to see a marvellous thing?" He asked with his beautiful long-lashed eyes and his rosy mouth, but the question might as well have come from the foul-smelling old man with the single tooth.

"Come to the byre this afternoon," he said. "If you're brave enough." She ignored the face he pulled, dragging down the skin under his eyeballs, extending his tongue. "But don't come in," he said, releasing.

"And don't let them hear you and don't tell them I told you to come if you get caught." He cackled. "A wonder, an unholy wonder. Like the Devil's balls."

The afternoon stretches away with nothing to fill it but the insistent fly.

In the pasture, a mule, startled at Chiara's sudden appearance on the path, lurches to its feet and brays once. Something brays back from Paolo's byre. Chiara approaches at an angle so that she will not be seen. The door stands half open, perhaps to admit light. Whatever called out, calls out more loudly now.

Chiara, with her hand on the wall beside the door, pauses. A black tide of dread and certainty is filling her. She feels it rising, cold inside her, filling every space within her, drowning her heart in darkness. It is knowledge without words. She does not formulate what is happening inside the byre; she has no need to. Everything she has ever seen or heard has led unswervingly to this moment: the knives hanging from the table; the lamps, the saws, the chains; the old man's tooth sawing a silken path; Ceccio's brute beauty; the searching eyes of Messer Paolo, the cruelty of his silverpoint investigating every line, every curve, every turn seen or unseen, every truth and every flaw, investigating every thing in all the world; the animals, sorry in their cages for the sins they do not know, the patient animals in the fields, the unknowing mule scrambling to its feet on the sunlit grass, the daisy crushed under its hoof; the eyes of the men on the quayside, the scream of the pen on the ledger book and a man's face — oh, she remembers now a man's face and the look on it as he watches, curious, excited. Ravenous for the unthinkable. But now she can hear Paolo's voice.

"*. . . for the diminution of discomfort of the beast that we be prompt in the performance of our demonstration.*" He is reciting or he is reading, and his voice continues over the intermittent cries. "*For this reason we make only one . . . incision . . .*" The scream is both unearthly and bestial. Paolo raises his voice.

"*. . . through the skin and the underlying muscle . . . taking care to stop just short of the trachea so as not to injure it . . .*"

Chiara steps quietly along to the door's edge as Paolo's voice continues "*. . . and as you see we may quite easily lift the trachea using only our fingers to separate it . . .*"

She sees everything before she runs. Paolo and Ceccio, Giuliano, the Duke, the ladies and a nobleman in black. Something on the table. A brute. On its back. The legs of it sticking straight up, quivering, through boards on each side. Lashed down with ropes extending to the rings on the floor. A pig. Its head held back with a chain that runs behind the teeth of its upper jaw, now its lower jaw. Paolo at its side. Ceccio sitting with his back to the table, his hands over his eyes to concentrate. Paolo speaking continuously. Paolo leaning over the pig, reaching into the wound that has opened its throat. The pig, the upside down pig, bucking against the boards.

Chiara is overcome with a shaking so violent that her knees buckle. But she is on her feet again already and running back down the path.

Inside the byre, her momentary presence at the door is already dismissed and all eyes have turned back to the fascination of the flesh. Paolo's voice, calm and measured, continues as if there were no interruption at all.

"*. . . as you may very nicely hear, when we sever the cerebral nerves on this side . . . the loss of the middle voice, so proving its source . . . located here in the throat . . .*"

⌐

CHIARA'S FINGERS CLUTCH tough, scrubby weeds. She is lying in a dip in the ground, pressing her face to the earth to stifle her bawling cries, an infant trying to find the breast, a young animal trying to melt back into the flesh of its dam, to hide in the fur. She grinds her face into the hard earth beneath the weeds, not for what she has seen in the byre, not that, but for her family, the image of them flaring behind her eyes, as she ran from the door of the byre. It is a vision of grief and terror both and it has risen from the dark place conjured by the screams of the pig. It belongs to her alone and there is no way to lose it. She turns her face from side to side as if she would grind the vision into the earth, and for a moment she succeeds. It retreats, thinning and diminishing, vaporizing like a dream, leaving only the long fall into a desolate void. She rolls over onto her back. Bits of grass and seed and dirt stick to her smeared face. Her eyes are squeezed shut.

The faintest of breezes begins to dry the salt tears. Chiara opens her eyes. Someone has lifted the sky all the way to Heaven. It is higher than she has ever seen it. She is a speck, a seed herself, a grain minute and insignificant as sand. And, oh, the distance, the vertiginous distance, as if she is lying at the bottom of a deep shaft. The blue sky so far above.

She gets herself up from the grass, wipes her arm across her face and begins to walk up the hill toward the menagerie. Her grief is soothed by the climb like a great rough wave receding. But even as she reaches the doors of the great barn, the wave returns, bearing its ruin. It is like a change in the body, physical like a sneeze, unstoppable, only this is terror. She knows it is going to happen again. It is — they are — returning and she is about to see it all again, eyes open, eyes closed, it will not matter. There is nothing she can do to avert it. A curious winding begins in her throat as she enters the barn, its darkness and its odours. She keeps her mouth closed against the sound, and it rises to a stifled wail, like someone far away crying in pain. Her presence sets up a shrieking and a chatter inside. She tries to open a cage but her hands are clumsy as paws, as useless as flippers. She crashes the sides of her fists against the wicker door. On the floor beside her is a hammer, left behind by one of Giuliano's men. A gift. She grasps it in both hands and moves from cage to cage, sobs lost in her throat, the hammer swinging.

The birds call to one another, the monkey shrieks, picking up her fear, picking up the filthy rinds of memory carried on the back of the flood she has unleashed, this tide of grief that has broken through its walls. She smashes at the doors of the cages. Splinters fly up and strike her face, and her hands bleed where she tears the wood away. Her breath comes in great gulping sobs, and she is shouting now her grief, each cry more protracted than the last, until she is wailing, her voice achieving its own terrible beauty as it ululates from deep within, from her soul itself, rising to unearthliness like the wind in a gale, in this gale of pity.

For she has seen her two brothers and her father. She is in a dark place but she can see them quite clearly, as perhaps she saw them through a crack between the boards of the wood box where she was hiding, or as perhaps she has created them from the voices that she heard that day, that she can still hear quite plainly. She has seen her sister and her mother. They are lit as clear as day. Her father, her sister and one of her brothers lie dead. Her mother is alive but she is on the floor. Her older brother also lives. He is kneeling. The soldiers are holding him. They are telling him to fall upon her mother, his mother, and he is weeping like a child, while her mother makes a strange noise behind the rag they have stuffed in her mouth. They say if he does not couple with her, they will cut off his ears and his nose. Her mother makes a small noise, it might be his name, over and over. They push him onto her but he will not move despite their shoving and their shouts. And then he is dragged off again, and in no time they have him up on his back on the table, a man tying his hands underneath, another standing at his head with both fists in her brother's hair. One of the men says, "See if you can hear your mother now," and another yanks the rag out of her mouth. Her voice rises like cloth tearing, like iron ringing, like a pig dying. Chiara closes her eyes at the sound and does not open them again until the room outside the darkness where she is hiding has fallen completely and utterly silent.

She climbed out of the wood box. She took in the room at a glance, her family just where they lay, and then she closed her eyes tightly again, squeezing them shut as if to keep out what she had seen. With her eyes shut and her hands clasped tight to her chest as if she was carrying there all that was left of her family, she began to walk slowly, carefully toward the door. She pushed her feet along the floor without lifting them for fear of treading on a hand, a leg. The packed mud of the floor felt unfamiliar, soft and slippery. Once she touched something and had to open her eyes to find her way, snapping them shut and continuing her dreadful shuffle toward the door and the sunlight. The weight of her aloneness in the world was the weight of the dome of heaven bearing down on her and she wanted to sink to her knees. There was a deep stillness all around, broken only by the noise of crows fighting. She did not want to look toward the house of their nearest neighbour. She walked, stumbling and tripping on the loose stones, down toward the river.

The birds have flown, finding the accident of solid air in the chaos of net, then beating against cages, against rafters until the constancy of the light drew them low out of the door. Chiara smashes now at the empty cages to destroy the silence which is death's achieved ovation. Stray feathers on the floor, like bright dashes of paint, mark the progress of the birds' panic. The monkey was quick to leap away, had watched from the back of its cage, alert and suspicious, while Chiara smashed the catch on the door and dragged it open. It leapt, squittering faeces, past her head, grasping the open door of the cage as it went and dropping to the floor a little way off. It made a motion there, as if throwing dirt back at Chiara, and then, with a shriek, swung up on the adjacent cage and up again to the one on top of that, and on up to the rafters, where it made one mad, squalling circuit in the shadows before hurtling down to the top edge of the open barn door and freedom. Chiara was left shaking. She has the door of the silver lizard's cage open now, the red silk trampled into the herbs under her feet. The door is hanging at an angle, but the lizard will not move and the cage is fixed.

A hand catches her wrist. There is shouting. Someone is striking her. She hears Maestro Paolo's voice. He is telling her attacker to stop. He is saying he will hold her. A man, one of Giuliano's men, is struggling to tie her hands behind her with a rope that fastened one of the doors.

Paolo says, "Look," and places her hands in front, joined, as if she is praying.

The guard ties them tightly and Paolo says, "Foolish, foolish girl." He would like to say he will take responsibility for her, but Giuliano's face is bloated with suppressed rage. It is not worth the risk.

Chiara is taken over to a small guardroom beside the stables and the door is locked.

⌐⌐

PAOLO STANDS JUST BEYOND the open doorway of the menagerie, waiting for the lizard to move. Little by little, as he watches, the sky to the west begins to alter. A new quality of light invades the blue, a premonition of colour, so that the blue is buoyed with it, lightened and lifted by it, the way the spirit is lifted at the first sign of morning. The new quality establishes itself by degrees until the colour is indescribable, neither blue nor pink, but both, and now there is another seamless shift as clouds appear from the south. He cannot see how they begin. They are simply there, multiplying in the furthest southern reaches as if the sky is spawning them. And this spontaneity, this continuous spawning, adds a new dimension to the sky, which exists now both in colour and in movement. Space becomes one with time. Paolo can see a whole bank of clouds in the distance, like a shawl being drawn up over the world. If he looks up, he can see how pieces from the leading edge of the shawl begin to break away overhead, like wool from a fleece, and are blown separately, airy floss from a magnificent rose-coloured vine. More break away, and more. They float in succession, borne by a wind stream high above him, floating against the blue and absorbing the pink light of this fantastic ceiling, great, weightless, rosy pieces of fleece in aerial procession above him. He is seduced, transported. He is ravished by their beauty passing over his sight, never ending, never ending, never ending.

His mind takes the loveliness into itself and begins to work its alchemy, creating something he has never seen before, something that has never before existed. It is like a window behind his eyes opening to a foreign land, giving on to a vista of a dream. He sees a procession not of clouds but of animals, a vision of harmony, a vision of Paradise before the Fall, and he is overwhelmed by his desire to have seen the captives move away, to have seen them process, the simplest thing in the world, one foot after the other. He would like to have witnessed their liberation, some walking, some flying, each according to its order, some fast, some slow, out of the door of the dark barn into the beautiful light. In his vision he sees them coloured by the reflected glow of evening, sees the jewels of the lizard's back catch fire, flashing as it moves slowly away to softer shadows, sees its fingered feet delicate and careful on the rocks, carrying it away.

Earlier, after Giuliano had hurried his guests back to the culti-vated order of his villa, Paolo had caught sight of the monkey loping across the yard over by the guardhouse. He had seen its bracelets flashing in the late sun as it climbed a vine next to the kitchen before it bounded across the roof and disappeared on the other side of the ridge. The guards were still searching for it. He had turned his attention then to the wreckage of the cages, had made sure they were all open. The lizard had not moved from the corner of its cage. He had carried it outside and set it down on a rock. He has been watching its progress. Now the low rays of the sun are turning its silver to gold. Except to blink, it has not moved for a long time.

One of the blue macaws that has returned to circle the barn flies close by Paolo's head with the sound of a fan collapsing. It lights on the roof of the shed across the yard and calls with a loose, throaty exultation. The lizard's body ripples. It stirs and moves slowly, one limb at a time, down the face of the rock.

Paolo is moved by the creature's efforts to save itself. To see a creature so obedient to its nature fills him with the same inexpressible tenderness that he feels in the face of beauty. Such perfect obedience. It is unchanged, is constant despite all that he has done to make the creature his. Every painstaking step leads him closer to the secret heart of knowledge where beauty and terror, like the two halves of a seed, lie in perfect balance. His compassion extends to every living thing. The awe that he felt in the presence of the unborn child returns.

~

THE TWO YOUNG MEN who ride down from Giuliano's are in no hurry.

"Stop at Orazio the painter's," Gaetano had said. "The daughter will have to come up at once."

But "at once" is a remote concept for the young men, who, when they draw near the town, hear singing and laughter coming from *La Cicogna* just outside the gates. Who could ride past? Not these certainly, who must go in and do not emerge for twelve hours, even then finding it suddenly necessary to visit the house of Benvenuto, an old friend who plays fine music for anyone bringing wine or a round of good cheese.

The young men have money to fritter and guzzle. They take their time along the way.

"Welcome! Welcome!" Benvenuto, thin as a rake and curly-headed as a sheep, ushers them in. "You are just the men we need." In his reception room, behind the laughter and the noise, someone is playing the lute and singing a sweet lament, a mournful drum accompanying with a single, steady beat.

"Take a look." Benvenuto points out Tassi. He is sitting at a window seat on the other side of the room with his back against the wall and one knee drawn up, his arms resolutely folded against all diversion.

Tassi turns to see his host and the two young men in all their finery, grinning. The carboy in the basket at their feet is full.

He cannot help but grin back in response, the night ahead suddenly as filled with promise as the fields of the morning.

As the afternoon wears on, the carboy yields its reliable harvest of rash promises, maudlin memories and bad deals — but no solace for Tassi. There is nothing for it, the young men decide, but to take him back with them to *La Cicogna*, where the women will just be getting up.

It is well past midnight and the gates of the city are firmly closed by the time Tassi hears about Chiara. No one understands his consternation.

And no one understands how or why a man who drank more than his share the night before can be up and away by dawn.

⌐⌐

TASSI CONSIDERS GOING STRAIGHT to *La Castagna*. But he stands little chance of being received at the villa. After what was said in the Court about the escapade with Chiara, it would be beneath Giuliano's dignity to release her to him. How can he plead for her? He has nothing to offer. He thought about selling his friend's horse, but in the aftermath of his drinking spree he forsees only too clearly the consequences of everything he does, and besides, it would bring him only a small amount, and that in vulgar cash. These men of substance never sink so low. They have to be wooed with more finesse. Lacking influence, a man needs to approach them with some gift of real worth. Sofonisba could do more. Women are made to plead. It increases their charm.

He will arrange for Sofonisba to intercede. He will force down his pride and turn around, ride right back to *Argentara* and inform her himself.

Does he think, too, that this act might somehow redeem him in her eyes, restore her faith in him, compensate for his base act? Make of her a compliant partner in the future conjugal bed? The only certainty is that Tassi does not look that far into the future; if he did, all he would see would be a long and fruitless journey, an arduous ride there and back with nothing to show for his pains but a worn out horse, an empty stomach, and an irresistible thirst for sleep. "No," the footman says. "*La donna* Sofonisba has returned to Firenze."

IN HER ROOM BEHIND the shop on Via del Cocomero, Sofonisba prays. She has been up early. Her two boxes are already on their way from the Porta San Friano to join the rest of a cavalcade leaving this day for Pisa. She will be travelling in the company of a number of merchants bound for Southampton. Tomasso himself has arranged for a trustworthy client of his to act as her protector. Now that it is upon her, the journey is daunting. Sofonisba has opened the tabernacle in her room for the first time in months and is kneeling before the gilded relief of the Blessed Virgin, the only celestial personage she really trusts, if truth be known. While Ser Tomasso waits patiently below, she prays, unaware of the sound of someone knocking at the door of the shop.

Reluctantly Ser Tomasso opens the door to Tassi. As if this unruly rake has not been trouble enough.

Matteo Tassi has a purposeful look about him, thrusting forward into the house, chest, chin first. For once he does not reek of wine.

"Have you heard?"

"'Heard? Heard?'"

"You have not heard. The girl. No one's told you? She has run mad up at Paolo Pallavicino's. She ran through Giuliano's menagerie and stove in all the cages. Let all the creatures out and killed them. Giuliano has locked her up. Where is her mistress?"

Ser Tomasso turns away. He keeps his back to Tassi. "Four hundred and eighty florins was the figure I heard."

"You do know, then."

"It's a serious matter. A collection worth that much. I'm not surprised he locked her up. Four hundred and eighty . . ."

"Damn his florins."

"It's the girl who will be damned."

"So why haven't you sent someone to get her back? Where is Sofonisba?"

"Monna Sofonisba is on her way to England."

"That can't be true."

Tomasso turns and gives Tassi a level stare without a trace of a smile. "Ser Orazio has asked for her. If you're so concerned, my esteemed friend, may I suggest you undertake the little business with *La Castagna* yourself?"

"But the girl belongs to Sofonisba. It's your business to look after her affairs."

"Don't be ridiculous."

"Why ridiculous?"

"She's your slave, Matteo. You own the deed of sale."

"Did Sofonisba know about the girl?"

Tomasso shrugs.

"You don't care what will happen to her?"

"I know what will happen."

Tassi kicks at the leg of the table. He would like to grab Tomasso by the neck of his tunic, the way he would a comrade. "You know this, yes. You know what will happen to her."

He walks round to lean close to Tomasso's face.

Tomasso stares him down. "You know this, too. She'll hang."

The silence between them is marked by a creak as the leg of the table settles back to its usual place.

"Sofonisba can't have known."

"She knew."

Tassi waits.

"She gave me no instructions."

"You are not a man of honour."

"And you are?"

Ser Tomasso rubs his hands together briskly when Sofonisba comes down.

"Madonna. Are you well prepared?"

"I made the sign of the cross fifteen times," she says, smiling. "Do you think it is sufficient?"

She hands him the key to her room, which he threads onto an iron ring.

"You take good care of us, Messer Tomasso."

Perhaps it is the compliment that goads him into honour.

"Matteo Tassi was here a moment ago."

Sofonisba glances quickly toward the door.

"He is gone now. He came with news. Of your slave." His voice carries the tone that hovers behind all unwelcome news, that says, *Be ready for this.*

She is frowning.

"She has committed a crime up at *La Castagna*. She has been arrested for it, I regret to say, and placed in Giuliano's keep."

"What sort of crime? A girl who spends all her days keeping out of the way of others. Not a girl to get above herself."

"I believe it was some crime against Giuliano's person. In any event there is nothing you can do, but it seemed only fitting you should be advised."

"I should go there."

"With respect, *Madonna*, you cannot."

"At least try to find out her crime, sue for clemency. Poor Chiara —"

"*Madonna*, this is a slave. Your first duty is to your father. If you delay now you will have no company to travel with for another week, perhaps more."

"Then —"

"I advise against it. Most strongly. Your duty, as I said, is to your father. Ser Bernadino now will be waiting."

He regrets that he had ever spoken. She seems to have abandoned all thought of the journey. Abandoned her senses. He watches her face.

"I will sue for leniency, *Madonna*."

"*Signor* Giuliano will never accept money." It is a crass imputation and prods Tomasso's irritation toward anger.

"You have none to give."

Sofonisba is looking desperately around now, as if she would rifle the supplies of the shop, and there is the *Judith* still under the oiled cloth that had wrapped it for transport from *Argentara*.

"I have a painting."

"Oh, a painting —"

"No, Messer Tomasso, please hear me. I have this painting," and to Tomasso's dismay, she is bending down to unwrap it. "It is not to be dismissed. It is the finest work I have done." She pulls off the oiled cloth.

"See," she lifts the piece of scarlet away. "See. It is something."

Tomasso can see that. He can see Matteo Tassi himself lying on his back, steeply foreshortened, his head foremost. Matteo Tassi as Holofernes at the moment of his most appalling murder. It is more brutal than all the elegant flayings and stonings and piercings with arrows that decorate the city's churches, contains more unnerving violence and terror within it than all the sublime crucifixions.

He coughs awkwardly.

"You could send this from me, Messer Tomasso. Send it to Giuliano with a note."

Tomasso raises his eyebrows, purses his lips and looks coolly about the shop as if to say, *Note?*

"I shall write one now."

She is at her father's desk.

Tomasso sighs and takes the small key off the ring.

When at last he watches her ride away beside Bernadino, it is a relief.

He returns to Orazio's shop, telling himself he must confirm once more that all is secure. But as soon as he is inside, he goes to look again at the *Judith*. Judith herself has the arms of a butcher, her sleeves rolled up to the elbow. Give it away for a slave? Some would pay handsomely for such an extraordinary painting.

~~

PAOLO PALLAVICINO IS WORKING when Ceccio comes in to his *studio* to say that Giuliano is coming down the hill. He is drawing. The porcupine, looking strangely deflated in death, is lying on the table in front of his drawing book. It is the only creature from the menagerie that did not disappear. Paolo likes to think of the others dispersed over the countryside like the creatures of the Ark, but the same intelligence that renders each quill faithfully in lead point on the page tells him that this is the only one of them that has not been eaten by birds or cats or, if any reached the hills, by wolves.

"I'm busy."

"My dear Maestro!" Giuliano is already in the door, trying not to breathe the unspeakable odour of decay. He has his arms open to embrace. "Let us console one another."

Paolo lays down his silverpoint and dutifully gets up, allows himself to be clasped to the expensive, jewel-encrusted doublet.

"Our animals, Paolo. Our marvellous animals."

"Better to work and forget. It is an accident, just like the fire," and he is already returning to his desk. He gestures to a stool.

"Sit down, sit down, *Monsignore*. An accident, not a judgement. They were already consumed." Paolo speaks without looking up. "They had served their purpose. Observation and investigation. Of the two, observation, if carried out with diligence and attention, is chief. But the girl? What are you going to do with her?"

"You ask about the girl before you enquire after *sua Eccellenza* Lucia? *Sua Eccellenza* Lucia was more unsettled than I have seen her in many a day. But by God's grace she will recover. We have sent the girl away."

"Yes, I can understand that."

"Cosimo thought it best." He seems to want to tell Paolo something else. "She went down this morning with one of his men."

"To?"

"To the *Stinche*."

The mention of the jail secures Paolo's full attention, but Giuliano has little to add. "It was for the best. She had done enough harm."

When he has gone, Paolo stops drawing. The girl will not last long in the *Stinche* with no one to speak on her behalf. Yesterday morning he had gone to see her up at the Villa. She was lying on the floor of a narrow room adjacent to the stable. She was sleeping, pressed close to the wall. Paolo watched her. He could hear slow, rhythmic breathing coming from the other side of the wall.

The guard said, "I can't let you in."

Paolo shook his head. "No matter," he said. "I just need to look."

Something like shame is opening him from the inside, exposing his heart. He might have spoken for her then when he saw her there. But there was her beautiful mottled skin, and there the tip of one wing and the turned head, all he could see of the white dove on her black brow. Her perfect imperfection. The mystery of her affliction, which he had thought to unveil. He considers how her body might be used were she to be executed. He is ashamed of the thought, stifles it like an unwanted child. It seems that, however wide his heart is laid opened, there is always something more terrible to see.

When he had caught Chiara's wrists at the height of her frenzy, he had looked into the furthest reaches of her eyes and had seen there something stronger than himself, something that had made the journey beyond its bounds, beyond law, and had disrupted the prescribed order. For a moment afterward he too felt liberated, as if she had freed him from the fetters of his work. But the feeling vanished as quickly as it had arisen. When he went the next day and saw her lying there, with the great bow-faced gentle mare, heavy with foal, breathing into the wall on the other side of the stall, he felt only the return of an obscene curiosity and the bonds of his greed for knowledge again constricting his heart.

⌐⌐

TASSI IS IN THE SQUARE to see for himself, and it is true. This morning, the boy who had worked for him in the spring came pounding on his door before he was even awake. He was still out of breath as he delivered the news. That slave of his, that girl that was all marked, well, she was in the *Stinche* and tomorrow they were going to hang her.

"No," said Tassi. "No, you've got it all wrong. They've got her up at *La Castagna.*"

The boy shook his head, puffed now with his superior knowledge.

"No. The *Stinche.* They've got the cart ready and everything. Go and see."

It was like waking into a bad dream. He pulled on his clothes and set out for the prison to see for himself, and then he had found himself running.

It is a crisp morning. Only the high roofs of the prison and the upper reaches of the windowless walls are in sunlight. The tall, bossed gates are shut. There are two arraignments nailed up. There is no mistaking the first:

> *The maleficent and impious slave, marked with the Devil's pitch and bearing a blasphemous white dove upon her brow, known to certain citizens of the* commune *as 'Chiara' and known to all for her wilful mischief-making at the* festa *of San Giovanni, at this time constrained by chains and confined within the secure walls of this prison for the safety of the* commune, *has of her own free will, guided by the merciful God in Heaven and his Holy Saints, confessed her heinous crime against the person of* Signor *Giuliano, cousin of His Excellency, Duke Cosimo de' Medici, in which she wilfully destroyed and desecrated certain of his properties to the value of five hundred and eleven florins causing* La Signora *Lucia, wife of the esteemed* Signor *Giuliano, to fall into a fit and suffer pains beyond endurance.*
>
> *Let it be hereby known that in the judgement of the venerable Podestà and all his court, the aforesaid slave Chiara is pronounced guilty of this and other hitherto undiscovered crimes that have rained misfortune upon the citizens of our fair republic, and that she is convicted and condemned to be dispatched from this life by hanging at the hour of noon on the twenty-second day of October on the piazza San Firenze before the doors of the Palazzo del Podestà.*
>
> *Let the Executioner be advised.*

It takes Tassi only minutes to get to the Palazzo, where he intends to pound his fist on the polished tables of secretaries. But of course he cannot. He knows this even as he is approaching. He will be out on his ear, in the gutter. So then he will go directly to the Duke, bypass the unapproachable Podestà altogether. He walks on to the *Signoria*, talks his way in, and gets himself directed through hall after splendid hall until he arrives at the door of Cosimo's own reception room, which is flanked by armed guards. It is his good fortune that the door is open and Cosimo, magisterial at a vast polished desk, says, "Get that fellow's name before you throw him out." Tassi, who has never given a thought to name, either good or bad, must now thank his reputation as an artist of the highest order for the fact that he is allowed to stand before Cosimo himself.

Cosimo, dressed in black except for his soft white collar and cuffs, exudes the power of secure wealth. By some miracle of comportment and for the first time in his life, Tassi, wild-haired, unshaven, manages to convey the wringing of a wretched cap — despite the fact that he has none — between his fists. But it is not for Cosimo, this stance, and it is not for himself. It is for Chiara.

Cosimo listens. He flicks at the white cambric at his wrists, says his hands are tied. It is not for him to challenge a plaintiff's charge nor to overturn a verdict brought down by the Podestà. He cannot.

"But, *Eccellenza*, if your Lordship found it in your Lordship's heart to obtain a pardon for the girl, I, Matteo Tassi, humble servant of your Lordship, would undertake to remove her from the city. In this way, the source of aggravation would be removed without recourse to the grave expedient of execution, so burdensome a matter for a compassionate and just ruler. Such a magnanimous pardon could only earn merit in Paradise for your Lordship's soul."

Cosimo is thinking how many times and in respect of how many cases, he has heard this same argument, when Tassi continues:

"Your Excellency's own well-being weighs upon me heavily and I would be remiss in my duty if I did not move to warn you of a danger of which your Lordship, in your Lordship's zeal for justice, might not otherwise be aware."

Cosimo's attention comes to heel.

"*Sfortuna*, my Lord. *Sfortuna*. I urge you to think of the unnatural events that might accompany the death of this strange girl."

Cosimo's whole life is beset by threats, worried and gnawed by them as by a pack of dogs. He has constantly to be on his guard against everyone, from the King of France to the kitchen scullions. There are exiles who might conspire against him, military commanders nursing grievances, cardinals spreading poisoned rumours, mistresses concealing diseased sweets. Even his own family. He does not like the unspecified 'misfortune,' has not forgotten the way it had struck so suddenly in the church of San Pier, had been for God the Father so irreversible. *Sfortuna* was always ready to take down the highest.

"No reprieve can be granted without a withdrawal of the charge on the part of the plaintiff, without, that is, his own pardon."

Tassi is not sure what to say.

"So fetch it."

A scaffold has already been erected in front of the gates to the Palazzo del Podestà, ready for tomorrow. It spurs Tassi on. It is as if he is waking from a dream where he has been whirled in all directions. He knows exactly what to do. Like a mother separated too long from her child, he makes straight for his house. He is running again by the time he reaches Via Rosaio, conscious of the amount of work still before him.

It is not only for Chiara that his blood is racing, his heart pounding. He has not forgotten, will never forget, the day his mistress went to the gallows — and he stood powerless. He is not a coward, but he is not a fool either. It was against Cosimo himself that her husband had conspired. Who knew her guilt? She was capable of conspiring. Yet still he would have tried to help her, but for something she said the night before she was arrested. "Never think," she said, "never say I loved you more. For my husband I will go through the fires of Hell." Had he made a move, any move, to speak on her behalf, it would have been a step into the flood, to be dragged under. It does not take much in this city to find oneself all at once dressed in the white of an old man's night-shift and walking the gauntlet of jeering faces. There is nothing he could have done, no word that would have saved her. The impotence of his position has weighed on him ever since, as if he should have spoken, offered himself, as it were, to accompany her.

When he reaches his house, he goes directly to his pantry shelf, finds the key tucked down behind the board and unlocks the chest beside his bed where he keeps Paolo's bronze. He carries it to his workbench and lays out his chisels and files, his saws and his hammer. And there is the mysterious child that has lain curled in its lapis sleep all these months.

How perfectly the casting came out, so crisp and clean! He picks it up and turns it. Perhaps for the first time in his life, Tassi feels his hands tremble. For he knows at last why he locked it away. From a great distance the knowledge comes to him, like a scent borne on the wind from a place he has forgotten — or not wanted to remember. He knows how Paolo acquired the foetus. He had not needed to ask where. He knew; everyone knew Paolo Pallavicino took the bodies of the hanged for his work. The most important question had never crossed his mind: he had not thought to ask when. He thinks about his mistress of that other year, who took him so lightly, abandoned him so easily. He thinks of her heart-breaking climb on the ladder, her heavy body, heavier than he had ever known it riding his own.

When his hands have stopped shaking, he sets to work. He takes up his finest chisel and whispers at the details of the eyes with its blade.

He does not want to stop until it is perfect.

In the small hours of the night he sleeps with his head resting on his arms, a small file almost hidden in his hand.

THE SCAFFOLD IS A CONCESSION to the citizens' lively interest in this human wonder. Dispatching her from a window would not give them what they want. It was settled that the gallows would be brought into the square, making the affair more public, more formal, so ending the continuing murmurs of ill luck. It was thought to be particularly important since her malign influence appeared to be edging constantly nearer to Cosimo himself. It was Cosimo's secretary who said in the end, "Give them what they want — a spectacle." Criers confirmed the unofficial rumour and anyone with anything to sell began to savour in his veins the pleasant quickenings of avarice.

⌒

IT NEVER CEASES TO AMAZE Giuliano how treasures seem to come his way. He has never gone out of his way to acquire wealth. It has simply flowed to him as water flows to the sea. A lodestone for riches, his father used to say. It is a small consolation for a wife who absents herself and a son who never arrives. He has been given all manner of gifts since his marriage and he has never tired of looking at them. It nicely disproves the teachings of certain ancient, goatish clerics he could name, who claim such practices not only damn the soul but dull the senses. Old men they are, who spend all their lives looking back in fondness to the days of the mad monk, the fanatical friar who preached austerity. But today. Today brings the strangest gift of all. The ruffian Matteo Tassi with his wild black curls (like a living satyr, for the love of God — he might sprout horns) bringing his marvellous gift, laying it down unceremoniously with a thud on the table and then asking the most fantastical of favours Giuliano has ever heard: that he pardon the wretched, perplexing creature who, it seems, will not cease to be a burden to him wherever she is. It is too extraordinary, not to mention something of a gift in quite another sense altogether. For, as keen as he is to bring felons to justice and to punish misdemeanours, he did lose enthusiasm when Cosimo took Lucia's part and said that of course the slave would have to go. It was obvious what it would mean. He had gone to see her lying there curled in the guardroom, with her strange markings giving her the look of a dumb animal, a calf, a foal. He remembers his delight when he had first seen her, how he was so sure of the pleasant change her presence would effect in his wife, his thought that she might even make a splendid buffoon. How deceived he was! And still she comes back, albeit in the aspect of Matteo Tassi, to haunt him. Cosimo said he should deliver swift and just retribution there on the spot, but he had no heart for it, none at all. He thought then, and still thinks, only ill could come of it. For how — and this is not a question he had asked himself while he was under the spell of her exotic charm — had she acquired the skin in the first place, the stains she wore, if not from some unholy union on the part of her mother? Old Paolo, when he tried to interest him in keeping her, said she was bought in Genoa and rumoured to have come from Circassia — that in itself a sign of deviltry when she looked like something come out of Afrika. Lucia, in her distress, had insisted the girl be taken away and locked up — in the city. She had been easy to listen to. To have the girl dealt with somewhere else, that was the attraction. And yet, when the girl had been taken away with the guard, his uneasiness had returned. It had all been most unsettling. What a fine solution, then, that this fellow Tassi should arrive at his door like an apparition out of the early morning mist and boldly ask for her pardon. But to bring with his request such sublime perfection!

He has first to delay his answer. It would be unseemly to grasp. His hands hover above the gift that lies before him on his desk. He clasps them as if above his dinner and says, "I shall have to consider. Carefully." But the man doesn't move. Instead he says, "*Monsignore*," and bows his head and shows, the scoundrel, no inclination to leave. Just stands there twisting the strap of his satchel.

"In private," good, dependable Gaetano puts in, and the man Tassi finally gathers up his satchel and backs out of the room like a fool.

Giuliano turns to Gaetano.

"Write a letter for Cosimo. Ser Matteo can take it himself. Tell him our wish is for the girl to be spared. And tell Matteo Tassi not to come within twelve miles of here in the girl's company. Tell him that when he comes back to our *contado*, he is to come alone."

Now Giuliano wants to look again at the lovely sad perfection of this thing in its nest of blue.

He lifts it from the blue velvet and turns it in his hands. The strangeness of this life amazes. The little fists are clenched, with the thumbs tucked inside. The feet are crossed, the small pads underneath inviting touch, making the mind believe, '*soft*' — but subject to no foul corruption ever. He will give it to Lucia when she comes in and she will be charmed and it will remain as perfect as any living child most assuredly will not. As he gazes on the face he can believe not only '*soft*' but '*living.*' The closed eyelids might at any moment flick and open, the small, perfect lips part to expel sweet, untainted breath. It charms and it repels for it is perfection and yet a thing unborn, both yet to be and never to be. It is as beautiful and as terrible as the world.

FIFTEEN

Orazio has been anxious for Sofonisba to come. He has been given fine apartments in a house overlooking the Thames at Richmond. It has a garden walled in yellow brick and it stands in the grounds of the new red brick palace — all angles and chimneys and gates and courts and inner courts — on the other side of a spacious level park. The palace is as busy and as noisy as a town, but the park, planted extensively with horse chestnut, elm and oak, has a serene quality. Orazio is grateful while at the same time grieving, for he knows that this is the place where he will die and he will have only his boy for company and the sheep that graze on the other side of the wall. The river here runs through a wide and open landscape. Here are no folding hills of blue, only occasional rises in the land abruptly flattened by the weight of the grey sky. But Orazio balks at the word 'sky.' There is no lovely, changing light, no fleeting shadows cast below, no blue above, only a grey vacancy that has usurped the blue field on which clouds might play. There are no clouds, no mounds of brilliant fleece, no purple thunderheads, only this heavy veil. Perhaps there is not even a veil, but only an absence that matches perfectly his sense of loss. He is lonely beyond belief. He has his boy but the lad is always tired, and if he is not working he sleeps, even when Orazio props him in a chair to talk to him. There is no one else to talk to. The workmen they have given him barely understand his instructions. And it is a wild, unbroken tongue the people speak, even at court. Orazio cannot grasp it, cannot rein it in. It gallops on and then rears and shies away at the last moment as if it has never before been spoken. Nothing rhymes. The emptiness of the sky invades all his days. Each day is an empty room he wakes to, and a pit has swallowed up his heart. For Orazio has achieved the fame he longed for and found it insubstantial and unrewarding as a dream that binds the dreamer, who, blinking, loses it. He has succeeded in all that he set out to achieve. He has renown that has spread beyond the borders of his home. He has the recognition of a foreign monarch. And it means nothing. The Queen smiled and stared at the ceiling while he spoke. She glanced at him and smiled once, twice, commending him in her appalling language, and disappeared again to the sound of laughter in the long panelled passage, leaving him to work on in the cold, sunless halls. How hard he worked all his life for that moment, and it was nothing more than walking to the horizon. But though he does not know it, in the muddle of his torments he is spared one affliction: never on his long walk to the nonexistent horizon has it occurred to him that he might have stopped and turned back for his friends.

Orazio wants only to see his daughter. He longs, longs to be at home in his city of yellow stone with its warring sun and shade. He has been sick and worsening ever since he arrived. The voyage was no good for him. His heart lapped rapidly against his ribs like the ripples on the backs of the waves as they passed the ship's hull and when he lay down the blood pounded in his ears. His persistent nausea abated soon after he stepped ashore at Southampton but the staggering gait he had acquired on board refused to leave. By the time he arrived at Richmond, he felt jolted and beaten and thoroughly ill at ease. Before two weeks had passed, he sent his letter to Sofonisba. All through the overcast days of summer he tried to work, conscious that his strength and vigour were leaving him. The two assistants, though he maligned them in his letter, were competent and worked with a will when he managed to make them understand. The boy, Tanai, learned a few words. One way or another, the work progressed. And then a week ago, Orazio was stricken with a sweating palsy. Certain that it was the plague, he wept and prayed all night, convinced himself that it was a punishment for his sins and so increased his fear and anguish, certain that he would see the gates of Hell before morning. But after a day the fit passed to his chest, where it began to do another kind of harm, racking him with such spasms that every breath caused pain. Now when he works he keeps by him a rag into which he spits some solid, blackish matter flecked with red. He would like to stop painting. He would like Sofonisba to come and lay cool hands on him, take away all this hot pain and this ugly emptiness that is cold and heavy as phlegm. He would like her to say sweet prayers for his soul so that he might be certain of seeing Heaven.

By the time Sofonisba arrives, Orazio's health is gravely weakened, his spirits at their lowest ebb. She is waiting for him in a small reception room in a distant wing of the palace. He makes his way slowly there from the assembly hall where he is painting his vast allegory, *The Union of Truth and Beauty*. When he sees her, it is as if all her youth and vitality are glowing from her face inside the hood of her great brown travelling cloak, and he weeps. She is the only light for him in this dark, panelled room.

It is all Sofonisba can do not to let her own tears betray her pity.

Her father's skin is grey and flaking, cracked and red around his nose and mouth. He is stooped and out of breath, a man who has aged five years in as many months.

Orazio says he will not work any more and sends Tanai to tell his assistants that he is finishing for the day. He takes Sofonisba's arm and walks with her slowly away from the palace and across the park to his house.

Sometimes, he says, he has not the strength to return to his house at all but sleeps on a pallet he has had made up for him in a corner of the hall. It is better. If he returns to his house, sometimes he cannot summon the strength to leave it again.

It is two days before Sofonisba sees the painting. Orazio walks back across the park with her. In the palace, he climbs the stairs to the assembly hall with difficulty. He has not the breath to speak until he has rested. Sofonisba examines his work.

She is glad to see how much is already accomplished. It is splendid work. Her father has captured it, that illusion every painter seeks, that manipulation of the sense of sight, the sweet confusion of space that lifts the veil between the artist's vision and the beholder's perception. Sofonisba sees that she can step right into his painting and complete it — not just complete but upholster, bolster its vision and infuse the stark tricks of sight with life. She can see where, she knows how. With careful attention to the faces, especially the eyes, she can bring the viewer to stand within the painted crowd that views this painted wedding. And if only one of the wedding guests can be made to direct his gaze away from the glorious couple and outward to the room, then the viewer will become a participant in the event, and a second and most real union will take place.

Orazio's breathing is raucous. It is like a wooden wheel churning over stone chippings. He gets up with difficulty.

"This. This is where you will begin, adding ornament here and here . . ." But even as he speaks, Sofonisba is looking at a smaller panel, reserved for yet another personal tribute to the Catholic Queen. She knows that is the place where she will begin.

"You will have Tanai . . ." Orazio is saying.

She corrects him.

"*We* shall have . . ."

"You will have." His gaze does not waiver, does not flicker once. "He will be no use to you for this stage of the painting, but you will have the two assistants given to me . . ." He closes his eyes and concentrates again. When he regains his breath, he points to the work table, the jars and dishes, the brushes standing ready.

"It will be well to adhere to the scheme." He taps the dog-eared notebook in his hands. "It is all here. All here."

In the evening, in a small room in the women's quarters of the house, Sofonisba goes through the notebook, carefully reading Orazio's prescriptions for colours and his directions for their application. His recipes for flesh tones are carefully written out, along with recipes for 'distant landscape without sun,' 'distant landscape with sun,' 'foliage, middle ground, sun' and much more. He has devised a scale for light and dark, with twenty gradations for each pigment. Every gem, every leaf, every ribbon of *The Union of Truth and Beauty* is prescribed a colour and every part of each an intensity. The darkest shadows in a blue robe are azure and indigo to the value of twenty, while the highest reliefs are azure with white lead to the value of one. The book is crammed with sketches and with numbers. A monkey could be trained to execute this work.

Three mornings later, Sofonisba is woken while it is still dark by a hammering at her door. A maidservant with rumpled hair is in the passage. Sofonisba narrows her eyes against the candlelight. The girl speaks in English and though Sofonisba cannot understand, she can clearly hear the anxiety in her voice. Tanai at the end of the long passage, signalling for her to come and now calling, "*Fretta, Madonna! Fretta!*" She turns back into the room to put on a night robe. She hurries, but she knows already that it will be no use. She knows before she hears it from the boy, breathless with fear, hurrying now down the dark passage, scared to say the words: "*Qualcosa di male avviene al* Maestro." Something bad. She knows already what it is, that it will be too late and that she will find her father already dead. She hurries only for the sake of Tanai.

Her father's cold flesh confirms her premonition. She crosses herself. His familiar face is a shell, a husk. Nothing there behind it. Nothing. She feels a rush of panic that subsides as swiftly as water falling down the face of a rock. There is nothing to be done. There is no one to save. She crosses herself again. He has already left them. Tanai says he was making a strange noise, "*Un ringhio arrabiato.*" He says he ran as fast as he could. He is in tears. His face has reverted to a child's: *It wasn't me, it wasn't me.* He says he woke straight away. As soon as he heard the sound. He says he could not have run faster. Sofonisba puts her arms around him, and he howls against her breast like a baby. Through the open door she sees four, five members of the household looking in, their eyes wide with apprehension to learn what these noisy Florentines are about. They begin to gabble among themselves and Sofonisba is about to hush them when she realizes it is not necessary.

She does not want the boy to stop howling, wants him to cling forever to keep her from looking again at her father's unseeing eyes. She pushes Tanai gently off, offers the sleeve of her robe so that he can wipe his face, then goes to the door and draws one of the women into the room so that she can see Orazio.

"*Prete,*" she says. She makes a cross in the air and joins her hands to make them understand. "*Prete.*" She points to her father.

Throughout the day, Sofonisba and the boy in turn kneel beside Orazio's body to pray for his salvation. Sometimes when her eyes are closed, it feels to Sofonisba as if the platform on which the bed is built might be a raft. She and the boy are kneeling on it adrift in the wide world. People come and go from the room and mostly fail to make themselves understood. Sometimes they bring food, grey and lumpen, ale that tastes like urine. The boy eats anyway. All the while, Orazio's waxen face seems to strain toward the ceiling, his head tilted back too far, his mouth looking as if he is about to speak.

And perhaps he, too, does have a need to speak, just as Sofonisba wants many times in this long day to address him, to reassure him that his work will be finished, that he will have a good burial, that he will go to Heaven. How easy to love the dead.

The Queen's chaplain arranges for a Mass to be offered next day for the repose of Orazio Fabroni's immortal soul. He sends a deacon to anoint the body. An old woman comes to wash it and waits patiently while Sofonisba, in the hope of finding some English coin, looks for the keys to her father's travelling chest. A carpenter comes soon after to make sure his boards will be long enough. They are pear wood and the hammering they require in the walled garden outside seems to last the entire afternoon. As the light fails and the winter evening draws in, Tanai leans against the side of the bed and prays or pretends to. Sofonisba sits close to the candles with Orazio's notebook and studies his prescriptions.

They buried Orazio the following day. An early winter fog suspended the world in its cold and damp. The escort promised by the steward of the household did not appear. Sofonisba and Tanai and the woman who washed the body accompanied the coffin. It was carried out of the park by the carpenter and three lads from the work sheds. The dark shapes of the chestnut trees loomed out of the white mist and melted back as they passed. A deer that had been grazing lifted its head briefly and continued.

Orazio, because he was not of the court, was taken to the church of Saint John the Divine in the town of Hampton. He was buried in the churchyard there, a stranger in his pear wood coffin, his notebook wedged under his crooked hands beneath the sealed lid.

Sofonisba sat the whole afternoon in the grey and white stone church, getting colder and colder, until the woman who had accompanied her got up and left and the boy said they must go back or the Queen's gates would be shut against them, and besides it would soon be dark and they would not be able to find their way.

⌒

SOFONISBA WROTE AT ONCE to Ser Tomasso and instructed him to settle Orazio's affairs. She wrote that she had no wish to return immediately and would not make new arrangements until the commission for the English Assembly rooms was completed. She instructed him to find buyers for whatever inventory remained, keeping the proceeds in trust for her return, when he would receive his fee. There were linens and plate she said, if nothing else. He was to sell all. She asked him to ensure that the shop remain rented to a reliable and hardworking craftsman and to see that the payment was made promptly. "And I beg you to send me, Ser Tomasso, when you write, news of my girl. Tell me, I beg you, if she was spared. I think about her almost every day."

It was more than three months before she heard any word, but she was content to wait. She had no wish to return and find Ser Tomasso, like a surrogate father, waiting to enforce her marriage. Here she could live in the world and be insulated from it at the same time, isolated by her language and by the white mists that overflowed the river in the night and hung all day heavy and still over the wet grass. In the very deep of the winter even the court was quiet, a hive with the queen removed. Sofonisba's appearance and her foreign manners attracted interest from the members of the household who remained — an invitation to a small dinner, an evening of music. She deflected it all. Desirous glances, intimate questions, disarming smiles all fell against her stockade of self-preservation. She walked often in the cold park accompanied by the waiting woman assigned to her and she painted assiduously, completing the painting begun by Orazio. She painted, too, another, smaller companion work, *The Progeny of Truth*, depicting certain regal virtues — Justice, Accord, Dominion and Mercy. Two unhappy figures languished in the right hand corner. "Dolour and Travail," she answered when anyone enquired of their identity. No one thought to ask their origin.

She thought often about Chiara, never forgetting to include her in her prayers morning and night and at every Mass she attended. In February, she at last received word. "The girl," Tomasso wrote, "was spared and another hanged in her stead, but before she was given safe conduct out of the city, *Signor* Cosimo had her driven three times round to satisfy the people's curiosity." In her reply, Sofonisba asked Tomasso to arrange for a Mass to be said in one of the smaller churches, whichever was not too dear. She would not, she added, be back for some time. She did not try to explain that she liked the isolation of this place, liked the role she had been assigned, a foreigner set apart from common custom.

By March, the second painting was finished, and still she delayed her return even though she felt the quiet, solitary temper of the days breaking with the weather. The birds each morning were raucous with excitement. Even the sheep were noisier, the presence of lambs among them making them behave like poorly trained troops, rushing and retreating, bleating terror before imagined enemies. When the Queen returned, the Court again became a place where it was difficult to follow a thought to its conclusion.

⁓

NICCOLÒ BANDINELLI, LEGATE to the new Pope, looking elegant in black with white lace in the Spanish style, listens to the Queen's Commissary, who looks in contrast as if he is still in the middle of the winter, bundled up with a surcoat trimmed with fur. He has been telling the whole sad story of Orazio Fabroni. He paces self-importantly in front of the *Truth and Beauty*, pointing out its merits, such as the way the viewer is drawn in by the eyes of the courtier who stands a little to the side of the main group with his hand extended toward the central figures but with his head turned away from them and into the room to meet the viewer's eyes.

Niccolò Bandinelli nods his approval, but wonders why the man seems to be claiming for this foreign court a talent born and bred so far away. He is too polite to voice his opinion that such talent is workaday in his own country. He would like to get on to the main business of this particular interview, this little addendum to the diplomatic matters that have occupied his morning with more important men. It is the daughter of the painter who interests the Pope. "If you can see her while you are there," he said, "bring her back. We can find work for her." Niccolò himself is intrigued by her. She is as dark as a southerner, with a heavy beauty about her shoulders and breast. She stands by and says little. He asks her which portions of the painting are hers, asks her if she has added or subtracted material. Her answers are elusive, and dismissive, too. She worked, she said, almost entirely from the notebook her father left her.

Niccolò asks if she has other paintings to show. He says he has seen a work of hers, *The Slaying of Holofernes*.

"In Firenze, *Monsignore*?"

"No. In Roma."

Sofonisba is not sure whether this is good news or bad. She had painted Holofernes' — Tassi's — undoing for the satisfaction of its being seen in his own town.

"It is a subject that interests me. I have a version of it here, intended for Her Majesty the Queen." She begins to explain something about the painting's derivation, but the Commissary cuts her short.

"It was not suitable," he says. He does not feel the need to repeat personal, confidential advice that the Queen received about the painting: that, despite its allegorical nature, this particular rendition of the Church triumphing over the State was simply too blood-thirsty, too inflammatory for even the most staunch Catholic, and could only rouse the most passionate opposition from certain members of her Court.

His interruption is just hasty enough to kindle Niccolò's interest.

"It is a simple matter to arrange a viewing," says Sofonisba. "I can have it sent over from my apartments."

Sofonisba stands in front of her new *Judith*. She has painted this version in oil on canvas. For the purpose of *Signor* Niccolò's view-ing, she has asked for an easel to be set up in front of the window of this small antechamber. She has taken care with its position, setting it at a slight angle so that there will be no reflected light from the surface of the paint. She senses that his is not an idle interest. If he asks her to return to Roma with him, she will go. When she looks at this painting, she is disgraced again. She feels the same raw emotion — the same tensing in the gut, the same furious, abysmal desire for revenge. To violate the violator. She cannot return to the same city as Matteo Tassi.

The composition of this painting is the same as that of the orig-inal, but the expression on the face of Holofernes is subtly altered. Here is no appeal for help nor any hope of rescue. It is the purity of this moment that has come to interest Sofonisba, for, despite the enactment of her own desire for revenge, the painting moves her less profoundly than a certain sketch she made at the killing of a calf. Probing for the moment of death, she had unwittingly touched a deeper mystery. The terror that she saw in the eyes of the calf transcended purpose, transcended finality and so was marked by a strange beauty: a reflection cast back by the flaring of compassion in the heart of the viewer. She had watched the animal's eyes, while at the same time her chalk had traced the edges of the wound in its neck opening cleanly like a mouth parting and something there inside, like a silver-blue satin slipper, throbbing. What she caught in the eyes was a perfect union with life itself — and then it was gone as the throat gaped and the blade met bone. After that it was all industrious purpose. The butcher brought his weight to bear on it with a rocking, hacking motion still grasping the tuft of hair. When the head was free, he held it up. The beautiful, intelligent tongue, that had once found the sweetest grass, now fallen back and hanging through the neck. The beautiful, flaring eyes already smoked over. But what if that power of reflecting back, that reflection of her own compassion for its plight, for the plight of us all, could be held, fixed?

Niccolò pauses as he steps into the room.

"Ah, but that is it. Exactly. You reproduce your own work perfectly, Monna Sofonisba. You have a consummate grasp of the subject. In your hands, this subject could be painted over and over, you have it so perfectly."

But Sofonisba knows it is not quite the same painting. The first had lacked the purity she saw — and depicted — in the eyes of the calf. It is a mystery — and a beauty — absent from the face of the first Holofernes, who, fulfilling Sofonisba's purpose, will always remain within those human bounds — and lock the viewer with him. His was a terror full of finality, painted to fulfil her own desire for revenge. She does not want to paint her own revenge over and over. What she has glimpsed is beyond finality, is sublime and therefore one with beauty, one with truth. It is why she will never stop painting.

"There could be work for you for a lifetime in Roma, Monna Sofonisba."

SIXTEEN

APRIL IN THE YEAR of 1555 is a benediction. Trade prospers, the land is at peace, and the people are content. The month has brought only sweet delight to the city of Firenze. No thunderbolts falling on the cupola, no *fuorusciti* conspiring against the government, or trees uprooted by gales, no packs of wild dogs devouring infants — only the lovely pear blossom and the plum, the clouds as white as lambs, and last year's vintage tasting sweeter than ever. It has brought two new lions to replace the ageing specimens in their cages behind the Palazzo Vecchio, a plenary indulgence from the Pope, and a cardinal's hat for Andrea.

The expense necessary to obtain the crimson cap was not excessive. Andrea knows that gold coins sometimes serve only to place one with the common crowd. A judicious gift, on the other hand, firmly fixes one's name in the memory of the great, keeps it forward in the mind when the time for honours comes due. Andrea wonders what has become of Sofonisba Fabroni. Her heated rendering of Judith murdering Holofernes was for strong stomachs only. He had hesitated to purchase it when he received the offer from Tomasso the notary. But it did provoke a certain visceral excitation, and the more he thought about it in hindsight, the more he realized what he had let slip away when Sofonisba left. He made Tomasso a modest offer, and the painting was brought back to *Argentara*. It remained with him for a month before he shipped it (along with a promise to transfer a piece of property to the Pope's nephew, a lad who was nothing but trouble) as a gift to the Pope: an allegory of the conquest of the Church over Satan.

He is sorry he made no progress with the woman while she was with him. But it is for the best. She would have been a trial. He remembers an unsettling tale told by one of his stewards after she left. It seems she had been speaking with the cook and had asked to be present at the butchering of a calf, and then once she was there she had made all kinds of demands, the strangest of which was that he was to slaughter it with its face to the heavens. The steward said he came upon them just in that moment. "And you know what?" he said. "She was still drawing."

Well, a woman like that. She is not worth the effort of seduction. In fact, he has grown weary of women altogether. He has derived more pleasure of late from the slender young men he selected to wait upon him — of which there has been a recent shortage, but fresh faces, he trusts, will be plentiful at his celebrations.

The preparations have been in progress since his appointment was first announced in Roma. Matteo Tassi has proposed a triumph to honour his success. The conception was splendid enough to outshine all competitors and secure his permission to re-enter the city. It is to be a supreme and glorious tribute, the triumph of the Soul, through Beauty, over the poverty and meanness of the Flesh. Everyone, he assured Cosimo in his letter, will understand it to represent the glorious line of the Medici. It will take place in the piazza at

Santa Croce, followed by a joust in the old style — followed, Andrea hopes, by a night of undiluted pleasure. The triumph that Matteo proposes will present a living boy of gold, of pure gold. It makes Andrea's mouth water just to think of it.

For someone who professes to scorn flattery, Tassi knows how to use it. With hardly any effort at all, he has engineered his return to the city and is installed in workmen's quarters behind the convent just off the piazza Santa Croce. He had spent the winter working on the doors of the small church of Santa Lucia in Arezzo and he had written to the *Signoria* as soon as he heard about Andrea's appointment. He had also heard another piece of news that interested him: Monna Sofonisba was expected to return to Italy in the spring. In his eagerness to believe, Tassi made no enquiries to confirm the rumour. The city fathers in Firenze were quick to reply to his proposal. They agreed to all the terms he had requested. But his satisfaction was short-lived. Almost as soon as he re-entered the city he learned that Orazio's house was still let, and that Tomasso had made over the shop to a book binder.

The prospect of the work that lay before him was suddenly daunting. He told himself it was not for Sofonisba that he had wanted to return. The order to make reparation through marriage still stood despite Orazio's demise, despite Sofonisba's refusal. But Tassi was not naïve; he knew exactly how it would be in the absence of her father: they would, both of them, satisfy the terms set by the Podestà, pronounce the vows — and turn their backs. He had never yet bedded a woman who loathed him. An order from the Podestà could change nothing. Yet it was for her, his return, this triumph, the golden boy. It was not Andrea's triumph, it was his, Matteo Tassi's. It was to represent — for Tassi at least — the consummation of his skill. He would amaze and astonish the entire city with his boy of pure gold. Only Sofonisba would be privy to his secret, when, at the end of it all, he would give her the 'boy'. But now the chief witness to this public testament of his art, the recipient of his gift, would be absent, and the creation of the golden boy nothing but a commission to be filled. No matter. He would have the whole city for a witness.

The quarters that have been assigned to him are reached through part of an ancient cloister, no longer used and open now to the sky, and consist of a single, large room above a portico. The room, reached by an outside staircase, serves as both bedroom and workshop. Its whitewashed walls are bare, its only furniture a pallet on the floor and a sturdy table with a bench. The space beneath, open on three sides, is given over to worksheds. It will house the triumphal car while it is under construction. The whole is sheltered from public view — and from the curious monks — by a high wall. The *festaiuoli* have provided a team of two journeymen carpenters and a painter to perform the labour. Each morning, they arrive noisily and set to work with Tassi to transform, with hammer and with saw, a simple wagon into a celestial chariot in the shape of a swan.

In the afternoons, Paolo Pallavicino arrives. Paolo is lodged in apartments in the Palazzo Vecchio. He has no love left for Tassi, who stole his glory so rudely, and no more interest in these entertainments. He comes as a special favour to the Duke. In accordance with Tassi's plans, the swan will carry on its back the dish of a giant scallop shell set on a raised platform designed to revolve. Paolo Pallavicino has come down to the city to assist with the workings hidden beneath the platform, the bladders and gears and screws that will cause a fountain to issue from the shell when the wheels of the cart begin to turn. When he is in the yard, Chiara stays out of the way. Sometimes she hears the boy Ceccio down there. Tassi has threatened her with a beating if she shows her face.

To fill the empty hours — for Tassi has no use for her until the day of his triumph — she takes up a piece of red chalk, holding it in her fist like a child, and draws on the limed wall at the back of the room where the shadow of the tree outside the window falls. When her hands are busy, she is happiest; the visions stay away. The saffron cloth she uses to wrap her head grows rusty with the chalk dust. Once, Tassi brings her a speckled thrush struck in mid-flight by the youngest workman, who has a knack of throwing his hammer in a clever arc. He lays it on the bench. Chiara rolls and rubs the chalk to a point, the way Sofonisba taught her, and begins to draw. Her eye follows the long sweep of the back first, it travels on, turns, sweeps back under the tail and meets the complication of the legs angled awkwardly from the body, the long toes with their claws curled in on themselves. It is difficult to concentrate here and the chalk must be kept sharp. It is a blessing. The effort of pinning the attention to complexity scours the mind's eye clean. There is only one other way to get to that place, and only Tassi can take her there.

The swan car is a sophisticated contraption. It is to roll forward while at the same time the fountain rises from the revolving shell on its back. It houses machines to make men curse and swear and fling tools down into the dirt. But then comes the day that the car is pushed forward down the walk and a jet of water springs briefly up to soak the man who is nearest. Tassi grasps Paolo by the shoulders and slaps his workers on the back and says he will buy them all a drink to celebrate. Paolo declines and retreats to his comfortable apartments.

Chiara is left with a promise of food to come. When darkness falls, she lights no candles. Eventually she sleeps. She dreams about the bird again. She dreams it now with spangles between its feathers, like a bird that has fallen into a fire and is kicked out, embers in its wings.

It is long after matins, almost light. Tassi slides out from beneath the largest of the two women who have been entertaining him. He pulls on his clothes, scrambles for his cap, his cape. He cannot find his knife anywhere. His purse is empty. A servant is sleeping across the door of the chamber. Tassi wakes him.

"Unlock the kitchen," he says, "and I will give you a ducat." The servant goes bleary-eyed to his mistress's keys, takes Tassi to the kitchen and unlocks it.

"And a knife," says Tassi.

The feast, which they barely touched, is on the table. The cat, satiated, is asleep like a cushion on the bench. Tassi picks up a roasted fowl. It is untouched. He cuts it in two, gives one half to the servant, wraps the other half and the knife, too, in a towel and says good night, even as the servant begins to argue.

His protests rouse one of the women who sits up unsteadily and calls, "Matteo?" The other does not stir.

Tassi grabs the boy's face and pinches his mouth in his big hands.

"Not in your interest. Not to your good," he says. "Not to your good at all. Now open the front door."

Before he leaves, he steps back to the bedroom, smiling, lifting the chicken to his lips, licking its crisp, oiled skin, and leans to run its savour on his tongue over the lips of the woman, pushing it through them and onto her sleep-sticky tongue as she lies back down. "Not a word," he whispers.

Chiara wakes to sunlight and the smell of roasted capon. And there it is beside her on the floor, a beetle chewing at it. Tassi is sleeping on his back on the pallet, almost a smile on his face. Chiara reaches for the capon and then changes her mind, leaving the beetle to its feast. She climbs onto the pallet and lies down beside Tassi.

"Tatilbi," she says. Tassi does not understand the word though she has repeated it often since the trouble at Paolo's. He thinks it might be a name. For a while she said nothing else. Lately she has

begun to speak again. It does not matter either way. She understands.
"Tatilbi."
Tassi, without opening his eyes, smiles and takes her in.

"NOW," SAYS TASSI. "Stand up. Raise your arms."
There are only three days of preparation left before the triumph.
Chiara is as patient as ever though she is naked and the room with
its unglazed windows is not warm. She lifts her arms high, elbows
bent like a water bird stretching. He no longer sees her pied skin,
though he knows it as a sailor knows his shores. He has a long piece
of linen, two hands in width, of the kind that is used to swaddle
infants, *gli innocenti*. He plasters one end against the side of her
breast and begins to wrap, holding the end in place as best he can
with her help. "Here. Put your hands here," turning her as he pulls
the linen tight, flattening her breasts.

"You are bandaged," he says. "After our battle." He grins. "Here,
take this." He has come to the end of the linen and leaves Chiara
holding it against her side. He steps back to view his work, looks
at her from the side.

"That's it," he says. "You are a boy. Done."
The flatness of her form is seductive, his hands must run over it,
turn her round and round again.

"A boy." He pushes her gently, supporting her, down onto the
pallet and turns her on her face. Kisses each buttock, kisses between
them so that Chiara thinks she will die at once for pleasure and for
shame and then, drawing himself up onto her back, he takes her
suddenly to the edge of pain. Afterwards, Chiara is still not sure
what happened and knows only that for a moment or two the room
turned black. It is what she seeks, this repeated oblivion, the
obliteration of sight that even sleep — especially sleep — cannot
provide. It is the trick she has come to need: to be taken to the edge

of terror and let fall into a chasm of heart-stopping bliss.

There is work still to be done. Tassi has already sent Emilio his order for twenty ounces of finely milled gold, to be placed on the account of the *Commune*. He has a few ounces to experiment with and tries all morning to find the medium best suited to transfer the gold to human skin. By the afternoon, he has settled on a glue rendered from the head and bones of the wolf-fish and coloured with ochre. The whole place stinks.

He pours a little of the warmed glue into a shell of finely milled gold and stirs it to a thick cream. It has the appearance of a lump of gold moments after passing the point of liquefaction.

He sits with Chiara and has her rest her mottled arm on the table. Using a ball of lint covered tightly with Gaza cloth he applies the paint, stroking from the middle of her upper arm down to the back of her hand. The cloth absorbs too much and he tries again with a thick round brush. It lays on nicely but the darker pigmentation of Chiara's skin is not wholly masked. He lifts her arm and tries some on her side where the markings are less pronounced. He decides to wait until it is completely dry to ascertain the effect. Chiara, meanwhile, wanders the closed room with her bandaged breast and her gilded arm. She pulls the meat from the capon and eats it. Tassi comes to play, licks her face like a dog. In a little while his neck, his shoulder and his ear on one side are gilded along with the bed cover, and the shadows on Chiara's skin have reappeared. The gold peels away like skin that has been burned.

Tassi says he must try something different. He goes outside to where the painters are working and comes back with a dish of realgar enlivened with cinnabar. He mixes the pigments with clear of egg and, using his finger wrapped in a rag, he wipes the colour in smooth strokes along the length of her other arm. He tries it on the swaddling. It grabs the cloth and stays. It dries quickly and Tassi applies the gold over it. It too takes hold. Tassi is pleased with the effect, the underpainting of red giving the gold a burnished, solid look. When it dries it does not come away.

Tassi leaves Chiara to clean herself while he writes another order for Emilio, this time for more of the red pigment. Chiara pours the sharply fragrant turpentine from a jar into a little dish and begins to rub away the gold. She is sorry to see her skin uncovered. She is an old and flaking, painted terracotta statue.

Next day, waiting for his order to be filled, Tassi is busy in the yard with the workmen. Paolo has asked more than once to see the lad who will represent the golden boy. Tassi tells him the boy is not to be revealed. All is in hand. The boy will know exactly what to do. "But you will have a trial first to see what difficulties you might encounter?" Despite himself, Paolo is beginning to assume a measure of responsibility for this undertaking.

"None," says Tassi. "It is easy. Look. Ceccio, get up there." He makes Paolo's already-golden boy climb up onto the car and into the shell.

"First he will crouch in its base — Curl up, Ceccio! — and he will be hidden from sight as we enter the square. Then at my signal," he bangs on the side of the car, "he will stand up — So! — with his arms extended. Like this, Ceccio —" He raises one arm in front, extends the other behind him. "The platform will turn to show him at every angle."

Paolo raises an eyebrow. He would not attempt the thing without a trial first.

Alone in the upstairs room, Chiara takes up a stick of charcoal and begins to draw on the white wall.

She draws first a bird in profile. It has a long back and a long tail. She fills in its form, leaving a round eye to see the worm. She draws another beside it, almost identical, and another beside that. The birds are not side by side as she had intended, but one behind the other. She is interested to see the way beside becomes behind. She draws four more and is halfway across the wall. Determined that the birds shall be sitting side by side, she draws the long lines of a bough beneath them, joins it to a tree trunk in the centre of the wall. Tassi still has not returned. The tree trunk grows boughs on each side, spreading farther than is possible in any tree. The limbs sprout heart-shaped leaves beneath and at their tips. The leaves are mapped with veins, each a perfect echo of the one before. And still Tassi does not return. Without him, Chiara is afraid. His absence makes a space where visions might enter, where memory might leak in. She fills the space with drawing. One moment fuses with the one before and melts into the next and Chiara can forget where she is, who she is. The birds follow one another across the wall. In obedience to the symmetry she imposes, the birds on the right-hand branch turn their backs to those on the left. Above them, on a higher bough, a new flock begins to alight. These have learned to turn their feet to grip the branch beneath them. They face in toward the trunk as do their counterparts that appear an hour later on the opposite bough. Time is charcoal dust vanishing in air. When there is no more charcoal left, a tree filled with birds fans out across the wall. On the topmost boughs the birds have their wings spread, ready for flight.

When Alessandro comes with the stoppered jars of gold and pigment hanging from one shoulder, a pair of scales from the other, Tassi is helping the workmen position the shell in its final place on the platform of the swan car.

"Leave them over there," says Tassi. He jerks his head in the direction of the workshop. Alessandro is walking over, when the men behind him send up a great shout as the shell locks into place. He turns to look, and at the same moment a figure appears briefly at the window upstairs. As he turns back, he catches just a glimpse of the figure before it vanishes back into the room. He puts down his order and waits for Tassi to sign for it. His mind is racing. There was no mistaking the saffron cloth, the white dove.

Tassi swings down from the car, smiling broadly.

"It is ready," he says, pointing back to the swan. He wonders why the fellow can't show some interest, let by-gones be by-gones.

Alessandro wonders why some people never seem to suffer for their sins, but always escape punishment. He has not forgotten the jeers of the townspeople, the lectures from the priest, the calluses on his hands from his own punishment — helping the Misericordia bury every wretch and scoundrel in the town that died destitute, from the day of the trial until All Souls. To his profound shame he is known now around the town as *Alessandro del Camposanto.* Alessandro of the Graveyard.

He nods. "Very good. Where is the boy?"

"The boy will leap into being on the very day. He will arise fully formed from the shell." Tassi slaps Alessandro on the back. "You will see. You will be astonished."

~~

"TELL ME AGAIN," says Chiara before she falls asleep.

"The boy will spring into being," says Tassi. "*Il ragazzo d'oro.*" He watches her face.

"Yes?"

"He will be as the waters of a fountain leaping."

"Yes?"

"He will rise up fully formed and shining like the sun."

Chiara looks deep into his eyes as if she will be able to see there this vision of the golden boy.

"His face will shine with the light of the sun in heaven and his limbs will gleam like the backs of golden rivers. Close your eyes. Now you can see him. His skin is burnished with its own beauty like fire. His frame is polished with an unearthly lustre. He will radiate loveliness. He will shine like a wingless angel, and his beauty will be beyond compare."

"Yes."

"And you must dream the rest. Now God keep you. Go to sleep."

IT IS JUST AFTER DAWN. If you were to climb the road leading northwest out of the city, stop to rest beside the wall that hugs the hill, and look back down toward the river, you would see that dull, gold ribbon that could be wheat turned now to livid bronze. The wind hammers at its surface. It calls to mind the late afternoon, this light, which nevertheless is coming from the east, streaming in under the clouds. The trick of the light is the gift of the coming storm. Clouds the colour of iron and steel, the colour of liver and ashes, are gathering fast, piling in to take the place of night, crowding, massing one on the other, so that it is obvious the sky will not be able to hold them. Already there is a sloping shaft of rain, showing only as mist, falling from a tear in the base of one and illuminated by the early sun. The coming storm has not yet obliterated the sun's rise, and the river still gleams. Down in the city, only the red dome of the cathedral and the top of the *campanile* have caught light. As the sun ascends the space between the horizon and the cloud layer, the shadows of the adjacent rooftops slide down the walls. It rained in the night. The tiles of all the roofs are a rich red. It will rain again before they are thoroughly dry.

In the whitewashed room, the side of the copper bowl that contains the measured gold briefly takes fire where the sun catches it through a missing lathe in the shutters. Tassi slept with the bowl next to his bed in case of theft. He is still sleeping despite the unrelenting convent bells. Chiara, who slept all night curled against his back, is awake. Tassi should have been up at least two hours before dawn. She prods him in the back. There is a man down in the courtyard calling for him. He sits up, startled, wild-haired and wild-eyed. He has the same look he has after a night of debauchery. He scrambles into his clothes.

At the bottom of the stairs, the overdressed young man who has come from the Duke is standing with his arms folded to signal, Tassi supposes, the displeasure of his employer.

He has come, he says, to inform Tassi that Cosimo himself will shortly arrive to view the golden boy.

"In that case," says Tassi, "his Excellency will have no unanticipated delight when the moment of the boy's revelation arrives. You would do well," he says, "to try to put him off."

The young man stops representing the Duke and gives his own opinion: a short, incredulous laugh through his nose. "And you would do well," he says, "to stop warming your poker and get to work."

Tassi takes the stairs two at a time. When he gets back to the room, the birds on the wall are nothing more than a cloud of dirty grey-black smoke. Chiara has the pitcher of water beside her and is rubbing at the wall with the balled up linen, terrified at the thought of the Duke's man seeing what she has dared to do.

Tassi sees only the blackened bandages and how they will ruin his paint. He yanks the bed sheet from the pallet and then changes his mind. There is no time. He throws some sticks on the fire and stirs the embers, throws on lamp oil and makes a blaze to warm the glue.

Chiara is sitting hunched in the corner of the room, her knees drawn up to her chest, her eyes red from crying, her mouth ugly with resentment and hurt.

"Get up. Get up."

But her nights with Tassi give her license to defy, which only enrages. The next time Tassi asks, it is with real fury. Chiara cannot move with fear, and all of it becomes an ugliness of pulling and resisting and flailing and hitting and again hitting, until she is on her feet, taking off her dress while Tassi wrings out a piece of grey, dirtied bandage. He plasters it to her breast with the fish glue, winding it round, flattening her profile, pulling it so tight she cannot take the great sobs of air she needs. She puts on the codpiece that Tassi has fashioned from varnished parchment in the shape of a cockleshell. Tassi pours the warm glue into the gold and mixes it with his finger. He wipes it across her cheek and down her neck, loads a wide brush of the kind he would use on plaster and, with the bandage still sticky with glue, begins to paint. He lays it on too hurriedly. Her cheek, her neck, her shoulder, her breast. It is trickling, dripping, giving her the look of someone rising from a muddy pool, or of a statue fouled by birds, and it is all too late. He works in a frenzy, covering her belly, her limbs, willing the insistent patches to vanish beneath the gold. They can hear the sound of people gathering, greeting one another in the courtyard. The voices down below are getting louder. There are footsteps now on the stair. Cosimo's man telling his master to watch his step, the stairs are very narrow.

"*Sua Eccellenza, il Granduca Cosimo di Giovanni de' Medici!*"

Cosimo and his man enter the room in a flurry, and stop. No salutations, no back-breaking bows greet their arrival.

There is only silence in the room. The last sound, the Duke's intake of breath as he was about to speak, hangs on the air like one of Chiara's vanished birds.

No one moves as he walks across the room to Chiara. He stops in front of her, frowning, cocks his head to speak to his man behind him.

"Take that thing off," he says, pointing to the shell.

Chiara closes her eyes. The servant coughs, walks behind her to see how the thing is attached and twists his hip, peering, not seeing any clasp. Tassi sighs with exasperation and steps forward, pulls the shell back, unties the cord behind it and steps away.

"There," he says and his tone verges on insolence, as if he had said, "Satisfied?"

Cosimo is too angry for theatrics. He turns to Alessandro. "Paolo Pallavicino will take over this commission," he says. "You can assist. Tell him to come at once, and tell him to bring that boy he has.

"Matteo Tassi, do not come back to my city again. Ever. Bring this disgusting creature within even fifteen miles of the gates and she will be hanged from the Palazzo Vecchio. We'll save the gallows for you."

⌇

THE RAIN THUNDERS ACROSS THE ROOFS, driving birds under the eaves, rats under the tiles, driving everyone inside to wait it out, watching the cobbles where a second small rain, the mirror of the first, dances up.

In the workmen's quarters behind the convent, Paolo Pallavicino sees none of it. He likes the insulation the noisy rain provides, sealing him in the room within its curtain of sound to perform the marvellous alchemy on Ceccio, who is more than willing to oblige. How easy to slip back to the satisfactions of the fantastical. He bends over the bowl of re-warmed gold, stirring it with a little stick. Something to make it adhere, something to make it fast if the rain this afternoon should wheel round and return. The *festaiuoli* sent a man to watch from a tower, and he saw clear weather following the clouds from the west — or that was what he said to his companion before he was struck by lightning and transformed into something resembling a blasted, twisted limb. A second man was sent up. He made the same prediction and was not struck and when the sooth-sayer at the *Signoria* released a pair of doves they wheeled and flew westward, which proved, well, *every*thing. The pageant will not be postponed. The evening will be fine, the streets washed clean. It will be perfect. Paolo Pallavicino nevertheless prefers to take this precaution. He mixes boiled oil of flax with the glue and brightens it all with yellow orpiment. Now the sheen of the gold is lowered and must be brought up again with a little quicksilver. It will be perfect.

He begins with Ceccio's hair and uses a comb to apply the gold. The boy's soft curls acquire a darkly metallic sheen. They fall limp under the weight of the paint. Even the shape of the boy's head appears altered. With a wide liming brush, Paolo works down the neck, the shoulders, though he leaves the face for now. It is a peaceful task, laying on the paint, slowly transforming the warm, living flesh to the appearance of cool, unyielding gold, restful here in the grey light of the room, the air freshened with rain.

"Turn round."

When Ceccio moves it is as if he is clothed in a foreign skin. The smooth skin of a golden frog, perhaps. There is a slight wrinkling at his armpit, his elbow, his knee. He is wearing the gilded shell; behind it, his genitals, unpainted, are more foreign still and vulnerable, like a pale creature under a rock that is suddenly lifted. Paolo works with love at the feet. The boy giggles. Paolo does not spare the gold, but paints even between the toes. Ceccio's body now is as smooth and graceful as Donatello's lovely boy, but until his face is painted it will seem at odds, hectic. It needs quieting.

"You will have to kneel down."

With a narrower brush, Paolo begins to apply the gold to Ceccio's face.

"You must keep perfectly composed."

Ceccio is all twitches and reflexes. He hiccups with suppressed giggles.

"Perfectly, or you will look like a cracked and crazed old man. Be still."

Ceccio takes a deep breath, feeling the pull of the drying paint on the skin of his chest. With effort, he composes his face and presents its lovely contours to Paolo.

"The eyes are the most difficult. We shall paint them closed and when they are almost but not wholly dry, I shall ask you to open them. You will open them very, very slowly, hair's breadth by hair's breadth. Do you understand?"

A small squeak of assertion issues from Ceccio's throat.

"Good."

Inside his golden darkness, Ceccio can hear the rattling of the rain on the broad leaves of the tree outside. He stands at the window. He is waiting for Paolo to tell him to open his eyes. When he opens them he will be able to see down to the river, but Tassi and Chiara, already soaked to the skin and stopped for a rest, will have long ago crossed it.

<hr>

TASSI HOLDS CHIARA beside him under his raised cloak. Her face bears the patient look of an animal waiting out the rain. Tassi's head, his shoulders, his back feel the dampness striking through. At the height of the storm, rain had streamed from the edge of his cloak like rain off a roof. He had been glad to find this rock with its slight overhang for protection. Chiara was farther back, trying to shelter in the lee of a steep drop of land beside the road. When he called she had come, bent, hurrying, with bits of wet straw and grass sticking to her, flinching at the gusted rain, to slip in under his — the rapist's, the drunkard's, the brawler's — arm, as comfortable as the kitten slipping under the cat. Tassi had accepted her as comfortably. She represents no claim on his affection, no bond, no chain or shackle; she, a slave, is guarantor of his liberty; she is neither spur to his conscience nor bridle to his desire; she is nothing — and so the one thing he can love without condition. She settles her head against his shoulder and makes a small noise of content. Tassi smiles.

How his fortune reverses time and again. Who plays this game with him? Against him? His fortune a coin flipped and flipped again in the air. He can see, as he rarely does in the town, the whole wide face of the sky; how its thunderous scowl is slowly lifting, the light on the horizon pushing up, making its own space under the clouds, diminishing them even as it glorifies their steely colours, their buried beauty.

His moment has gone, but so be it. He has half his fee and a pocketful of milled gold. And the road looks good.

Firenze is nothing without Sofonisba. She was the reason he risked all he did to return. He had always believed she would become his wife or, better, that she would marry a wealthy man. He did not doubt he would be allowed to climb then, welcome, into her bed while her husband played elsewhere. It had been a savoury dream. But it had ended when he took her in anger. He knows it now. It is not to be. This wet ditch beneath the rock is his awakening.

He will begin again. In Urbino they will appreciate him. They do not have so fine a sculptor. His talent is the one thing he can never lose. No one can take it from him. He will find work, set his own terms. He has his model with him. Who has begun to snore. He will wait a little while. He does not have to hurry.

⌒

IN THE AFTERNOON, the cheering is so loud a traveller on the road to Lucca might hear it. The people are like birds after rain, shouting for exuberance. They have hung bright banners from the rails under their windows, and the washed city is criss-crossed with colour, has become a prism in the sunlight. The musicians decked in ribbons enter the Piazza Santa Croce from the east side and assemble in front of the basilica. The Piazza is a rectangle both long and wide, with the basilica at its eastern extremity. The buildings on either side stand shoulder-to-shoulder as if always ready for a spectacle to begin. A single trumpeter announces the beginning of the triumph and what he is announcing is the cessation of quarrels, the suspension of grudges, the forgiveness of petty affronts and the forgetting of past rebukes. Twenty more trumpets repeat and amplify the call. At the west end of the square, in front of the Serristori's old palazzo, a red and gold baldaquin stands in the centre of a curtained platform under the protection of a wide awning. The canvas roof has been kept from collapsing under its own weight by two men who were stationed under it in the rainstorm and worked to keep the water from collecting. Some lessons are learned over time. The curtains around the dais are not yet drawn back. Behind them, at the corners hang long linen sacks, their necks closed with cords on whatever is still moving inside. The Duke has his own pretensions to theatre. It is why he loves Giuliano's Paolo and his friends. He takes his seat on the dais to the right of the baldaquin where Andrea is enthroned, resplendent in red satin. Cosimo nods and his major-domo sends a signal to the men who are managing this piece of stagecraft. They draw back the curtains and at the same time release the cords on the necks of the sacks. Four hundred white doves that have been held captive for the duration of the storm fly out from under the awning. The music outside is drowned in cheers. Some of the birds tumble, bleeding, to batter at the feet of the seated guests; but all eyes in the crowd are tracking the birds that fly free to briefly decorate the sky.

"It was difficult work, of course, but brought off successfully I think you'll agree." The triumphal car, with its giant swans and its cockleshell, its freight of water which will cascade down behind the golden boy, has been drawn up in the grounds of the monastery beside the basilica. It stands hidden from view by gates that open directly onto the piazza. The four white horses are skittish with apprehension. Alessandro's voice is unnaturally loud. He has given it a deeper register and an urbane gloss.

"I might have improved the car, had I more time." Though he knows the car to be magnificent and likely to win acclaim.

Paolo is looking at the car with that way of his, his mouth clamped shut, his bearded chin jutting. His eyelids, hooded as always, do nothing to disguise his hawkish look. Alessandro tries again.

"I did what I could at the last minute, but with time I could have made this swanly wagon a celestial chariot." Which makes the hooded gaze slide in his direction again. The clamped mouth is resolute.

The men open the gates and lead the horses through. Paolo observes how the central fountain is revolving quite smoothly as the carriage is pushed forward. He is pleased. The fountain works less erratically than it did on the rough ground of the yard, the wheels then turning more slowly. He is satisfied with its appearance. Tassi always knew how to manage workmen. The swans have a grace not easy to achieve with such intractable material and in subjects larger than scale. Their surfaces have a pleasingly soft appearance. It was a brilliant touch to affix the down, and fortunate that the city was prepared to foot the additional cost. The thought of engaging in yet another begging session for his disbursements only adds to Paolo's irritation with this dolt of a man beside him. He turns to Alessandro.

"It's Tassi's car. It is his achievement, and you know it."

Alessandro glances at the spectators, mostly boys, who have come to the gate, liking to be the first to catch a glimpse, some already running away with the news of what is approaching. No one hears the rebuke. The sight of the car is too rousing.

Ceccio, at the base of the fountain lies curled like a gilded snail undetected in the shadow of a leaf. Perhaps he is taken for a sculpted form, for no one, it seems, has any inkling of his presence. As the car gets underway and the jet of water rises higher, there is a satisfied ring to the cheering. No one expects any further surprise. A fountain in motion is delight enough. Ceccio hears the voices and has an urge to stand, but he knows he must lie without moving until the moment comes to reveal himself as the golden boy: the prosperity of the House of Medici in all its youthful beauty and glorious lustre. It is as well to lie still, for his limbs are suddenly lead, his head heavy clay, and in place of his stomach someone has left a bucket of eels.

The swan car swings in behind a cavalcade of helmeted soldiers bright with green and gold livery and silver breastplates. They cross the square in front of the basilica. Pennants flutter from the tips of their lances as they wheel to ride past the spectators on the north side, wheel again to cross in front of the dais. Paolo and Alessandro keep pace among the boys who have squeezed through the wattle fences to run alongside. Ceccio's face has begun to ache intolerably in the nose and forehead and around the eyes. He is cold. And how the car jolts and sways! If a spectator now could see the expression on Ceccio's face he would believe him in a wagon on the way to the stake. His eyes are closed against the ache and his mouth is pulled to one side in his discomfort. His tongue is as dry as dirt.

Something in Ceccio's stomach is dissolving in a thick and rising pool. His shivering does not stop though waves of heat are washing over him. The car is turning again. He does not know whether they are travelling up or down the square. He can hear a steady wall of voices on one side as the car passes. Through the wall of voices he can hear Alessandro spitting at him in his excitement. "Almost finished. One more turn, then a straight run down to the dais. Be ready."

None of it matters. Ceccio wants only to climb out of this dire feeling of unwellness, would happily stand and spew the whole bucket of eels.

"Can you hear me?" Paolo's voice is close beside the car. Ceccio has trouble forming a reply with the thick tongue bumping on the dry walls of his mouth.

On the last turn of the square, the sky grows noticeably darker. The spectators grumble at the clouds, at each other, pull on hoods and prepare for rain. The first drops fall as the horses come to a halt in front of the dais and one of them, as if in commentary, shits.

The boy who has been engaged specifically for this eventuality runs forward, not minding the jeers, pleased to have his place in life, or at least in this triumph. He shovels the droppings into his bucket.

Ceccio is stalled by the laughter. Paolo growls and growls and at last, not because he hears him but because he feels that the laughter is somehow his, that he is part of what is going on, Ceccio begins the effort of will that will bring him to his feet. But something unsettling has happened. Though his eyelids stretch taut in answer to the muscles of his face, they do not open. It is hard for him to find his balance as he uncurls himself. He stands, sure that once he is upright his eyes will open. Steadying himself, he holds out his arms, one raised in front, the palm upturned, toward the dais, the other extended to the side and back a little in balance. Paolo is hissing again. "To the left, to the left. Toward me. Turn, turn." He is heard this time by all around him, for the crowd has fallen silent as it takes in this apparition. Paolo succeeds in getting Ceccio centred in the shell so that his rear parts are not exposed to the crowd as he bows before the dignitaries.

Ceccio comes up from the bow, his eyelids pulling stickily apart. He sees Cosimo, who is turning to speak to Andrea, explaining something, his hand outstretched. Andrea is not even looking in his direction. He sees the mass of faces of every shape and size, every colour and form, slide into view as the platform beneath him turns, first to the right, then to the left and back again. The sea of faces is all movement. The rain is falling faster and the people are dragging capes and cloaks over their heads and beginning to look about for shelter. Ceccio has difficulty keeping his balance; the movement of the crowd and the movement of the platform combine to bring about a sickening dizziness. He feels as if he has begun to spin and cannot stop. It is only when Cosimo has stopped speaking that Andrea finally takes in the golden boy, perfectly still, perfectly poised, his gilded limbs glistening everywhere with a thousand drops of rain that bead before they roll and slip away.

He thinks that he has never seen a sight so beautiful and longs to consume it.

～～

AS IF IN A MILITARY MANOEUVRE, the rain has indeed wheeled round and for several hours has concentrated its assault on the town. There is no break in any direction. The joust and the fireworks and the rest of the festivities have been postponed. Andrea's personal procession of triumph was a hasty scramble up to Cosimo's new palace on the slopes of San Giorgio. Cosimo's hospitality is lavish; Andrea and his entourage have been assigned an entire wing. The feasting begins early. Andrea, rankled at the heavens' inconsiderate display, quickly drinks himself into a state of morose disaffection and retires.

Behind his bed curtains he is alone and wide awake. He knows his mistress will send her attendants to sleep in the passage. He knows she will have only one lamp burning to light his way to her bed. But his thoughts are elsewhere. He has sent a message to Alessandro to attend him with the golden boy. He closes his eyes, and his vision plays over the boy's limbs. It licks at the wrists, at the inside of the elbows, biting at the sweet tendon there and flicking away to search behind the gilded knee for its counterpoint, the strong sinew in its curtain of fine flesh. He lets his mind's eye travel down to the ankle bones and his teeth can feel the thick tendon there behind. He is wildly aroused, can barely keep still while he holds on to himself and groans softly. In his mind, he travels the length of the shin bone, rubbing his chin against the knee as if he were a cat, postponing the moment when he will take what he wants, finding the warm groin and smoothed, shaved root place, finding what he wants, a reflection of himself there but gilded — oh, he hopes they have gilded all, the prick, the balls, the entry to eternity — and strong and lovely. Finding himself as he longs to be

— beautiful. He will stretch out upon beauty and it will melt into him, he into it. There will be no division and no difference. All shall be consumed.

~

A SMALL RIVER IS RUNNING down the Costa Scarpuccia straight for the apothecary's door, for his shop stands opposite the spot where Via Scarpuccia sweeps into Via Bardi. Most of the stream rushes on; the rest flows under the door, spreading to a pool on the stone flags before continuing through and out of the back of the shop where Ceccio sits. Alessandro's father shouts at him to leave Paolo to take care of the boy; better still, get him out of here before he has to be carried away on a bier. It will do his reputation no good, no good at all.

"Look at him. He's sickening. Leave him," he shouts, "and come and help."

He wishes they had come here sooner, but when they left the square they were fêted. They became their own procession as youths and children ran out in the rain to get a closer look at the gilded boy borne through the streets on a litter all wet and shining. And then they passed Tassi's whore who had a crowd of friends with her in the loggia next to Torrigiani's house. She pulled the heads off the marigolds that were growing in a pot by the great door. Gold for the golden boy. She tore the petals and scattered them on his face. By the time they got back, the house was awash.

Emilio stuffs a long bolster up against the bottom edge of the door, but the water still makes its silent advance.

The boy in the back is sitting limply on a stool. He is slumped with his shoulder to the wall and his head drooping, his arms hanging at his sides, his hands limp, his mouth slack. He has thrown off the blanket Paolo gave him and it lies on the floor. Across his thigh is a linen towel and at his feet the basin of turpentine that Paolo is using to wipe away the paint from his neck and his chest. The clattering of the rain outside is not as loud as the knocking and grinding of the boy's teeth.

It sets Emilio's nerves on edge. Alessandro sweeps vainly, trying to reduce the spreading pool. The rivulet continues to flow.

Alessandro and his father both think they hear thunder until they realize that someone outside is pounding on the door.

The messenger appears to be standing under a downspout, there is so much water streaming from his hat. He stands with one shoulder drawn up against the rain while he delivers his speech. The water swirls round Emilio's feet.

"Come in and wait," he says when he has heard what the messenger has to say.

It is the perfect opportunity to get Paolo and the boy out of his shop. Even Paolo won't refuse a message from the Cardinal. Emilio goes through to the back of the shop.

Ceccio's teeth suddenly stop their chattering. He thrusts his lower jaw forward, gasps for breath and grinds his jaw again as if he would eat the air. Emilio and Alessandro watch as he repeats the motion. His neck is longer surely than any neck can be, his chin thrust up toward the ceiling. The messenger coughs and Ceccio turns his head. He looks out through slits as red as any knife wound and his mouth opens wide on a black tongue.

Emilio and Alessandro whisper and hiss and glance at the messenger. It does not take long to reach a decision, nor does the messenger need to be persuaded to leave the boy. Alessandro throws a cloak over his shoulders and follows the messenger out again into the blinding, deafening rain.

By the time he reaches the corridors of Cardinal Andrea's house, he will have thought of a suitably verbose and grovelling excuse and he will welcome the opportunity to deliver it personally. And then what else will he do but submit to the offered embrace, believing, as he does, that this must be the opening of Fortune's very door?

CHIARA, HUDDLED AGAINST Tassi before she gave in to sleep, knew there would be no other moment for her ever: to stand, beautiful to behold in the eyes of others, to wear a skin of gold so beautiful that taunts and jeers would fall away. To be seen to be beautiful. It was a dream spun on an afternoon in a white room. If Tassi left her now she would be finished. She would be stoned to death. She settled deeper against him. On the long road to Urbino she will do anything for Tassi. She will stand on a table in a tavern and display her body if it brings them coins to buy food, to stay together.

It has stopped raining. The day dawns without any hint of fire. The night lifts. The world returns, the great hills first, then the ghostly shapes of the trees rising from darkness to meet the eye, assuming first a darkness of their own and then reflecting light, answering the blessing of light with the gift of sight. The inky sky lightens, greys, and unmistakably begins to glow. The sky to the east is alive with the coming day. The world begins to shine from within.

Chiara opens her eyes.

Tassi says, "I suppose you're hungry."

EPILOGUE

In the years to come, Emilio and Paolo will sit together sometimes in the shade and talk about the unpredictability of life, for
Emilio likes to visit, perhaps to get away from his ailing son. He
often wonders aloud if he might have done better to consult his
astrologer more often, if perhaps his son's affliction might have
been avoided. But who was he to know, to even guess, that the
French disease could strike so quickly or so ruthlessly? Better to
work and to forget, is all the reply Paolo will offer. Who has his
own grief to tend. Better to work and forget. Paolo knows this. If
he did not work, he might open his own veins in grief and remorse.
But he has his drawings. Work for him now is only drawing. He
wants nothing more than to lay Nature honestly before the eye,
having buried all desire either to dissect or to enhance when he
buried Ceccio. He drew the face of the beautiful Ceccio again and

again when the boy was alive, ungilded, unadorned. He sees now that it was enough. The faces blaze with beauty. Paolo will go to his grave believing their light belongs to Ceccio. Were it put to him, he would not accept that it is his own love he renders on the page. He spends his days in his house at *La Castagna*, absorbed in his drawings of small creatures — before they take wing, or dart to refuge — and the finest details of plants. Hours at a time, he will sit in contemplation of the crenellations of a leaf, the whorl of a snail's shell. Then he will lose all sense of his own existence within the bonds of time and will know only the thing itself revealed as beauty, though it is nothing more — or less — than love.

He has only one project awaiting completion. He has fashioned in wax the figure of a laughing boy reaching up. There will be a bird about to fly from his hands. He does not know whom he will ask to cast such delicate work. Tassi was always the best. Perhaps one day he will send it to Urbino.

Giuliano is resigned to seeing his generous support bear little fruit. He likens Paolo to an old apple tree bearing less each year and he continues with good grace to keep him, expecting nothing in return. There is little anyway that he wants of late, his interests turning as they have to horticulture and the nurture of the most delicate and rewarding plants. He will give away much of the plate and coin and the bronzes in his collection, donating it to the navy Cosimo equips against the Turks, much of it to be foundered for cannon. He will keep the bronze foetus. It will pass from hand to hand as a thing of beauty, until at last it, too, is sacrificed to the ruinous ambition of the next deluded potentate who declares that times are desperate. Then it will be foundered, its high pewter content forgotten, and recast to cannon. The gun will pass, according to the fortunes of war, across borders and through three generations, the hairline crack developing in its muzzle undetected, until another century, when, somewhere in Circassia, it will backfire, killing on the spot the drunken soldiers who have trained it on a farmhouse in the valley.

And Sofonisba? Sofonisba is in Roma. On her return from England, she remained in Firenze only long enough to settle her affairs. Ser Tomasso helped her sell the shop in Via del Cocomero, glad to close his book on the Fabronis who had caused him trouble unequal to their worth. In Roma, where Niccolò Bandinelli has established her, Sofonisba's reputation grows. Niccolò, who has never allowed his ties to the Papacy to stand in the way of his pleasures, has turned his attentions elsewhere, but follows Sofonisba's progress keenly. It seems to depend on her consorting with the rakes and rogues among the painters. Niccolò does his best to curtail the ugliest rumours. He might have taken her for a mistress had she been prepared to lead a less conspicuous life. She has a place in his affections still.

Sofonisba is happy in Roma. She likes the warmth of the city — even its stone is warmer — and she likes the painters and sculptors who live in the quarter by the Castello gate. As time goes by, however, her need to live alone is questioned, dividing those who know her into two camps. By some she is marked as a harlot, dangerous to the order of the city that knows in general where its harlots are at all times. Others praise her as a fine practitioner of the art of depiction. It will not be long before she confounds her detractors by producing a child, a daughter, both confirming and overturning their opinion. She will not send the child out to nurse, will not lose her in a fall or to some swift and savage plague visiting in the night, but will keep her close, delighting in her company. There will be times when she will come upon her daughter absorbed in her games. Her heart will stop for love, and she will sweep her up and kiss her roughly on her small brown face. The first thing she will teach her to draw will be a dove with its wings extended.

Fortune, having once shown Sofonisba that she is no more inviolable than a leaf at the mercy of the wind, will be kind to her now, letting her go gently. She will live a long and happy life, run a successful business and love her daughter more than herself. She will travel — with her daughter — to Bologna and to Napoli to fill commissions. She will never take a husband. When she receives an invitation from Urbino, she will decline.

ACKNOWLEDGMENTS

I should like to thank the Canada Council for the Arts and the British Columbia Arts Council for assistance in the completion of this work.

I should also like to acknowledge the very friendly assistance of Dr. Nicoletta Barbarito Alegi and Prof. Caterina Ricciardi in Rome; my thanks also, to Steven Kronenberg and to Joe Rosenblatt.

I am especially grateful to Ada Donati for her generous, patient help, and to Mandy Naismith and Michael Mintern for their expert advice. Grateful thanks, too, of course, to Hilary and to Marc. And, as always, loving thanks to John.

AUTHOR'S NOTE

A number of highly regarded women artists were at work during the period in which *Beyond Measure* is set. Their details are easily accessible in various excellent works and on the internet. Artemisia Gentileschi, who painted several versions of 'Judith and Holofernes', and whose life I have blithely ransacked for my plot, was working at a later date.

The slave Chiara, whom I thought was all my own invention, will be born — I've since learned — two hundred years later in Cartagena, on the coast of Columbia: the 'Piebald Black Child', Mary Sabina.

Date Due

JUN 15 2004	